I0579460

HUNTER'S MOON

A Hunter's Universe Novel by David Michael Martin

HUNTER'S MOON Copyright © 2016 by David M. Martin.

All rights reserved. Printed in the United States of America. No part of this book may be used or reproduced in any manner whatsoever without written permission except in the case of brief quotations embodied in critical articles or reviews.

Original Draft copyright by David M. Martin 8/19/2013

This book is a work of fiction. Names, characters, businesses, organizations, places, events and incidents either are the product of the author's imagination or are used fictitiously. Any resemblance to actual persons, living or dead, events, or locales is entirely coincidental.

For information contact:
Bent Briar Publishing L.L.L.P.
Sahuarita, AZ 85629
www.bentbriarbooks.com

Book Design by Freelance Creative Support Services

Kidahin on Ibeetu
Original artwork by Roy S. Seger

978-1-942665-03-8 SC
978-1-942665-04-5 HC
978-1-942665-05-2 eBook

First Edition: September 2016
Revised Edition: December 2018

10 9 8 7 6 5 4 3 2 1

This book is dedicated to the ring-tailed lemurs of Madagascar. Without them, the Eyloni wouldn't be who they are.

Acknowledgements
Let me first thank Dr. Anne Goiran-Bevelhimer, Sunday S. Smith, Wendie Thomas and Laura Kathleen Sutton for their help in making this book possible. I would also like to thank BetteRose Ryan and everyone at Bent Briar Publishing for their tireless efforts. Their work is greatly appreciated.

Table of Contents

PROLOGUE

Crouching on the balls of her feet, tail swaying just enough to keep her balance, she listened. Her clan, the Uahua'asee'a Eyloni, petitioned the La'huaset Tribal Elders to bless her adulthood ceremony. They always gave a blessing. Making the request was a sign of respect. Once given, all of her immediate family's females would dwell on an emotion of their choosing. Those emotions would strengthen the potency of the pheromones that clung to their scent. Pheromones produced emotional images creating an empathy web, and once caught in the web she would turn inward to face the Oyya of the spirits.

Excitement shivered through her. When would they begin? Danger lurked in adulthood ceremonies: immediate and extended family females had warned her many times already. She was surprised to see all thirty of her immediate family's males standing with the Tribal Elders. Thirty males in one place among over two thousand females heralded an important event. Of the three female phenotypes expressed in Eyloni biology, the

Hunters lent her their close support because she too had been born a Hunter. Many Warriors milled through the crowd singing encouragement to her while keeping an alert eye on the males. Even within the massive trees her immediate and extended families called home, Warriors stewed and worried only a fraction more than Hunters did over male safety. Her immediate family's few Comara walked an *ell*, the length of a male's tail, beside their chosen males. In a crowd, the yellow skinned, blond haired, tailless Comara gave themselves away by the wide berth given them. Born mute, their pheromones sent out dire empathic warnings.

She changed from crouching to sitting, adjusted her balance, and waited. She could hold this stance for days if necessary. Outside, a storm beat an insistent rhythm. Heavy black clouds boiled up over the jungle canopy. They turned the auroral twilight sky into night. Rain pounded the leaves in torrents, and the wind made boughs tens of forest trails thick creak and groan. She heard crackles and snaps, smelled metal in the air, felt static brush against skin the color of forest leaves. Lightning bolted across the sky, flashing lingering blue strobes in the blackness. She watched a sea of colorful leaves, a fury of oranges, reds, and yellows, writhe around her. Thunder clapped in pursuit of the lightning's tail, rumbling through the hollow living spaces of the great tree.

Jolting awake, all around her healthy leaves the size of a warship's hull plates turned from their bright warm colors to death's shades of green. Dreary rain beat on them. Dampness and mold closed around her. A fungal odor bit at her nose. Something felt wrong. Where were the empathic images she had been taught to expect?

The canopy turned metallic silver. The mighty tree swayed in a wind that did not touch her. Wood squeaked like rusty hinges. The sharp squeals hurt her sensitive, delicately pointed ears so much so that she folded them down and back against her head to muffle the agonized screams.

This tree had sheltered her numerous immediate family members for thousands of years. Now every branch reminded her of ragged teeth waiting to rip and tear at her.

Jumping ten ells to the massive branch below, she saw no one. Had all of them abandoned home? Had they abandoned her? Was something wrong with her adulthood ceremony? Gliding to the outer trunk, she slipped through a hole and crawled along a twisted path. She found one of the tree's many natural hollow spaces, a communal living area large enough to hold a hundred people and their belongings. It was empty. Empty as if it had never been occupied.

Scrambling around the room she entered the tree's central spiral path. A hint of sawdust rode on the air. Alarmed, she ran back to the abandoned room, slamming her head against an overhanging aerial root, and fell to the inclined, gnarled path. She cocked an ear sideways and listened but heard nothing. She looked at her bare feet. Her nails, adult crimson, had once been infant deep red, almost black. She remembered how sharp infant nails were. Her fingers and toes had itched while they shed, and the adult ones grew. She once clawed them along the living handrails and paths, seeking relief. In doing so, she peeled curled shavings from the living wood, causing it to weep the spicy aromatic sap that alerted the family to what she had done. The shame she felt for harming her home had stalked her for months.

Her people called home, and trees like it, *elleiu*. The notes of the name sang a form of the word for home. A healthy elleiu tree had broad yellow variegated crimson and orange leaves, each one resembling a shovel blade two ells wide. Rough, shaggy, brindled, orange bark covered its trunk, branches, and aerial roots. Those aerial roots hung from the underside of limbs and extended into the ground. Over the centuries they grew into secondary trunks, buttressing, supporting, and concealing the main trunk like a suspension bridge. They formed vaulting arches and hollow recesses that sheltered family groups with ease. Interior paths and interconnecting rooms twisted around and up through generations of accumulated aerial root growth that reached into the tree's crown. The oldest aerial roots spiraled down around the main trunk, twisting a bloated corkscrew that formed the tree's wide central path.

Thunder rumbled, shaking her from the memory of trees. She listened to the beating rain that made the tree thrum like an idling combat vehicle.

She felt damp. She should not have. Elleio's rain forest climate never penetrated this far into the tree. Her eyes played tricks: she caught a glimpse of something sharp, jagged, and disjointed. She sang a low whine. Coward! She scolded herself, and snarled: dark red, nearly-black lips drew back, exposing her equally dark gums and brilliant white teeth. She felt childish and stupid, but she could not shake the feeling that a predatory reptile lurked in the tree's hollow spaces. Boles stood out around her, silent judgmental sentinels that frowned derision and contempt down on her. Who was she to think of herself as an adult? She jumped through one of them, ran through another vacant room, and out onto another broad branch.

Shadows lengthened. She found nothing but rain and wind. She padded back to the tree's spiraling central path. The air glowed foggy whiteness. It filed the tree from the ground up like water filled a sinking ship. The scene below her turned hazy. The mold smell rose on the mist. The jungle concealed many deadly predators. If one of them had come through the ground entrance with the mist, then it was her duty to kill it.

She did not want to go down there. The damp fuzzy mist tickled her bare feet with runnels of water. If she lost her footing here, then walking down the twisted bark's spiral trail would turn from a gentle descent into an uncontrolled crash. She remembered playing on these paths with other infant females; cornering one of the infant males; learning how to protect him by stalking from a distance; watching without upsetting him.

The smell of rotting wood banished the happy memory. Seeping, cloying, it rose up from the wide, gnarled fused path. Fungal, damp fingers drifted on the still air. She stepped down with caution. Cold bright light from the dense fog streamed into the tree far below. She twisted her tail for balance and increased her pace. She brushed an opening with her *pons*, her tail's ringleted tip, and fell into empty space. Jumping aside, she spun her tail to keep her balance.

Stepping into the tree's ground level central chamber, she sat on a twisted knot of roots and stared at the wood chips covering the ground. As with all elleiu trees, this level boasted meticulous care. Flat natural stepping stones paved heavy traffic areas. Wood chips covered bare ground from the central trunk, around the hollow interior spaces, and all the way to the outer columns formed by the youngest of the fused aerial roots.

Her immediate family met here for communal events. They should be here, but they were not. Foggy mists billowing through the central bole brought its own cheerless light. Its glow reminded her of the seldom used, eye-straining, harsh white of fluorescent lighting. Stepping through the foggy mists, she entered the untamed jungle. Her world consisted of great oceans and small continents covered to their shores with rain forests. Undeveloped by both custom and Tribal Compact decree, the jungle's plants, animals, and even the terrain itself concealed dangers both subtle and magnificent.

She felt trapped in a dream. When would her adulthood ceremony begin?

The jungle glowed. Edges blurred. Bright tree shapes blasted out pale light that punched through the dense fog. She felt better exposed to the dangers of the wild than she did in the safety of home. The fog made her feel weightless. She held out her hands. Her long, four-jointed fingers looked solid. They felt solid. Everything she touched felt solid, too. She thought of the spirits.

The spirits? The spirits had no form. She saw her body. She saw the trees shining in the fog. Her people did not visit the spirits until they died.

She glided back into the tree's communal area and found it filled with filigree opalescence. She felt strange, weak in the knees. A palpable, insistent urge tugged at her from all sides at once.

She longed for the beckoning jungle, its features lost in a white haze. A multitude of soft gentle voices sang potent songs from its depths. The music comforted her and reminded her again of the spirits.

The spirits! Glancing up the twisted path she saw a dark hole in the preternatural fog. She raced back up the bark-covered spiral. Her weight returned. The smell changed. Dead things rotted. Death clung to the tree. Its cloying denseness filed her nose like a stuffy cold. Dampness made the rotting wood and dead fungi smell stronger still.

Frozen to the bark, she stared at the Ni'zakhonii, the alien reptiles from another star.

She heard a male's mighty singing voice ring out deep bass notes from the fog.

She felt it important that she wrap her tail around the puzzling melody. The song dropped in pitch, whispering to her from below, where the white fog had made her feel weightless and insubstantial. She blinked: the vision of the Ni'zakhonii and her family had vanished. But she remained. The spirits must have taken her outside of time to show her the future, and now she was back in the Oyya's eternal now. She had been carried along by her people's empathic visions. Why had the Oyya not ejected her? Was she lost? It was possible to get lost during the adulthood ceremony if you chased after the spirits instead of remaining grounded in physical surroundings. Home represented physical reality for her.

A tumbling white blob floated out of a bole. From it, shimmering streamers of mist floated past her. They ignored her and caressed the living tree. Where they touched, the wood died. She could not smell the reptilian invaders, but she felt certain they controlled this thing somehow. She steeled herself and resisted the urge to bite her tail.

She pulled a black and red flint knife and rushed the hovering white blob. She struck creamy fog, and her concerns melted away; she did not care one way or the other about anything. Nothing mattered anymore. All seemed well. Momentum alone pulled her from its grasp. Mindless and indifferent, she tumbled off the wide branch.

Arboreal instinct forced her to stretch arms and legs wide and aim for a large orange variegated red leaf. She hit it and four others in rapid succession, decelerating with each impact. She hit a final leathery leaf and rolled onto a wide bough like a raindrop rolling from its tip. The white blob did not follow.

Primitive fear yammered at her. Instinct warned her to beware, least she become prey. She feared being eaten alive. Every creature consumed matter to live. Even her people, vegetarians without exception, ate living fruits, vegetables, seeds, and nuts.

A pheromonal scent triggered an empathic emotion, an image of unnatural feeding. She thought the emotion implicated technology somehow.

Her people knew technology was a loose tail that needed a strong fetter. They harnessed technology to provide abundant clean energy and power faster-than-light warships, but its use on Elleio was limited to protect the climate and the environment.

Had technology gotten away from them? She doubted it. Where had the males gone? Had technology killed them?

A creeping coolness radiated from home. The tree pulled warmth from her like a lonely winter night. She understood: sickness and not technology acted here. Technology produced astounding medical advances. Medical technology kept death at tail's length.

The cloudy form surged out of a bole in front of her and wrapped its tendrils around a bough. Wood waterlogged and molded before her eyes. Lacking structural strength, the bough sagged with a shrieking moan.

Enraged, she charged the fluffy phosphorescence. She jabbed her flint blade through its soap bubble skin. The force of the strike carried her close: she smelled pheromones.

She froze as her mind translated the chemical odor.

"You must hold the high ground," its scent told her. An unintelligible song pounded an insistent background beat. Around her, leaves soughed in time with it.

"What?" she stammered.

"The first song of all Eyloni is in your hands. The first song has saved, saves, and will save. I am Death. I cannot change though the spirits will it. You must embrace the high ground."

She staggered away from the apparition.

What did it mean?

Old sawdust and urine odors seeped from the ruined stump. The fog ball dropped below her branch, extended a fuzzy tentacle, and stabbed another branch. An aura formed around it. It wavered and pulsed in time with the subdued strange song echoing through home.

She smelled the reptilian invader. It sought the singer. Its scent formed an empathic image in her mind that she connected with territorial squabbles.

She ran into the vast tree's living areas.

The path vanished in a sea of twisted fluffy white threads that wove an Oyya web all the way down to the ground. That way led to the spirits. The music echoed up from there. How? Spirits lacked gender, but the song projected a male identity.

How? Spirits were pure forms. The male image must stand for an archetype. Was she to bring a male singer into the world? Astounding! Male births were rare. If she was to give birth to a male, then this web must lead the way.

Why not? When in season, females mated in the hope of delivering a male. She ignored her clan's warnings not to follow the spirits and ran down the misty spiral heedless of her safety.

The song faltered, and she gasped as though thrown into a freezing river as she found herself standing on a narrow branch high in the tree's crown.

She growled a challenge. The great tree moaned in sympathy. *Enough!* She must find out what high ground she held and how to use her superior position.

As though they had waited for a sign, the spirits surrounded her. They had no form, but she knew they were there, nonetheless.

"*Ki*, Kida," they sang.

She stood with the spirits. They called her by her infant name, Kida. Her clan had not prepared her for this!

She faced them and sang a formal greeting.

The spirits seemed to hesitate, seemed to listen.

She perked her ears forward. They listened to the singing male. Females always listened to males singing, but spirits lacked gender.

Around her, a mouth opened in the whiteness. Sharp teeth receded into its throat, a tunnel that sloped down to the ground.

The web had turned into a predator's gullet! She shuddered in revulsive spasms and thought of prey. Filled with shades of green, the color of dying vegetation, the gullet smelled of mold and decay. The scent called forth an empathic vision of finality.

The male's odd music beat against the gaping horror, made it vibrate. His song hurt it somehow.

She stepped forward.

"No," the spirits sang, "You hold the high ground. He holds all Eyloni in his hand. If you capture the low ground, he will falter."

"Males never fight alone," she spluttered. "No female ever lets a male face danger alone!"

The spirits sang to her: it was of no consequence that the male fought alone.

The spirits wasted her time, stalled her.

The reptile's pheromones drew a clear picture in her mind: it devoured males.

Defiant, she ignored the spirits and stalked into the yawning web. A wrenching force pulled her sideways, as though she ran and someone grabbed her tail and yanked her aside. She tumbled off the branch and fell.

Fog surrounded her.

"Why are you here, Hunter?"

"This is my adulthood ceremony. I know I am in my clan's Oyya web. You are the spirits," she accused.

"We are who are."

"Please let me help the singing male," she said.

"He must fight this battle. Although it is not natural for males to fight without female support, you may not help him in this battle while you are in the Oyya's web. You must hold the high ground."

"What does that mean? I am a Hunter who holds onto a decaying home. I could sing strength to him!"

"No, Kida. Instinct and social norms urge you to protect and defend the male, but in doing so you would distract him from the battle."

"That is obscene! No female ever leaves a male defenseless. His song lacks female accompaniment."

"Males are fearsome fighters. You know that. His song echoes through all Eyloni. He holds them in his hand, and you hold the high ground. He does battle on the low ground. Remember basic strategy. Are you an adult or not? An adult should know what it means to hold the high ground."

"Battle on low ground is folly if the high ground is not secured first," she said.

"Yes."

"But I do nothing but leap from branch to branch. I make no contribution to the battle, and I let a male face danger alone."

"He is not alone. Uncounted females watch him always."

"I smell no females here, no female association that follows a male, and no occupational society of females that associates with a *sire cairn*, a battle leader," she said.

"They respect male autonomy, as all females do. Just because he battles alone does not mean that female eyes do not follow him. Even now Hunters, Warriors, and Comara keep jealous watch over him,"

"Comara? Not just a single Comari? A Comari cares only for her chosen male to the exclusion of all others."

"The male singer is the beloved of all Comara."

The response rocked her back on her tail. Comara females were even rarer than males. A Comari fixated on a single male and protected him throughout her life. The male chosen had no say in the matter. Why would all Comara take an interest in the same male?

"Why do the Comara care for him?" she asked.

"Because he sired them."

The reply made no sense. Her people traced their history back to the beginnings of the first songs, well over one hundred thousand years ago. How could a single male sire all the Comara that ever lived?

She remembered: the singing male was a gender archetype. She traveled along her clan females' Oyya web; their empathic feelings came to her through their pheromones. This was her adulthood ceremony: she had been warned.

"The singing male is not an individual male," she accused.

"He is an individual male, the embodiment of the male gender, and the progenitor of the female gender's inherited phenotypic characteristics. He is all three because of you: you hold the high ground."

Their words confused her. They smelled of false trails and hidden meanings. Immediate and extended family females had warned her: logic in an Oyya web followed the emotions of the participants.

"How do I hold the high ground for an archetype?" she asked.

"We are who are. We are like the jungle. We grow wild. We do not weep for every leaf that falls to the ground. The fallen leaf renews the soil. We do not tell you why or how: you hold the high ground."

"And if I fail to hold the high ground?" she asked.

"Then it will be as if you had never been, and it will be as if all Eyloni everywhere had never been."

What did that mean? She had been told the imagery of the adulthood ceremony was filled with abstract meaning.

"Go." the spirits said. "Your time has come. You are an adult Hunter now."

The world wrenched sideways.

She stood on a narrow branch among the topmost branches of home, looking out across a sea of leaves and their varied ocher shadings, from pale gold to orange to red, all of them trimmed in yellows. The colors blended together until the patterns matched her own unique natural skin tones. The leaves heaved in the wind as though a muscular male flexed his shoulders.

The male's odd song remained. The spirits had said he was the embodiment of all Eyloni males, and that she held the high ground for him. She looked down. Far below, gold and orange grasses and crimson jungle vegetation waited among the lesser trees surrounding her towering home tree.

Above her, the sky turned black, blacker than Elleio's days-long night sky. Here and there bright wisps sparkled in a vision of deep space. The stars became the multitude of her people. They gazed down on her. Around them, the reptilian Ni'zakhonii either died of starvation or devoured those of her people who stood on the fringes of the gathering. Groups of tailless people, not Comara, the people the Tribal Compact of the Ten Tribes of

Elleio had only just discovered either sang with her people or helped them beat the Ni'zakhonii aside. Some of them even seemed to help the Ni'zakhonii in some obscure way!

The stars around the vision's edge pulsed in time with the male's fading, haunting melody.

The empathic vision dissolved around her, and she found herself balancing on the balls of her feet before her immediate family members, representatives of her extended family and clan, and the Tribal Elders.

In silence the Tribal Elders presented her with a veined, black-and-crimson-flint adulthood knife, the outward symbol of her adult status, on this the twelfth year, twenty-fourth month, and tenth day of her life.

In silence, they waited for her first adult decision.

"I will submit myself for selection by a warship's society," Kidahin told them.

"So be it." The Tribal Elders sang.

1

ABOARD THE COMPACT WARSHIP HUNTER'S MOON

Kidahin twisted her tail around her chair. She had been doing so for hours now. Four months had passed since the warship's crew made her their youngest member and declared her their *huluhar*. For weeks she had received lessons on ship history from the Mistress of Saga and trained day and night at the command helm and navigation station with Trebithia, the Mistress of Pathwalking. She counted herself lucky every time she got a full four hours of sleep. Today's assignment placed her at the warship's helm, but the Mistress of Pathwalking supervised her from the navigation console.

Kidahin wondered again why the crew chose her. Doubt and excitement warred within her. That was bad: doubt killed. She called up the warship's navigation plot and reviewed the data about the area they patrolled. The Nikkiolo Expanse, a volume of space named after its central star, was a ribbon of free territory standing as a buffer between Compact space and the Ni'zakhonii, a hostile race of bipedal reptiles. They filled her with loathing. When her people first contacted them over 130 years ago, the Ni'zakhonii showed no desire to establish peaceful relations. Survivors of the Ni'zakhonii attack said they watched in horror as their captured loved ones were eaten alive.

She was glad the recently discovered humans were nothing like the Ni'zakhonii.

They surprised and intrigued her people. They intrigued because when the first human warship visited Elleio, 102 infant Eyloni females followed a human male infant everywhere. The child's mother and the other humans were surprised and thought it strange that infant females even a few weeks-old herded infant males away from dangers and protected them from predators. Why the humans thought normal female behavior strange was a mystery to her. After all, as much as it had surprised the Eyloni, the human male infant had sung to them, and when his mother had taken him to go visit another clan, the females had crossed several thousand ells of heavy jungle to maintain their association with him, only to find that he had been returned to his ship. This upset the Eyloni infants and adults.

Kidahin brought her thoughts back to *Hunter's Moon*. Looking at the navigation plot again, she reassured herself that the helm controls remained in their correct settings. She leaned back into her chair. They were cruising at the warship's normal readiness condition: Action Ready. Crimson red status indicators reported all systems nominal. No emerald green warning lights showed on her console. Good.

Her lessons with the Mistress of Saga had taught her the history of the ship. He was a good ship. All warships were male, of course. The Compact Fleet classified *Hunter's Moon* as an elite class assault battle cruiser, a hybrid that combined the features of a destroyer and an assault forces carrier. Several Hunter societies from two hundred clans of the La'huaset Tribe had financed and built him. The warship belonged to them, not to the families, not to the clans, not to the tribe, and not to the Compact. The Hunter societies chose the original crew and gave the warship to them.

The builders had done their best to mimic the living spaces found within the elleiu trees growing in the rain forest jungles of Elleio. Quarters, bays, and compartments resembled rooms formed from fused aerial root structures. Warship passageways resembled jungle trails. Holographic projections added to the illusion. Jungle smells of soil, of leaves, of grasses, and of flowers drifted on random breezes.

The deck plating modeled uneven jungle terrain. They felt like roots, rocks, and earth but did not crumble like the real thing. Indeed, they resisted wear. Kidahin scrubbed her bare feet along the uneven surface, gripping it with her opposable toes, and sighed with pleasure.

She leaned further back and stared up at the ceiling. Yellow sunlight seemed to shine through jungle canopy. Gold, yellowed orange, and red light filtered down on her. Shifting her bright amber eyes from left to right about the command center, Kidahin snuck glances at the Hunter and Warrior crew. Their hair, fluorescent orange, bright red, or deep red grew in tight ringlets on their heads and on their pons. They all had tails as lengthy as they were tall. Their differences showed up in their skin coloring. Warriors had unique dominant orange and yellow variegations overlaying their reddish skins. Deeper red tones highlighted their musculatures, giving them an airbrushed look. Hunters like Kidahin had less orange but more elaborate yellow variegations covering their reddish skins.

Everyone wore waistwear; hip-riding thongs covered by a short outer loincloth adorned with varying clan and tribal colors. Their neckwear looked like necklaces of loose braided colored knots that fell across their breasts. The circular web in their left earrings proclaimed their military rank, accomplishments, and commendations.

Phelindra, a tall willowy female, caught Kidahin's attention. Seated at the security station, the Mistress of the Watch held the highest Hunter social rank aboard ship: Eldest Huntress. She also held the highest military rank. The gold circle hanging from her rank earring framed the intricate web patterns, the lobed honor knots, and the tiny mission beads that proclaimed her status.

Like the Eldest, Kidahin was also a Hunter—the lowest ranked one. But they shared similar traits: both were tall and slim, with typical Hunter skin color patterns common to the Hunter female phenotype.

She looked forward. Three ells from her console was the warship's command and control station. Sitting there at stiff attention, Melkorka, the Mistress of the Ship, rested an unsheathed longsword across her thighs just above her knees. Her tail wrapped several times around the sharp blade. The sword belonged to Kalinn the ship's Warleader. He picked her to command the warship. Her rank was inferior to the Eldest's, but holding his sword declared her authority over the ship for as long as Kalinn lived. Her short, slim, muscular build and skin pigmentation marked her as a

Warrior. Her bright orange hair drew eyes to her: she was quick to anger and slow to tolerate failure.

Shifting in her chair Kidahin looked over Melkorka's shoulder. Her eyes froze on Warleader Kalinn. He was their strategist. He was also the essential male presence who served as the focus of all female fighting power aboard ship. Females loved males and were their fierce protectors. A male increased their combat aggression in proportion to the danger they felt he faced. He held no rank but commanded anyway. As on all warships the entire crew, without exception, chose a male and gave him absolute control over their ship. At the moment, he hummed a comforting melody which she knew echoed throughout the warship. Every word he uttered, every song he sang, was always transmitted for their benefit. He had just given Melkorka a gentle caress and was crossing the command center to brush his tail against Phelindra's pons.

Kidahin's delicate ears swept back as she felt Kalinn's emotions. His scent projected calm assurance through her people's pheromonal empathy. She dwelled on the mental image his scent conjured in her mind. It troubled her, but she did not know why.

She wore the adulthood knife, but she retained a juvenile's instinctive irrationality. Youthful instinct mattered in a crew's search for a huluhar. Infant and juvenile females fixated on males with an obsession lasting until a year or so after coming into season for the first time. She retained, for the time being anyway, vestiges of her juvenile instinct. As the warship's huluhar, she alone must pick, for several thousand females, the most acceptable male replacement for Kalinn if he should die. Although the unanimous choice of the crew selected a warleader, they trusted her judgment in making that choice.

She contributed her instinct to her crew. She felt they had not chosen well in picking Kalinn to be warleader, for no matter how well he sang, she was put off. He made her feel uncertain, hesitant.

Kidahin made stronger empathic contact with others when she touched them, or when she sang with them. Music formed the basis of her language and had ancient cultural roots. Music triggered emotions. Emotions triggered pheromones. Pheromones blended with scent, and scent stimulated empathic centers in the brain.

As huluhar, she served in the command center to experience empathy with the warleader. It bothered her that she felt uncertain around him. The last emotion she should expect near him was uncertainty. Kidahin watched Kalinn a moment longer before turning her attention back to the helm controls. She knew Trebithia's navigation console overlapped with hers in double redundancy and that they both saw everything was still nominal.

Kidahin knew their mission was classified. Kalinn had said that they were to test Ni'zakhonii military capability and, if possible, capture an enemy ship for analysis.

Kalinn felt the huluhar's empathic fingers flutter about his temples.

"We will strike within the next thirty-four to forty-one hours," he said. He spoke to her, but everyone aboard heard him as always. "The search pattern leads us near the Surutia and Nikkiolo star systems. We will prepare an action plan that considers a series of probable faster-than-light jumps. I do not want to waste time calculating a likely FTL jump at the last minute."

"To where? How many?" Melkorka asked from her command chair.

Kalinn activated the tactical viewscreen next to her. "Here, here, and here," he said, tracing his orange and red four-jointed index finger along the projected navigation plot.

Melkorka choked. They could prowl for some time, days between jumps, hoping to detect and capture an enemy ship without pounding him into useless junk.

"Mistress," Hlinlodyn, the Mistress of Tactics, interrupted, "Sensors detect a neutrino anomaly consistent with that of a Ni'zakhonii FTL wake."

"Can you type the ship and plot his course?" Melkorka asked, her tail snapping.

"Yes, Mistress. The neutrino mixing angles and emission rates are consistent with a Ni'zakhonii frigate or smaller ship under V-band FTL acceleration. The projected plot suggests he will travel near the Nikkiolo and Surutia star systems in just under two days. Mistress, the enemy ship could make for either system, or he could continue on into human territory."

"Where do you think he goes, Hlinlodyn?"

"Nikkiolo, Mistress. Ni'zakhonii FTL drive physics forces him to follow a series of arcs course through a subspace manifold. The neutrino mixing angle tells me that they come from a hydrogen-antihydrogen fuel source. The particle decay rate betrays his velocity and approximate course. I cannot say for certain which system is his destination, but I am certain no mere scout intends to cross the extreme edge of Compact territory and enter human space."

"Any reason why the Ni'zakhonii would go to Nikkiolo?" Kalinn interrupted.

"No Kalinn," Melkorka said. "We have nothing there. The Compact claimed the system over a hundred years ago. They sent a probe to scan the system and nothing came of it until a few months ago, when the evaluation team sent there encountered the human warship *Alexandra Witze*. The system has one habitable moon orbiting a gas giant, just as Elleio does. While the survey team understandably paid more attention to the humans, they did report that the moon was covered with healthy *green* leaved trees--disturbing, I know—and that it had a thriving ecosystem."

"Could a Ni'zakhonii survive there?" he asked.

"Yes, but not in comfort," Melkorka said as she scanned the exoevaluation team's report. "There is too much seasonal temperature variation, but they could survive there with minimal logistical support."

"Territorial grab," Kalinn mused aloud.

"That is possible," the Mistress of the Ship said. "Nikkiolo and Surutia both follow the extreme edge of Compact territory and face human space. Nikkiolo is 4.2 light-years closer to the humans than Surutia, and it does have the habitable moon."

"You think the Ni'zakhonii might use Nikkiolo as a staging area for raids into both Compact and human space?" Eirmilla, Kalinn's Protectress, asked in her usual blunt manner.

"No. Why would they provoke war on two fronts?"

"Then what do you think the Ni'zakhonii plot?" Eirmilla demanded.

"I think they have sent a small ship out to test human detection capabilities because their drive emissions barely stray into our territory. The spirits have given us the opportunity to capture an enemy ship," Kalinn said.

His enthusiasm caught on. Pheromones wafted throughout the warship as the crew anticipated killing the enemy and capturing their ship intact. Kidahin took the initiative and called up the navigation data needed to plot a jump into the Nikkiolo star system.

The Mistress of Pathwalking gave Kidahin a fond indulgent smile and turned to review her navigation plot. She watched the young Hunter lash her tail, smelled her quivering excitement, and knew she yearned for her first taste of naval combat.

Kalinn considered options. The Ni'zakhonii ship would reach Nikkiolo in two days. They would jump ahead, wait, and plan the attack, then fire on him the moment he reentered normal space.

"Trebithia, plot a course for Nikkiolo. Set vectors and spool up the drive for a jump to the system's heliopause," Kalinn said.

"By your command," the Mistress of Pathwalking replied in the traditional manner and passed the task on to Kidahin.

Compact FTL technology differed from Ni'zakhonii drive physics. A Ni'zakhonii ship fell through the void between dimensions. Compact warships used gravity lensing to create a quantum singularity. A warship could jump up to a maximum displacement of 3.043 light-years. Warships of *Hunter's Moon*'s class could recharge and jump again in a little over a day.

Kalinn watched Kidahin plot the warship's jump data as he thought about the enemy ship. His warship outclassed the Ni'zakhonii ship by a significant margin; the engagement would fall far below even that of a wargames exercise. Kalinn twitched his tail with confidence; his pheromones conveyed pictures of victory celebrations.

The huluhar's tangy pheromones formed youthful, exuberant pictures in his mind.

Kidahin. She was very young and biased toward instinctive behavior. He thought about her for a moment and concluded that she would have a challenging time curbing her impulses.

He considered her lingering pheromonal discomfort. It puzzled him. Eyloni took comfort from close contact and communal living. Kidahin seemed to have adjusted to her crew's society, to the Hunter society aboard ship, and to the helm operator's society, but she remained standoffish with him. He had tried to win her confidence ever since the crew had chosen her. Females took comfort from a male presence. She took comfort from him too, but an occasional empathic tremor rang through her scent.

Adolescent jitters, he concluded. Her clan must have petitioned for her adulthood ceremony too soon. Eyloni infants walked and climbed trees within hours of birth. For the first three years of life infants relied on instinct alone, like animals in the wild. When their skulls grew large enough to house a bigger brain, hormonal changes let them learn at fantastic rates until they reached sexual maturity around twelve years of age. Eyloni remained instinctive creatures until puberty. Once a female came into her first mating season, her clan sent her into the jungle naked and alone for three months. When she returned from the survival ordeal, her clan petitioned their Tribal Elders for permission to conduct her adulthood ceremony.

Kidahin had been awarded the adulthood knife hanging in its curved sheath tied below her left breast. The colored knots on her neckwear displayed clan and tribal affiliations along with her status in various female hierarchies. Because the knots concealed nothing, her breasts bobbed behind eyeball-sized openings, and her skin pigments showed between the braided knots. The simple web in her earring declared her low military rank.

"Sublight drive is shut down," Melkorka said, "Vectors set. Jump drive standing by," she added.

"Prepare to jump the ship," he said.

Kalinn began to sing. By doing so, he incited the entire crew to battle readiness. He reviewed his strategy. The enemy's drive signature implied a small ship. Experience showed such ships lacked dense hull plating and relied on particle weapons for attack with radiological shields for defense.

Hunter's Moon boasted both heavy weapons and interleaved defense shields. The ship employed particle shields to spread enemy strikes across his hull's surface area. Even if shields weakened, the hull plates sapped energy from particle beam attacks by ionizing electrons and boiling the wasted energy into space. It would take much heavier weaponry, prolonged bursts, or coordinated weapons fire to defeat his warship.

Kalinn knew they could handle anything a frigate or scout ship could throw at them. He planned a simple strategy: jump into normal space at the predicted point, wait for the enemy ship to arrive, fire to disable his engines, lock tractor fields onto him, quantum translate a boarding party into the ship and kill his crew, secure the ship, tractor the ship into the combat operations bay, and return to Elleio.

"Jump," he said.

"By your command. Jumping the ship to Nikkiolo, a low threat Action Zone. Set jump parameters to maintain attitude and disposition and null exit velocity. Jump displacement is 2.331 light-years. Mistress of Pathwalking, commence jump," Melkorka said.

"Affirm, acting," Trebithia said. She checked her instrumentation and nodded permission to Kidahin.

Kidahin made a swift obsessive scan of her navigation plot and pounced on the jump control.

Thirty billionths of a second after she hit the switch, the warship exploded into starry blackness ten light-minutes from Nikkiolo's heliopause and staggered as though punched with a massive fist. Violent shudders rippled through the ship as structural integrity fields saved the bow from crumpling like a crushed can.

"We have been fired upon by three Ni'zakhonii destroyers in attack formation three million ells off our bow," the Mistress of Tactics said.

A second particle weapon barrage slammed the warship 341 degrees onto his left side. Multiple fusion torpedoes erupted from the enemy task force, sped toward them, and proximity detonated off the warship's bow.

"Battle Status!" Kalinn shouted, "Evasive left. Initiate damage control measures." At the same time, a volley of radiological torpedoes detonated a mere two hundred ells off their right flank.

Damage reports came in. Emerald green status indicators highlighted damage control alerts. Hull breach warnings flashed. Forward Fire Control and Forward Torpedo Bay-2 had been hulled. Forward Torpedo Bay-1 had been blown open to space, with the loss of the entire bay crew. The forward weapon targeting systems and the forward primary particle weapon systems dropped offline. An electromagnetic pulse torpedo detonated mere ells from the forward kinetic railgun coils, causing them to overload. The EMP also crashed right quarter forward main and forward auxiliary power systems. Radiological shields overloaded as they reflected hard radiation away from the hull.

The damage control station reported good news with the bad.

Judging by the soothing red indicators on the defense systems console, secondary shields held at half power. The overlapping tertiary shields stepped up to three-quarter strength to carry the load. The radiological shields would reactivate within the minute.

"Navigation shields are down, Kalinn," Kidahin said.

"Hlinlodyn, what is the tactical situation?" Kalinn asked.

"The enemy destroyers hold the points of an inverted equilateral triangle 22,000 ells on a side. They focused on our battle-hardened forward sections, and their concentrated firepower cut into our hull and disrupted several key systems," the Mistress of Tactics reported.

"Melkorka, ship's status?"

"Damage control parties are working to reestablish minimal navigation shields. The jump drive is offline because the armatures are misaligned in the gravity lensing system. There is minor buckling of the hull in Power Systems and Propulsion." The Mistress of the Ship paused in her report to read from the tactical systems command console. "All forward primary offensive weapon systems are offline, but forward point defenses are undamaged," she paused again. "A recorded message from the Mistress of the Decks reports that she had to blow the emergency airlocks and purge the forward antihydrogen fuel compartment to extinguish uncontrollable fires. Fire Watch reports all fires are out in Forward Fuel Reserve-1 and the loss of at least 114 females, including the Mistress of the Decks." An alert flashed on the screen from the warship's chief physician. "The Mistress of Healers reports Health Center at full strength and ready to receive casualties. She reports minor injuries so far, but she expects that to change."

"Ki, Melkorka. Auxiliary power to the forward shields. Hlinlodyn, plot firing solutions and execute. Fire control is at your discretion," Kalinn said.

"By you command. Targeting," the Mistress of Tactics replied. Her electronic countermeasures panel flashed a warning.

"Incoming fire! Multiple torpedo spreads!" the Mistress of Tactics reported. "Enemy ships breaking formation and closing on independent attack vectors." She scanned the data relayed from Combat Analysis Center and yelled, "Emergency evasive! Lead ship. Multiple particle weapons swinging to bear..."

The defense shields had already withstood a massed proximity torpedo spread. They needed a small but critical amount of time to redistribute and radiate the sudden influx of energy. The Compact warship suffered a glancing blow, and the overloaded shields struggled to absorb the additional load. Two particle beams hit the forward left dorsal hull, brushed aside the weakened shield, entered a massive hull breach, and ripped inward through eleven compartments. One thousand and twenty-one females died as the burst tore through Environmental Control Central, shredded the Forward Nutrition Center, and blew two forward primary particle weapon mounts into twisted wreckage. Bouncing between metal frames, charged particle streams ricocheted down passageways killing hundreds. The tail of the strike missed the Combat Analysis Center but slashed through the containment grid controls in Forward Fusion-2, one of the warship's four fusion power plants, forcing the reactor into emergency shutdown.

"Helm, evasive right. Pitch the ship to decrease the angle on the forward left quarter," Kalinn said.

"By your command. Maneuvering," Kidahin said as she coaxed her sluggish helm over to protect their damaged forward left flank. She began her maneuvering arc as another torpedo salvo hit them. Pulsed particle beams raked the warship's ventral right quarter and continued down his flank.

The Mistress of Tactics fired a targeted strike from the right broadside particle weapons. Using the wisdom of experience, she did not fire on all three enemy ships but instead concentrated all broadside firepower onto the nearest Ni'zakhonii destroyer's power systems and propulsion hull.

"Direct hit, right side, aft. Sensors show moderate to severe damage to their hull. Readings detect metallic debris, outgassing, and severe buckling in their hull. Combat Analysis reports the enemy ship's FTL drive has taken severe damage and their shields are down. I have locked onto them with the secondary particle weapon system and continue to fire at will," the Mistress of Tactics said.

"Incoming fire from the other two destroyers," Melkorka said.

"Hard about," Kalinn ordered, "Come to low ground, minus twelve relative, and fire pointblank as we pass through their angle of attack."

"By your command," Kidahin replied. "Kalinn, enemy ships are turning with us. They are attempting to lock onto our battle damage!"

"Evasive," he cried.

"Lead ship targeted. Firing," the Mistress of Tactics reported.

Against three Ni'zakhonii destroyers, *Hunter's Moon* held the strategic edge in an otherwise even match. However, the enemy had numerical superiority: three lesser ships could overwhelm a single but more powerful ship by forcing him to attack and defend against independent targets.

On the main holographic display, a destroyer blossomed in silent fury.

Kalinn sang a note of cheer. One ship damaged and unable to navigate and one destroyed. They had to disable or destroy the last one.

"Kidahin, set a collision course for the remaining ship. Ramming speed," Kalinn ordered.

"By your command."

Hunter's Moon had the armored bow and reinforced keel of an assault destroyer's forward hull. His builders had designed him to kill enemy capital warships, and he could survive a ramming attack if the situation warranted it. In Kalinn's opinion, the danger outweighed the risk. The Ni'zakhonii commander could still punch a lucky shot through one of his ship's large hull breaches.

"Closing on collision course at ramming speed," Kidahin said, "Impact will occur in four, three, two, one, zero."

The warship staggered as the huluhar counted zero. The inertial dampening field failed to mesh with the structural integrity field at the point of impact, pitching the command center crew into their consoles.

"Fire forward secondary weapons pointblank. Reverse maneuvering thrusters. Back us out," Kalinn said.

"By your command. Firing forward secondary weapons," the Mistress of Tactics said.

"Maneuvering thrusters at full reverse," Kidahin said.

The Compact warship withdrew from what remained of the crippled enemy's bow. Harsh, rending metal sounds, grinding noises, and explosive concussions followed them out.

"Maintaining fire," the Mistress of Tactics advised. "Moderate damage reported on all forward dorsal hull plates. Minor damage to the forward secondary particle weapon emitters from repeated pointblank firing. Minor hull breaches on all forward decks. Emergency force fields have activated at all hull breach points."

Melkorka read reports from the damage control station. Green pictographs flashed a warning across the screen, an alert from Combat Analysis Center.

She cringed. She froze for a heartbeat. She screamed.

"Full emergency reverse…"

The rammed Ni'zakhonii destroyer exploded. The shock wave pitched *Hunter's Moon*'s bow up and over into an uncontrollable roll.

"Helm does not answer," Kidahin said, struggling to keep her seat, her tail lashed around both it and her. "Navigation shields are offline again. Maneuvering systems are offline. Attitude and reaction control systems are offline. The ship is not free to navigate. The jump drive remains offline. Sublight engine power levels are holding at half power, but…" the young Hunter left the obvious unsaid.

Without the helm or maneuvering systems, moving the ship under sublight propulsion was suicide.

"Melkorka, what is the remaining enemy ship's status?" Kalinn asked.

"Adrift. Sensors report heavy loss of life and environmental system failures. Readings indicate that they have localized their repair efforts to the destroyer's FTL drive. Kalinn, they will no doubt flee the moment they complete minimal drive repairs. They must know they have no chance once we reestablish a weapons lock on them," Melkorka said.

"When can I expect helm or attitude control restored?" he asked.

The Mistress of the Ship conferred with a Warrior at the damage control station.

"Fourteen minutes," Melkorka estimated.

Kalinn growled a negative and snapped his tail.

"Too long. Translator status?"

Melkorka consulted the red status indicators on her command systems monitor. "Operational. Do you intend to translate aboard the enemy ship?"

"I do. I want that ship. Have the Mistress of Battle assemble two boarding parties at the amidships assault translation station. I am on my way there now."

"By your command," Melkorka replied and relayed the order to the Mistress of Battle and to the Mistress of Arms.

She glared at her command chair. She had doubts. No tactical reason demanded that they board the enemy destroyer. He was not going anywhere anytime soon, and he lacked the power to punch through their unshielded hull plates.

Melkorka knew Kalinn was furious, smelled it in his scent, saw its empathic image in her mind. Everyone in the command center smelled just as angry, but their empathic images also told her that they followed the battle's rhythm. Kidahin projected an image that jumped between youthful inexperience and focused excitement. Kalinn's scent, however, caused unease to crawl up her tail. At a loss to understand why, she glanced at the Mistress of the Watch.

Phelindra flexed her ears in response to the question the Mistress of the Ship's looping tail implied. She also thought the boarding action was unnecessary and irrelevant. *Hunter's Moon*'s damage control parties would restore helm control and targeting systems in ten minutes. Once free to navigate, they would lock weapons onto the enemy destroyer and kill him.

But Kalinn was Warleader. He had a mission to accomplish. If they could capture the destroyer intact, then they could salvage his key systems. She twitched her ears, signaling her acceptance.

Melkorka growled, causing Kidahin to flinch at her helm.

Melkorka's frustration was understandable. Females protected males as a rule and did so to obsession when they placed themselves at risk. Over four hundred Warriors and forty Hunters would translate with Kalinn aboard the enemy ship. They would all die before allowing him to come to harm.

"Mistress, the Mistress of Conveyance reports that the assault teams have translated aboard the enemy ship," Hlindredreda, the Mistress of Communications, said.

"Understood. Kidahin, status?"

"Pitch rate unchanged. Helm and attitude control remain offline."

"Ki, Kidahin," Melkorka said. She knew the word for strength, *ki*, was not enough, and so she comforted the huluhar with a gentle brush of her aromatic pons.

"Mistress of Tactics, continue scanning the enemy ship and report any changes."

"Affirm."

Kidahin conferred with Trebithia a moment and then addressed Melkorka.

"Mistress, I believe I can use the auxiliary gravity generator to null our uncontrolled tumbling."

"Continue your investigations and report when you arrive at a solution," Melkorka replied and entwined her tail with the huluhar's a moment in affection.

"Affirm, acting," Kidahin said. Pride filled her as she bent to her task with tail held high.

✦✦✦

Kalinn and his assault teams materialized aboard the Ni'zakhonii destroyer. Eirmilla arched her dappled tail around behind him. She did not embrace him, but her tail set a perimeter no one would dare cross. They had translated into an intact main passageway that ran the length of the enemy's amidships hull. It resembled the view of a green plant's stem from the inside.

On Elleio, a green plant was a dying one.

Flickering light filtered dim and pale along the passageway. The air smelled of spoilt fruit and reptilian musk.

"Assault teams report ready, Kalinn," Eirmilla said.

"Ki, Eirmilla."

The Mistress of Battle stood before them, her amber eyes somber and serious; her tail whipped high behind her. She swiveled her ears forward to follow his every word. At her side, a portable electromagnetic pulse device, a thumper, pumped out modulated, powerful EMP bursts.

"Are you ready, Brelioranda?"

"Yes, Kalinn. The thumpers are operating at full power. Scans show full EMP coverage over a one hundred ell radius. That should kill ship's comms and sensors, portable comms, scanners, and energy dependent small arms in the area. Assault leaders report ready."

"Ki, Brelioranda," Kalinn murmured. Thank the spirits Brelioranda was his Mistress of Battle. She had over thirty years of experience leading boarding actions.

"Get me a combat link to Melkorka."

"By your command," Brelioranda replied.

Kalinn waited a minute before the secure communications tone sounded in his ear. The Mistress of the Ship's holographic image solidified before his eyes.

"Melkorka? Comm check."

"Kalinn? Comm clear. Translation lock established. Maintaining vigilance."

"Ki, Melkorka. Executing action." He flicked his left ear to deactivate the comm device affixed there.

"I will press forward and take the ship's command center. Brelioranda, head aft and seize the power systems and propulsion hull. Move out."

Brelioranda and her team made their way through twisted wreckage. Prowling through the shattered amidships corridor reminded her of crawling through thorny jungle vines. They met little resistance and made steady progress. Here and there twisted bulkheads bristled with jagged crystal shards. They climbed over a maze of shredded decking and found a sealed blast door.

"Demolition crew blow this hatch," Brelioranda ordered.

With calm efficiency, the demolition team slapped shaped charges against the massive crystalline iris.

"Ready!" a Hunter's voice filtered over the assault group's open comm.

"Do it," Brelioranda grunted.

"Demolition in progress!" the Hunter yelled.

"Hot! Hot! Hot! Hot! Hot!" the demolition Hunter sang in warning scale.

Taut silence hung in the air, followed by a dull concussive thud. The heavy crystal hatch crumbled to the deck with the sound of shattering icicles.

"Kalinn? Brelioranda. We have penetrated the power systems and propulsion hull. The compartment looks intact. The corridor leads into a crystalline jungle. I can see the reactor and the power systems command center from here. Aft of the reactor is the engine complex. To the right is a scaffold structure fused into the bulkhead. I think the scaffold contains the propulsion command center. Should I hold the reactor, or should I take the propulsion command center?"

"Brelioranda? Kalinn. Take the propulsion command center. If we control the power systems and propulsion navigation systems interface, we can pilot the ship from there."

"By your command."

Brelioranda smelled Ni'zakhonii, a lot of them, hiding in the engineering spaces, waiting to jump them.

"Kalinn? Brelioranda. We have made contact with organized resistance, too many of them for propulsion and power plant crew. I think that the survivors have evacuated aft and are attempting to control the ship from the propulsion command center."

Kalinn stopped. If the surviving crew held the power systems and propulsion hull, then the primary command center must have been destroyed or rendered uninhabitable. Combat sensors aboard *Hunter's Moon* should have been able to discriminate between habitable and uninhabitable areas of the ship. The bulkheads may have blown out after they translated aboard, or the scan may have been indeterminate at the time it was made.

In any event, he had divided his forces for nothing. Doubtless he would need both assault teams to pry the enemy from the most critical control centers of the ship.

"Brelioranda? Kalinn. Do not engage them until we arrive."

Too late. Brelioranda had already committed her force in compliance with Kalinn's previous order. Warriors slashed black ceramic combat knives into the hated enemy. Hunters climbed the scaffolding and picked off opportunity targets with bows and arrows as they held the high ground. The ship's defenders found their weapons inoperative and charged the Eyloni, slashing naked flesh to ribbons with cruel knives and wicked claws.

"Brelioranda?" Kalinn repeated.

The destroyer's crew fought to hold the power systems and propulsion hull, while Kalinn's voice filtered through the now dead Brelioranda's commlink. Obeying the Mistress of Battle's last command, the Compact assault force cut the Ni'zakhonii down to four. Those remaining reptiles, amber scaled and wearing red smocks, turned their backs on the advancing females. They huddled over a long, wide, shallow console filled with glowing multicolored crystals. The crystals seemed no bigger than a flattened hand. The Eyloni rushed the Ni'zakhonii, victory certain. One of the four, rather than turning to defend itself, pulled two soft blue glowing gems from the console and smacked them together.

On contact, the crystals exploded in a flash of blue light, pulverizing everyone and everything within four ells.

The hydrogen-antihydrogen fusion reactor escaped the blast, but its control systems had vanished along with the remaining crew and the invading force. Without its fuel sequencing and emergency stop systems, the reactor ramped up to full power. Open circuits produced positive feedback that fed into the reactor's plasma containment control system.

Kalinn and his assault team rushed through the blown hatch and into the smoking wreckage at the same moment the containment force fields failed.

✦✦✦

Tactical scanners aboard *Hunter's Moon* detected the explosion in the destroyer's reactor control spaces and flashed a bright emerald warning to the Mistress of Tactics' threat assessment display.

"Mistress! Power surge in the enemy's reactor. The reactor is going critical!"

"Translate them back here now!" Melkorka ordered.

"Acting! Locking in. Translating," the Mistress of Conveyance said over the open comm.

The reactor exploded at the same time the boarding parties began to dematerialize. *Hunter's Moon* staggered as the shockwave hit, spinning it through four distinct axes of rotation simultaneously, crippling the warship's power distribution network. Artificial gravity faltered, inertial dampening fields fluttered. The helpless crew slammed against bulkheads and passageways. Casualties mounted. Main control consoles crashed, and lighting failed on all decks.

"Auxiliary power!" Melkorka demanded.

"Auxiliary power is unresponsive. Emergency battery power is coming online now," the Mistress of Tactics reported.

Battery power brought command center illumination back to a dim, weak, fluttering pale orange. The holographic projections that gave the ship his illusion of Elleio jungles had failed as well. Green status indicators painted emergency displays everywhere, betraying heavy damage.

"Mistress, all weapons systems are offline. Primary, secondary, and tertiary shields are offline. The sublight drive is offline. Translation systems are offline," the Mistress of Tactics said.

"Mistress of Conveyance, report boarding party status!" Melkorka demanded, as panic gnawed into her breasts.

"Internal comm systems are down, Mistress," Hlindredreda said. She wrapped her tail around her waist, seeking comfort.

"Send a scout to the amidships assault translation station. Find out if Akenallin got them translated off that ship!"

Eternal moments passed before Akenallin's voice fluttered over the open, intermittent comm channel.

"Mistress? Akenallin. I recovered only thirty-four Warriors and twelve Hunters. Kalinn has been lost. The Warleader is dead."

Stunned silence filled the command center. It hung there for an instant before anguished keening filled the warship.

A male had been lost. *Their* male had been lost.

On a world of rare males, the loss of a single one was devastating. His safety belonged to them, and they had failed him.

Melkorka stared at her command chair. She no longer held the title of Mistress of the Ship: it depended on Kalinn's preference and had died with him. For the moment she retained command by the simple inertia of habit and the nature of the continuing emergency. In a few weeks, petty hierarchical squabbles would degrade the warship's command structure.

Melkorka conferred with Phelindra, the highest-ranking female aboard in actual fact now. "We must find safe harbor around the habitable moon. A stable orbit is preferable to drifting in interplanetary space. We cannot attempt interstellar travel with the gravity lensing armatures misaligned."

"I concur," the Eldest said. She agreed that Melkorka should maintain the duties of Mistress of the Ship. In this she did not act either magnanimous or gracious: she considered Melkorka the most capable Mistress of the Ship she had ever known.

Far more important though, the ship remained at Battle Status and prudence dictated no changes for the time being.

Kidahin's novel use of the auxiliary gravity generators halted the warship's tumbling, but it would take days to restore helm and attitude control.

"Mistress of Pathwalking, plot a course for the habitable moon at best velocity," Melkorka said.

"Affirm, acting," Trebithia said, "Course plotted and transferred to helm control."

"Kidahin, execute course change," Melkorka ordered.

"Acting," Kidahin acknowledged.

The Compact warship limped further into the Nikkiolo star system, headed for the unnamed gas giant and its forested moon. Melkorka transmitted a general distress signal using the jump radius coverage FTL hyperlink transmitter. It would take them some time to reach standard surveillance orbit around the moon and repair the primary FTL scanners and hyperlink communication systems.

Whether or not they could repair the warship's FTL jump drive while they remained in a potential Action Zone she preferred not to dwell upon.

2

01h20: Senior Chief Warrant Officer Delwyn Wyrnette Marsch sighed. He watched men and women pile into the alphafortress troop transports waiting in their launch tubes. Only he knew that the alert was a wargames exercise.

His Action Response Teams lugged their weight in gear on every mission. They had to be ready for everything the nasties could throw at them. Everyone wore the Special Operations Group Working Uniform Type-II. The uniform—camouflaged with random shades of grass, moss, and sage green; each color a thumbnail square in size—included a carbon composite helmet. That helmet could take an antipersonnel railgun slug without a scratch. Of course, inertial dampening field coils embedded in the helmet nulled the slug's impact, but he repeatedly told the ARTs not to wear the chin strap in an Operation Zone because if a kinetic round hit the helmet, then the residual momentum transferring to the chin strap could rip their heads off.

Everyone carried a personal medikit that contained gauze packs, liquid bandage, plasticast, laser scalpel, pain meds, antibiotics, a staple gun that fired dissolvable staples for wound closure, and Mercy, a small euthanasia capsule for just such an emergency.

Too often now he thought about Mercy.

Missions seldom coincided with warm dry weather. Everyone packed a Uniform Type-II poncho. Thin as paper, in a pinch it could be used as a pup tent, a stretcher, or a body bag.

Standard weapon issue included an M-414 sidearm, an energy weapon that fired a particle stream: imagine a seventy-five-meter-long lightning strike focused to a fine beam. Various team members carried one of three other favorite weapons: The M-303 railgun that threw projectiles at supersonic speeds; the M-88 particle weapon assault rifle; or the M-707 grenade launcher that fired grenades and guided them to their targets. These weapons tended to fail if the enemy fired EM Pulse countermeasures so the standard Fleet 9mm pistol was a necessity. A plain and simple firearm, it worked when modern stuff died.

Special Operations Group missions came under the "if it needed to be done, then the ARTs could do it" category. ARTs established Forward Operations Bases, infiltrated enemy bases and ships, and carried out the majority of all covert operations.

Special Operations Command fell under naval jurisdiction but was a combined services organization. Every planet in the Coalition of Earth Colonies supplied volunteers from their own elite combat forces. Volunteers came from enlisted, noncommissioned officer, and warrant officer ranks: no commissioned officers. Only the top five percent volunteering qualified for special operations training, and those qualifying had to shake out in the top one percent to earn a Special Operations Group duty assignment. No one volunteered for Special Ops duty unless they didn't care if they died.

Marsch wanted to die.

Eight years ago, after retiring from Special Operations as a noncommissioned officer, he, his wife, and his three little girls had bought into an agricultural cooperative on Valhalla, a moon orbiting a planet in the Mu Arae star system. Bigger than Mars and having a heavy molten iron core, Valhalla's climate resembled the North American central plains. It had been a beautiful little world on the edge of Coalition space, a mere 50 light-years from Earth.

Each cooperative supported several hundred colonists and put out thousands of hectares in soybeans and winter wheat, the only two Earth crops that would grow well in Valhalla's soil. The cooperatives sold their inventories as fast as they were harvested, and all signs pointed to the moon becoming a major agricultural commodities exporter.

Then the Lizards came.

They attacked without warning. A small task force of unknown origin assumed high orbit around Valhalla and launched massive missile spreads over the cultivated plains. A planetary distress call was sent to the Coalition Fleet base in the Mu Virginis system.

Orbital strikes rained down on Valhalla for hours. Scanners detected volatile chemicals in the upper atmosphere that precipitated out over green fields, reducing them to pasty sludge. None of the imported Earth crops survived the weaponized alien herbicide.

Then the Lizards landed in force and slaughtered men, women, and children. The homesteaders who rode out the attack in enclosed vehicles and farm equipment returned home to find their friends, families, and neighbors disemboweled, dismembered, or even worse still living but so badly mutilated from being eaten alive, the survivors had no option but to offer Mercy to them. The Lizards hadn't spoken, warned, or otherwise made known the reason for their vicious, unprovoked attack.

Marsch returned to his ravaged home to find four bodies. Little remained of them, yet two of his little girls stubbornly clung to life. He gave them Mercy, and then crumpled. He had failed as a husband and father in the worst conceivable way. He had not kept his family safe.

The bedroom resembled the killing floor of a slaughterhouse. He couldn't stay there. He staggered out of the room. He couldn't think. Why hadn't he been here with them? Why was he alive and they weren't? He should have been here for them, should have protected them, should have died with them.

He poked through the debris, looking for toys, gifts, family pictures, anything to banish the horror lying in the bedroom.

The Lizards broke everything. They took nothing of value or use; everything had been broken beyond repair for the sheer joy of leaving nothing intact behind.

Marsch found a single hologram of his three daughters. Of his wife, no image survived to wipe the gruesome visage of her body from his mind.

There would be no burial. The fleet was still several hours away.

He set what remained of their home afire, the blaze a fitting pyre for them. The fire would wipe away all evidence of what had happened here. His family's ashes would scatter across the ruined fields.

They would remain here forever.

He watched the fire burn until it finally burnt itself out. It took a long time. Fleet personnel found him staring into the dying embers. He refused to move from the spot until a commander gave an order: "Senior Chief Petty Officer Marsch, report to the alphafortress for immediate evac!"

"Aye, aye, Sir," had been his numb reply.

Aye, aye, Sir!

After the Coalition battle group had evacuated the survivors and jumped into hyperspace, Marsch accessed the Naval Recruitment and Retainment Center's network site and reactivated his military status.

01h57: Marsch watched the troop transports land. The ARTs exited the alphas and moved out on their objective.

✦✦✦

A soft breeze blew across the winter wheat. The smell of death followed in its wake. Silence shattered. Screams echoed off into the predawn night. Veiled bodies laid here and there on the ground. He looked on the torn bodies of a woman and her daughters and froze: a farmer, filled with survivor's guilt, he stood confused and afraid, and wondered what had happened.

Marsch took a step forward and felt the soft, torn grass at his feet. In a far corner of his mind he heard a distant gonging, an alert siren, maybe? He dropped something from his hand as he spun around and around, seeing only madness. Next to him in the bloodstained grass lay a third girl no more than ten, skin torn to shreds by clawed hands. Her ripped-off head kept its unbroken, accusing glare. Weapons fire raged throughout the chaos. Gray sludge covered the ground like a blanket, cloaking desperate people, smothering their resolve.

He ran a hand over his face, felt the sweat, tried to get control of his breathing before he lost it. *I am NOT there!* he told himself repeatedly in a mantra of hope.

The stench of spilled blood and torn bowels filled his nostrils. His stomach churned as he watched young men and women on his left and right being cut down by suppression fire. He glanced upward, impotent. He peered up at the Valhallan flag that hung limp behind him. He pulled his damp, heavy head around, too slow to meet the bullet meant for him.

The round found PFC Serena Butcher's head instead. Her mouth a crater, her teeth blown across his lap. A bruise the size of a dress shirt's button colored her closed eyelid. Her cheek was gone…

***

"Commander? Sir, are you all right?" PFC Serena Butcher clutched his arm.

Marsch opened his eyes and scanned the hanger bay with a bewildered stare. He looked at the young woman.

"You were screaming, Sir."

"What? Oh yes, I guess I was."

Marsch bent over and picked up his helmet. He noticed the live fragmentation grenade lying on the deck, picked it up, pocketed it, and stepped onto a makeshift stage. Glancing overhead, he stared a moment at a holographic banner spread across the bulkhead that read, "CECS Henri Edda (CFA-81) Home of SOG-444 Special Operations Group."

"Be seated," he told his teams.

The men and women sat as one and faced forward. Delwyn Marsch commanded the carrier's SOG division. The ship supported fighter squadrons and a company of Marines, but most of the small footprint, high-risk missions were assigned to Special Ops ARTs. They got the job done when it needed doing. Marsch tended toward a calm direct intensity and had little to do with anyone outside of his command.

The trauma he suffered while on Valhalla had given him Posttraumatic Stress Disorder. The symptoms didn't inhibit his tactical and command abilities, but his off-duty hours were filled with flashbacks that made him dangerous and unpredictable. Dr. Kerchival had him down in sickbay at least once a week in therapy.

He took medication. Without it, he might kill someone without realizing what he was doing.

SOG-444 personnel shared an unshakable loyalty: they didn't care if their commander had an episode aboard ship, and he never had a flashback while on a mission. They all knew his story and kept quiet about it.

Even the carrier's commanding officer, Captain Winters, considered Marsch the best tactical special operations commander in the Fleet. Marsch had leadership qualities that made his teams want to follow him. He felt for his people and refused to order them to perform a task that he wouldn't do himself. He enforced that maxim on his NCOs, telling them "What you order done, you better be willing to do the same yourself."

Marsch held the rank of senior chief warrant officer, which in today's navy meant his rank paralleled that of a commander. Marsch had been an NCO and came up through the enlisted ranks. He was an enlisted man at heart. The Fleet had forced the rank of warrant officer 3/c, third class, when he reactivated: his expertise was sought for mission-critical assessments, but the gulf between officer and noncommissioned officer ranks made tactical planning difficult. The warrant officer rank gave him the freedom to speak his mind, overrule the high-styles, and yet work with his NCOs and enlisted personnel without an officer's rank getting in the way. The men and women of SOG-444 didn't much care for Fleet officers and their 'I read it in a book' tactics.

Marsch turned to the bulkhead holographic display and replayed the wargames log, stopping it often to point out mistakes and lecture his people on corrective options. The panoramic display followed the action from a particular unfortunate's perspective, alternating between the soldier's forward view and the OZ's overhead scan.

Heads up and eyes riveted, the ARTs listened to their intense commander.

Marsch leveled scathing criticism as the wargames log switched from one person to another. He pointed out doubtful moves and counted off alternatives on his fingers. His soft, deep voice captivated their attention and drew them in.

The exercise had begun at 01h15: an alert notice came from the bridge to the SOG Ops Center, ordering the ARTs to report to the flight deck for alphafortress deployment. The alphafortresses, armored troop transports, launched and cruised for about fifty minutes before returning to the ship. They landed on a flight deck covered with holographic trees, rises, tall grasses, depressions, and buildings made solid using force field generators. There, they received final mission briefings and moved out.

Marsch yawned in the middle of his exercise critique. He'd been awake since 01h00.

He had added the unscheduled exercise at the last minute at around 22h00 yesterday before hitting his rack. Winters signed off on it and left orders for gamma shift to drop the ship out of hyperspace and issue the alert. Landing on the flight deck had reminded him of dropping onto rolling fields of hay three hundred meters from a field command bunker. The ARTs accomplished their mission but took simulated casualties they shouldn't have.

And he'd lost it again, right there on the flight deck. This was the third training exercise that had triggered flashbacks in the past month. This time he'd nearly thrown the frigging frag grenade!

He had to get them under control before the ship's Chief Medical Officer bumped him into a teaching assignment or put him behind a tactical planning desk at headquarters. Only Captain Winters stood between him and a permanent ground assignment.

After the exercise debriefing, Marsch ordered his division to resume the morning's standard training regimen. He nixed the forty-five-minute PT exercises and started off with a ten-klick run around the hanger bay. He composed a report for the morning intelligence briefing while he ran. As the carrier's SOG commander, he had to sit through, listen to, and comment on issues that impacted Special Ops. Most of the time it turned out that new intel was old intel sprinkled here and there with retooled BS.

Military intelligence is a contradiction in terms. Marsch muttered the old cliché as he jogged. What he found interesting lately had more to do with their alien guests, the Compact co-ambassadors.

The two Eyloni, a man and a woman, preferred the terms male and female when referring to gender. Eyloni had funny ideas about gender identity and considered the terms man and woman offensive. Marsch thought their complaint turned on species identity, but the report said that the term 'woman' implied a chimeric composite, wo-man, a female-male. He wondered why the same logic didn't apply to the word 'female'.

He had learned from earlier briefings that the Eyloni female gender broke down into three types: Hunters, Warriors, and Comara. If he understood the briefing materials, then the different female types passed their characteristics on to their female descendants like racial traits that bred true along the same female type. Unlike the females, Eyloni males passed on a uniform set of traits to all succeeding male births. A fragile sex chromosome was said to vary female gender types and prefer female births by 20 to 1.

The two Eyloni held the authority of a single ambassadorship for the Tribal Compact of the Ten Tribes of Elleio. Scuttlebutt had it that they were Compact military and not career diplomats.

Marsch completed his fifth klick and checked his watch: 06h35—good time—no stragglers.

Rumor hinted that Honorius Alphonse Harrison, the Coalition ambassador plenipotentiary, was about ready to chew through a bulkhead. There hadn't been a meeting of the minds so far between Harrison, Anlann, or his Protectress, the female Hunter Seralin. It sounded to Marsch as though the co-ambassadors had weighed Harrison's character and found it didn't measure up to their standards of honorable behavior.

Humans speak with forked tongue. Marsch chuckled. An image of a fork stabbed through Harrison's tongue formed in his mind.

Marsch thought he understood their reservations. He knew something about cultural tribalism. Valhalla's cooperatives had been based on modified tribal rule, where small groups of people living close together decided what was best for them. He believed in that type of cooperative rule. Marsch didn't care for the Coalition's slow descent into federalism, where a strong centralized government told everyone what was good for them. He had heard that Percy Parakh, the Coalition Cultural Attaché working with Harrison, was pushing the federalist program by painting rosy pictures of a Coalition/Compact alliance that would present a united front to the Lizards, establish economic markets, and secure basing rights for each other's' ships. But images of beads and worthless treaties persisted in Marsch's mind all the way to the end of the ten-k run.

After the run, he ordered his NCOs to put the ARTs through a series of individual and group unarmed combat exercises that would last until Flight Ops began fighter launch and recovery drills at 08h30. As he sparred with his exercise partner, Marsch reconsidered his mangled metaphor. The Eyloni reminded him a lot of Native Americans. Remembering what had happened to them reinforced his doubts about strong federal management. Federal systems had a knack for elevating liars into positions of 'great negotiators', all of them passing out promises when none could be guaranteed. Coalition Government officials had made reassurances to the colonists going to Valhalla. They swore that the Mu Arae region harbored no dangers. A lot of good those assurances had done Marsch's wife and daughters.

08h25: Sweating after his workout, Marsch had his NCOs form up the ranks prior to dismissal. He had just enough time to clean up before the daily briefing.

08h30: Fighter pilots arriving in the hanger bay gave them the universal sign in a parting salute that said, "Get the hell off of our flight deck!"

His ARTs savored the departmental rivalry and responded in kind.

09h00: Seated in the briefing room, Marsch glanced through the xenocultural report on his omni while waiting for the meeting to get underway. The pages covering the initial intel briefing said that the Eyloni belonged to a primitive tribal culture. They had soft, textured skin, like fine suede or velour, colored with shades of orange and red with yellowish highlights that reminded him of fall leaves in Pennsylvania on a sunny day. Their skin color patterns let them blend into their homeworld's rain forest foliage. They believed in spirits and were a warrior people.

Marsch keyed the omni's audio and heard the pronunciation of the word 'Eyloni' in their language. To him it sounded something like an *a cappella* trio and woodwinds combined. He wondered about that: hit the wrong notes when you were trying to say their name and who knows what you might have called them. The report stipulated that humans were to identify them as *ee-low-nee* to avoid accidental insult. The co-ambassadors understood that humans lacked an Eyloni's vocal range so they took no offense from the human pronunciation. The word Eyloni meant The People and applied to them no matter where they lived, but when a specific tribe's people were meant, then the word was modified by the name of that tribe.

Marsch turned a page. Harrison's standing order prohibiting all musical expression aboard ship while the co-ambassadors were aboard was underlined, capitalized, and printed in red letters. It was feared that Anlann and Seralin had been offended when someone had tried to pronounce their species name. Marsch knew there was a rumor going about that knives had been drawn. To avoid misunderstandings, Ambassador Harrison had ordered everyone not to sing or play music.

Eyloni wore minimal tribal clothing. The male co-ambassador wore a short tan loincloth that looked tie-dyed, a fine braided multicolored rawhide necklace on his otherwise bare chest, and a gold button earring embossed with a triangle pierced into the tip of his left ear. A black obsidian knife hung from his hip.

The female co-ambassador wore a similar loincloth with blues, indigos, and violets in a tartan pattern. A simple arrangement of colorful braided knots hung from her neck down to just over her breasts, clearly not meant to conceal them. A wicked flint knife hung along the curve of her left breast. From her left upper ear, a pierced earring similar to Anlann's, but with three embossed superimposed inverted triangles, beckoned. The circular web hanging from her left lower earfold resembled an elaborate dreamcatcher. It held several webs studded with small colored beads and a collage of tiny knots, like bugs caught in spider webs.

Eyloni had body hair only on their heads and tips of their tails. They didn't even have eyebrows or eyelashes.

Attaché Parakh entered the room. Everyone gave him their surprised attention. "Ambassador Harrison sent me to go over today's information. You are reminded again not to sing, hum, or play any musical instrument while the co-ambassadors remain aboard ship. It is believed they are offended by the misuse of music or song. Not long after the light-cruiser *Alexandra Witze* entered orbit around Elleio, Captain Lahiri teleported to the surface and met with the Compact Counsel. She brought her toddler son with her. While she spoke to the Counsel, twenty infant Eyloni females surrounded the child. The kid sang a nursery rhyme to them. The song affected the infants somehow. When Lahiri visited a neighboring clan, those infant females—some as young as seven weeks old—crossed 2.6 kilometers of wild jungle to remain with the boy. Lahiri feared they might take her son into the jungle with them and had him returned to the ship. A quick diplomatic lie saved the Coalition from a diplomatic incident before talks could even begin."

Marsch wondered about that. Ignoring for the moment just how weeks old infants crawled hundreds of meters anywhere, let alone through a rain forest, he wanted to know more about the presumed musical link between the Eyloni infants and Captain Lahiri's little boy. Why had evacuating the child caused the Eyloni so much grief? Marsch frowned. In the meetings he'd been to so far it had not yet been made clear why singing within earshot of the Eyloni offended them. It couldn't be just a fear of giving offense. When asked, Ambassador Harrison had suggested, with a roll of his eyes, that singing upset their spirituality in some way.

"Remember that the Eyloni use a base-five counting system. They count '1, 2, 3, 4, *10*, 11, 12, 13, 14, *20*' and so forth. For example, if an Eyloni male sees ten Eyloni females and one walks away, then both you and he sees four females remaining. Their numbers also get bigger much faster than our decimal numbers do for the same absolute quantity. An Eyloni 100 is our 25; their 1,000 is our 125. Don't be tempted to cut Eyloni numbers in half: that guesstimate works only for numbers between ten and forty. Divide Eyloni numbers between 100 and 400 by four and divide numbers between 1,000 and 4,000 by eight to get an approximate decimal value," Parakh said.

Roger that, Marsch said to himself.

"The Eyloni measure distance in units based on the average male tail length. Called the ell, it measures 1.778 meters exactly. The ell is also the radius of an Eyloni's personal space. Seralin may issue a challenge if you get within two meters of Anlann."

Good to know, Marsch nodded.

"Elleio is about 60 percent of Earth's size, or about 1.2 times the size of Mars. Due to its mass, its gravity is 0.877 of Earth standard. Although the Eyloni evolved in a 0.9 gee environment that does not make them weak. They have little body fat and greater muscular density, and that makes them three to four times stronger than a human of the same build.

"Elleio is the only moon of the gas giant Tyreniioroneo in the HD10180 Hydri system 127 light-years from Earth. Thought to be a rogue captured by the gas giant's gravity in antiquity, over millions of years Elleio has de-spun into gravitational equilibrium with its adopted planet. For the non-astrophysicists among you, that means the Tyreniioroneo/Elleio system resembles our Earth/Moon system. Elleio is tidally-locked with Tyreniioroneo so that the same hemisphere always faces the gas giant. Elleio has a nearside and a farside with most of the land mass on the nearside.

"Unlike the Moon's 28-day period, Elleio orbits its planet once every 12 days, 16 hours, 21 minutes, and 1.96 seconds. That means Elleio's day is also 12 days, 16 hours, 21 minutes, and 1.96 seconds long. This fact has made Eyloni time standards a trial for us. Eyloni do not synchronize their clocks to their world's rotation. They derive time from physiological references.

"Eyloni have two-time standards. One is called Elleio Standard Time. The other one is called Tyreniioroneo Standard Time. Elleio standard, or EST, is based on a female's average at rest heartbeat. Tyreniioroneo standard, or TST, is based on a male's average at rest heartbeat.

"An EST day and a TST day are both twenty-five hours long, but a TST hour is not as long as an EST hour because male and female heart rates differ. An EST day is 11.4939 Earth standard hours long, but a TST day is only 10.2592 standard hours long.

"Eyloni use the TST standard regarding all male activity, for male ages, for all the sciences except biological and medical sciences, and for most events that take place beyond Elleio, including ship's standard time. They use EST for all female activity, for female ages, for all ritual timekeeping no matter where the ritual occurs, for all biological and medical sciences, and for their homeworld's standard time.

"The Eyloni do not divide the surface of Elleio into time zones. Elleio Standard Time is set to the prime meridian, the eastern terminator, when all nearside is in darkness and all farside is in sunlight. Standard time is the same everywhere on Elleio no matter where the sun is in the sky. For them dawn, noon, dusk, and midnight are not synchronized to a regional time."

Marsch smiled: telling an Eyloni to meet him at noon, when he meant twelve o'clock, would be meaningless because noon occurred at different times, depending on where you stood on the surface.

"In the Eyloni counting system and in TST," Parakh continued, "co-Ambassador Anlann is forty-three years old, yet he is actually seventeen in Earth standard. Co-Ambassador Seralin, in EST, is one hundred years old, yet she is only twenty standard years old.

"If you speak to the co-ambassadors about timed events, remember to think in and use Earth standard minutes. A standard minute is within one second of a TST minute. They will refer to TST time when dealing with humans, but you must remember that Eyloni males and Eyloni females use the TST and EST standards according to social conventions. They may forget and describe a duration to a man in TST and the same duration to a woman in EST," Parakh said.

That's interesting, Marsch thought. They must relate the two standards like we relate time zones or twelve- and twenty-four-hour clocks.

The briefing continued with nothing else new or interesting. By the time it ended, Marsch had just enough time to pick up a quick lunch before returning to the training center for an afternoon of live fire exercises in the rough terrain combat bay.

He bolted from the briefing room hatch and ran for the port side amidships galley. Absent an alert he wasn't supposed to run, but he was in a hurry. Rounding an intersection, he stepped into the approaching male co-ambassador's path.

Marsch twisted his step into a standard avoidance maneuver and stopped a respectful distance from Anlann's territorial Protectress.

The female spun and interposed her body between them and faced him, her long tail arching up and curving around behind Anlann like a shepherd's crook. Not touching him, she gave the impression of a woman putting her arm around her child's back. Her rusty red hairy tail tip turned slow circles in warning. She locked eyes with him. Her twitching elfin ears cocked sideways for a moment before flicking back flat against the sides of her head.

Marsch knew that look. He'd owned cats as a kid and teased them often. Cats telegraphed their moods through body language. Their tails, their postures, their eyes, their ears, even their hair bespoke their feelings. The briefing he'd just left made it clear that Eyloni were most like lemurs and not cats, but her ears and tail sent a feline message: back off!

The cultural report described Eyloni as a direct people; they considered coy glances from anyone other than an intimate associate evasive. The report also stressed that looking away conveyed either disrespect, or an attempt to hide nefarious intent.

Marsch looked into the female's larger than human amber eyes and acknowledged both her presence and her overt challenge before turning to meet Anlann's deep yellow ones.

"Good morning, Ambassador Anlann."

Anlann winced at the sound of the title. Ambassador Harrison derived importance and status from it. He had no need for either. As the only Eyloni male present, he held first male on scene precedence. He returned the human's courteous stare and considered his smell. The human's scent filled his mind with an awareness of a male presence, one clinging to restraint. This male was a sire cairn, a battle leader.

Anlann remembered. When he first arrived aboard this warship, he had stopped next to him believing that he was the ship's warleader. Although human pheromones were normally quite weak, his scent screamed in Anlann's empathic mind.

It had shocked him to learn that the sire cairn was not the warleader here. Captain Winters held that honor through some Warpact arrangement with the other human males that remained unclear to him. He could not grasp human male rank hierarchy. They obsessed on it as much as Eyloni females did. The human hierarchical command structure applied to both males and females while in the course of their duties, unlike Eyloni females, who were always conscious of rank and status.

Remembering courtesy, Anlann rippled his tail in a gesture of chagrin and brushed his pons against Seralin.

"Good morning, sire cairn," he said. He sung the presumed rank and gave it the formal stress and musical projection an Eyloni male used when stating another's rank.

I like this human. I cannot point my tail at why, but I do. Empathic honesty filled Anlann's mind. He flicked his ears, frustrated by the human's inability to convey feelings through body language. The sire cairn lacked most of the usual indicators that betrayed character and intent. Anlann had to rely on smell alone, but human scent produced images that did not always agree with what their body language or their words said.

Seralin relaxed. The human intended no attack on her Warleader. He had met her eyes, and she saw no subterfuge or hostile intent. She listened as he and Anlann talked, twitching her ears in search of the subtle change in tone that heralded a lie, and found none. The human smelled more male than any human male she had yet met.

"Good morning, sire cairn," she sang on the tail of Anlann's belated greeting. "We are on our way to a meeting with Ambassador Harrison. Would you care to join us?"

Anlann twitched his ears at that. Odd, he thought. Females enjoyed male company, true enough; however, they were not trivial creatures either. He had known Seralin for many years and knew well her scent of curiosity. The empathy resonated within him, reinforcing his own curiosity.

"Uh, no. Thank you for asking. The Ambassador wouldn't appreciate my presence, and I'm no diplomat. I have duties and responsibilities that require my attention. Maybe when I'm off duty we can spend some time together."

"We would enjoy your company," Anlann said. He noted Seralin's pleased scent. He felt a tingle in his thoughts, a subtle difference in the sire cairn's scent, a momentary empathic touch.

How was that possible? The exobiology report said humans lacked an empathic sense. Exotribal analysis found no evidence of a singing culture in their adults and no mechanism for them to share deep emotions.

"Until another time, good day Anlann, Seralin," Marsch said.

Both Eyloni watched him lope down the corridor and enter a lift. Ambassador Harrison chose that moment to arrive and begin his usual probing questions.

Seralin fluted a soft complaint beyond human hearing. She flicked her ears at Anlann, who took her meaning: the ambassador did not ask direct questions. He pried with evasive words as though he sparred with them in verbal battle.

Harrison jabbed and parried words with Anlann, ground his teeth, and tried his best to put forth a polite face. He followed the diplomat's art of war: he saw no moral fault with dissembling or prevaricating. White lies served a purpose in diplomacy; they were expedient and expected, and they shaded meaning to provide plausible deniability. The co-ambassadors had no flair for artful negotiation. Why, they even considered dissembling a character defect. How could he help these people? The Coalition provided an opportunity for them against the growing Lizard threat. With a Coalition/Compact alliance in place, the Lizards would have to search elsewhere for prey. Bound by treaty, the Compact would also help defend Coalition borders. The Eyloni concept of combat honor baffled him.

Anlann sighed with relief as he stepped into the lift. "Bridge," he interrupted.

Harrison stumbled. Not the bloody bridge again, he screamed in silent fury. Anlann visited the bridge more often than he met with him for diplomatic talks, but if he wanted to visit the bridge, and if that made him more amenable to negotiation, then he would wipe the scowl off his face and smile.

The lift door opened into the carrier's bridge, a large round room with an oval island in the center and about two meters above the main deck.

Anlann stepped out of the lift to one side and looked around the warship's command center. Three sets of stairs connected the main deck to the raised island, one on each side and one in front of him.

Humans did seem to have a fascination with stairs.

Captain Winters stood next to a redheaded female at the communications station. Harrison pushed past Anlann to stand behind Winters and breathed over his shoulder.

Anlann's eyes swept the command center again, and he shuddered at the odd thrill of violating a social taboo: that of standing on the deck of another male's warship.

And not a single human female cared! They did not try to kill him, or even spare him so much as a glance. If Winters had pulled a similar stunt aboard *Surefooted*, his warship, then his female crew would have killed the captain before his foot touched the deck.

Anlann listened as Winters and his Mistress of Communications conferred. He watched Harrison and sighed. The ambassador did not enjoy crew status aboard this ship. A Compact warship's crew killed an outsider for territorial trespass. Exceptions did occur: sometimes a male had to be conveyed and sometimes two warleaders had to meet in person. Otherwise even a male risked death from a female crew, who would believe his mere presence was meant to foment mutiny against their own warleader.

Ambassador Harrison argued with Captain Winters. The disrespectful display unnerved the Mistress of Communications: Anlann could smell her distress. His fury grew. A warleader held absolute command over those aboard his ship by the crew's own choice and under Compact law. Harrison's actions mocked the principle of male autonomy. Anlann sought the comforting touch of his outraged Protectress. Her scent told him how she felt. Females took insults aimed at males poorly and tended to avenge insults directed at the males they associated with. Her scent gave him a mental picture of her questioning human female inaction.

"I've got that signal back again, Captain. Audio only," the communications officer said.

"On speakers," he said.

"Aye, Sir."

Seralin twitched her ears. They must have arrived in the midst of a situation. She cocked questioning ears at her warleader.

Anlann answered her out of habit, "The Mistress of Communications has picked up a garbled transmission."

A weak audio signal filled the bridge. The voice sounded both melodious and feminine.

"Record, enhance, and run it through linguistic analysis Lieutenant Romaine," Winters said.

"No need, Captain," Anlann interrupted, twisting his tail in abrupt jerks. "The transmission is a distress call from *Hunter's Moon*, a Compact warship. His Mistress of the Ship reports that they have taken heavy battle damage. Their FTL jump drive is offline. They are headed into the Nikkiolo star system. Your navigation references label it the…the…the Iota Horologii system."

"Hyperlink communications turnaround time, Lieutenant?" Winters asked.

"Just over six days there and back at this range, Sir," Romaine said.

Seralin's mood matched her Warleader's. Her ears flipped forward and backward nonstop in sympathy with the distant female's voice.

"Something is very wrong Anlann," she said. "I hear it in her voice, something much more serious than their propulsion systems."

"I know. I hear it too."

"Navigator! Plot a course for that system and engage at maximum hyperdrive velocity," Ambassador Harrison demanded.

Both Eyloni glared at Harrison. He dared to usurp Winter's command, and he dared to order entry into Compact territory without first asking respectful permission. Those who were ni'zakhon, outside tribal law, did not venture into Compact space uninvited.

"No, Mr. Ambassador, not without the permission of our guests," Winters said. "Ambassador Anlann, Ambassador Seralin, have I your permission to enter Compact space and render assistance to the distressed ship?"

Calming, Anlann nodded. "I grant you Warpact status. You may proceed, Captain."

"Warpact status?" Harrison blurted. "You will disregard that, Captain Winters. You don't have the authority to enter into military alliances, not even temporary ones. Only I may approve an agreement between a

Coalition ship and the representatives of the Compact Counsel. Ambassador Anlann, Ambassador Seralin, I hear your plea for assistance. Be assured that the Coalition will render any and all assistance necessary to aid the distressed ship."

Harrison turned back to the helm. "Navigator, I told you to plot a course for Iota Horologii at maximum velocity. Do it!"

Seralin seethed. This pompous fool did not have the right of command aboard this warship: Captain Winters did. How could the females present tolerate the indignity of having their captain overruled by another male?

Anlann smelled the respect Winters had given him despite Harrison's blatant disregard for Compact territorial integrity. He faced the Captain, perked his ears forward, and held his tail erect.

"Captain, I give you permission to enter Compact space under Warpact, but only upon your order and no other. The Compact Counsel shall consider it an aggressive act if this ship enters Compact territory on any order but your own."

Anlann turned on Harrison, "I shall break off diplomatic talks with the Coalition if you interfere with this ship's warleader again."

"Thank you Ambassador Anlann," Winters said. "I hereby enter into Warpact with you for the express intent of crossing Compact space and rendering assistance to *Hunter's Moon*."

"Accepted," Anlann said.

"Witnessed," Seralin chimed in ritual response to the formal declaration of intent.

Harrison held his tongue and let Winters have his way. He had his hook set in the Eyloni now. By accepting Coalition assistance, he had the bargaining chip he needed to convince these spirit-worshipping, non-human primitives that a diplomatic alliance benefited them.

He hoped the Compact ship had suffered severe damage and heavy loss of life. The more dire the need, the more he could maneuver the rescue mission to his benefit.

"Lieutenant Carstairs, plot a hyperdrive course change for Iota Horologii at maximum velocity," Winters said.

"Aye Captain. Change in course plotted. Ready, Sir."

"Very well. Execute."

"Aye, Sir, Executing."

Anlann brushed his tail against Seralin's pons. Flicking his ears back a momentary twitch, he signaled his need to put as much distance between himself and Harrison as he could get.

Too bad the human females could not put Harrison in protective custody like Eyloni females did to that rare unwanted male visitor aboard their warships.

"What are your thoughts, Anlann?" Seralin asked, smelling his change in mood.

"I do not know. Let us return to our quarters for now, unless you have a better suggestion."

"I feel the need to prowl. Humans are strange. We would learn more about them if we watched them interact with each other," she suggested.

"I am not so sure. Only one human aboard this ship smells normal."

"The sire cairn. Yes, I know. We could seek him out, ask his opinion."

"No. He has responsibilities. We cannot impose on him."

"True," she admitted. "However, he did say he would spend time with us when his duties permitted."

"We should find his quarters and ask him when he will be free to visit," Anlann said.

The crew of *Henri Edda* had been ordered in advance to take every opportunity to put on smiles if the co-ambassadors asked for assistance. Since the location of Marsch's quarters didn't raise security issues, the pair had no difficulty finding and cornering him there.

It didn't take Marsch long to figure out that the diplomatic corps didn't know what they thought they did about the Eyloni. The co-ambassadors treated him like an old friend. Affectionate, they brushed their tails against him often and in a coquettish manner.

He kept feeling imaginary cobwebs brushing at his face. The longer he remained in their company, the more his PTSD symptoms retreated. In fact, he felt like he'd just finished a huge holiday meal. The two Eyloni smelled, well, like family. Their vague, musky scents reminded him of the smell of his old childhood pillowcase. He couldn't explain it.

Anlann, ever curious and polite, devised several subtle ploys that let him move about the sire cairn's quarters. Swords mounted on the walls drew his attention. How he wanted to feel the grip of one of them in his hand. Painted images hung there, too. His work? What did that writing on the desk near Seralin mean? It had rows of horizontal lines filled with small circles, some were hollow, some were filled in, some had tiny vertical lines, and some were joined together at the top. Beige dust covers hid four lumpy items on stands resting against the bulkhead.

Anlann's curiosity burned as the sire cairn described the warrior tribes of his people's past.

Seralin, sensitive to males, scented the human's pheromones. Anlann was correct: the sire cairn smelled more male than any other human male did. His scent was laced with pheromonal signals. Suspicious, she focused on the two as they fell deeper into an animated discussion concerning all things male. As Anlann's Protectress, it fell upon her to keep the lovable fool out of trouble.

Excited male voices rose around her, and she sighed: the male mind was a universal annoyance to all females everywhere.

Alert, she concentrated on the odors in the room, examining each one until she isolated a tingling thread of questing emotion. It did not come from Anlann: she knew his empathic scent. These smells projected a different empathic identity.

It came from the sire cairn. She had never smelled its like from a human before. Empathy! He possessed pheromonal empathy. She felt certain of it.

A momentary rush of savage affection tumbled through her.

Marsch's attention wavered a bit from Anlann's excited voice. He felt a curious presence hovering around him. He smelled vanilla and nutmeg in the air and thought of his daughters lacking the mental pain that laced the memory. He glanced at Seralin,

Her eyes shot wide open, and her ear tips tried to caress the ceiling. She sat in the presence of a male who lacked a female association! How was that possible? Many females walked the decks of this ship. She concentrated on altering her scent.

Marsch felt the odd presence vanish. He grinned at her—like a baffled idiot—before turning back to Anlann.

Oblivious, Anlann continued through to his story's climax.

After the co-ambassadors left, Marsch couldn't sleep. He could still smell the Eyloni's homey scent. Something worried them. How he knew, he wasn't certain. He could feel it, almost see it in his head. He jumped out of bed and paced the length of the bulkhead while looking at the oil painting hanging there. His latest, it depicted twelve small birds huddled together on a branch in a snowstorm. He thought about the birds, took out a pencil, and penned a poem.

Marsch felt like writing music for the first time in weeks. He hummed a tune that followed the meter of his stanzas and tried different rhythms before choosing one. He pulled a dust cover from a stand, considered the ivory and ebony keys for a few minutes, and struck a chord.

The Coalition carrier drove through hyperspace toward Iota Horologii. Hyperdrive ships could cross 4 light-years per day. For 6 days, 13 hours, 43 minutes, and 6 seconds the ship plunged through hyperspace. During the trip Marsch, Anlann, and Seralin had plenty of time to become quite close friends.

"Captain? We have arrived at Iota Horologii's heliopause, about 35 billion kilometers from the system's gas giant," Lieutenant Carstairs reported.

"Very well, Lieutenant. Lay in a course for the second moon of the planet at maximum orbital approach velocity for standard geosynchronous insertion," Winters said.

"Aye, Sir."

"Captain?" An officer interrupted from the tactical scanning station, "Sensors detect substantial debris just outside the system's heliopause, 941,000,000 kilometers distant. A lot of wreckage, Sir. Readings are consistent with a mass of at least two capital ships."

"*Hunter's Moon?*" Winters asked.

"Negative, Sir. Sensor sweeps of the system have located the Compact ship maintaining orbit around Iota Horologii B-2. I'd say whoever tangled with them lost here, Sir."

"Lieutenant Carstairs, set Condition-3."

"Aye, Captain."

A shrill whistle pierced the air, followed by the navigator's voice: "Security alert. Security alert. Set Condition-3 throughout the ship. Security alert. Security alert. Set Condition-3 throughout the ship." The soft bong-bong-bong of the alert klaxon started as his voice stopped.

"Flight Operations, bridge." Winters said into his command handset.

"Flight Operations, aye," the air group commander replied.

"CAG? Launch a probe mission of two fighters into the system's heliopause and investigate the battle debris there. Have them make a fly-by at maximum velocity and transmit scans to Combat Information Center for analysis before reacquiring the ship and continuing inbound as escort. Inform the pilots that they will receive coordinates from bridge navigation once they clear the launch bay."

"Aye, Captain," CAG Commander Guthrey said.

"Sir, all stations report Condition-3. The ship is at Condition-3," Carstairs said.

"Very well."

The ship continued on into the system following a long, seventy-seven-hour shallow deceleration curve from 0.5 cee toward the gas giant. Coalition ships could not enter or exit hyperspace near a star's gravity well. The hyperlimit gradient varied with a star's gravitational strength and a ship's mass. The more massive the ship, the further away from the star the hyperlimit.

Winters watched the moon swing out from behind the gas giant. The outline of the two equatorial continents surrounded by a light aqua blue ocean dominated the main viewscreen.

"Lieutenant Carstairs, give me a capsule summary of the Iota Horologii system."

"Aye, Sir. Iota Horologii is a GOVp class yellow dwarf star approximately 56 light-years from Earth. Using Earth's sun as a reference standard, Iota Horologii shines at 1.64 standard. Its surface temperature is 6,080 degrees Kelvin, making it 300 degrees warmer than the Sun. Iota Horologii's radius is 1.16 standard, and its mass is 1.25 standard. The star makes a complete rotation in 8.6 days, and it has a 1.6-year magnetic activity cycle. By comparison, our Sun rotates once every 30 days, and it has an 11-year magnetic cycle. Sensors detect a metal-rich spectrum with an iron abundance 50 percent greater than that of the Sun. Iota Horologii is only about 625 million years old."

"How can that moon have evolved plants and animals already?" Winters interrupted. "It took the Earth 625 million out of 4.5 billion years to get around to producing us."

"That probably is what brought *Alexandra Witze* here to study, Sir," Carstairs ventured.

"No doubt, Lieutenant. Continue."

"Yes, Sir. The only planet, Iota Horologii B, is a J class hot gas giant having a mass of 2.48 Jupiters. Its year is only 307 standard days long, and it orbits at an average distance of 0.91 AU, about 136 million kilometers, from its sun. The planet has a modest orbital eccentricity that swings the planet between 1.12 AU and 0.69 AU from its sun. That means the orbit varies from somewhat larger than the orbit of Earth to about the distance between Venus and the Sun. Orbital analysis suggests that the moon has moderate winters but hellishly hot summers.

"Our destination, Iota Horologii B-2, designated Ibeetu, is a DN class inhabitable moon. It is 8,647 kilometers in diameter, about 28 percent bigger than Mars. It has a dense nickel iron core, about 0.89 of Earth's, which explains all the upper atmospheric activity. It has a lot of EM activity going on in its Van Allen belts, Sir."

"From the star?" Winters interrupted. He bet that during the star's 1.6-year magnetic high Ibeetu's atmosphere would light up with frenetic auroral activity.

"Partly Sir, but the gas giant companion also has a huge magnetic field, High EM field discharges too. I bet Ibeetu has some real pretty lower latitude auroras, Captain."

Winters smiled at that. He'd seen auroras in Alaska once. The data suggested that these might even be visible from Ibeetu's equator.

The carrier yawed and pitched around for her deceleration burn. When the ship slowed to Ibeetu's escape velocity, she pitched around 200,000 kilometers from the gas giant and made an orbital approach for a standard geosynchronous orbit near the Compact ship.

"Lieutenant Carstairs, once we're in orbit, maneuver the ship ten klicks abeam of the Compact ship and hold position there."

"Aye, Sir."

As the Coalition carrier settled into orbit, Winters gazed at the view on the tactical display. The greens of forest vegetation covered both continents. High boron and cobalt traces gave the foliage a bluish tint that looked more kelp green or marine green than Earth's normal greenery. Scanners picked up the usual insects and a thriving ecology. No primate or higher animal life registered on the sensors except for the 254 Eyloni and their Forward Operations Base on the surface.

Winters eyed the Compact surface presence with a tic in his eye and thought it might be wise to send down the construction engineers and establish their own bridgehead some five or six klicks from them.

He considered the damaged warship off his starboard beam. Moderate to heavy damage to the ship's bow and forward port quarter was evident from the images on the viewscreen. Sensors reported that the warship was well under repair. Maintenance crews and support shuttles worked on the hull. Manipulating scanner magnification, Winters saw sparks and flashes as wreckage was cut away and replacement hull plates were welded into place.

"Lieutenant Romaine, hail the Compact ship."

"Aye, Sir. Hailing them…Captain, the ship's Mistress is standing-by."

Winters faced the main viewscreen as a Warrior appeared, seated at her command station. Like co-Ambassador Seralin, she wore a series of artistic, colorful knots from her neck to just below her breasts and was otherwise bare except for a multicolored loincloth draped over a thong.

"This is Captain Alan Dean Winters commanding the Coalition of Earth Colonies carrier *Henri Edda*. We received your distress call and have entered Compact space under co-Ambassador Anlann's Warpact. Do you require assistance?"

Melkorka studied the human male. Warpact? Co-Ambassador Anlann? Had her distress call diverted his diplomatic mission here? She had been on Elleio when the Coalition warship *Alexandra Witze* had left word that this warship would bring a Counsel Elder to speak with the Compact Counsel. Had she inadvertently poked her tail in the eye of Anlann's mission?

"I am Melkorka. I speak for the society that is the Compact warship *Hunter's Moon*," she said with grave courtesy. "Captain Alan Dean Winters, may I speak with Warleader Anlann?"

"Of course, Mistress. One moment."

Winters turned to his communications officer. "Lieutenant Romaine, call the co-ambassadors to the bridge."

"Aye, Captain."

"Mistress Melkorka, do you need any medical assistance or repair materials?"

"Our Health Center has injuries well in-hand, Captain Alan Dean Winters. I have repair personnel on the moon's surface fabricating replacements from local raw materials. We could use your help in locating several rare elements. Our planetary scanning capability is not yet up to full capacity."

Winters thought he saw her grimace every time he addressed her as Mistress.

The co-ambassadors arrived on the bridge, and Winters let them speak with the Compact ship's commander. He watched and listened as the Eyloni spoke in their musical language. As they talked, he noticed the two females waggling their fingers at each other.

Sign language? Winters wondered. If so, it seemed odd to him that Anlann never made a single gesture the whole time.

Melkorka told Seralin in Battle Language about the circumstances that brought them to the Nikkiolo system. She ran through the warship's battle damage and stalled for as long as possible the humiliating news that Kalinn had been lost.

Seralin's ears drooped in sympathy and accepted the Warrior's sad tidings. She signed details of their diplomatic mission aboard the Coalition ship. She included her opinion of humans, their oddities, and a blistering commentary on the human ambassador: she refused to use his name or accent the first note of his title, an Eyloni sign of disrespect. She sung a stout endorsement of the ship's sire cairn and with all tact mentioned that he lacked a female association.

Melkorka took note of the vital information. A human sire cairn? And one unattached to an association? *Hardly!* Males were too valuable to be left unattended and too unstable to leave unattached. Unattached males were unpredictable and dangerous, a sire cairn even more so. He must be important for Seralin to have gone out of her way in mentioning him in so positive a fashion.

She shook her head and gave Seralin an estimate of when they would complete minimal repairs sufficient to let them jump their way back to Elleio and the repair facilities of Wrathsee'a Anchorage.

The drive repair problem centered on the mechanics of Compact FTL technology. The gravity lensing system relied on electromechanical assemblies. The primary drive elements consisted of twin rotating, linear oscillating armatures that generated the lensing fields. Without the gravity lensing system, the warship could not create the quantum singularity that let them jump at apparent FTL velocities.

The drive also depended on superior hull integrity, and jump calculations required a known mass figure—down to within four hundred Eyloni bodyweights—of the ship and everything aboard. Removed wreckage, vaporized materials, atmospheric losses, and crew sucked into space or disintegrated by particle streams affected the ship's total mass. The buckled hull compromised its integrity.

Even more serious, the lensing armatures were massive and had to be precisely aligned, a procedure requiring a repair station's heavy lift equipment. Space made the armatures weightless, but that did not mean they were massless. It took an equal and opposite push to shift a weightless mass into motion and the same push in the opposite direction to null its rate.

Without the armatures, there could be no inertial dampening fields and only minimal artificial gravity. It would take the power systems and propulsion crew forty days by hand to make repairs that took a mere forty-two hours of nonstop work at a repair base.

If they could manage it at all.

The realigned armatures had to spool up properly, too. Like an unbalanced wheel, battle damage that altered the angular balance of the armatures would cause them to shake the gravity lensing system to pieces before even one quantum singularity could form. Instability would cause the ship to translate anywhere within the jump radius. Destination and displacement depended on the spin velocity, spin angle, and charge of the singularity. Severe damage to the armatures could introduce the spin and charge errors that led to critical navigation errors.

The question that plagued both females remained unsaid: when would the Ni'zakhonii return?

3

AN OATH IS GIVEN

"Ship's log, 25 September 2172, 1055 hours, Commander Judith Arleen Rodgers, Executive Officer, recording. It has been forty hours since we entered standard geosynchronous orbit around Ibeetu. We are maintaining orbital position ten kilometers off the Compact warship *Hunter Moon*'s starboard beam. The ship's Mistress tells us she expects the Compact warship *Fearless* will arrive in 230 TST days. She said the figure, 27.785 standard days exactly—after converting her base-five number and accounting for the length of a TST day—was only a reasonable guess.

"We have arrived during Ibeetu's equatorial spring. The climate resembles the cool rain forests of the northern Pacific States of America. The Landing Zone is damp and covered with occasional mists and fog. The atmospheric content breaks down to 17 percent oxygen and 70 percent nitrogen, with traces of chlorine and halogen compounds. The current surface temperature of 22 degrees Celsius is on a slow and steady rise toward Ibeetu's broiling summer. In a month, the surface temperature becomes stifling and in six weeks will exceed human tolerances. The gas giant companion follows an eccentric orbit, giving Ibeetu's equator a mean summer temperature of 51 degrees and a mean winter temperature of -5 degrees. Both means drop about 12 degrees from their extremes within the gas giant's umbra, which shadows about 73 percent of the equatorial land mass. The Eyloni might fare better here since Elleio's summer heat is much warmer than Earth's.

"Medical surveys have found two viral and five bacterial strains harmful to humans on the surface. Dr. Kerchival reports that he will have sufficient vaccines made available for the entire crew by fourteen hundred today. Captain Winters has approved surface recreation for all vaccinated off-duty personnel. A maximum of 240 slots have been allocated, each lasting seven hours, or about half of Ibeetu's 14 hour and 37-minute day.

"Senior Chief Warrant Officer Marsch has assumed command of all surface reconnaissance forces. His ARTs have established an Operations zone surrounding the LZ. Marsch has designated the OZ a potential hot-zone pending a review of all initial contact ARTs situation reports. He requested, and the Captain has approved, an ARTs rotation of eight teams every two Ibeetu local days.

"Captain Winters has ordered the construction of a Surface Operations Base on the larger continent some five kilometers from the Compact Forward Operations Base. About the size of Greenland on Earth, the continent has an impressive mountain range similar to the Rocky Mountains, deserts, vast forests, and meadows covered with either thick-and-short aquamarine grass that looks like manicured golf course sod, or tall serrated grass that reminds me of large cross-cut saw blades.

"Captain Winters, the Compact co-ambassadors, and Ambassador Harrison have been meeting with the Compact warship's commander and her senior staff at the LZ since zero nine hundred this morning." Rodgers paused the log entry a moment and wondered when she'd get her chance to run barefoot through soft grass.

On the surface, Melkorka, Phelindra, and a few others paid Captain Winters a formal visit at the Coalition SOB. They abounded with curiosity, but many humans in the construction and supply crews struggled to overcome mild xenophobia. Their rare encounters with the Eyloni had gone no further than brief sightings of Anlann and Seralin aboard ship. Melkorka's command crew of mistresses, their tails, their body language, their brushing and touching, and their subtle hierarchical rank posturing made them too abrupt of an alien experience for the humans.

Unfamiliar with human scent and human behavior, the Eyloni smelled contradictory emotions, which translated into empathic impressions of being unwanted. When the awkward meeting ended, a confused Melkorka and her mistresses left, disappointed.

Marsch began his first local Ibeetu day with his ARTs as they secured the LZ and reconnoitered a buffer zone of three klicks into the OZ. He ordered extended patrol sweeps in all directions except past the midpoint distance between the Coalition SOB and the Compact FOB. Marsch understood the tribal, territorial mind: sending his ARTs into the Eyloni's security zone might be seen as both disrespectful and distrustful.

The ARTs settled into the routine of maintaining a combat presence, brushing up on jungle training, and sending random security sweeps into the forest. Marsch found he had about an hour or so of free time at the end of Ibeetu's short day. He spent the time coping with his hyperawareness by wandering off on his own solitary patrols. He scouted out the local terrain, examining every bush, tree, and grassy patch in the area. By the end of the second day, Marsch found himself drifting over the midpoint between the two temporary bases.

On the evening of the third day, Marsch hiked through the dimming forest to an overnight, naturally occurring, well-protected watch site. The forest trail wound along a smooth and even path that eventually fell into a depression near a ridge that rose up and curved around the Compact FOB some two klicks away. The ridge ran along a rocky wash that carried spring runoff from the distant mountains.

Fine rain began to fall in spurts. By the time he reached his primary objective, the sun had already set. He patrolled the area before taking up his post. It rained on and off all evening, the water sometimes streaming down his Type-II poncho. Rain tended to lull the mind and mask sounds, but his training prevailed. He found the rain's rhythm, the soughing leaves, and the whistling wind, followed them for about five minutes, and then pushed them aside. The forest fell silent to him.

Fog appeared, puddles splashed, the storm carried on.

Everything standing wore cloaks of water. The sky turned charcoal, and rain fell from metallic, heavily laden clouds. The lightning came in hot yellow flashes, brightening the area like brief starburst flares. Golf ball raindrops splashed against sopping trees.

Plopping above Marsch's head, drops struck leathery leaves, interrupted by the occasional hammering thunder that boomed as loud as a concussion grenade in an empty warehouse. He peeked out from his dry poncho and joined the wet night. The leaves captured the wayward watery gusts that swept past.

From the poncho's warm embrace, he struck his hand against a nearby tree trunk. Icy water ran down his arm, soaking the sleeve down to his elbow. He shivered. The wind, breezy and cool, blew against his face. In the darkness and cold, the storm and he became one.

Mist arrived about an hour after local midnight. Marsch hated mist. Mist was evil, deceptive. It stole through familiar landscapes, dampened sounds, blurred vision, and called up paranoid superstitions and fantasies that trapped minds or made them cower.

Without landmarks, perspective and perceptions changed.

***

The ridge, shrouded in luminous pockets of mist, made the Valhallan trees seem to float in gray cotton candy. The mist, like a mountainous landscape, arose around him, floating on the dense gray air. It concealed and revealed. Ponds and streams became slate paths. Familiar scenes loomed like specters in the thickening air. Marsch paused and glanced back at the trees again. Everything the mist touched turned into gray sludge. He thought he saw crouching figures and twitching wisps around them in the cold light. He checked his surroundings over and over again. Mist paved over drops and voids. Danger lurked in the mist. He walked through a battlefield filled with subtle gray smudges. He heard the sound of the Valhallan dead, and smelled the musk of…

♦♦♦

Marsch flinched. The vision vanished mid-flashback.

What had he been thinking about? Oh, yeah, the mist, mist raised hairs on his neck every time he moved through it. It personified stealth and was filled with crafty wraiths. Hard to see through while in the field, mist spoke to Marsch of loneliness.

When day broke three hours later, the skies had cleared. The gas giant dominated the early morning sky, filling it like a brown, red, and maroon aggie one hundred full Earth Moons across. Marsch moved out. The forest smelled of rotting leaves and damp earth. Moisture gathered over the next hour. Drizzle turned into another downpour; the game trail turned into a stream. When he arrived at the SOB perimeter, drenched and exhausted, he eyed an old, damp, slippery log with suspicion. It led across the knee-deep lake that filled the defensive zone between the base and the trees.

Over the next five local days, the weather varied from fog, to drizzle, to driving rain, and back again.

With each sortie, his curiosity grew.

✶✶✶

Melkorka stood before the FOB security center's panoramic viewscreen and wondered. Her prowling Hunters told her that the sire cairn had skirted their perimeter several times over the past few days. What was he doing? He had almost caught the Warriors shadowing him in the mist. If he caught a solitary Hunter flanking him, she would sing laughter in Phelindra's ears. Everyone reported the same empathic temperament: his pheromones painted visions of loneliness, concern, hyperawareness, combat readiness, and a manic preoccupation with safety.

Melkorka knew well the smells her scouts reported: normal male scent. Captain Winters and the other human males lacked the sire cairn's bold signaling. The scouts all said he had the smell of a male in constant worry for the females that associated with him, but Seralin had said he lacked an association. The prowling Hunters all reported that his scent drew images of Eyloni in their minds.

In Eyloni culture several females formed an association with the single male of their choice. That male's personality traits and empathic mindset sharpened the female's instinctive need to protect males. Males who projected concern for females during a crisis attracted unattached females. With Kalinn dead and no unattached Eyloni male nearby, and since the other human males lacked the pheromonal cues normal in Eyloni males, the unattached females found themselves fascinated by, but uncertain about, the human sire cairn. He smelled almost right to them.

Melkorka wanted to meet this sire cairn. Seralin had spoken well of him.

"Phelindra?"

"Yes, Mistress?" the Eldest Huntress replied.

"Go into the forest and stalk the sire cairn. See what you can learn about him."

"Affirm," Phelindra said.

On the tenth local day, Marsch crawled through heavy jungle on a security sweep some five klicks from the SOB. He scouted along an animal trail that wandered through a wildflower meadow and up to the top of a low hill. From there, the scene unfolded into a dramatic view hidden from below: a vast field of sawtooth grasses that stretched out to a rocky outcropping in the distance. Along the trail flocks of ebony, delicate, winged insects poured over patches of maroon fairy cilia.

He climbed up and over the hill to the other side. Winding down the hill's flank at a steep grade, the trail found its way to a small ravine where water babbled and gurgled over black polished stones before running through a crack in a massive granite slab poking out of the hillside.

He dropped down into the shallow gully and traced its course back to the trees. Marsch wasn't a bird watcher, but he counted more than a dozen reptilian flyers the size of squirrels riding the thermals in the pale, sage-green sky. The gas giant, waxing over the tall dark green trees, made a beautiful background for them. He watched them soar over the canopy. Once the gas giant's south pole cleared the horizon, the flyers wheeled over and strafed the branches before swooping to land nearby.

Marsch froze.

A handful of the avian lizards either hopped or crawled to a soggy group of large puddles hidden in the grasses. Their fine, iridescent, gold and violet scales shimmered in the sun. They hopped, alert and defiant, toward the beckoning water. No ripples stirred the puddle's surface; it lay quiet in its grassy solitude. The little flyers hopped into the water, splashing about as they played. Their antics failed to divert Marsch's attention from one flyer in particular, a wounded one that took its ease by a nearby puddle's edge. It stood and crept over to the others, stumbling on its feet, its wings akimbo. A second flyer pounced on it, scolding furiously. The wingsprung flyer fell away from the puddle, ducking and dodging nips and wing buffets. The aggressor, sensing a wrongness about the lone flyer, chased it away from the others. The crippled avian tried in vain to rejoin them.

It came close to Marsch. Its wing was dislocated, easy to pop back into place. Moved by pity, he stepped toward the puddle's edge. His boot broke the surface at the same time a clawed and fanged animal lunged into the water, snagged the screaming flyer, and bounded off into the woods.

Marsch listened to the flyer's fading shrieks. Lost in thought, the feelings he felt for the doomed flyer shook through him: yet another he couldn't save.

His distress did not go unnoticed.

Marsch began his eleventh local day knowing for certain that a rain forest world was the last place he ever wanted to live. The forest harbored red millipedes that spanned the length of his footprint, leeches of all sizes, and spiny-stemmed shrubs that shredded his tough Type-II uniform.

Pausing his sweep through the forest, he watched about fifty of the leeches between a grain of rice and a string bean in length leap onto his boots. Attracted by his body's electrical field, they looped upward like supercharged inchworms. Leech socks made from the same slippery material as the Type-II ponchos stopped those climbing onto boots from attacking his feet. Others continued upward until they found bare skin and sank their teeth into flesh. As they did, their salivary glands secreted an anticoagulant that caused the wounds to bleed for hours.

Yet he smiled: his blood killed them like salt killed slugs and snails on Earth, but much faster. A stifled chuckle barely cleared his throat when an eerie squeal, half song and half shriek, bounced off the trees.

He tensed as adrenaline poured into his bloodstream, readying him for battle.

He whipped around and locked eyes with an older Eyloni female, a Hunter, not ten meters from him.

In the dimly lit dark green background, under aquamarine skies, her red hair blazed like a setting sun.

Leeches covered her from bare feet to breasts. She scraped them from her skin with a curved flint knife, but others raced up from the ground to take their place.

"Come here, you! Right now, dammit!" Marsch demanded.

Phelindra heard the sire cairn, smelled his concern for her, but had no time to give a formal greeting. She had to get back into the trees, where she could scrape the painful bloodsuckers from her skin.

Marsch watched and waited. The Hunter's blood didn't kill the leeches. Her blood chemistry didn't affect them as badly - or as quickly - as his had. She ran for a tree but stopped to shave leeches from under her loincloth.

He needed saltwater, had none, didn't have to piss, and didn't have time to wait for the solid saline block to dissolve in the medikit's IV bag.

"Come here, damn you! Right now!" he demanded and charged the Hunter.

Phelindra's natural instinct reacted to the male's pheromones: she ran to him.

Marsch pulled his long combat knife, focused on her, and sliced his palms. Grabbing her with bloody hands, he smeared his blood across her breasts, over her waist, and down the small of her back, her hips, her thighs, her calves, and her bare feet.

The leeches foamed like baking soda in vinegar as they either dissolved or dropped from her body.

Marsch bit his cheek and concentrated on getting the job done.

Phelindra glared at him with her deep amber eyes, searching for every nuance of strength, weakness, and character by employing an idiosyncratic piercing scrutiny unique to Eyloni females. Ignoring the blood smeared on her body she eyed the sire cairn for several minutes and considered his scent. His raging emotions filled her mind with clear pictures as she sang him a formal greeting.

Marsch smelled her body odor. It reminded him of spice, scented candles, and something familiar—dogs, maybe? It quenched his driving hyperarousal impulses like water on a fire.

Marsch looked round about him a moment and nodded to himself.

"Climb up through the trees and out of this area. These leeches come up from the ground and don't hide in the leaves of the trees. I think the flying reptiles eat all they can find, so the leeches have adapted to life underground. You'll be fine once you're out of the marshy soil," he said.

She eyed him and sang a complicated melody.

Marsch nodded to her and continued his security sweep. He strode off into the jungle, spraying his palms with liquid bandage as he walked.

Phelindra watched the sire cairn continue his solitary prowl. She inhaled his bloody scent, his pheromones, searching for more clues that revealed his intent.

She smelled maleness, a persistent raging protectiveness, and the pheromones of an Eyloni male and female. Those pheromones painted a picture of affectionate acceptance. She recognized the two scents: they belonged to Warleader Anlann and Protectress Seralin.

Four more local days passed by without incident. Marsch expanded his solitary sweeps and made incremental headway through the SOB's northern flank. He soon became a regular feature near the Compact FOB. Several times now he caught glimpses of the same old Hunter stalking him. From time to time he saw fall colors keeping watch over him from the trees. That they gave themselves away demanded that he reciprocate. On the rare occasions he found them first, he stepped out from cover and spoke to them. They always sang the same complicated melody back to him.

Two Ibeetu days later, several Hunters came to him as he sat a watch in the jungle. They took turns talking to him, singing earnest-sounding comments and flexing their ears, awaiting his reply. He didn't understand their songs and assumed they reported individual variations of *all clear ahead*. He got an overwhelming feeling that they enjoyed listening to his voice. He must have made an impression on the Hunters. They seemed to cross his path more often than the Warriors did. Their patrol patterns and watch positions coincided with his sweeps and watch sites. When a Hunter spoke to him, he made a comment or two about her patrol area using pantomime and scratched diagrams in the soft soil.

The next day he skirted along the edge of the Compact FOB and was mobbed by females. They seemed excited by his presence, but their work kept them busy and as soon as one left, another took her place near him. He walked between two temporary machine shops and listened to servomotors whine and heavy sledgehammers beat wrist-thick wire around an 8-meter-wide trapezoidal core made from 121 laminated plates about as thick as a pencil each. He stopped, looked the work over, nodded, and made encouraging sounds. He turned to slip through the brush back into the forest only to run into the warship's commander.

Melkorka faced the sire cairn. She knew enough human language to speak on Kalinn's behalf if they should ever happen upon a Coalition warship.

"Why do you come here?" she demanded.

Females gathered around them.

"I'm Senior Chief Warrant Officer Marsch. I command the Coalition ground assault teams. I'm making a security assessment of the area."

Melkorka scented the air, smelling him, his scent, his pheromones, and considered the empathic images they drew in her mind. His words and his scent rubbed against one another. One image linked his notes with a name, but the weaker image called to mind visions of swampy ground.

"You are a wetlands commander?" she asked. The repair facility did not sit in wetlands. His fragmented scent did, however, make clear his concern for them.

"No, Mistress. I am Senior Chief Warrant Officer Marsch."

"A marsh is a span of wetlands, yes?" she asked.

Marsch pushed his impatience aside. "My name is *Del.* I have a few questions to ask about your patrol patterns."

Melkorka's ears twitched as the sire cairn surrendered his birth syllable. In Eyloni culture, the male present at a birth gave an infant female the first two syllables of her name made up of two chords. An infant male received a single syllable chord from his mother. An adult male who offered his first syllable to a female signaled either a desire to enter into an association with her, or advised her that he had not yet been declared an adult and given additional chords to his name. The lingering familial scent of the co-ambassadors on him made her certain he was indeed an adult. Both Anlann and Seralin had marked him with binding friendship pheromones, something no adult ever did to an infant.

She glided alongside him and smelled his confidence: he had no fear, he hid nothing.

It didn't take long for them to gain a following.

He led Melkorka through several approaches into and out of the Compact FOB, chatting with her as they strolled through heavy jungle cover.

"*Why* did you come to us?" she asked.

Fine cobwebs seemed to brush at Marsch's forehead. Strange emotions—dawning hope and mortal anguish—and the contradictory smells of fragrances, spices, and beagle puppies smothered him.

"To see for myself that you are all safe."

The large group closed ranks around him. Each female followed her own independent, convoluted dance. They didn't run into each other or him, but they managed to brush their red tail tips' short curled locks against his arms, his hips, his chest, his back, and even his face.

Melkorka studied Del's scent. Seralin had been specific in her Battle Language assertion that he did not have either a personal or an occupational association of females attached to him, and true enough she did not smell even a hint of either on him. Yet, he watched over them. He took an interest in their well-being. This sire cairn walked alone. They should claim him. Eyloni females always found a male alone intolerable.

She had demanded that most of the repair party complement take appropriate turns stalking him over the past several days, studying him. Now he walked among them. They repaid his candor and concern by making ritual personal contact with him, and he had moved through them, accepting their touches. The ritual greeting completed, they relaxed their formality and accepted him as the temporary personal male presence until the Eyloni males arrived for them to make an occupational choice.

The following morning Marsch ranged out in a slow circle through vines and thorny undergrowth with an eye toward testing a blind approach to the Compact FOB. Along the way lay soggy ground surrounding a spring. Subterranean aquifers discharged rills of cold water into a small wooded clearing, creating a saturated haven for water plants. He almost expected to find tadpoles swimming in the cold shallow water and smiled at the childhood memory. After working his way around the small, shallow pond, he entered the Compact FOB.

Melkorka and a petite female, a young one, greeted him.

"Del, this is Kidahin, our huluhar," Melkorka said.

Marsch gave the young Hunter a dismissive nod. Was the word 'huluhar' a rank, or was it the Eyloni word for child? He let the aimless speculation die and turned to brief the Mistress on her security problem.

Melkorka listened hard and concentrated on his scent, trying to make sense of his words and grasp both the defect and the corrective action he demanded. The image her pheromonal empathy formed reminded her of an overexposed back and the need to turn and face the threat. She quizzed him several times, ears twitching and tail stabbing, until she was sure she understood.

"By your command," she sang out of habit and in her musical language.

The young Hunter lurched in shock. She spun so fast she tripped over her tail and stumbled into him.

Marsch reacted without thinking and grabbed her, arresting her fall.

He didn't notice alert ears twitching.

Melkorka tensed. Muscular, hard-faced Warriors in short waistwear and flimsy neckwear froze, tails balance checked, and hands hovered over the flint knives that followed the curves of their left breasts. Squatting Hunters, tails held high, pons twitching like catkins in the wind, riveted their eyes onto Del's hands.

Marsch steadied the youngster and gave her a brief, complete assessment. She looked fine, no twisted ankles or knees. She stared at him in open curiosity, wrapped her tail about her waist, and absently rubbed a length of it. Her ears flittered, delicate flags semaphoring some message.

Kidahin found herself the center of attention. She smelled no threat. In fact, his touch reassured her. At a loss to explain why, she glanced at the Mistress of the Ship for a helpless moment before turning back to the human male.

Marsch held the young Hunter away from him and gazed into her large amber eyes. Captivated by her expression, he reached out with a free hand, brushed her right ear, and spoke. Her soft, burnt orange suede-like ear fluttered in his cupped hand like a trapped hummingbird.

Kidahin flipped her right ear down and then perked it forward, letting it swivel against the cage that was his fingers. Her ear tingled, sensitive, as the sire cairn's gentle touch brushed it.

"Cute kid," he told Melkorka.

Kidahin tried to capture pheromonal empathy from him and found his scent hung about him—a raging fragrance—not unlike Eyloni males. The human smelled male, but he smelled different too—alone, driven. Olfactory and empathic centers in her brain triggered youthful instincts that struggled to make sense of the coalescing visions in her mind's eye. She attuned herself to his scent and saw his hyperdriven concern for their safety.

She submerged herself in the exotic, bold wonder of his scent. She concentrated, letting her empathic sense build up a series of idealized halting images, more feelings than visual scenes, and realized he saw her as a child. She amused him in the same way an adult regarded a precocious infant. And Melkorka, she realized with rising anger, smelled amused at his amusement of her! She seethed, her pheromones broadcasting her rage to those around her.

Melkorka growled under her breath, amusement warring with her warning.

Marsch looked at the two females. The younger one smelled of elusive spices. He had a feeling; some fleeting intuition that called to mind flushing embarrassment. He focused on the young Hunter. She resembled a willowy, mature twelve-year-old girl, but he knew from the cultural briefings that she wasn't much over six or seven standard years old. He smiled kind encouragement at her and smelled a subtle change in the air that reminded him of indignant outrage.

"Del says you are an endearing child," Melkorka translated with a smile.

"Endearing child?" Kidahin whispered, blushing dark red. She stood rigid and still. The Hunters and Warriors smiled in fond enjoyment of her discomfort before turning to wish the sire cairn well on his way.

Kidahin watched the nauseating greenery of the forest swallow him and wondered. She smelled his meaning. His scent triggered empathic visions in her mind, visions that translated into feelings she could understand. She had made a strong empathic bond with the human male. How in the spirits had she done that?

Minutes passed. Her mind raced.

Rash instinct and her juvenile sensitivity to males hammered at her.

Curiosity teased her. She had to learn more about him.

Excusing herself, she turned around and strolled across the compound with feigned disinterest, broke off between two supply buildings, and ran into the forest.

Melkorka wrinkled her nose and frowned after the retreating huluhar.

The green leaves and grasses left little for Kidahin to blend into. She stalked in the shadows and around brown tree trunks, using their cover to break up her red and orange outline.

Twenty ells into the forest, she circled around the repair base until she intercepted the male's trail. With silent footfalls, she closed on him, working her way deeper into the shady forest. She increased her pace and soon found herself several thousand ells from her people.

She stopped, surrounded by unfamiliar dark shadows and green shades.

She lost him.

Impossible.

He had not backtracked, had not turned aside. Kidahin tensed and listened to the rhythm of the forest. She smelled the air. An indifferent breeze caressed her back. She turned through a tight circle and saw nothing. She stood there in stunned amazement.

Where did he go?

Marsch had stopped. His combat experience gave him a situational awareness; a sixth sense that marched alongside his hyperarousal. Something trailed him. An Eyloni making her patrol sweep, maybe?

No. He had met them often enough by now to know they always made an effort to declare themselves.

One of Ibeetu's predators? Xenobiology surveys had reported bearlike predators in the forest that preyed on the giant rodents that fed on the tough tree bark. And here he was without his sidearm. He stopped wearing the energy weapon soon after making Ibeetu landfall. Anlann and Seralin had warned him that Eyloni didn't approve of personal advanced weaponry. They considered such weapons the mark of a coward.

He had knives, but they would be ineffective against the creature's thick hide.

Marsch glanced up at a stout branch hanging across the path. The wind felt right. If an animal tracked him, at least it couldn't smell him.

He jumped and grabbed the heavy limb, levered his body over it, and stretched out along its length, hugging its contours.

The branch looked about as thick as his shoulders were broad. Not thick enough to hide his outline, but in the dark green dappled shade he doubted that a trailing animal would look up and see the overlapping growth that was his bulk.

The trees around him stood like columns of smooth aspens overgrown with giant leaves, pear shaped and grayish. A few minutes passed before he caught sight of a red and orange figure trimmed in yellows moving through the underbrush, the young Hunter he'd just met: Kidahin.

She closed on his position. The lithe female padded barefoot through the brush with exaggerated care. She wore a perplexed expression.

She stopped right below him.

Her stomach and chest muscles rippled under skin resembling a collage of fall colors. She stood still and tense, her long four-knuckled fingers flexing; her elfin ears perked toward things unseen. Clearly puzzled, she struck a listening pose, delicate beautiful ears flexing about, searching for the slightest sound. She held the pose for a few minutes before turning to look back and forth in apparent confusion. She sniffed the air again and seemed at a loss.

Marsch couldn't believe she didn't just look up. She did belong to an arboreal species, after all.

Does she think I can't climb a tree? He wondered.

No sound betrayed him as he rolled under the smooth branch and hung there. Gripping it with his thighs, he let go and extended his upper body down close enough to almost touch her short curled red hair. He pulled his combat knife and waited to strike.

Kidahin felt stupid. Doubts about her crew's wisdom in choosing her surfaced. Poor tracking skills proved her unfitness for warship duty. She felt like a child rather than the adult her knife signified.

She turned back the way she had come and put a foot forward. As she did so, pain blossomed from her scalp.

A startled *yip* squeaked from her throat. Surprise and pain triggered her combat reflexes.

She jumped back, her tail spinning. Adulthood knife drawn, ears folded against her head, and teeth bared, she exhaled a soft, sibilant undulating melody not unlike a whistled hiss, and looked up.

The sire cairn hung upside-down from a thick branch above her. He peered down at her, arms crossed, a heavy battle knife clenched by its sharp tip between his thumb and index finger, its broad handle pointed at her.

He had hit her with that handle!

The look on his face matched his scent: disappointment, disgust.

He shook his head at her. His voice carried at scold pitch. He swung down, repeated the scolding notes, and sheathed his knife.

She gaped at him as he put out his hand, stubby three-jointed fingers stopping just short of her left breast.

Her ears wilted. Her tail drooped until it almost touched the ground. She knew what he demanded. He saw her as a child and demanded she surrender her adulthood knife.

Hanging her head in shame, she untied the sheath from her neckwear, placed the knife in it, and gave it to him.

Marsch reached out, accepted the knife, grabbed her by the shoulders, turned her around, and shoved her forward.

Kida marched back to her extended family, her society. The sire cairn followed holding her sheathed knife and never let her range ahead more than an ell from him.

She considered her plight. How had he evaded her? She was a Hunter! How stupid could she have been? She should have looked up!

Her head smarted. She sulked. She flexed her ears backward and listened to his long tirade. She did not understand a word he said, but his tone of voice and scent told her what he thought of her stalking skills. His tone, his scent, his face, and his posture projected flat disapproval.

Kida winced at the sound of each cracking stick and snapping branch. She tried evading the obvious brush, branches, and sticks in an effort to lead him from the noisy undergrowth, but he foiled that strategy by weaving back and forth behind her, stomping, breaking, and snapping through the brittle undergrowth with even more vigor then if she had just kept to the trail.

Males are strange, she recalled the indulgent female maxim. He revoked her status for being inattentive while on the hunt and for displaying poor skill in tracking.

That he bothered to do so at all made her wonder. *Why? The human was male, was he not?*

Of course he was male. She smelled the gender's signature in his pheromones. He treated her in the same manner any Eyloni male would have under similar circumstances.

She preferred his treatment to what her society would say for displaying incompetence in the field to the sire cairn who had taken an active interest in their well-being. Her inept stalking would reflect on them, too. Not only had she humiliated herself, but she would cause her huntress society, her helm and navigator's society, and her crew's society acute embarrassment. Her favored standing among them would not excuse her poor performance.

Marsch followed the young Hunter. Her tail drooped, its ringlet tip hovering about a hand's span above the ground. If her tail signaled her mood, then she was not happy. He'd seen enough of the Eyloni over the past twelve standard Earth days to grasp their feelings and attitudes by how they postured their ears and tails.

He thought that she even smelled humiliated.

Marsch reckoned the youngster should have been a far better tracker based on his observances of other Hunters prowling through the forest. Her rank of huluhar must be equal to the Fleet rank of apprentice crewman. She must be a recent recruit, too. The other Eyloni carried themselves with an independent dignity, but they had hovered around her the moment he touched her. Their body language, subtle, hinted at some significance she held for them: the kid everyone watched over. He doubted she was a child if she served aboard a combat vessel.

He debriefed her as if she had just completed one of his wargames exercises. But it was different, too. Thoughts and memories of his daughters intruded, as if they had been the ones he had smacked on the head. Fear for them enraged him as he worked himself up into a fury.

"I thought you Eyloni were natural hunters and trackers! Skilled hunters my ass. Don't sneak back, Kidahin! No point in being quiet after you've been killed. Some stalker you are. They shouldn't let you walk alone in the forest!"

He heaped scorn and insult upon her in ways only an NCO could. She flipped her ears back and listened to every word he said. Her tail drooped more and more the louder he yelled. She didn't complain, didn't stop, didn't look at him. She paced in silent footfalls back to her people.

"Let's let'em know you're coming!" he yelled. He stomped through brittle brush and kicked old sticks, making their passage more than obvious to anyone in the area.

A nearby scout heard them coming well before she spotted them. She recognized the human sire cairn's voice. He never came to them from this approach, and he never made noise. He traveled into the wind, and she could not smell his intent, but she heard him well enough to guess. Not him, but them, he walked with another. One stepped with a light foot, but the other one tore through the undergrowth. He yelled, too, and his tone quaked with fury.

She turned and signed Battle Language to her prowling partner, and together they watched with astonished interest as Kidahin paced a near straight line ahead of the human. Unhappiness drifted from her pons like a flower's fragrance.

The sire cairn followed her by less than two ells, and he held a weapon at her back!

Startled, one of the two scouts, Nynava, turned and sang a short, high pitched warning. She watched the two make their noisy way past. Kidahin did not wear her adulthood knife. The sire cairn held it. Shocked, she wondered whether he had fought Kida, for Kida she was now if he had demanded her adulthood knife. And yet, Kida did not carry herself like a defeated Hunter. She wore an aura of shame about her. The sire cairn smelled furious with her. He screamed a continuous percussive rant at her back. His scent and voice conveyed doubt, and Nynava understood that he doubted Kida's adult status and wanted them to witness her embarrassment.

Kida twitched her ears to the left and then flattened them against her head.

Marsch saw her reaction and smiled. They'd attracted the notice of at least one Eyloni and Kidahin wasn't happy about it, either.

After several thousand ells of loud noise and yelling, Kida broke into the clearing surrounding the Compact repair base. She smelled all 1,401 females standing there, everyone assigned to the repair teams had dropped their work and came in reply to Nynava's warning notes.

The crowd watched in silence. They felt no reason for alarm, but they were concerned. The huluhar's posture and scent radiated shame. The sire cairn reeked with both angry disappointment and familial concern. He did not smell at all worried about marching her into their midst and worried he certainly should be if he had acted dishonorably.

He had not hurt her, and he had not taken injury, either. Yet he held Kida's sheathed adulthood knife. He must have demanded it from her, must have considered her a child for some reason. She was *Kida* now, an adolescent child and not an adult by the standards of their culture.

Melkorka stood before the gathering and watched the sire cairn and the child approach. Kida lowered her eyes the moment they surrounded her. Marsch stopped scolding her.

Melkorka relaxed and twisted her tail to let the crowd know all was well. She sighed. Kida had shown much promise, but a male had found her either not ready for, or unworthy of, adulthood status. It fell to her to discover why he felt that Kida was unprepared. Her failure reflected on all of them. They chose her, and they must not have perceived the lack he found in her.

They would never allow a child aboard their warship. Melkorka stepped forward, confronting Kida, but addressing Marsch with her imperfect grasp of his tongue.

"I regret you find her unseemly," she faltered. "We accept that you find in her no adult, but only a child. We take back her adult chord, *hin*, and leave her with the child name Kida."

"It's not that I find her to be a child, Melkorka. She's not what I had come to expect from a Hunter."

Kida watched him, ears perked forward.

Marsch admired her poise. She wasn't defiant. She was embarrassed, but she maintained her dignity.

"Kidahin, tell Melkorka what happened. Leave nothing out."

Kida cocked her ears and gazed into the sire cairn's small brown eyes. She did not understand him, but she found his meaning in his scent. He demanded she reveal her faults. To disobey him was as unthinkable to her as was lying to her society. She began speaking before Melkorka could finish translating the order.

Marsch watched the warship's Mistress for some sign as Kidahin made her report. He had no idea whether she told the whole story, a sanitized version, or an outright lie. He listened to her, but he noticed subtle shifts in Melkorka's stance, noticed how her ears flicked forward, relaxed, flattened, and then flicked forward again. As she listened, her tail twisted in slow tight circles.

Marsch looked at the people surrounding them. They paid Kidahin attentive respect and didn't interrupt. They mirrored the same concern, disappointment, and surprise Melkorka had. They glanced at him often, their ears twitched to the rhythm of Kidahin's singsong voice. She stood stiff, ears cocked wide to include her audience, and held her tail still. It sounded to him as if she reported the incident with calm detachment. She could have lied, made up a trivial incident, and accused him of overreacting.

Yet apparently she didn't. The two hundred or so Eyloni present alternated between regarding him with cautious respectful approval and glaring at her in distaste.

Kidahin stopped speaking, and Marsch turned from her to face the Compact warship's commander.

Melkorka flattened her ears against her head and fumed in silent anger. A child could not perform a huluhar's duties. When they most needed one to help them choose a warleader, they no longer had an adult young enough who had the juvenile instinct that responded to male temperament.

The sire cairn's bass voice pulled her from a chasm of depression.

"She shows promise, Melkorka." Marsch didn't know why, but he thought Kidahin needed an advocate. "I think she has great potential. Maybe a bit more training is needed. If only I had her for five days," he held his open hand up to stress the time, "I could give her special training like she's never had before."

Melkorka rounded on him in flabbergasted surprise. Her ears pitched forward and pointed at him as she translated his words to the crowd.

They focused their eyes and ears on him and ignored Kida.

Stammering, the Mistress of the Ship struggled to form clumsy human words, "You have declared her a child. You believe she can learn from her mistakes and be rehabilitated. I accept your judgment in this matter and thank you for expressing an interest in both her and our well-being."

Marsch smiled. Melkorka had pounced on his words, and the crowd watched him with animated interest. Just when he thought he'd made a point, Melkorka fired a terse order at Kidahin.

The young Hunter turned and fled into the FOB.

Now what? Marsch wondered. Was she restricted to quarters? Ordered back to her ship? Ostracized? He ran through what he knew about tribal cultures. They might even exile her for causing harm to tribal unity, but they'd do that once they returned to Elleio, wouldn't they?

Females surrounded him, and he got a sudden fluttery feeling in his gut—the one that hinted at a problem he hadn't been aware of at the time— and it was already too late to do anything about it.

The Eyloni didn't seem hostile. In fact, they looked relieved, pleased.

What in the world was going on?

A blur drew his eyes. A running Kidahin returned holding onto a waist pack.

Exile, he sighed. He should have let her pass him by, dammit.

Melkorka looked Kida over with exaggerated care and nodded.

Another female, the old Hunter he had saved from the leeches, stepped out from the crowd and stood next to Kidahin.

While Melkorka and the old Hunter conferred, Marsch wondered whether or not she was Kidahin's mother.

The old Hunter turned to Kida and gave her a short lecture lasting no more than a minute, stepped away from her, and faced him.

"Phelindra and I thank you for taking an interest in Kida. We entrust her into your care for the days agreed," Melkorka said. "We will not interfere, nor will we object to the method you select for her training. She is special to us, and we are happy that you do not enter into this duty lightly."

Marsch turned to the old Hunter. Phelindra? Her intense expression didn't quite distract him from Melkorka's halting words, and his heart skipped a beat when they finally penetrated his thoughts.

Waitaminute! She's assigning Kidahin to me? How did that happen? I'm no Eyloni!

The Mistress's pronouncement provoked an instant response from the crowd. They seemed pleased, as though things like this happened all the time. They gave Kidahin barely a glance but smiled and nodded at him in open gratitude. Their clear approval baffled him.

Kida's heart raced, had been racing since the Mistress of the Ship told her the sire cairn had demanded he train her himself over the next four weeks. Melkorka stressed the honor it was for him to take a personal interest in her, that he saw great potential in her.

Melkorka also had made it quite clear that she had no choice in the matter.

Like she would have refused! Males, rare and always busy, had many special social duties to perform. For one of them to take a familial interest in a female not of his tribe was a high honor. They did not have time for trivial matters best left to the various female hierarchies. A male of the same tribe occasionally gave a female further training. Not in the hope of mating her, of course, but to attract her and other females into associating with him, for his protection.

Kida remained stupefied. She could not believe that Melkorka and Phelindra, let alone the others, had agreed to let her leave with the human male.

She felt honored. She felt apprehensive. She stood there and savored the moment until Melkorka spoke a slow, intense, rhythmic sentence.

"Del, we entrust the safety of our huluhar to you."

Marsch made a snap assessment: this gathering had taken on the sudden appearance of a ritual, no doubt about it. He had no idea how to respond to either a rite of formal leave-taking, or to the guardianship of a Compact tribal member. He struggled to recall all he could about tribal societies. Many demanded some binding ceremony to seal special agreements. Most ceremonies featured feasting or oathtaking. They expected him to take Kidahin with him now, so there could be no feast, no parades, and no long ritual ceremony. That left some kind of simple oath or promissory statement made to a spirit who witnessed the oath and gave it its binding nature.

The cooperatives on Valhalla had sealed agreements with a witnessed handshake. Craftsmen and farmers there nicked themselves so often that they started sprinkling blood on their fields or blooded their tools. Both acts were popular superstitions that, like cutting Halloween pumpkins, was done out of social habit and in the spirit of community participation. He had done it himself too, although the many cuts he got from equipment made his voluntary bloodletting mere show. He did know how to offer his blood in sacrifice.

But would they accept his oath?

He watched feet shuffle in the awkward silence. The crowd grew restless. He had to come up with something plausible before they perceived some slight to their honor and attributed it to his delay.

A warrior people respected blood. Eyloni used knives and revered spirits. He had a small boot knife, but he needed a spiritual reference. The war gods Ares, Mars, and Tiwas came to mind, but what if Eyloni considered their spirits female? The one female war spirit he knew of by name was the Valkyrie Sigrdrifa, the woman of victory depicted on Valhalla's flag.

He pulled his boot knife. Hundreds of amber eyes followed the backup blade as he played for time.

How does a blood oath look to an Eyloni, anyway?

Marsch cut his left palm and let the blood flow. His abdomen clenched, and he ground his teeth, forcing his heart rate to slow, and showed them the bleeding wound. He excluded Kidahin because she wasn't in a position to object.

The crowd grew by the minute. Their ears flexed forward, eyes focused on him; their tail tips twitched like cats eyeing a slow, fat mouse.

They arranged themselves in a weird branching pattern around him and waited in complete silence.

It made sense to him. They just wanted to hear his oath.

He held the knife flat against the cut and rubbed the blade into the blood.

"I say before Sigrdrifa the victory spirit that I will care for and keep safe the Hunter Kidahin and give her the training she needs. I will return her safe and well, but for any injuries she might receive in the course of normal combat training, as judged by the Hunter Phelindra. Thus do I accept Kidahin into my care."

The oath spoken, he sheathed the small knife and presented it to Phelindra. It made sense to give the knife to her. Her webbed earring made it clear she was the highest-ranking female present, a Hunter—like Kidahin—and he still wasn't quite sure whether or not she was Kidahin's mother.

Melkorka's tail twitched in surprise. The sire cairn had given the ritual knife to the Eldest. He must have known it was much more appropriate for Phelindra to accept the fosterage oath. His meaning was clear: Del vowed to assume guardianship over Kida, protect and train her, and return her to them unharmed—or Phelindra could kill him with the weapon.

An impressive oath. It reassured them: the trust they placed in him required an equal display of honor, and Eyloni placed offering one's life as hostage to an oath in high esteem.

With such a small blade, Phelindra could drag his death out for weeks.

Marsch turned to Kidahin and held her black, red-veined handmade flint knife out to her.

She refused to touch the weapon, or to even look at it.

Stubborn! Marsch grumbled under his breath. He stepped up to her and tied the sheathed knife to the dyed braided knots dangling just below the swell of her black-nippled, red and orange, yellow-shaded left breast.

Kidahin let him lace her adulthood knife to its customary place. By his action, he reinstated her adult status before witnesses.

Marsch looked at the crowd. He took his time and met each pair of eyes before turning to Melkorka and Phelindra. Nodding to Kidahin, he stepped into the forest. He did have a security sweep to complete, after all.

"Come on, Kidahin,"

The huluhar gave the crowd one last look before following the sire cairn—Del, his name was Del—out of the repair base. She felt their eyes on her tail as she caught up with him.

She wondered what they must all be thinking. Excitement prowled the trail alongside her.

Worry stalked behind her.

Loneliness tweaked at her pons.

She would make her society proud of her, would make Del proud of her.

She followed him into the ugly green forest, her heart hammering in her ears.

4

A TEST

Marsch moved out and soon put the Compact FOB far behind him. He pushed Melkorka and her people from his mind by thinking about the forest. In many ways, it reminded him of the woods he played in as a kid. The soil smelled of old moldy leaves, damp deadwood, and smashed mushrooms. He dug his heel into the soil, disturbing the crimson worms that toiled under the bluish sod. At least they weren't leeches.

Marsch knew from his survival training that a creature's bright colors could mean poison. He wouldn't have to work hard to find food here. Edible fruit grew from the prolific broadleaf trees on this continent. Their fruit resembled the hedgeapples that fell around his childhood home. About the size of a green softball, they had a warty skin that made him feel a little squeamish about eating them at first, but it turned out that they had a mild sweet flavor that reminded him of a honeydew melon.

Marsch watched the young Hunter, Kidahin, step with nimble grace through the brush. She leaned forward as she stalked through the forest, tail counterbalancing her upper body. She made no sound and stepped without brushing so much as a stick or a leaf. Barefoot, her opposable big toes grasped the ground as though she climbed it. Her toes and balls of her feet seemed to caress the soil. She stood on her negligible arches and heels only when she drew herself to her full height. She twisted through the undergrowth with the flexibility of a rhythmic gymnast. Several times now she had turned to check on his progress, twisting her waist through three hundred degrees without effort.

Her ears flipped about all the time, listening. They pricked forward, flattened, flexed backward, twisted aside, twitched, folded back, and then pitched forward again, searching for sounds. Her tail idly swayed as she listened. Sensing his eyes upon her, she turned again, perking ears at him. He smiled, nodded, broke eye contact, and continued on his course.

They hiked through grass, brambles, and burdock-like bushes covered in rosy burrs. The path continued up a small incline and twisted around a pile of rocks covered with aquamarine vines and more briars. Kidahin seemed to enjoy weaving about Marsch's path, venturing out ahead at random some thirty or forty meters at a time before circling back behind him for just as far. She followed him, then flanked him for a minute or two, then either surged ahead, or angled to one side or the other. She didn't stay for long in the same flanking position.

A small, winged, iridescent, violet blur jumped in raucous surprise as Marsch stepped on the flyer's grassy roost. Ferns and grasses flanked him on both sides all the way down the slight grade. The ground leveled out and opened into a small gully. There, the creek and its eroded bank wove along the contoured landscape south a few hundred meters before dumping into a small creek.

Kidahin veered to Marsch's left and scouted under broad canopies. The trees stood some distance apart with nothing much growing among them except for a downy purple moss that resembled mold. The canopy barely touched in places, and direct sunlight trickled across the mosses. Oddly enough, she liked it here. The trees reminded her of the late autumnal season on Elleio, when—one at a time—the La'huaset tribal land's leaves faded from their warm reds and golds to shades of green before dying and falling to the ground. Only the permaleaf trees kept their leaves, but they too turned dark green, almost black, as winter's cold embrace shrouded the extreme northern latitudes of her tribe's continent.

These trees, much shorter than those on Elleio, grew no more than one hundred ells or so into the sky.

Be careful, she warned herself, familiarity kills.

She turned around and prowled awhile along Marsch's right flank before falling back a short distance to reassure herself that nothing followed him.

She stalked him, watching him twist around trees and obstacles. He followed a pattern, something Eyloni instinct said not to do. Patterns signified laziness. An attentive enemy could predict movement by observing repeated stalking patterns. As she watched him, he broke the pattern and started up a low hillside as if he had heard her mental critique.

Kidahin watched him from cover, studying him. He stood the length of her pons taller than she and was half again her width at the shoulders, or about a thumb's length broader in the shoulders than an Eyloni male. His hands looked deformed, a little wider than hers at the palm, and thicker; he had short, stubby fingers with only three joints each and thin translucent nails. Like other humans, his skin lacked color patterns. His skin pigment cloaked him in a uniform tan with minimal shading. His hair gleamed a wavy, shiny black that always looked damp. His eyes, smaller than hers, sparkled with black pupils surrounded by brown irises that did not completely fill his eyeballs, leaving them with white borders. His nose squatted on his face larger and softer than hers. His jaw sat squarer and broader than her sharper and more angular chin did. They shared similar mouths and lips: his, pale pink and hers, blackish red. His teeth were like hers too, but his teeth were pale compared to her brilliant white ones, and his upper canines evenly matched his other teeth, unlike her slightly longer ones. Hair grew above his eyes, from his eyelids, and even in his nose. Sparse black hairs covered his bare arms. He wore clothing to excess that covered his torso and lower body with patterns that broke up the solid lines his plain skin made against the foliage. His footwear suggested a wider and longer foot than hers with tiny stubby toes useless for climbing.

She scanned the hill as they climbed. Short bushy trees grew everywhere. The thick canopy here prevented sunlight from shining onto the forest floor. Moss and thin, short bladed grass grew around tree trunks. Vines crawled up them and into the branches. She gazed at the trees, overgrown with vines, and wondered at how healthy the trees looked despite their greenish colors. On her homeworld green vines like these burrowed into trees and leeched sap from them, parasitic. These vines anchored themselves by wrapping around the trees and using them as trellises to climb up into the sunlight. As she crossed behind and to Marsch's right, she wondered what the trees got out of the symbiotic arrangement. The vines infiltrated the trees so much they should have crowded out their leaves, and yet the trees most overgrown with vines had bigger leaves and more branches than those with fewer vines.

Marsch stopped and listened. He couldn't hear her, but he had a good idea from where she kept watch. He didn't have to guess, either. His heightened awareness gave him a reliable feel for such things. He turned through a slow circle until he felt where she should be.

Kidahin watched Marsch pan about. His gaze tracked her movement along his flank. She silent-tracked him, and she should be undetectable by a human unaided by a scanner; yet, he tracked her unaided, his eyes offset to her right. He looked to where she had been, but he cocked his head to where she stood.

Impossible. Her warship's Huntress society had said a human's hearing truncated the Eyloni norm in both range and pitch. Eyloni heard better than four times the human high pitch range and almost two times below their low pitch range. Eyloni also heard sounds in tonal layers for up to thirty or forty thousand ells away. She remembered everything she heard and could filter selected notes from her memory and replay the sounds in her head. Humans lacked her people's exceptional hearing, so how was he always finding her?

She stopped. He stopped. He inclined his head and watched her. Frustrated, she checked off possibilities from a mental list.

Marsch stared where he thought the Hunter hid. She stood still. He grinned, turned, and continued up the gentle rise. She kept a watch on him all right, studying him. He bet she was still sore at him for rapping her on the head.

She had been overconfident. Had he been an enemy, she'd be dead. Better she learn caution and be curious than be sloppy and headstrong.

Marsch glanced at the cloudy, turquoise sky. Ibeetu's short day flew by. He had an ARTs briefing in an hour or so. His return to the Compact FOB had taken time he didn't have to spare.

Kidahin spied out Marsch from where she squatted in the jungle and swore when she realized that he had found her again.

Marsch settled into a direct line advance toward the Coalition SOB with Kidahin pursuing from his right flank and watching him dodge around trees. Intrigued by his scouting technique, she noted every detail and his concern over minutiae. He stopped often, cocked his head to the left or right, probably compensating for his ears, and listened to the forest. She inhaled his male scent, considered his soft footfalls, and followed, awed.

She wanted to prove to him that she was an adult female, one who could rise to the call of battle with him as her male fighting focus.

Kidahin stopped, confused.

Marsch was a human and could not in any way be mistaken for an Eyloni male, yet his scent kept alerting her to a male presence. It did not match the intensity of an Eyloni male's on a wide range: yet, not only was it a male's scent, but it overpowered her on many of the narrow signaling peaks that were the most important. Eyloni and human biochemistry must run along similar lines: pheromones were pheromones, after all. Cursing her lapse, Kidahin shook herself and snapped back to the task at hand. She circled behind Marsch and stalked out along his left flank until she paralleled him. She matched his pace and let her mind wander as she prowled.

She wondered how well he fought in battle. As the Coalition warship's sire cairn, maybe he would let her participate in a wargames exercise as a part of her training. If he allowed it, then she could watch him lead others.

She wondered whether he fought only with bladed weapons. He carried knives in sheaths at his hips. She saw the slight bulges in his tunic that hinted of hidden knives. She hoped he fought with traditional weapons, but she knew that humans preferred personal energy weapons.

Anyone can be brave hiding behind the trigger of a particle weapon, she sniffed in disdain.

But Marsch did not wear an energy weapon. Was it possible that humans recruited their sire cairns from a blade society?

Kidahin heard him call out to her. She turned to find that he had stopped and was watching her as she continued in a straight line. She had gone tail chasing, and he had caught her at it. He must have watched her for a minute or two before calling out. She had wandered off the trail and was stalking parallel to the Coalition base perimeter.

Not the way to make a good first impression, she grumbled on her return. What was wrong with her?

"What's the matter, Kidahin? Lost? The trail goes this way," he pointed.

They closed the distance to the base perimeter. The soil looked less claylike and felt soft and spongy under her bare feet. The trees had thinned out and tended toward the coarser brindled dark bark ones with wide, dark green leaves.

Marsch watched the Hunter, concerned. She wanted to scout into the next sector. Why? How capable was she in battle? Could she fight? She hadn't impressed him much so far. Could he surprise her in unarmed combat as well?

Marsch wondered how he was going to explain her presence in the SOB. He had put himself smack in the middle of the diplomatic mission. Her presence would distract the ambassadors from their negotiations. Besides, he had duties of his own to perform. Where could he put her then? From what he remembered of the cultural briefings, Eyloni honored their agreements. Would Melkorka consider it disrespectful if he refused to let Kidahin accompany him everywhere he went?

What would he do with her when he returned to the ship?

He ducked under and around branches as he thought the problem through. He of all people should not have gotten involved with the Eyloni at all. He wasn't in the executive chain of command and he wasn't a diplomat: a good field commander made a poor liar.

He had overstepped his authority by making a personal agreement with Melkorka and Phelindra. He hadn't intended that his rhetorical comment be taken as a literal offer to train her himself.

They had assumed he demanded to train her and had entrusted her into his care for training as he saw fit for five standard days.

That would make the next 120 hours tough. Maybe with some luck he could drop her into an ARTs recon patrol. That would keep her out of sight of the captain and the ambassadors and keep her training in low profile.

Kidahin wondered about human organization. No doubt Marsch had duties to perform. Maybe she could watch other humans perform their duties. She wondered how their hierarchies worked. She had been told that humans did not have tribes or clans. They had nations: tribeless compacts.

How did human females command their males, or even each other? What must happen before a human male consented to the Warpact command of another male? How could Coalition warship crews act as one if they did not have female social hierarchies? How could human females have their fighting instinct enhanced when the many males aboard their warship distracted them?

Why had Del assumed responsibility for the Eyloni on this moon? Why had he insisted on training her? Why had he sworn such a dire oath? Raging interest, curiosity, and an impatience for answers filled her as they broke through the jungle and into the clearing around the Coalition base.

Kidahin watched him with respectful reserve and forced down her youthful impulses. He had not shown her any specific skill she did not already know—but that did not matter—at times training repeated what was already known. She had to prove herself worthy of his singular care, be patient, and wait.

She walked up a shallow incline into a grassy clearing and a thrill shuddered through her. She saw camouflaged field buildings laid out in a set pattern. Main buildings sat atop the rise, and she could see a few outlying structures from where she stood. The layout bothered her. It did not blend into the landscape; rather, it stood out and advertised its presence, called attention to itself.

Marsch stopped to look at the grassy incline behind the SOB security center. He called Kidahin over to him and pointed forked fingers at his eyes, hoping she understood: watch. He held up his hand, palm outstretched in the universal sign to stop. He strolled across the bluish grass and paced out a large circle.

Kidahin waited, curious. She watched his every move, but she also listened to the activity around her. She heard two thousand humans rustling about the base, but no one seemed to have noticed their arrival. Satisfied, she perked her ears at him and wondered.

Marsch scuffed up the grass from the soil using his booted heel. It was time to see just how much the young Hunter knew, and he needed an area large enough to allow for a variety of strategies using both offensive and defensive single combat maneuvers. He considered several options as he looked his work over, checking for holes or objects that could cause serious injury. The ground gave somewhat. It was still damp, and its short grass and thick thatch should absorb impact like a thin exercise mat.

Kidahin's interest rose as Marsch dug out a circle in the grass. He waved her to join him at its center. She glided over to him, ears pricking with curiosity, and wondered what he planned. Her nose told her that he had something in mind. Why else would he bother scuffing out a circle in the ugly grass? She tingled all over the whole time he made hand signs to her. Those signs made it clear that she was to defend herself and hold the area within the circle. If she retreated, or was forced out, then she was defeated.

Marsch made eye contact with the Hunter and pantomimed the rules of engagement for the impromptu training session. He pointed to her flint breast knife and made an explicit, violent negative gesture, hoping she understood it wasn't allowed.

Kidahin congratulated herself. She knew it, knew she had smelled him right. Marsch would begin her training now. Excited, she focused on his movements. He pointed to her adulthood knife and made a second negative gesture. She placed her hand on its sheath a moment before continuing to include the swell of her breast and looked him in the eyes.

"*Entiki*," she sang under her breath.

"Begin," Marsch said.

Kidahin tensed, wary. This male had significant combat skills. The title sire cairn implied that its holder had expertise in fighting and battle tactics. But Marsch was human, and she did not want to hurt him. He was a male: she wanted to impress him.

Stepping back three paces, Marsch set his stance and nodded to her. She watched him and sought an opening. She circled him; her undulating tail gave her the balance she needed to make exaggerated feints without having to overcorrect her thrusts. She had the advantage, for he had no tail to help him offset the inertia of an attack or a feint.

Marsch watched her stalk him, tail whipping behind her. He focused on that tail. It telegraphed her moves. As a balancing organ, it shifted opposite to her intended thrusts to keep her body stable. A natural tree climber, she should conclude that he'd have no idea of its uses in combat.

Kidahin pirouetted around him again and froze. His bunching muscles and glancing eyes told her that he was about to lunge at her right flank. She twisted sideways to counter the strike to her jaw and set herself up to grab his arm and use his momentum to take him down.

When her fingers brushed his fist, however, he shifted parallel to her strike, grappled her, and flipped her over his shoulder.

Kidahin landed on her splayed long toes and pivoted, cursing the spirits for being duped on the first try. She fired off a backswing, catching him in the jaw.

Marsch, anticipating the backswing, turned with the blow; her elbow skidded along his jaw, tearing his lip as it streaked past. The momentary contact bled off her inertia and slowed her follow-through at the same time it accelerated his turn.

Marsch swore. If he had turned any earlier, she would have dislocated his jaw. If he had turned any later, she would have knocked molars out of his head!

Bleeding from his torn lip, he spun to face her exposed back. Before she could turn to face him, he grabbed the base of her tail with one hand, reached under her armpit to grapple her collarbone with the other hand, and threw her.

She hit the ground, and Marsch jumped on top of her. She rolled aside at the last second and swung her legs, catching him behind the knees and knocking his legs out from under him.

Marsch swore again. The youngster moved quick and had incredible physical strength.

Kidahin rolled onto his chest and looked him in the eyes. He was not even breathing hard! Her ears swiveled forward. She had no experience reading human body language, but she smelled clearheaded cunning in his scent. She had him down and the advantage was hers.

She laced her tail under and around Marsch's knees, anchoring herself to him, and lunged for his exposed throat.

Anticipating her attack the moment he felt her tail grapple him, Marsch overrode the instinct to defend his neck. Instead, he flung his arms out, not to intercept her blurred hands, but to slap cupped fingers against ears that twitched sideways as they tracked the air whistling around his hands.

He felt her tense an instant before he cuffed her delicate ears. Amber eyes flashed in surprise as she squealed, stunned.

Marsch tried to roll her off his chest, but he found himself fouled in her tail. Grabbing it by its red ringleted tip, he did to her what he used to do to his pet cat Fuzz-Fuzz: he rubbed it in her face.

Kidahin hissed with indignant anger and rolled away from him, furious.

Marsch, ignorant of Eyloni social customs, didn't know the significance of his act. For the Eyloni, her pons meant to her what pubic hair meant to a human. He had done the equivalent of shoving a woman's nose below her waist as if to say she should smell herself.

Kidahin jumped at him from her semi-prone stance.

She tried to overbear him onto his back, but Marsch used her anger against her, catching her in mid-leap with a punch under her rib cage, below her left breast. As she buckled, he reached between her legs, under her buttocks, and threw her up into a midair flip meant to bring her down on her stomach.

Kidahin, stunned by the human's beefy fist, relied on pure instinct to twist her tail in an effort to resist being flipped.

As she passed over his head, Marsch realized he couldn't flip her. Like a cat twisting its tail to land on its feet, she prevented him from flipping her over.

Marsch's mind worked overtime. He'd never fought a tailed opponent before. Her tail could unravel several unarmed combat moves if he wasn't careful. He needed to find a solution, fast!

As her upward motion slowed, Kidahin grew confident. He could not flip her.

She kept up her tail's vicious twisting. Instinct had saved her, but now she varied her tail's speed and position, a practiced balance maneuver she had learned while still an infant.

The countermove gave her the fractions of a second she needed to think. He would either let her drop, or he would try to slam her back into the ground. Either way, she could snap her tail and let the momentum roll her away from him and up into a ready stance. He would be vulnerable the instant after she rebounded.

The Hunter made Marsch sweat. She didn't sweat dammit, but she didn't have him at a disadvantage, either.

When Kidahin's upward motion stopped, Marsch snapped his wrists, and she flipped the other way.

Kidahin's eyes widened in shock. She found, too late, that her tail now helped Marsch overcome her resistance. She flipped over and slammed into the ground, on her stomach, air blasting from her lungs with such force that her breath abandoned her and would not return no matter how desperately she tried.

Kidahin panicked. The powerful male grappled her as he settled onto the small of her back. He drove his fingers into her armpits, jabbing at nerve centers that controlled her hands and arms.

Fear consumed her, but her rational mind clung to the certain knowledge that no male ever willfully harmed a female.

Her lungs paralyzed, her arms paralyzed, her defenses paralyzed, she laid there helpless.

He grabbed her by the head.

She knew Marsch would snap her neck. Her breath came in ragged gasps as feeling returned, too late, to her hands.

He was going to kill her.

She stiffened as he twitched his hands. She had lost.

Marsch heard shouts. He saw people running, towards them, close.

Kidahin, resigned to her defeat, relaxed to let the sire cairn know that she knew he had killed her. She laid there rerunning the exercise through her mind until the sound of charging feet roused her from her disappointment.

A pair of feet pounded up to them, and Marsch's weight flew from her back.

Her attitude changed from detached chagrin to protective outrage in an instant.

They attacked her male!

Possessive anger and the bitter loss of having something of value taken consumed her. Eyloni females had peculiar ideas about who could touch the males they associated with. They always defended them and even stopped them from fighting amongst themselves if they carried it to extremes. Exceptions existed only for points of honor, betrayal, and failure to abide by the conventions of a Warpact.

Petty Officer 1/c Nelson held Marsch by the shoulders and dragged him away from the enraged young Hunter.

Crap! Marsch thought as he struggled to free himself. This crowd will draw the wrong kind of attention.

"Sir! Sir! Stand down, Sir!" Nelson said.

"What do you think you are doing, Petty Officer? Stand yourself down!" Marsch demanded.

Kidahin rolled over, jumped to her feet, and forced her body between Marsch and his attacker, driving them apart.

She spun, pulled her adulthood knife, and set her sights on her target.

A surprised Marsch stood behind her. Her tail brushed him often in its frantic whipping.

The hairs on Nelson's neck crawled with the sudden realization that the Eyloni female stalked him.

Whatthehell? Nelson gaped. Does she think I'm robbing her of her prey?

Kidahin trilled a sharp, ominous growl at him: a final warning.

Nelson heard running. He glanced up at the Compact co-ambassadors heading toward them.

"Stop! Stop! He is testing her. A combat test. A practice fight," Anlann yelled in his accented standard. "She will kill you if you do not withdraw. She thinks you are attacking Del! She is defending him from you. You must withdraw!"

Nelson heard the female co-ambassador shouting in her language at the stalking Hunter.

Protecting the commander? From him? *That's crazy*, Nelson thought. He had pulled Marsch from her before he could break her neck. *She should be thanking me for saving her life, dammit!*

The Eyloni female stalked Nelson until he retreated. Kidahin backed up into Marsch and pressed her pons under his chin. An instinctive need prompted her to wrap her long tail around them both. She glared at the gathering crowd with arms out, hands up, long fingers splayed wide, fingernails brandished like claws, adulthood knife held between her left thumb and forefinger.

Marsch put his hands on her shoulders and said, "Easy, Kidahin. You did well."

Kidahin relaxed at his touch. His voice sounded strong, commanding, comforting.

He did not speak in the derisive tones he had used when he had demanded her adulthood knife. She looked over her shoulder and met his eyes. She pricked one ear toward him in reassurance and the other back to listen to Anlann and Seralin and track the gathering crowd.

Marsch thought he'd better calm everyone down a bit.

Too late, Ambassador Harrison and Captain Winters ran down the grassy rise at breakneck speed. Anlann and Seralin were already here, calming Kidahin.

"Senior Chief, report!" Captain Winters ordered as a livid Harrison gulped the thin air.

"You stupid grunt!" Harrison screamed. "What the hell do you think you're doing? If you've caused a diplomatic incident, I'll have your warrant!"

Winters considered Harrison's hysterical voice a moment and sighed. He already had his fill of the ambassador and didn't need incidents like these bringing them together any more than was necessary to carry out the mission. Now he had to do something before he lost the best special operations commander in the Fleet to a jealous bureaucrat's administrative revenge.

But how? Winters asked himself. He needed time to think.

"Report to my office in ten minutes, Senior Chief. Dismissed," Winters said.

"Aye aye, Sir," Marsch said, spun on his heels, and headed for a shower and clean uniform. Everyone stared in open-mouthed astonishment as the young Eyloni Hunter followed him.

Everyone, that is, except the co-ambassadors. They watched her retreating tail with irrepressible curiosity.

5

A GUEST IS ACCOMMODATED

"What the hell did you think you were doing, Mr. Marsch? On whose authority did you include the Compact Forward Operations Base in your security sweeps?" Winters demanded.

"Mine, Sir!"

"Yours, Senior Chief? What put that idea in your head? Do you think that they can't patrol their own territory without you?"

"No, Sir. Of course not, Captain. That's not the issue Sir," Marsch said.

Harrison broke in, "Then just what is the issue, Marsch? The Eyloni don't need your help. They didn't ask Captain Winters for security assistance, and they damn well didn't relay any such request to me through their co-ambassadors. They have their own security personnel. Hell Mister, they have everything they need aboard their own ship!"

"Not everything, Mr. Ambassador. They need a battle leader, *si-re ki-re*," Marsch said, singing the musical notes that spelled out the title Melkorka and Kidahin had attributed to him.

Both co-ambassadors leaned forward at that. Anlann appeared to be lost in thought, judging by his averted expression and relaxed ears. Seralin glanced at Marsch a moment before turning to stare at the warship's huluhar. The young Hunter stood near Marsch, arms folded beneath her breasts, watching him. She listened, her ears following the voices around her, but her eyes ignored everyone in the room but him.

Seralin inhaled Kidahin's scent, smelled her jumbled feelings. Impotence and irrational fury radiated from her in waves. The huluhar's latent preadolescent instincts made her unpredictable and dangerous.

Seralin wondered what in the spirits was going on with Kidahin's shipboard society. They would never have allowed her to leave them for a trivial reason, not now. With Kalinn numbered among the dead, her part in choosing a new warleader made her indispensable. What had they smelled in Del's scent that convinced them to allow her to go with him?

Kidahin had made it quite clear that she would kill anyone posing a threat to him. Like all Eyloni females, her violent nature flared up the moment she believed a male was in even the slightest danger. Why? Seralin had to find out. The reason might be critical to the covert mission assigned to her by the *Be'atika Senge*, the Compact Counsel.

Seralin stared at the young Hunter and concentrated until Kidahin noticed the changing scent and looked up. Seralin signed a query in Battle Language. Kidahin replied in kind, telling Seralin how she had ended up in the Coalition base. The huluhar's account stumped Seralin: the possibility of danger and death lurked in even routine combat training, and the drill had been no playful tail yanking.

Anlann wondered what all the fuss was about. Marsch had tested the young Hunter in single combat skills. So what? Males tested females every now and then just to see what they had learned from their hierarchies.

Ambassador Harrison's bizarre jealousy over Marsch's expanded security sweeps made no sense either. The Ni'zakhonii attack had killed Kalinn, and any unattached male would look in on his crew and show an interest in their welfare. No doubt they noticed Marsch's interest and had accepted him as an unattached male, an impressive one too, judging by his ability to pry the huluhar from their affectionate grasp.

Anlann studied Kidahin. She had greeted him with formal dignity before turning back to watch Marsch. Ambassador Harrison tried to exclude her from this meeting, but she refused to leave, her glare pure violence. Anlann could still smell her seething fury. His empathy connected with her scent and drew a picture for him in his mind that suggested broken social taboos, violated territory, and theft.

He understood her anger and empathized with it.

A male did not interfere with another male unless he exercised Warpact status over the other male for the duration of a serious event. Males enjoyed an almost absolute autonomy, unlike females with their many complicated hierarchies. The human male who interfered had no claim of Warpact rank over Marsch. Besides, no male would ever dream of interfering with a female and male exchange. A female's clan, society, or tribal hierarchies would avenge any wrong done to her in their own dire fashion. For a male to interfere with another male insulted the honor of all parties involved and violated social etiquette. The human, Nelson, should thank the spirits that Kidahin had not killed him outright.

Anlann focused on Harrison's equally offensive public display.

"So you decided that you could train one of those people better than they could train her themselves?" Harrison demanded, flushing deeper shades by the minute as he tried to get a grip on his rising temper. It was bad enough trying to negotiate with these primitive animals under ideal conditions, but incidents like these made his job even more difficult.

The admission of the Compact into a Coalition alliance held top priority on Harrison's political agenda. He would not allow his greatest diplomatic triumph to be derailed by Fleet sticking its long nose into the personal lives of these backward natives he negotiated with! Familiar contact made them people, not things to be manipulated. He didn't want any direct contact between the warship's crew and Fleet personnel unless he arranged the meeting himself, monitored the event, and consented to any agreements made. And here this amateur, this moron, had walked right into the Compact base, shot the breeze with the warship's commander, brought their youngest crewmember here, and beat her down the moment they arrived! That Anlann, Seralin, and Melkorka now called Marsch 'Del' infuriated him all the more. The co-ambassadors had taken Marsch's side; they even ignored him and addressed Marsch directly.

Kidahin stood behind Marsch and shook. Her training interrupted before it had begun, she had to force down her instincts and restrain herself from killing the human male who attacked Marsch. Had he not reassured her of his safety, she would have dispatched the interloper then and there, and she would have been within her rights to do so, too!

Kidahin's ears followed the voices in the room. She struggled to understand the human tongue. The three human male scents hinted at some territorial dispute. She signed Battle Language to Seralin and asked what all the serious vocal tones were about.

Seralin caught the huluhar's wistful query and began signing a running translation.

"Warrant Officer, didn't you know that your presence in the Compact FOB could have fomented a diplomatic crisis?" Harrison asked.

"No, Mr. Ambassador."

"*Senior Chief* Warrant Officer Marsch," Captain Winters said. "I understand the need for the inclusion of the Compact base perimeter in your security sweeps. I also tend to agree that you had to make courtesy contact with the Eyloni you met while in the field. But did you have to meet with the Compact warship's Mistress of the Ship?"

"Yes, Captain, I did. Not only did I coordinate sweep parameters with our security center and expand our patrol area into their territory, but I also briefed the Eyloni on security issues and got a bead on how things stood there. Besides Sir, they changed their patrols to overlap ours, giving us better overall coverage."

"Don't give me that bull, Marsch!" Harrison interrupted again. "Even if security protocol does justify sweep integration with the Compact force, it doesn't authorize you to make formal agreements with the commanding officer of a Compact warship."

"I beg your pardon, Mr. Ambassador, but no formal agreement has been made. We only have an informal status-of-forces agreement concerning free-movement in each other's patrol areas," Marsch said.

"Then what do you call *her*?" Harrison screamed and jabbed an assaultive finger at Kidahin, "She's no informal understanding! They agreed to let you remove a member of their crew from their control and bring her here, with you assuming responsibility for her. That's damn formal. You take her back where you found her!"

"I'm sorry, Mr. Ambassador, but I have Kidahin in my care for five days."

"No!" Anlann interrupted, "The agreement between Del and Melkorka is binding on him and the warship's crew. Compact warships are autonomous. Their crews have the right to make independent agreements and fulfill honorable obligations so long as they do not violate Compact traditions and interests."

"No!" Seralin added, "Del has begun Kidahin's training, training Melkorka must have felt the huluhar needed. The agreement binds their honor to his word."

Kidahin grew tired of being the ignored center of controversy. In a temper, she interrupted them by singing a lyrical string of notes. She sang for some time. Winters and Harrison both froze, wary. Remembering what the cultural report said about the Eyloni considering music sacred, they listened as the young Hunter sang a long, defiant complaint.

"What's she saying, Ambassador Seralin? She is involved, and I'd like to hear her side of it," Winters said.

"Kidahin says Phelindra ordered her to go with Del for a training period of ten human days to correct a field stalking inadequacy he had found in her skills." Seralin paused and locked eyes with Harrison for a moment before continuing. "Phelindra is the Eldest Huntress aboard *Hunter's Moon* and holds even higher military rank than Melkorka. Kidahin tells me that she did not come with Del against her will. She desires the training as well." Seralin flicked her ears at Kidahin in dignified delight.

Harrison glared at Marsch, his bald spot sweating.

Anlann turned his back on the ambassador and casually addressed Marsch.

"You may have meant five days, Del, but Melkorka mistook your open hand reference to mean ten. She told Kidahin that you meant ten as humans count, and that you meant standard human days. By now, Melkorka's crew knows that you have their huluhar for ten Coalition standard days. That is four Elleio standard weeks, a long time for them and for her. If you do not mind my asking, what did you do to get them to entrust Kidahin into your care?"

"I swore an oath in blood that I would keep her safe."

Winters blinked in confusion.

Harrison heaved a sigh of relief and chuckled. "A voodoo oath? What superstitious hogwash! It's meaningless! Send her on her way home Marsch, and I won't mention this matter in your permanent service record."

The room turned cold as both co-ambassadors glared at Harrison.

"The oath Del made with Melkorka is binding on him and her crew. We hold oaths in high regard and honor them throughout the Compact. Any assault you bring against this oath will precipitate a diplomatic incident, Ambassador," Anlann warned.

Harrison stewed in silence and glanced at Anlann, then Seralin, and then a flat-eared Kidahin before he settled on the true villain here: Marsch. Harrison's silvery eyebrows narrowed in thought. He had an idea: stall. "Very well, I see no reason to take diplomatic notice of an apolitical agreement between a young woman and a mere warrant officer. The agreement shall be strictly constrained to personal combat training for her lasting ten days. That means no contact with the Eyloni command staff, Warrant Officer Marsch, understand? None! Now, Ambassador Anlann, Ambassador Seralin, shall we return to the discussions at hand before we were interrupted?"

Kidahin made a possessive, gaudy show of entwining her tail around Marsch's waist.

Seralin smiled; Anlann turned aside and struggled to keep a straight face.

Harrison's eyes narrowed in sudden realization that he'd lost a point with the Compact co-ambassadors. He swallowed his rage. Vengeful, he locked eyes with Marsch, opened his mouth, but paused. For the first time he truly saw Marsch and gauged his demeanor. For all his outward, calm reserve, he had an intensity about him, a presence that commanded notice. The man's stony gaze told Harrison all he needed to know: this was a dangerous man.

Winters rolled his eyes at the ceiling, shook his head, and tried not to laugh now that the crisis had abated.

Seralin and Anlann brushed tails and flexed ears at one another. Both wanted to speak with Marsch about his oath and hear how seriously he took it. Harrison's telltale pheromones in his scent had made it clear that he did not. The co-ambassadors had not exaggerated: Marsch's oath had the binding power of Compact law behind it. No fosterage oath was ever a mere agreement. Such oaths had far-reaching obligations, but this one was laced with dire consequences.

Anlann liked humans, most of them anyway. They fascinated him. He did not want to see them harmed through their own ignorance, but unless they exercised care, the Compact warship's crew would tear *Henri Edda* apart if Harrison tried to interfere with Marsch's oath in any way.

"Carry on, Mr. Marsch. Dismissed!" Winters said.

"Aye, aye, Sir!"

Marsch turned and walked out as fast as military courtesy permitted, Kidahin following on his heels. Once outside, he considered what to do next. He had to find quarters for her. He met her attentive gaze and waved her to follow. On the way to the quartermaster, he stopped in at the mess hall.

Inside, Marsch grabbed a tray and a cup, poured some coffee, scooped the dregs of lunch's whipped potatoes from a shallow pan and plopped them on the tray. He showed Kidahin the food and beverages still available from what little remained of the shiptime lunch buffet and let her make her own choices.

Kidahin's sensitive nose twitched; she smelled something delicious. What was that hot drink Marsch sipped? She inhaled the black liquid's odor, and her mouth watered. She grimaced at the pasty gruel lying at the bottom of the pan. It looked and smelled like emergency carbohydrate rations: flat smell, no texture, and probably no taste, either.

The few base personnel remaining in the dining area watched the Eyloni female explore. They knew the co-ambassadors could show up at any time and were prepared for a chance encounter with either of them, but the young Hunter surprised them even though scuttlebutt had already placed her with the SOG commander. Their eyes followed Kidahin's progress until she froze, flicked her ears at them, and looked back at Marsch.

"Excuse me, Sir. May I ask a question?" Apprentice Crewman Avalis said.

Marsch looked up from his coffee and nodded, "Fire away Apprentice Crewman."

"Ah, well Sir, what's she doin' here anyway?" Avalis asked, gesturing at the exploring Eyloni.

"Basic training, Avalis. She's going to be with us for a while. Problem?"

"No, Sir!"

"Very well, carry on," Marsch said.

"Aye, Sir,"

He'd better carry on, too. The delay notice he posted would expire soon. He had to get the ARTs security briefing underway, and he still had to get Kidahin supplied and quartered.

"Come on, Kidahin. We've got to go."

The Hunter looked up from her coffee cup. She took another cautious sip of the wonderful smelling hot liquid, sputtered, and swallowed the bitter brew. She took another sip and made a face. Her ears folded back before flipping forward in a half-perk. Her eyes followed Marsch's back across the room.

Must be an acquired taste, Kidahin decided as she scowled into the cup. Maybe she could learn to enjoy it as much as he seemed to. He drank enough of it.

She glanced at the few remaining humans. The female who spoke to Marsch wore a different shade of clothing than he did. The difference suggested to Kidahin that the human was common crew and not one of his elite combat females.

That female must have inquired about her, for Kidahin smelled an empathic reference. The female's scent seemed to suggest that Marsch had given her a perfunctory response and then dismissed her.

Kidahin gulped the last of the delicious-smelling, bitter-tasting drink and raced after him.

They strolled along a gravel path to the quartermaster, where Marsch requisitioned a standard ARTs ground forces duty pack for her. It included the usual Type-IIs, bedding, linens, toiletries, and other items necessary for camp life. He reckoned she'd not want, or need, the clothing: she would find them too confining.

They left the quartermaster and stopped at the SOB's hygiene facility. There he introduced Kidahin to its complement of sinks, toilets, and showers. Unlike the latrines of old, modern field toilets had plasma torch emitters a meter below each seat. Powered by the SOB's portable fusion generator, they zapped everything that fell into them to vapor and vented it first to a catalytic converter and then outside. He worked with her, showing her how the device operated, worried she'd dangle her tail into the commode and suffer serious injury. The waste torch vaporized everything that passed a sensor, but safety features scanned for the occasional futile hand that plunged after dropped personal items. Even then, the plasma torch would disrupt skin cells a good three or four millimeters deep before the safety mechanism could shut it down.

Kidahin watched Marsch make the proper demonstrations with no thoughts of modesty. Compact necessary facilities operated on similar principles, but she could not understand the idea of, or need for, toilet paper. She had no difficulty operating the showers, the body dryers, the sinks, or the hand dryers.

Marsch took Kidahin to the Administration building and requisitioned guest VIP quarters for her. The petty officer in charge put her in the quarters next to the co-ambassadors.

The quartering process should have been a quick, simple, and easy task, and it had been until they stopped by the VIP quarters, where Marsch tried to explain that the quarters were hers.

No! her expression told him. She launched into a singsong argument that trailed off into a short series of sour notes. She dropped her gear and glared at him, tail snapping. She complained, and Marsch felt his temples jump in nervous ticks throughout her tirade. He smelled a mild odor around her that reminded him for some reason of porch gates and playpens.

Kidahin knew as soon as she entered the room that Marsch meant for her to shelter apart from him the whole time she remained on the human base. She spent ten minutes explaining to him that she had been assigned to him and would be sheltering with him, too.

Marsch recognized an ass-chewing when he heard one. She was offended, but at what he had no idea. Some misunderstanding he'd have to ask Seralin to sort out for him after the ARTs briefing. No, scratch that, the routine PT and jungle combat training came after the briefing according to his revised schedule. Then he had a strategy meeting with his senior NCOs and the Fleet/SOG liaison staff.

Kidahin took mental notes of all the sights, sounds, and smells surrounding her. They painted a picture in her mind; a map that marked important buildings, paths, and security teams throughout the base. She heard several wheeled vehicles rolling down adjacent paths, nearly silent.

But they were not noiseless, and she grumbled about them as they walked. The low but audible whine of servomotors set her teeth on edge. She would have to tell Marsch that rollers lacked stealth. Compact surface combat vehicles crawled on six legs. They made no noise except for the sound of brushing through jungle foliage. Heavy mandibles mounted forward cut brush and small trees where necessary, giving the vehicles variable terrain access, unlike these wheeled vehicles. Looking around, she saw a hovercraft—another poor choice for jungle terrain—an armored troop transport, and a suborbital vertical takeoff aircraft.

Marsch led her into a large semi-cylindrical carbon composite shelter, open at each end, standing in a grassy clearing.

"Special Ops Commander on deck!" a petty officer announced.

Heads turned as Marsch stepped inside.

"Have 'em form up on deck, Senior Chief Johnson," he said.

"Aye, aye, Sir! All hands, form up on deck!"

"Aye, aye, Senior Chief! Forming up on deck, aye! Sog-Ops!" They yelled in unison.

Marsch performed a quick inspection before turning them over to Johnson and her petty officers.

Kidahin watched Marsch receive several reports. She counted almost as many males as females in the combat force. More than one male commanded the same females, and some of the females commanded the males. She knew humans had a unisex command hierarchy, but seeing it in action was odd, unsettling, and worrisome.

After the briefing session, Marsch ordered physical training. The PT session lasted well over two hours before Marsch broke them up into small groups and began drilling them in unarmed combat, knife combat, and particle weapon exercises.

Kidahin ground her teeth throughout the energy weapon scenarios. She considered any reliance on the coward's weapon a potential weakness. Such weapons violated her people's strong personal combat ethic. Of course, Eyloni operated armor and artillery pieces. They fired the heavy projectile and energy weapons mounted on military assets, but no Warrior ever used personal weapons more advanced than piercing, bludgeoning, or slashing primitive hand weapons. No Hunter with any self-respect carried weapons more advanced than knives or bows and arrows.

The people in Marsch's elite combat forces treated her with respect. She recognized them as assault forces by the way they looked her in the eye, could smell it in their scent. She saw no flinching, no glancing aside. They remained centered, alert, confident, and they jumped every time Marsch yelled at them. What more evidence did she need? He was the Coalition warship's sire cairn. Kidahin tailchased an intriguing idea: Marsch and his fighting hands made up the blade society aboard his ship.

She listened, ears cocked wide, to a report Marsch received from another male. She speculated. Marsch commanded elite combat forces and not routine Fleet security or combat personnel. His teams reported to him on a wide range of issues. His time was valuable. Why would he waste it prowling personal security sweeps?

It soon dawned on her that no other human male ever bothered to make a security sweep into her people's base perimeter. Marsch's forays into their territory had not been a part of normal assault force operations. He had gone out of his way to patrol their territory. He had taken it upon himself to look after them. He placed them under his protection. *Had Melkorka known? Had her society entrusted her to him because of it?*

"All right Senior Chief McCain, form 'em up on deck! In squads!" Marsch yelled, jolting Kidahin from her tailchasing.

"Aye, aye, Sir! You heard the Commander! Form up on deck. Eight-man squads! Move! Move! Move!" Senior Chief Petty Officer Joann McCain bellowed.

"Aye, aye, Senior Chief! SOG-444 forming up on deck. In eight-man squads! Sog-Ops!"

Kidahin watched as males carried out the female's orders.

"Team," Marsch began, "I can tell by the distracted performances I've seen this afternoon that you have taken an interest in our visitor." He turned and invited Kidahin to join him.

The Hunter flicked her ears up and forward in surprise, coiled her tail, curious, and glided over to him.

"This is Kidahin," Marsch introduced, "a Hunter serving aboard the Compact warship *Hunter's Moon.* No doubt you've heard about our scuffle earlier today."

Heads nodded, and some of them smiled or chuckled. Kidahin learned from Marsch's scent that she had been introduced. She perked her ears up and forward, flipped a casual tail, and met their eyes.

"Team, Kidahin is one of her ship's most junior crewmembers. I've decided to include her in our training exercises. She has a few tricks to surprise you with, and her anatomy gives her unbelievable control of her body when she's off the ground."

Some of the ARTs members nodded or murmured in appreciation, while others reassessed the lean, muscular young Eyloni in a new light. They saw a willowy 175-centimeter-tall, 55-kilogram, redheaded woman with matte velour skin splashed with fall color patterns. Her lips, tongue, gums, tear ducts, and nipples were so deep a red they could pass for black. They took in her thong-riding short loincloth, her breasts bouncing behind draped columns of colored knots, her black and red flint knife hanging under her left breast, and her single hooped earring and its simple web in stride: a soldier was a soldier as far as they were concerned.

Kidahin withstood the scrutiny with patient dignity and examined them just as keenly as they had done to her. She wondered how well they could move with all the restrictive clothing they wore.

"If I can," Marsch continued, "I'll ask Kidahin to give you a short hand-to-hand combat demonstration."

Kidahin's ears kept time with his voice's rising and falling notes until he spoke her name, and then she flicked them at him. She smelled the pheromones in his scent, grasped his meaning, but she struggled to connect the feelings with his words. He turned to her and cocked his eye ridge hairs as if they were ears. She lacked his hairy brows, having instead brick red shades around her eyes, her eyelids, and her brows that feathered down across her upper cheeks into the oranges of her face.

Shaking her head to clear the facial comparison from her mind, she took his cocked eyes for a gesture to follow. She padded after him onto a large square floor covered with black mats, suddenly wary.

Marsch jogged to its center, the Eyloni female following close behind.

Ah, Kidahin realized, Del is going to train me here to see if I make a mistake while others watch.

She whipped her tail in crafty eagerness.

Marsch smiled as the Hunter stalked across the cushioned practice deck and assumed a ready stance.

Given the 'go' signal she had picked up from watching the afternoon's single combat matches, she circled him, seeking an opening.

Ten minutes passed as they probed each other's defenses with several feints before launching into an arms, legs and tail free-for-all that ended with Marsch on his back. Using her left thumb, Kidahin lightly jabbed the base of his skull, 'killing' him.

The ARTs personnel clapped their hands, impressed with the fox-faced woman's moves.

Marsch left the training area with Kidahin in tow and arrived at the Admin building for the daily intelligence briefing with the senior command staff.

Time dragged by as Kidahin stifled a yawn and paid attention, while Marsch talked at great length about things she could only guess at. He sat at a beige oval table large enough to accommodate twelve people, An embedded holographic projector rested in its center and displayed maps, rosters, and reports necessary for the briefing. She sampled the many scents in the room and from them delved initial impressions of the other humans in the room. One male represented base security. The female next to him supervised security aboard the Coalition warship. Another female, wearing different colored clothing, represented a combat society called *Marines*. The two males next to her had some connection with the warship's command crew, and the last person, another female, commanded the warship's science society. The science female seemed to take more of an interest in her than in the meeting.

Inattention to duty, Kidahin flattened her ears in disapproval.

The briefing turned into a rotating discussion on key matters: surface base operations, ground features, and her people. Kidahin swelled with pride upon seeing Marsch's opinion sought after and discussed often, further confirming her society's suspicion that he was the warship's sire cairn.

Marsch listened to the reports made by Tactical Operations Commander Millford and Marine Colonel Kelley. The ship's Chief of Security, Lieutenant Commander Allendale, made one short, four-word sitrep, "Maintaining Condition-3 Security Alert."

No kidding! Marsch thought and mentally rolled his eyes heavenward. They remained in Compact space and in the same system where Kidahin's crew had engaged three Lizard ships. Captain Winters was taking no chances. A recent battle invited reinforcement, or at least a recon patrol, and so they remained at Condition-3.

Marsch turned to the Marine colonel. Cairn Kelly's inclusion at this briefing smoothed over force integration issues. Her Marines could handle any planetary combat or large-scale boarding actions if the Lizards came looking for their task force.

"Your opinion, Mr. Marsch?" Commander Millford asked.

"None, Commander," Marsch replied automatically, the Tactical Ops officer's voice snapping him from his daydreaming. "I've got my senior chiefs forming up a few ARTs for reconnoitering all SOB heavy jungle approaches. I noticed the Eyloni have mounted their own heavy patrols when I passed through their territory earlier today. I've raised my concerns with SOB security, and I recommended that twenty-four SSB Mark-52 automated surveillance sentinels be sown throughout the forest. The Mark-52s will upload perimeter integrity data to both the ship's Surface Force Tracking Network and SOB security's Threat Detection Grid."

"Have you received any actionable intel from your Eyloni guest?" Millford asked, nodding to the young Hunter.

"No Commander, and I doubt I'd get much out of her. She's apprentice crew. From my jaunts into their FOB, I'd say they're preparing for a high-threat incursion. Makes sense, they lost their warleader, their captain. I think they expect a Lizard assault any time now."

Kidahin felt a fleeting empathic brush with Marsch's thoughts—an image of inclusion—when the others looked at her a moment before they turned back to him. She listened to the voices for a few minutes before turning her attention back to the holographic display.

She studied the orbital plots of the two warships. Both held station-keeping distance relative to each other as they orbited the moon. They maintained fixed-target surface surveillance orbit, which meant both ships kept pace with the moon's rotation above the bases on the surface. The scan covered the entire hemisphere, with the Coalition base acting as the sensor web's focal point.

Kidahin studied the outbound plot as it extended from the surface to the edge of local space, the volume within a sphere that contained the moon and its gas giant. The planet and its moon interfered with tactical scans, a minor inconvenience addressed by multiple passive combat assets launched from both ships.

She considered her ship's indicated disposition in the plot. He held his orbital position relative to a jump point within local space. As her warship's helm operator, she knew her ship's normal fixed-target surveillance orbit attitude and saw a deviation. The plot told her that Melkorka expected to engage the Ni'zakhonii in local space, and that she intended to support the Coalition warship in the event of enemy attack. Whether an attack was pending or not did not necessarily mean anything. Her people always considered battle options, but her warship's attitude change had been recent—within the past few hours.

Kidahin glanced at the Coalition warship's orbital plot and considered his orbital disposition. Reading the plot and making educated guesses, she concluded that the Coalition ship held his right broadside parallel to the moon's surface. That made her wonder about the human warleader's defective strategy.

Why use broadside fire to cover the surface installations?

Should the warleader not reposition his ship so that both broadsides covered all threat vectors and orbital arcs at once? He could still fire on the surface from his forward primary weapons and cover his hyperdrive coils with his aft batteries and point-defense systems. Kidahin puzzled over the orbital disposition problem and by the time the briefing ended she had worked out the tactical rationale.

Compact FTL quantum drive technology allowed a warship to jump within a gravity well. In contrast, the Coalition ship's hyperdrive created a wormhole in normal space, but the ship had to pass beyond a star's hyperspace gravity anomaly before he could open a stable wormhole. Local gravity destabilized the wormhole's event horizon and made entry into hyperspace hazardous within a certain variable threshold distance. The Coalition ship's attitude and disposition cleared it for maximum sublight orbital departure without having to execute delaying orbital maneuvers.

Marsch watched Kidahin pour over the tactical scan data. She had insisted he bring her to this meeting. She must be bored by now. She spent the whole time behind and to his left, listening and looking around.

Whenever he spoke, those ears of hers swept around like little dish antennas and gave him their undivided attention. At times, she would nod to herself as though she kept time to a rhythm running through her head. When he said certain words, she would nod in satisfaction. Judging by the increasing frequency of nods, she already understood many of his words and was making rapid progress.

Marsch checked the time: 20h00. Time for him to return to his command. He grinned. His XO wanted some time on Ibeetu and had probably paced a groove in the deck by now. Marsch figured he'd give him a few hours relief by standing the XO's watch until the end of beta shift.

He stopped smiling.

Kidahin.

He glanced at the Eyloni studying the plot. She stuck to him and made it clear she wouldn't allow him out of her sight.

He'd have to get clearance before he could bring her aboard ship. No problem there, the ship already hosted the co-ambassadors.

Marsch pulled a device resembling a pack of playing cards from his belt and tapped it, activating the *omni's* comm systems.

"Marsch to Captain Winters."

"Winters here. Go ahead, Senior Chief."

"Captain, I need to report to my command. Request permission to bring Kidahin aboard, Sir."

"Kidahin? Oh, your Eyloni trainee." Winters paused a moment. "Permission granted, Mr. Marsch. I'll pass the O.K. on to the bridge. You should be set in five. Comm the bridge when you're ready."

"Yes, Sir. Set in five, aye. Marsch out."

"Winters out."

Five minutes, less than that if he knew his captain. And Marsch knew his captain. He had served under him for three years, ever since his promotion to senior chief warrant officer.

Kidahin flinched and spun toward Marsch, her mind reaching for his fine empathic threads. She saw his feelings better, but the effort of matching his words to them reminded her of trying to hear someone yell through a waterfall. She learned his language the same way all Eyloni females acquired the language of a male who spoke a divergent dialect: she compared his words with the empathic pictures his scent brought to her mind.

Her eyes narrowed: something troubled him.

She stepped away from him and assessed his personal perimeter, puzzled over the feelings his scent presented to her.

She realized that he recalled a sad memory. Her concern deepened. She growled, a complex rhythm far beyond his hearing.

Marsch fled his past only to catch the Hunter focused on him, her amber eyes narrowed, her ears flattened, her nose sniffing the air around him.

Dammit! She must think I'm a mental case!

"Kidahin, I must return to my ship and check in with my command. Do you want to come with me?"

Kidahin flexed her ears, perplexed. She fought to match his words with the mental images her sense of smell drew in her mind's eye and put them into her own words. He pantomimed them rising into the sky, giving her the context clues she needed to unlock his meaning.

She jumped to him, ears pitched forward, tail held high, and nodded.

"*Yesss*. War. Ship. Go. I. You," she said in a clear voice, quite pleased with herself.

"Good, come with me."

Marsch nodded absent approval. She was picking up on some of his language. Seralin told him back aboard ship how hard it had been for her and Anlann to learn Coalition standard. He had complemented them on their language skills, and they told him how they had to learn the human tongue by brute force and still had difficulties with it. Standard made them feel tone deaf. They explained to him that Eyloni language followed a system of pitches, rhythms, and melodies. Eyloni grammar, mechanics, and syntax followed a complex series of musical sharps, flats, and rests. The same series of notes sung at different beats or octaves pronounced different words. It hadn't been easy for them, which made Kidahin's rapid grasp of it seem gifted.

The five minutes were up. Marsch tapped his omni.

"Marsch to *Henri Edda*..."

"*Henri Edda*. Lieutenant Alexander. Go ahead, Sir."

"Two for teleport, Lieutenant, myself and an Eyloni from the Compact ship."

"Acknowledged. You are cleared for return to the ship. Teleportation is standing by for your order, Sir,"

"Very well. Thank you, Lieutenant."

"You're welcome, Sir."

"Teleportation? Marsch."

"Teleportation, aye, Chief Kidwell here, Sir,"

"Two for teleport, Chief."

"Aye, Sir. Teleporting."

6

UNFAMILIAR TERRITORY

The Coalition carrier's personnel teleportation system opened a Mobius point around Marsch and Kidahin, and they vanished. The teleporter swapped the two volumes of space they occupied on Ibeetu with equal volumes aboard ship, and they arrived on separate pads in a chamber outfitted with sixteen similar ones.

"Permission to come aboard, Chief?" Marsch asked, in accordance with standard boarding protocol.

Chief Petty Officer Kidwell glanced up from her console and nodded. "Permission to come aboard granted. Welcome back, Sir."

"Thank you, Chief. Chief Kidwell, this is Kidahin, from the Compact Warship *Hunter's Moon*."

"Welcome aboard *Henri Edda*, Kidahin," Kidwell said with a smile.

The Hunter cocked her ears, looked the female in the eyes, and answered with a halting, lyrical, "Thank. You. Chief. Kidwell."

Kidwell nodded absently as she shut her station down. Marsch raised an eyebrow at Kidahin's expanding vocabulary. Kidahin peered about the chamber, wary and suspicious. Humans and human things made her jumpy. The odors throughout the base had put her on constant alert because human scent said things unbecoming in Eyloni culture. And now she felt nauseous. Her stomach fluttered as if she had passed through an artificial gravity generator's unstable graviton field.

Marsch led her past Kidwell to a closed door. Its sensors registered his presence and whisked open, and she followed him out into a world of harsh fluorescent lights.

Kidahin's eyes darted everywhere at once. She felt exposed, vulnerable. She focused on Marsch, the only Eyloni-like constant in an otherwise alien world.

A durable dull black padding embossed with ten-point stars covered a deck far too flat for her bare feet. The corridor stretched off into the distance on her left and right in seeming unrelenting regularity. Colored conduits and pipes ran along the ceiling, interrupted by more lights. Rectangular seams outlined hardware access panels along the walls. Marsch and she passed by closed doors, hatches, and other intersecting corridors.

Unnatural! her instinct screamed.

Every intersecting corridor led off into its own uniform parallel lines. A glowing yellow band ran at breast height along the left wall. Ribbed frames formed walls along the deck, and every bulkhead that intersected a corridor had stenciled swinging-door hatches. The hatch frames extended above the deck just enough to house a mechanical seal.

Marsch led her deeper into the ship and his bare utilitarian corridors. His builders cared nothing for him or for his crew. Dull carbon composite casings, burnished metal panels, gray bulkheads, polished stainless-steel hatches, harsh fluorescent lighting interrupted only by narrow yellow panels, and colored conduits ran down every corridor.

The Coalition ship both stressed and disappointed her.

Her nose wrinkled in response to an odor. It reminded her of a Health Center's medicinal cleanliness combined with the aromatic lubricants more at home in a maintenance bay.

This ship did not smell like anybody's home.

The striking contrast made Kidahin yearn for her society, homesick. *Hunter's Moon* was her home, and his internal layout ran nothing like this. His pathways wove around and about, mimicking a rain forest's subtle twists and uneven terrain. Main paths meandered along forest trails covered with simulated rocks, exposed roots, and uneven hard soil. Side paths resembled the narrow crown branches of elleiu trees, which led into quarters and compartments designed to remind everyone of the rooms back home, the ones formed from the elleiu tree's fused aerial roots.

Red, orange, and yellow leaves hung from branches that varied from brown to deep orange. The holographic trees surrounded solid rugged pathways overgrown with gold and orange grasses. Ceilings of warm forest colors smiled down on her as simulated leaves filtered the sunlight of *Elle*—Elleio's sun—giving the ship's trails and pathways their soft natural light. Shipwide illumination rotated through Elleio Standard Time, synchronizing circadian rhythms and following the orbital phases of Elleio around Tyreniioroneo. His aquamarine glow, the bright stars, and brilliant auroras flashed throughout the simulated night.

Kidahin counted twenty-four frames before stepping into a dead end. They turned right and followed another corridor, passed three more frames, turned left into a stairwell, climbed four steps to a landing, walked off the back of the landing and down a corridor for two frames before entering a lift that took them down three decks and then shifted them aft for some distance.

Kidahin grumbled to herself about all the ups and downs as she listened to Marsch talk. Horrified by the ship's unrelenting regularity, she remained alert and absorbed every feature she saw. They walked on, and she wrestled with his words and the smells his scent conveyed.

Hunter's Moon had no stairwells and no personnel transport lifts. Heavy lifts existed aboard a warship for the transport of ordnance and heavy equipment throughout the ship. Her people quantum translated most bulky or heavy items directly to their destinations. While her ship did have occasional vertical passageways, an Eyloni scaled them in the same way she would climb a rocky cliff face on Elleio. There were a few crawlways aboard ship that had rung ladders, but they were reserved for tight machine access, where physics and technology demanded utilitarian straight lines and angles.

Surely humans did not put up with this harsh light all the time. The room in which she arrived had not been this bright. On her warship, duty stations and pathway lighting followed standard daytime illumination. During the days-long night, station lighting slowly shifted from the prolonged sunset's pastel twilights to the auroral shimmers of the night sky and continued into the dawn's slow orange sunrise. During Battle Status station lighting shifted to a heart-racing emerald green no matter the time of day.

The few humans she met walked their ship's deck. They did not prowl him like her society prowled their warship. The humans are not one with him! They do not own him! She was shocked, and she shuddered in discomfort. To not care about, or for, her surroundings was foreign to Kidahin. It was as if humans had abandoned the natural world rather than live with it. Such a concept frightened her! That humans seemed to ignore the natural environment and had replaced it with *this* vision of despair pounded home the otherworldliness of her surroundings. She felt apprehensive and distrustful: Human constructions and human scent seemed to complement one another.

Why then did Marsch stand out in contrast to all of this? The humans they met either nodded or spoke to Marsch but gave her rude stares that piqued her already overtaxed territorial instincts. Every time they glared at her, she would lay her ears flat against her head and corkscrew her tail in a warning twist. On occasion she even hummed a shrill warning growl, apparently unheard, when they invaded her personal space.

Her warship's pathways meandered about, and uneven relief broke up solid lines with random forest landscapes. She could hug her ship's pathways and stalk or prowl along the simulated trails with supreme confidence.

She had no such confidence here. If an enemy boarded this ship, these straight corridors would offer neither her nor the crew any cover or camouflage. She doubted humans could hug flat walls or stalk their way along open decks. Why, an enemy had an uninterrupted line of fire along the entire length of the corridor! Was it possible that the frame hatches sealed off sections during enemy boarding actions?

Kidahin's people had designed *Hunter's Moon* with aesthetics in mind and hid his bulkheads in sculptured relief. They sealed pathways during Battle Status with force fields. When extreme circumstances demanded it, they quantum translated hull plating from ship's stores across a pathway, fusing it to the deck, walls, and ceiling better than any weld.

She glanced again at the yellow panels that marched alongside her, glowing faintly against the deck's harsh white illumination. The human homeworld, Earth—their word for dirt, not for Home—had green foliage, or so she had been told. She failed to see how a simple yellow strip substituted for their sun's rain forest leaf-filtered, greenish-yellow sunlight.

A triple tone pealed down the corridor. She froze, alert. The yellow panels began flashing in short pulses. The harsh ambient light dimmed a bit, and she heard a female voice speaking over the combat address system.

Kidahin glanced at Marsch, watched him tense a moment and then relax. They continued down the corridor for another two or three minutes before stepping into a niche that hid a wide spiral stairwell. Marsch led her down the stairs and onto a broad deck that was sealed at one end with wide reinforced hatches built into a heavy, shielded bulkhead.

She recognized blast doors, knew what they meant. On her warship, blast doors barred unauthorized entry into airlocks, Power Systems and Propulsion, Health Center, Command Center, Auxiliary Command Center, Armory, Ordnance Bays, Combat Deployment Bay, and other critical areas.

The blast doors slid aside, and they stepped out onto a huge hanger deck. Several single-seated and dual-seated fighter craft lined both sides of the flight deck, aimed into their broadside launch tubes. The flight command center tower loomed several ells above her. Looking forward, she saw the fighter recovery area and more broadside launch tubes. Looking farther ahead, she could see that the flight deck extended forward until it passed through the atmospheric containment force field that shuttered the oval opening in the bow. The Coalition warship reminded her of an eleven thousand ell long axe grasped by the middle of its handle and held at arm's length, blade pointing down. The warship's hyperdrive coils ringed all but the forward quarter of his length like a textured grip. The fighters entered the axe's eyelet and flew down the hollow interior of the handle a third of its length to land where she stood.

No fighters took off or landed at the moment, and she sighed in disappointment that no familiar combat action stood ready to soothe her nerves.

Marsch passed a row of fighter maintenance bays, opened a manual hatch under the Flight Operations Center tower, and held it open for Kidahin. She stepped through, and he dogged the hatch behind them before leading her into another lift.

They descended through a few decks before stopping. The lift doors whisked aside, opening into a hallway about twenty ells long that came to a dead end.

There, two hatches faced one another, each covered with its own mysterious script and symbols. One of the symbols matched the design on Marsch's shoulder insignia.

Kidahin's tail curled with excitement as she watched Marsch step up to a scanner built into the bulkhead next to the hatch and waited while the security system verified his identity. He felt like a tour guide. He hadn't taken Kidahin on the most direct way here, giving her an opportunity to see more of the ship. The opposite hatch led into Marine country. Like the Special Operation Group, the Marines had their own compartments carved out of the bowels of the Fleet carrier. The SOG division main hatch opened, and Marsch invited the Eyloni female into his command.

Special Operations had its own command center, planning center, combat information center, arsenal, training center, briefing room, ARTs quarters, and the command staff's day cabins. It even had its own makeshift galley, more a briefing room kitchenette than anything else, but at times it was much more convenient than hiking to the galley.

The SOG division Command, Combat Operations, and Mission Planning Centers filled a tiered structure built into the ship's bulkhead. The Special Operations Group division occupied several compartments that spanned a number of frames. They contained a jumble of rooms, bays, catwalk decks, lifts, and ladders. The SOG spaces had no pretty paneling or sub-decking. The place looked as if a kid had built it with an erector set.

They climbed up a railed metal stairway to the Command Center on the top tier. Marsch wondered what Kidahin thought about it all. She had wrinkled her nose and flattened her ears several times on the way here. He bet the ship looked quite different than hers did, and he wondered if he'd ever get a chance to see it for himself. As they stepped into the Command Center lobby, a short stocky man looked up and gave Marsch a businesslike nod.

"Good evening, Commander. Who's your friend?"

"Good evening, Les. Chief Warrant Officer Leslie Wayne Cummings, may I present Kidahin, a Hunter from the Compact warship *Hunter's Moon.*"

Kidahin perked her ears at the sound of her name, made eye contact with the male, and spoke a careful reply, "Presented I am to you Chief Warrant Officer Leslie Wayne Cummings."

Cumming's eyebrows rose in surprise. He hadn't expected the Eyloni female to understand him, let alone return his greeting. Nodding politely to her first, he then turned to Marsch.

"I heard about your little combat demo. Killed you quick, did she?" he chuckled.

"Yeah, well. She's good in unarmed combat drills." Marsch's voice turned businesslike, "Chief, anything happening that I need to know about? I heard the ship go to heightened Condition-3 on my way down here."

"Well, Sir, you know how them Fleet types are. They know something when we tell 'em about it. I received a security status bulletin from Combat Information Center that warned of sporadic neutrino activity within local space. Not strong enough for a Lizard FTL signature, or so CIC says. What's it like standing around trees and on grass and things?"

"Well, it's nice walking on a world that has forests like those on Earth for a change. You'll see odd shades of green, weird leathery leaves, pretty flying lizards, and creepy predators, but it's still nice. The chlorine trace in the atmosphere made my skin feel like I just stepped out of a swimming pool. The lighter gravity lets you go and go without getting tired but watch your mental fatigue. The new shapes, colors, and thin air will get to you. Oh, and use your omni to take a chlorine gas scan before you venture into small confined low-lying areas."

"I'll go down tomorrow for the daily briefing rotation, so don't spoil it for me, will you, Sir? I want to discover the change of scenery for myself, if you don't mind."

"Oh? I thought I'd let you get a two- or three-hour preview. You may go now. I'll stay here and mind the store."

"No thank you, Sir. I don't want to start enjoying it just to come back up here and then go back down again tomorrow. Besides, it's local night now, isn't it? I want to see it from the dawn."

"Okay, Les, if that's the way you want it. I have some Admin paper-pushing to finish that can't wait until morning. I think I'll relieve Alannah, send her down, and let her look the surface Combat Ops setup over. Besides, I have an ulterior motive. I want to give Kidahin some time to look around. Carry on, XO."

"Aye, aye, Commander."

Marsch led Kidahin into the SOG Command Center.

"SOG Commander on deck!" Lance Corporal J.A. Lyons barked.

"As you were," Marsch announced. "Report, Master Chief."

Master Chief Petty Officer Alannah Deering was a thick, no-nonsense woman. Kidahin thought the female resembled an overweight Warrior: bulky and muscular. She made a point of looking the human female over, weighing her physical presence against her hypothetical combat effectiveness. This was Marsch's Mistress of Battle. Kidahin laid her ears back; her possessive nature warred with the fact that she was the guest here.

"Aye, Commander," Deering replied, eyeing the Eyloni female with distaste. "Shipwide heightened Condition-3 is now in effect. Duty security maintaining heightened C-3 throughout the ship in response to anomalous neutrino readings within the ship's security perimeter. Division readiness is at Echo-2 per your standing order. All division stations are manned and ready. Sidearms have been issued, and the arsenal is secured. No casualties and no damage reported. That ends my report, Commander."

"Very well, Master Chief. Since the XO and I are both here, you may as well go down to Ibeetu and take a quick peak. While you have the chance," Marsch added, pointing to the flashing yellow status strip running the port side length of the Command Center.

"You don't have to tell me twice, Sir. I need to get some things from my quarters, and I can be out of here in a squirt. It's 20h42 now. Okay if I don't report back until the end of beta shift?"

"Fine by me. Gunny Watkins has the gamma shift watch. In the meantime, I can get some administrative paperwork done and Kidahin can prowl around and satisfy her curiosity."

Kidahin drifted back to him, staring daggers at the human female. Eyloni craved a sensory diet, a compulsive set of activities that ensured their sensory needs were met. They found momentary casual contact comforting because it let them exercise their inherent empathic needs. The Mistress of Battle kept frustrating Kidahin's attempts at touching Marsch.

"She doesn't care much for me, does she, Commander?" Deering asked, staring at the sulking Hunter's whipping tail.

"I don't think that's it, Alannah. It's just the structure of her culture. They had only one male aboard their ship, and they were quite attached to him. Her crew lost him, and I think that because of her age she's a mite protective of any male. I doubt she intends any insult."

"Oh, okay, makes sense I guess. I'm ready to be relieved, Commander."

"Master Chief, I relieve you."

"Aye, Commander. I stand relieved."

Marsch watched Deering bolt from the CC with alacrity. He smiled after her fleeing form and hoped she wouldn't fall down the open stairs in her haste to feel grass beneath her feet.

He caught Kidahin looking at him askance.

"It's okay, Kidahin. She'd gone."

The Hunter brightened at his tone, thankful that the human female had left. She knew the female was under Marsch's command, understood it from a rational point of view, but she felt uneasy about her and had from the moment they met. The Master Chief smelled *wrong*! Kidahin's wariness grew. Memories of Kalinn came unbidden, and she remembered how his scent had troubled her, too. Was it the human female she doubted, or was it the unease she felt from being aboard the Coalition warship? She did not understand her strange feelings and contented herself with the certain knowledge that Marsch was nearby.

He commanded here. She sensed the subtle empathic threads that emanated from him now, smelled his feelings, and experienced his emotions. So unlike Kalinn that, for the first time in weeks, things felt normal.

For the next hour, Kidahin prowled about the CC, COC, and the MPC. Marsch's elite combat forces stood their duty stations, alert and ready. Their courtesy, the respect they gave her, rivaled the glares she had received on her way here. They asked her questions, and she answered them as best her growing but still limited command of the human tongue allowed. She explored the tiered command complex, prowling back at random to check on Marsch. She paused at times to watch him sit at his station in the Command Center.

It all seemed routine to her until Marsch started playing with glasses of water.

As the end of beta shift drew near, Marsch started slapping at imaginary itches, impatient to return to the surface. Deering had at most another twenty minutes before the end of shift, and he was bored.

He strolled over to the Command Center's kitchenette, filled a pitcher with cold water and grabbed a glass.

I should pour this over my head.

The glass felt comfortable in his grip. Heavy, it reminded him of leaded glass. Grown from a single crystal, it was nearly unbreakable. Even if he smacked it with a sledgehammer, it would break into no more than two or three pieces, shed no slivers, and produce no sharp edges.

Marsch flicked a finger against the rim of the glass and dwelled on the loud ping it made.

He sat there and stared at the glass for a short time, thought about the sound, and headed back into the kitchenette.

Moments later, he returned to the command console with seven more glasses.

He poured water in all eight glasses, some more than others. Then he struck each of them. Unsatisfied with some of the tones, he filled or emptied the glasses until he heard the sounds he wanted.

Convinced he had them tuned, he played notes by snapping his fingernail against the rim of each glass, pinging his way up the scale.

Marsch checked the status boards again. Satisfied, he dabbed his fingers in water and circled the rim of each glass. As he rubbed wet fingers against the glasses, they vibrated, producing haunting, ringing musical notes.

Marsch adjusted the water levels a few more times before judging the tones adequate and then played "Row, Row, Row Your Boat."

Kidahin, examining the displays, consoles, and the logistical and tactical wall plots in the Combat Operations Center, heard the first random pingings. She dismissed them at first, thinking them nothing more than the chirps and beeps of instrumentation. Humans seemed to rely on noisy equipment to alert them when something was, or was not, happening.

Minutes later she froze as a musical scale rang though the center, clearly not console audio alerts. Her sensitive ears zeroed in on its source: three ells above and twenty-two ells behind her, in the Command Center where Marsch sat.

Kidahin ran between consoles and tactical plots, passed startled people on the lower COC combat analysis deck, and raced up the ten-step companionway leading into the Command Center lobby. She stopped. The music began again. This time it continued into a simple melody.

The Eyloni female stepped up into the Command Center and froze, shocked. She stood there and watched as Marsch made music from a row of water glasses.

Kidahin had been told that humans lacked pheromonal empathy and had no singing culture. How could an emotional species survive without the empathy boost that music gave? She had sung uncounted times in her short life. She sang with her clan, with her Hunter society, with her tribal members, with her intimate friends, and of late with her warship's society. A male's music, combined with female accompaniment, produced a metamind that filled everyone singing with an emotional awareness of all those who sang. She had been told several times that humans lacked this ability.

And yet Marsch played music! Human adults had musical ability, or at least some of them did.

She followed the simple melody as he played on the makeshift instrument. She could sing the same notes that he played with ease. Her triple voice box—amounting to a set of three panpipes—could easily weave a melody around his notes, freeing him to sing while her voice replaced his instrument. Certainly he could sing if he could wring notes from thirteen water glasses.

Kidahin remained frozen at the sight of a male playing music. Nobody noticed her presence on the main command deck; they focused on their duties and listened to his music, just as Eyloni females would.

"Commander?" Gunnery Sergeant William Watkins interrupted.

Kidahin fought the urge to join him in song and hoped he would not stop.

"Yes, Gunny?" Marsch replied, cursing the minor distraction.

"Well, Sir, I wonder if you should be playing 'Row Your Boat'."

"Yes, Gunny?" Marsch prompted.

"Well, Sir, didn't the ambassador's posted orders say something about not playing music, or singing, anywhere near the Eyloni?"

Marsch swore. He'd forgotten. Parakh's story about Captain Lahiri's son flashed alerts in his head. That explained the captain's five-minute lag before he could teleport aboard. The bridge had alerted the crew that an Eyloni would soon be arriving aboard.

His playing violated diplomatic protocol.

"You are absolutely right, Gunny. I've had Kidahin with me all day, and I've come to think of her as a team member. Her voice sounds so musical that I've gotten used to it. Not to besmirch our illustrious ambassador, but I'm not so sure he has the bead on the Eyloni that he thinks he has."

"What makes you say that, Sir?" Watkins asked with a wicked smile, enjoying the implied insubordinate conjecture. He had, along with the entire Special Operations Group, and almost everyone else on-board ship for that matter, understood that the Coalition Ambassador had a functionary's gift for ignoring certain inconvenient truths and was deluding himself with his own sense of self-importance.

The Compact co-ambassadors tended toward genuine friendship and had shown insatiable curiosity. They enjoyed the diplomatic run of the ship and sometimes seemed to wander around in aimless confusion, searching for elusive answers—answers not apparently forthcoming from Harrison. And yet, from the time Watkins had first met them, he couldn't shake the certain feeling that something disturbed them—something lost in communication.

Wasn't a lack of communication a failure in diplomacy? Watkins wondered.

Maybe the Senior Chief knew more now that an Eyloni female accompanied him.

"Commander? What do you think she has to say about all of this?" Watkins asked, nodding back toward the lobby's main hatch.

"Hmmm?" Marsch murmured, his eyes following Watkins's nod.

Kidahin stood there, frozen, trying to parse their words. Marsch stood his watch. She would have to wait until they returned to the surface before she could ask him about his music. Once she learned his tongue better, she would pin him down on his use of music.

"Not much, Gunny. She's apprentice crew and not connected in any way with the diplomatic mission. Although I'll bet a month's pay she's the more honest face in the mix. Same goes for the women aboard the Compact warship. From the time I've spent with the co-ambassadors, I'd say they're good people, too. And yet, I keep thinking that those two and Harrison are talking past each other's purposes. Harrison is a bureaucrat looking for his place in the history books, and the co-ambassadors aren't even diplomats. Anlann is the warleader of his own ship and Seralin is his Protectress, his personal bodyguard. They're Compact military. The way I read it, they should be negotiating with Captain Winters, captain to captain as it were."

Kidahin ambled over to Marsch, faking casual innocence and feigning indifference. His intense voice sounded serious, and she did not want to interrupt. Her ears perked on hearing the co-ambassadors named and reasoned that they discussed the diplomatic mission. She knew Anlann and Seralin already endorsed Marsch by their words at the Coalition warleader's tribunal. Their scent still drifted from him, but now she took precedence. Her training came from his interest in her society's well-being and his oath, giving her the higher priority claim on his time.

Kidahin spent a final few minutes speculating about Marsch's music and how to raise the matter with him.

The bosun's pipes announced an incoming call from the bridge, followed by the communications officer's voice.

"Bridge to SOGCC."

"SOGCC, aye. Gunnery Sergeant Watkins."

"Gunny, is the Senior Chief with you?" she asked.

"Yes, Ma'am. Stand by."

"Marsch here, go ahead bridge."

"Master Chief Petty Officer Deering has just arrived aboard and is on her way down to you, Sir."

"Understood. Thank you, Ensign."

"You're welcome, Sir. Bridge out," the relief communications officer replied.

"SOGCC, out," Marsch said.

Several minutes passed before Deering arrived in the Command Center.

"Reliving you, Sir," she told Marsch.

"I stand relieved, Master Chief," Marsch said, completing the ritual of relinquishing command.

"Have fun down there, Master Chief?" Watkins asked, envious.

"Loads. You have got to take an R&R slot and get down there, Gunny, before the Compact ship fires up her FTL. Oh, Commander? SOB Security Ops reports sighting Eyloni scouts skirting the base perimeter."

Marsch frowned a moment before coming to the obvious conclusion.

"They're looking for me. I make a quick pass through their FOB before going off-duty. Today's unscheduled events trashed my normal routine, and I guess they're wondering if there's a problem. I bet they're powerful curious about Kidahin, too. I may have some explaining to do come morning. Speaking of which," he added, "I'm out of here!"

Marsch smiled, turned, and exited the Command Center, taking Kidahin on a more direct route back to the teleport station.

Kidahin did not mind the shortcut. She had enough of the Coalition warship's monotonous parallel corridors, stairs, lifts, and harsh white lights. Besides, she had more important things to consider now. She wanted to tell her society that their sire cairn had music, and she wanted to tell them as soon as possible.

Eyloni females valued honor and privacy. Public matters belonged to public concerns, but private matters remained between those involved. Many a Compact warship had his secrets, shared only among his female society. Many such secrets revolved around tribal or clan interests, but the most personal ones dealt with their warleader. Kidahin viewed Marsch's musical ability of significant interest to her society. A male's music fulfilled ritual and social needs and represented a cohesive element in her culture, more so given that Marsch had assumed responsibility for them.

They entered Teleport Station-4 and took their places, where Kidahin carefully mimicked Marsch's foot placement on her pad. Marsch gave the teleport chief the order, and seconds later she found herself back on the moon's surface.

Kidahin gazed into the night sky and marveled at how fast this moon's sun rose and set. During the daylight, the sun had crossed the sky so fast that she could see it moving: a distraction. Even now, the gas giant glowed in fluorescent browns, oranges, and maroons—reminding her of a speeding Tyreniioroneo, *the Hunter's Companion*, the planet Elleio orbited—as it raced across the sky. Occasional auroras shimmered, cloaking the bright stars.

Shaking her head in wonder, she padded off to her assigned quarters.

Surprised by her willingness to abandon him over any distance, Marsch wished her departing back a good night and took a slow stroll around the SOB to his quarters. He took his time and enjoyed the clear night sky and its strange constellations, the giant glowing aggie beaming down on him, and the rolling green and yellow auroras.

He turned to his quarters, opened the door, stepped into the room, reached behind to pull the door closed, and felt it smack against something solid and immobile.

He turned around and saw Kidahin standing there carrying the metal, single bed frame and mattress with the quartermaster issue and her waist pack laying on it. The heavy load was stopping the door from swinging closed.

Marsch gaped at the ninety kilogram load she held at waist level against the door and for the first time fully appreciated just how strong the young Hunter was. Taken aback, he wondered if she had been pulling her punches earlier.

He glanced over her shoulder and down the dim path. A few curious people watched them standing in the doorway, but one of them stood out.

Co-Ambassador Seralin, Anlann's Protectress, gave Marsch a warm, open smile.

"Do not be concerned, Del. Kidahin has been assigned to you. She will remain by your side always. This is normal behavior," the co-Ambassador confided.

"Is it? I don't understand, but I'll deal with it somehow. Thank you, Seralin."

The Protectress twitched her ears, nodded, and melted into the night.

Marsch sighed. This day had been nothing but one surprise after another.

"All right, Kidahin, you can come on in."

The Eyloni Hunter charged into the room, thanking the spirits for Seralin's opportune words. Her jealousy flared, however, at the co-ambassador's ability to speak with him so well.

Kidahin stepped into the center of Marsch's quarters, brushing her tail against his arm in passing. He touched her shoulder, prompting her to turn and twitch an ear at him.

"Kidahin, go ahead and drop that bunk anywhere you want along the wall."

The Hunter flicked her other ear at the open space indicated and snapped her tail in acknowledgment. Her eyes darted around the room, taking in the simple and functional beige and blue working quarters. Marsch's bed rested against the far wall. A smooth soft blue blanket stenciled with darker blue script, numerals, and the Coalition seal covered it. A large blue pillow rested on the blanket and against a headboard. Two small tables flanked each side of the headboard. A holographic display filled with glowing symbols rested on one table, the other held a personal energy weapon. Kidahin hissed at the coward's weapon, ears laid back. She wondered why a sire cairn had need for such a thing until she remembered the humans she saw training with the same weapons earlier. Of course he had one. How could he not be competent in the same weapon that his elite combat forces drilled with? Her eyes followed the yellow light shining on the weapon back up to its source—a yellow panel—and thanked the spirits it did not emit the harsh white light that had filed the Coalition ship.

Kidahin prowled the room, getting a feel for her territory. She stopped next to a long desk that ran along the right-hand wall. A recessed opening allowed the room's only chair to roll beneath it. Closed drawers ran up both sides of the chair recess. A soft protective cloth concealed three lumpy objects on the desk. A shelf ran along the wall above it, filled with obscure objects.

She looked at each strange item until she found a small holoimage and paused. Within it floated the images of three infant human females.

Kidahin smiled. Infants touched the Eyloni heart. Everyone in the clan had a hand in raising them. Infants formed the social center of clan life. Females always mated when they came into season. The drive to bear the rare male, or more females to protect him, came from both a powerful biological imperative and a fact of social life.

She examined the holoimage, curious. The infants appeared preadolescent, and they bore an uncanny resemblance to that most dangerous of Eyloni females: the Comara. The infants' skin reflected a uniform paleness; their hair, platinum blond, gleamed long and straight, flowing down their backs. Like Comara, they lacked tails. Only their ears, human-expressionless, distinguished them from the deadly females. She tasted a momentary tangy metallic fear and thanked the spirits that she had not blundered into a room with three Comara. Had she done so, the mute, permanently preadolescent females would have killed her on sight rather than risk harm to their males.

Kidahin pulled her eyes from the holoimage with difficulty. She weighed the defensibility of Marsch's square, single-exit quarters and glared at the door before lifting the bunk again and setting it up against the wall. She fussed with its placement; her instinct prompting her to shove it around several times. Finally satisfied, she turned to find Marsch busy at the desk, his back to her.

Reassured, she made her bed, sat on the blanket, and unpacked the quartermaster items first, placing them just out of her reach. Next, she pulled the waist pack onto her lap. She removed and inspected each item. She had packed light, grabbing basic hygiene items: hair pick, skin oil, oral care, and a few other items. She laid out two spare waistwear, two spare neckwear, a pair of archsoles, a sheathed flat-black broadblade, an unbreakable ceramic battle knife, a spool of fine wire, and her spirit pouch. She placed the items in a branching semicircular pattern that spread across the blue blanket, each item touching two others.

When she finished the meticulous placement, she opened the spirit pouch and pulled out a rolled-up square of supple bleached white hide. With deep reverence, she removed the remaining objects and placed each one on the leather square in a predetermined order and dwelled on the spirits of her people.

Marsch shook his head at the idea of Kidahin staying in his quarters. That her presence passed for normal in Eyloni eyes did not make it necessarily so in human ones. He knew where Winters' view ran regarding cohabitation. Regulations prohibited familiar relationships among people who shared the same duty station or who occupied different levels within the same chain-of-command. The regulations did not seek to prohibit personal relationships aboard a combat vessel, but rather to prevent disruptive cohesion issues in shared duty stations and abuses in shared chains-of-command.

Captain Winters, no doubt, would view Kidahin's assignment to him as a shared duty station.

Besides, the Condition-3 security alert prohibited recreational cohabitation among the crew for the duration, unless they maintained current civil—read: marriage—contracts.

Marriage. Marsch remembered. His wedding ceremony had been held on a raft in the middle of a river. His wife's idea, she had loved the water. The raft had been covered with so much white lace and baby's breath it resembled a large ice floe. The bridesmaids and ushers rowed oars; his best man played orator, beating a drum to time their rowing. As he exchanged vows with his wife, the haunting strains of *Row, Row, Row Your Boat* echoed across the water.

The memory came back to him in vivid detail. Bits and pieces had been flashing through his head since he started playing that song aboard ship.

Marsch touched the holoimage of his daughters. After a few minutes, he jabbed a control, pulled off his outer shirt, removed a vest and bandolier, and set them next to the control pad. He opened a small drawer and took out three small sheathed daggers and set them next to the holoimage. *Would he use them tonight?*

He reached into an inside pocket and withdrew a pair of drumsticks bound together by his wife's high school graduation tassel.

He pulled the dust cover from the desktop, looked at the three daggers, and meditated on how sharp it was, the knife that severed short lives.

Kidahin, distracted, dwelled on the trinkets that hallowed her spirit pouch. The little bits served as reminders, pieces of Elleio meant to stand in the stead of her people, the Uahua'asee'a Clan of the La'huaset Tribe. The items came from her immediate and extended families, her clan, and her intimate friends. She fingered braided ringlets of pons hair, small dried flowers, the first arrowhead she had knapped, a polished blue stone from a creek that ran through Uahua'asee'a clan territory, a tooth and a claw from her first kill, other small mementoes, and her *oyya*, her spirit web. The oyya resembled a female's rank earring web, but it was much bigger, about the size of her splayed hand. Its intricate weave of webs, knots, and beads reflected in miniature the Oyya of the spirits. By tracing a strand of web throughout the weave, answers to questions appeared.

She remembered her adulthood ceremony. The pheromones given off by the participating females had produced emotional images that created an empathy web that caught her up into the Oyya of the spirits. The empathic vision tested females and gave the Tribal Elders a pherornonal link into her mind. They used the empathic feedback from her to decide if she was worthy of being declared an adult. She had been warned not to chase after the spirits because it was possible to lose contact with the physical body and drift in the mind forever.

And yet the visions she experienced made her headstrong, and she sought them out anyway. The spirits had told her that she held the high ground for a singing male who fought on the low ground. They said that he held all Eyloni in his hand, and if he fell in battle, then all Eyloni would vanish from history as if they had never been. She argued with the spirits, demanding that she be permitted to defend the male, that it was obscene for a female to let a male fight alone. The spirits declared her an adult Hunter and left her. But before the empathic vision collapsed, she saw a sign in the sky above her immediate family's elleiu tree. Shapes resolved into images of her people, humans, and the Ni'zakhonii. The questions her adulthood ceremony raised inspired her first adult decision: to submit herself for selection by a warship's society.

And with the spirits' own luck the society of an elite warship had chosen her! That fortuitous event had brought its own share of questions for her oyya.

And now she walked with a human sire cairn, which brought even more questions to mind.

Kidahin held her oyya as she sought answers, answers to the questions she had been asking herself all day. How had she been assigned to a human sire cairn? Why had she been assigned to him? Why had Melkorka and her society felt so at ease with him that they allowed her to leave? Why was she so comfortable in his presence? What about the music she had heard him play on the water glasses? Why did the haunting notes he played sound so much like the song the singing male had sung during her adulthood ceremony? Was it his singing that made him a sire cairn among his people? How could her people not know about singing adult human males?

She meditated on the answers her oyya gave, and as she did so, she felt a faint empathic sigh of distress nudge her consciousness. She ticked her ears back at Marsch in reflex. Her concentration broken, Kidahin smelled his scent, felt empathic waves flood her mind with impressions that drew stark, painful pictures.

She leapt from the bunk and spun to face him, concerned. Moisture fell from his small brown eyes. Did he have something in them? Dust perhaps? No. She saw no dust. What had happened to him?

Eyloni did not weep, did not shed tears in response to intense feelings. They conveyed basic emotional expression through body language and vocal pitch. For them, however, the core emotional experience expressed itself in pheromonal activity. They cried by unconsciously varying their pheromonal chemistry. They smelled the scent changes in others, and by doing so they had shared access to another's feelings through empathic contact. Eyloni felt the joy and pain of others with an intensity that dwarfed human experience.

Kidahin glanced at the small daggers placed next to the holoimage and understood. Eyloni, males and females, received adulthood knives when the Tribal Elders declared them adults. Marsch must mean these daggers for the infants' adulthood ceremonies, did he not?

Kidahin scented the air and focused on what his pheromones were telling her.

What is wrong here? Adulthood ceremonies are happy occasions!

Images resonated in her mind, and she strove to understand what his scent said he felt. Concentrating on his scent and its possible meaning, her eyes widened upon realizing what he held.

Drumsticks! Engraved symbols marched along their length. Spirit writing? An ornate, tasseled cord hung from them. An Eyloni male engraved his drumsticks with spirit writing and carried them wrapped in a cord of twine woven with the colors of his clan and tribe. Marsch's had obscure symbols etched on them. A red and gray cord wrapped them together, the hanging tassel, twice as long as her pons, was half red and half gray. A gold ring bound the tassel. The small gold medallion hanging from it was embossed with two symbols, symbols resembling markings that covered the hatches on the Coalition warship. What did they mean?

An Eyloni male etched his drumsticks with spirit writing to give them power. Her people used pictographs, idealized drawings, to convey the written word. Strict social custom reserved spirit writing for spiritual matters: no exceptions. The looping doodles flowed in intricate designs along the curved rim of her oyya, a tree branch bent into a circle, dyed with berry juices, and polished to a light ochre. She had carved them into the wood herself. The words linked the oyya to her and to the Oyya of the spirits.

Kidahin did not remember seeing the symbols that patterned Marsch's drumsticks stenciled anywhere aboard the Coalition ship, which had to mean that Marsch communed with the spirits through music!

The way he held them shocked her even more. He readied himself to play, but where was the drum? Curious, she crept up behind him and sat on the floor, crossed her legs, and curled her tail into her lap.

He struck a beat, and she understood. Part of the desktop contained a percussion synthesizer.

She watched him strike the desk's surface and followed his beat. A warleader played a similar device at the Warleader's Watch on a warship's command center.

Marsch began to sing.

His voice sounds so beautiful, she judged, moved despite Marsch's limited vocal range.

Eyloni read feeling in musical expression. In ancient times, songs communicated feelings over distances better than scent. The more ancient pheromonal vocabulary hijacked the brain's musical centers to augment Eyloni empathy. Much later, overlapping notes led to syntax and vocabulary more complex than simple human language. Kidahin knew Marsch's music would convey much more emotional and aesthetic meaning to her senses than word alone. She smelled his scent and listened for the emotional meaning he gave to his music. She made empathic ties with his mind. She considered the images in her mind, and his words finally fell into place.

Kidahin quailed in panic. This was no song of joy, this was a song of misery! She clenched her tail and followed Marsch's singing harmony and drumming rhythm. Her brain sorted out the patterns in his music, the emotional cues in his scent, and matched them to her own life experiences. The music amplified the emotional content of his scent, and she began to learn his language at an exponential rate.

He sings a Death Song!

Kidahin knew a Death Song when she heard one, knew he sung it in memory of these three infants. Pain reverberated through the expressive song. She moaned along with him in sympathy, strangled her tail, and ground her teeth.

He hovered near a crisis point, and that realization hammered home the fact that Marsch was unattached to a female association.

The song cried out to her. Males never sang for their sole benefit. On her homeworld, the fact that there were far too many females and far too few males prohibited it. A singing male attracted listeners over long distances, and those who came would wait patiently for a chance to join him in song. A male's music implied a chance to sing in a public setting, and sometimes to find a male to associate with.

Kidahin had no permission to sing in accompaniment with Marsch. His back to her, immersed in his grief, he smelled to Kidahin as though he considered *himself* the enemy!

The Hunter followed the music and knew the song's refrain approached its end. The melody told her to expect another verse. As it began, she joined him in song, seeking to intervene somehow.

The music tore through her. Because Marsch lacked her superior hearing, she sang well above his presumed hearing range so as not to be heard. As she sang, she remembered the deaths aboard her warship. With Kalinn dead, no male lived to sing the Death Songs for them. Thinking about her society's dead, she added her pain to his and forgot her caution.

Marsch felt the pain and loss drain from him as the music unfolded, He imagined a flute, a clarinet, and an oboe playing together as he sang. The notes, so clear, so melancholy, and yet so true to what he felt that he followed where the haunting melody led. When he reached the end of the song, he experienced a release, a joyful one, more intense than he had ever felt before. How had he imagined instrumental music he'd never heard before in his life? How could he listen to music he'd never heard before?

Listened?

Marsch spun around to find Kidahin sitting on the floor, singing, her legs crossed, tail in a death grip. She rocked there, eyes closed, ears twitching in time to her voice.

Kidahin stopped singing and opened her eyes. Seeing Marsch staring at her, she looked down at the floor. Her ears drooped, and her pons twitched. She gripped her tail in a choke hold.

Marsch knelt beside her and put his arms around her. "Kidahin, your voice sounds so beautiful."

She hung her head in shame. She had sung into his music without permission. She had been caught up in the empathy of the Death Song. Would he send her back to her people for her bad manners? She gazed into his eyes and flicked her ears back against her head. She had to ask.

"Death Song?" she moaned.

"Yes."

Kidahin wrapped her tail around him and pulled him close to her. She glanced up at the holoimage and pointed her ears at it.

"Your clan's infants?" she asked.

His eyes followed her pointing ears, and he nodded.

"How dead?" she murmured.

"Lizards!" he roared, throwing the drumsticks across the room.

The empathic image from his scent matched her emotional memory of the Ni'zakhonii. Hatred tainted his scent, and she regretted recalling his notice to the holoimage. He was unattached, and she did not know if her pheromones alone could restrain his hyperengagement. She put her hands on his cheeks and turned him to face her. Direct or prolonged eye contact among Eyloni carried a significance beyond simple notice. Twitching ears signified polite interest, but direct non-evasive eye contact conveyed intimate meaning.

"You have music! You sing! You drum! Sing more now please Del, yes?" She begged.

Marsch looked at her in wonder. She wanted him to sing to her? He'd just violated standing diplomatic orders by singing within her hearing. Shouldn't she be outraged? Wasn't that what the cultural report had said?

"You enjoyed my music? I thought your people disapproved of impromptu singing."

"No. I love your music. Male singing is comforting. It is not natural for you not to sing," she told him with her increasing fluency.

He looked into her eager amber eyes and saw that it was true. Her ears pricked forward in a face he recognized as open and serious. She all but quivered with impatient excitement. *Well, here is another fact Harrison and the diplomats got wrong. Poor Anlann and Seralin must think humans are inhibited.*

"Please sing more," Kidahin said. She worked toward double purposes now. She had to pull Marsch away from his suicidal thoughts of death and remembrance, and she wanted to learn as many new songs from him as possible. Eyloni females loved to learn new songs and gained in social rank through the number of songs they learned and shared. She also wanted to share the new knowledge with her society at the earliest opportunity.

She shook with such an intensity that Marsch relented. Orders or no, she'd already heard him. He retrieved the drumsticks, returned to the electric drum set, and held them ready. She sat on the floor at his feet, tail wrapped across the tops of her thighs, its fuzzy tuft twitching. He played a new beat, and she closed her eyes, set her ears, and followed the rhythm.

He began the first of many songs they would sing that night. Kidahin wove her singing voice below, with, and above his hearing range and increased her volume to match the music and his voice.

7

CONCERT FOR AUDIENCES UNKNOWN

Seralin heard it first: a subtle melody that wove around a muted beat.

"I hear it too," Anlann said in response to her listening pose.

"Music?" she asked.

"Yes."

He heard a muffled drumbeat, accompanied by the unmistakable sibilant melody of an Eyloni female. The muted bass beat sounded close and alien, its striking rhythm pulled the female's high notes along with it.

"It sounds unique. I think someone is composing a new song," Seralin said, after listening to a few measures. "How could anyone in Melkorka's society sing at a time like this?"

"I do not think they have any part in this song. I think this singing is much closer, somewhere within this base."

"How can that be? They would not come here and not make themselves known to us first."

He grinned at her like a fool.

Males are simple, she thought the affectionate empathic tail yank at him before it dawned on her why he grinned.

"Kidahin?"

"Unless I am mistaken, yes. Kidahin sings—and so does Del," he said.

"Del? How is that possible? Adult humans have amusia, congenital neural tone-deafness."

"It seems not. Come, let us go and investigate this oddity," he ordered.

Seralin darted out the door and tracked the song by ear. Anlann paused to grab a small scanner, tuned it to the irregular, murmuring song, and pelted off after her.

It did not take them long to find its source.

Seralin grunted. Marsch's quarters, and she had been here not so long ago.

Anlann fiddled with a flat, thin, black disk the size of his palm and read its fine print pictographic summaries as he listened to the muffled, whispering music.

"Sonic screen," Anlann announced, "It nulls out most of the aural frequencies. My scans show a filter wedge negating the low audio band down close to the upper infrasonic. Even the subsonic harmonics fall to zero a few ells from here. I am surprised we heard the audio artifacts from Del's drumming. Kidahin's voice carries well above the screen's operating range. No doubt her society hears her." He gave Seralin a long, meaningful look.

Seralin smiled affectionate tenderness back at him. "I think they will invent 'accidental' encounters when they see Del in the forest tomorrow morning."

"Would that not be interfering with Kidahin's training?"

"Not at all, unless they interrupt in some way. They can always sign Battle Language and ask her about his singing. Kidahin will tell them about this discovery." *I want to report this discovery to the Compact Counsel myself!* "She will want to teach them the songs she learns tonight," Seralin said.

"I think Del's popularity will increase over the coming days," he laughed. "They will make up excuses to keep him in their sight."

They shared another secret, knowing smile and listened to the singing for a time before returning to their quarters, thoughtful.

Marsch listened. He discovered by accident that she sang with him just like partners danced. His tempo set the rhythm for the music, and she sang three separate melodies at the same time along with him. Curiosity got the better of him, and he improvised. He played an irregular beat, and she sang the notes he thought only musical instruments could play.

Kidahin rocked from side to side, tail twitching in time to her voice. Her eyes remained more than half closed in concentration. Marsch remembered the day his grandfather taught him how to whistle, how hard it had been to pucker his lips just right and blow to produce a note. Kidahin's singing voice sounded like she whistled multiple notes from deep in her throat. The intense concentration required to do so was evident on her face.

Marsch realized that Kidahin memorized the song as she sang it. He knew it by the expression on her face; her ears twitched to the beat like a tapping foot kept time.

He altered the tempo and wound the song down to the final refrain.

Kidahin opened her eyes and gazed at him in wonder. What new music would he share next? She could not believe her luck. Eyloni males often led females in song. They sang during tribal gatherings, for important clan events, before hunts and warfare, and to the spirits. They also sang to the females who joined with them in occupational societies and social associations. Warleaders and sire cairns formed emotional ties with the females who associated with them by singing with them. The male singing voice reassured, focused, calmed, but also incited. Many songs fulfilled ritual needs, and males performed them often before large gatherings. Males played new music stingily, preferring to wait for important social events or for emergencies. Males did not often sing more than one or two new songs at a time.

She watched him wrap the tasseled cord around his drumsticks and sighed, disappointed. She started to get up when his voice stopped her.

Kidahin watched him unroll a leather-like strip across the desk. Once flat, it became rigid. A row of white and black rectangles lined the bottom edge.

Kidahin stared at it, confused. Marsch placed his hands above the white and black narrow rectangles and rapped his fingers on them in rhythmic patterns.

Music flowed from the instrument.

Curious, she listened to the notes. They sounded somewhat like what a *kietl* produced. Few males mastered the kietl, a circular instrument an ell across with thin, tuned metal triangle bars set into its rim pointed at a hole in the instrument's center. A male made music on it by striking the metal triangles with drumsticks; their tips covered with soft boots to prevent the wood's rap from souring the note.

Marsch played. His melody flowed through Kidahin. The rectangular instrument impressed her. By using his fingers, he played complex chords and magnificent music. No male could accomplish as much on a kietl.

Eyloni prowling a night perimeter watch froze and listened to a subdued rhythmic melody. It sounded strange, but the voice belonged to Kidahin. The obvious male presence made himself known only through her joyful singing. Hunters on solitary prowls and Warrior pairs hearing the muted music knew at once that Marsch taught Kidahin his songs.

Within seconds, they called in, one after another, to report the unexpected and important discovery to base security. In their haste, they forgot that if one heard the music, then all heard it. The entire base complement cocked their ears toward the human base and listened. Distracted by the music, it took someone's wistful wish to share the comforting rhythms with those in orbit for priority calls to start flooding into the warship, where a harried Mistress of Communications struggled to make sense of the multiple urgent, excited calls about music. Before she could relay their reports to Melkorka, the news concerning a singing Marsch had already sped through the massive warship. The ship's society speculated. Males did not teach music on a whim or to pass time. Deep social and cultural ties always accompanied the teaching of new songs, and those cultural ties deepened when a male taught new songs to a single female.

Melkorka listened to the music as it filtered into her quarters and sighed. They needed to find a way around the audio shield that squelched the signal.

"Mistress?" Hlindredreda's intercom voice repeated, for the third time, from the command center, "I have pinpointed the music's source. It is within the human encampment, in a structure surrounded by a weak aural nullifier."

"Can you tap into the audio signal without disrupting the field?" Melkorka murmured.

"Yes, Mistress. The Mistress of Tactics says that if she targets the field with a low power resonance beam, then she can initiate a feedback loop that will propagate the audio signal back to us without disrupting the field or registering on the Coalition warship's sensors."

"Good. Proceed as described, but when the music ceases, you will disengage the probe," Melkorka said.

"Affirm, acting," the Mistress of Communications acknowledged. Of course she would disengage the probe when the music stopped. No female ever spied on another of her own society, and they never spied on a male but for his own good. They had to keep an eye on Marsch. Everyone knew that males needed minders.

What they did, what Melkorka allowed, breached social etiquette. Kidahin had the right to teach or share the music she learned. Custom prohibited them from singing the songs they heard without the huluhar's approval, unless Marsch sang them in public. The right to privacy favored the sire cairn and the huluhar, and Compact law did not bend in this matter.

The Mistress of Communications locked onto Marsch's quarters and bled off audio signals from the oscillating field like a phonograph needle pulled sound vibrations out of a record album's groove. She transferred the recovered music to the combat address system.

Marsch wound down the piano set, an enthusiastic Kidahin singing along with him until he came to the last word. Too bad he didn't have her endurance. Her strange and soothing melodies relaxed him. Just for fun, he decided it was time to scare up a few eye-opening martial beats before bedtime.

"Do you want me to keep playing, or are you tired?" Marsch asked her.

Kidahin squinted at him.

Tired?

It took an instant for her to fit the empathic image she smelled into his words and understood.

Hardly!

She never, nor any female for that matter, ever tired of music. She would rather sit and sing until she dropped from exhaustion than succumb to fatigue. She flicked her ears back, made a derisive noise, and shook her head.

Fighting the need for sleep, she refused to show Marsch either weakness or disinterest. If a male taught songs, no female in her right mind ever hinted at being too tired to sing with him.

She grinned a lopsided smile, realizing he tested her endurance. She looked at him—amber eyes twinkling—and shook her head again.

"Not tired! Sing more?"

Marsch sighed. She didn't want to stop. Did she think they sang a one-time-only session? He looked at her, and she began to wring her tail and rock from side to side.

"Okay, if you're not tired, we'll do two more before going to sleep."

He turned back to the electric drum set, unwrapped his drumsticks, and began to beat out a rhythm, an old satirical military campaign song. Soon after he began the striking stentorian rhythm, he noticed a change come over the Hunter. She grew tense. He continued, and her large black pupils vanished, leaving her eyes solid amber. Her breathing came in rasping sighs. Her singing tapered off into silence, and her ears shifted from their singing posture to one of riveted attention.

***

Aboard the Compact warship, pandemonium broke out a few measures into the sire cairn's Battle Song. No Eyloni slept, either aboard ship, or down on the surface, while the unexpected treat played around them. Melkorka relaxed, drifting in and out of tailchasing in time to the alien rhythm. When Marsch's beat shifted into combat-imminent tempo, she catapulted from her bedding wide awake, landed on her feet, and raced to the command center, yelling "Combat warning! Combat warning!" on the combat address system as she ran.

"Battle Status!" she yelled as she slipped into her command chair.

"Affirm, acting!" the Mistress of Tactics said as the crew scrambled to answer a male's combat-imminent warning.

***

Kidahin's fevered eyes followed Marsch's every move.

It was the beat, Marsch knew. He did this thing to her, whatever it was he was doing. She tracked his most subtle movements, watching him with the same intensity his ARTs teams did when he conducted mission briefings.

He swore. He should have known, should have understood. A warrior people, Eyloni must respond to musical cues whenever they marched into battle. After all, Earth's military history had several similar examples: the fife and drum, bagpipes, and cadence drills.

How could he calm her down?

Could he calm her down?

Did she see him as an Eyloni male, goading her to fight? He hoped not!

Marsch compared her demeanor to his posttraumatic stress disorder experiences. His symptoms moderated when near the Eyloni. Something about them caused it. Could he moderate her symptoms somehow? He liked her. He felt responsible for the young Hunter. Her fixated stare made him think of a hair-trigger waiting for the slightest touch.

Maybe if he mellowed out the tempo, then she'd snap out of it.

Marsch somehow knew she'd kill anyone stepping through the door. He blended the beat and his voice into a low and slow melody.

Kidahin relaxed. Minutes later, she started to sing again. She knew what had happened but didn't seem too concerned about it. Her quizzical expression stared back at him, and he wondered what to do next. Tempo and rhythm must affect all Eyloni in the same way. The Diplomatic Corps had tied music into Eyloni superstition. They sounded lyrical even when they spoke Coalition standard. What if their language included music, like standard had its formal, colloquial, and dialectal forms?

"Why do you stop?" Kidahin asked.

"Why? Because I didn't want you hurting yourself."

Or anyone else.

"Not hurt. Battle Songs are important. They set the proper mood," she gushed out the melodic words. "This is normal—true—correct. It is necessary for you to sing true," she said.

"Necessary? Aren't you afraid it might happen again?"

"No. You know how to excite battle and how to entice calm. Your Battle Songs are better for me to learn now than later," she said.

Kidahin knew that what just happened had been extraordinary, for all her casual words. Males sang Battle Songs before and during combat to improve female morale, focus, and combativeness, but it took time for a female to adjust to a new song or to a new male singer. All females responded to such arousing songs in the same way she had, but it had not been normal for her to respond to Marsch's Battle Song in so forceful a manner. She felt more confused than alarmed. She responded to his voice as though he had been her sire cairn for a long time.

A new thought occurred to her: could he affect the others in the same way he had just affected her?

***

Melkorka focused on the alert.

"Status?" she barked at the Mistress of Tactics.

"All surface personnel except for Kidahin have been recalled, Mistress. All stations report Battle Status." She touched several controls on her console. "Warship is at Battle Status. All defensive shields read nominal, all available weapon systems read nominal, sublight drive reads nominal. I have a green light on the FTL."

"Status of the Coalition warship?" she demanded, glaring at the vessel floated in the command center's panoramic holodisplay.

"No change. I detect no other warships in local space."

"Nothing at all?" Melkorka demanded, perplexed. Why did the sire cairn sing a Battle Song if no threat appeared to… She let the rhetorical thought taper off. She turned to the Mistress of Communications, who flexed her ears in shared amusement.

The spirits! Melkorka swore, smelling Hlindredreda's empathic giggle.

"This is what we deserve for spying on a male while he teaches Battle Songs." Melkorka vented a deep sigh and announced to the crew what had just happened.

"Neutrino anomaly detected, Mistress!" the Mistress of Tactics interrupted.

"Verify!" Melkorka said.

"Confirmed, Mistress," the Mistress of Pathwalking said from her station.

"Identify!"

"Decreasing signal-to-noise ratio. Signal degrading. Losing positive lock. Signal lost, Mistress," the Mistress of Tactics reported.

"Signal loss confirmed," the Mistress of Pathwalking interrupted, stepping on the Mistress of Tactics' tail. "Mistress, I have tracked the anomaly into the atmosphere."

"Spatial phenomenon or artificial origin?" Melkorka demanded.

"Unknown without longer sensor contact or multiple contacts over time. You are thinking about the Ni'zakhonii FTL wake that lured us here?"

"I do not know what to think!" Melkorka snapped. "Contact the Coalition warship and ask them if they have detected any ambiguous neutrino emissions since entering orbit."

"Affirm, acting," the Mistress of Communications said.

Melkorka eyed the panoramic display with suspicion. Perhaps it had been a good thing after all for them to listen in on Marsch's singing, if it turned out that a Ni'zakhonii warship lurked about.

***

By the time Marsch and Kidahin finished singing, the night had passed well into early morning.

"It's time for bed, Kidahin! I've got a morning stint at the base security center, and you're coming with me, I take it?"

The Hunter nodded. "Yes, is training all day and night. Ten days training for everything, everywhere!" she said.

Kidahin knew they should have gone to sleep soon after returning to the surface. Marsch tired, and he had duties soon enough. She tired, too, but she doubted she would get much rest. She had too many things to think about. She ruffled the mattress and shoved the pillows and blankets into a nest and then reached behind her shoulder blades to unfasten her neckwear. She sat on the bunk and scooted around to face Marsch.

Marsch felt her eyes on him and turned into her causal nudity, shook his head, and sighed. Her culture saw no embarrassment, she showed no embarrassment, so he shouldn't feel embarrassment for her, either. He turned back and continued inspecting his equipment.

Kidahin bit black lips between white teeth and considered Marsch's drumsticks. Humans must know the spirits. The drumsticks had spirit writing on them. She padded over to his bed, sat down, and watched him lay out his equipment. He had many knives. She saw standard battle blades, but the others looked more like dueling or throwing knives. He cleaned each one, she noted with approval. He opened a drawer under the foot of the bed and withdrew a long and narrow, brown, polished wood case. He opened it, and she moaned at the sight of the odd curved sword resting in its case.

Marsch thought about taking the old saber with him when he hiked into the field later that morning. It had belonged to an ancestor of his, one who fought in the American Civil War. He pulled the saber from its scabbard, inspected the edge, and then rammed it home.

The Hunter sat close, wearing only a short loincloth over a thong. Exotic and beautiful, she had sharp angular features, pointed ears, and a tail—as long as she was tall—that twitched and flexed like a cat's.

Kidahin stared back at him without seeing. She played the memory of his odd music over and over again in her mind. It called to her, made her want to live it, find meaning in it. So different, and yet so familiar. It lacked the range and depth of Eyloni singing, but it expressed a wide range of feelings within its limitations. Her mind drifted through the memory of his music.

Marsch grasped her by the shoulders and felt her flinch in surprise.

"It's late, Kidahin. We have to get some sleep before we scout the morning patrol, so lights out!"

She nodded and flexed her tail in lazy loops. Ears slightly pricked, she levered herself from his bed and glided back to her bunk.

Marsch watched her swaying tail. Its fuzzy tuft curled up, wrapped under her right armpit, and rubbed between her shoulder blades before she curled the tail around her waist.

Marsch stretched out on his bed, pulled the light blanket around him, and thought about her tail as he drifted off.

Kidahin dreamed. She knew that she dreamed because the images in her mind had no short-term memory empathic signature. She dreamt of her adulthood ceremony again. She heard the singing male's music echoing through her clan's home elleiu tree. The Oyya of the spirits surrounded her.

You hold the high ground…

You may not help him in this battle while you are in the Oyya's web…

It is not natural for males to fight without female support…

Kidahin jerked awake. She felt a disturbance, something wrong. She sensed fighting! This was no dream, either. She knew the difference between dreams and sensed reality.

As Marsch rolled and groaned, she raced to his side. Her night vision reduced the room to sharp, gray images. Marsch's clenched fists and twisted body told her that he fought with the nature of a male's mind.

Mind battles occurred often in Eyloni males until they formed female associations. Females did not suffer in the same way when they were deprived of male company. Research had advanced the theory that unattached male hyperarousal caused them to relive prior combat experiences during sleep and primed them for combat. Their minds hyperextended reflexes to increase combat effectiveness in future battles, while still deprived of an association's protection. But, Eyloni males never expressed physical signs of mind battles.

###

…Marsch found himself back on Valhalla, running toward his family, trying to beat the Lizards to the house, when he felt a gooey mist fall on his head, arms, and shoulders. The defoliant dissolved his arms as he watched the Lizards gut his oldest daughter from throat to crotch, claw out intestines, lungs, and the still-beating heart…

###

Kidahin watched the subconscious battle, helpless. Clearly, his suffering resulted from the prolonged deprivation of an association's pheromonal balance. He needed her. She jumped back to her bunk, lifted it to her breastbone, and carried it back to his bed. Rolling across it, she leaned against his body and caressed him with her pons, calming him with her spicy pheromones, marking him with her scent.

She watched him relax and fall into deep sleep. Satisfied, she curled her tail over her hip and placed it between them. She fell asleep, pointing her pons at the ceiling. It twitched: a warning to others not to violate her territorial space.

###

Melkorka sat at her command station in an ill mood. She did not like puzzles, did not like not knowing, and did not like the unknown. She no longer had a claim to the title of Mistress of the Ship under any reading of Compact custom and law. After the crew chose a new warleader, he would select a new Mistress of the Ship from the ship's society. The new warleader might even keep her in the position just to maintain continuity, but the choice remained his alone. He could even choose Kidahin if he felt her in some way more qualified than anyone else aboard.

Kidahin. The sire cairn taught her his Battle Songs.

Melkorka envied the huluhar. No, envy implied a covetous desire.

Marsch felt strong—through his music—to her.

The Battle Song had made her, and everyone else aboard, hyper alert. They prowled their warship with careful scrutiny.

Spirits, but she wished she could quantum translate him aboard, so they could all feel as reassured as Kidahin no doubt felt right now.

"Mistress?" Akenallin's voice whispered.

Melkorka sighed and hit the comm button, "Yes, Mistress of Conveyance?"

"Ready to translate personnel back to the repair facility on your order, Mistress."

"Approved."

"Affirm, acting." Akenallin said.

"Mistress of Communications, open combat address." Melkorka said.

"Affirm, acting. Combat address system open, Mistress."

"Resume Action Ready Status," Melkorka announced.

Nodding to herself, Melkorka leaned back into her command chair, ground her teeth, and meditated on Marsch's music. He sang with moving power and deep meaning. She stared into nothingness and fixated on the human male, his music, and their dead.

She swore to herself.

She hated the unknown.

And she did envy Kidahin!

Phelindra translated back down to the surface with the first two hundred, all Hunters. They scouted the repair base before moving out. With savage finger-wagging, she told them to break up into standard patrols, take care, beware, and extend their prowls out to the human base perimeter. She raged in silent fury. *Melkorka!* Why, for the spirits' sake, had the Warrior stood them down from Battle Status to Action Ready Status so soon?

She speculated. Marsch not only taught the huluhar his songs to teach her his language, but he also conveyed his tactical empathy to her and prepared her for battle if he needed her. Males taught females Battle Songs all the time without triggering their combat reflexes. The sire cairn must have had a good reason for singing the Battle Songs the way he did.

I want him with us! She spotted three hefty rocks each the size of her fist and kicked them, one at a time, her bare foot launching them up and over tens of ells through the forest. She ought to do something. But no, she would not. Melkorka's say mattered; her character and force of will spoke for her.

I will not usurp her. Phelindra sighed. Besides, social compacts and crew composition issues came into play. Few Hunters served aboard relative to

Warriors. That, along with all the tribe, clan, society, and rank posturing in the multiple hierarchies of ordinary female life, made managing the crew a thankless task. She would rather eat rocks. The burden a mistress of the ship suffered overwhelmed; it was an onerous trial swamped with stress: she commanded the warship, dealt with the crew, and worked tails-entwined with the warleader. Warriors made up most of the crew, and it made good force management sense to let Melkorka deal with them. Hunters worked best alone on solitary prowls and grew impatient with large groups, but their caution and stealth made them the more thoughtful at times when Warriors charged blithely into danger.

The Eldest Huntress thought a second look, a stealthier second look, mattered now, and so she veered off into the forest on agile feet. Soundlessly, effortlessly, she crept through the forest's dim predawn light. The dark, leather-like, marine green leaves blotted out most of the approaching dawn. She prowled along the human base perimeter, circling it once, and noted the increased patrol activity there.

Good. Melkorka's call to the Coalition warship had put them on alert.

Phelindra squatted in the ugly green brush and listened to the forest. Stray predawn sunlight made her eyes glow deep yellow in the dark, an obvious but small price to pay for night vision. She remembered people's skin and forest foliage patterns and could compare them to what she saw. Even in the dark, her night vision's sharp gray vision let her compare what she saw to what she remembered of an area's visual pattern.

Human patrols dispersed around the base. Prudence demanded Kidahin's society also keep watch on the area for the time being and into the foreseeable future. If an enemy assault came, Phelindra intended to grab her huluhar and the sire cairn, move them to safety, and to the spirits with custom!

She stood up in complete silence and backtracked before shifting parallel to the base perimeter. She stopped next to a stout tree, scented the air, listened, then climbed into the tree's high branches. She stretched out along a narrow branch and looked between large heavy leaves. She watched the Hunter Andralea make stealthy progress to her place along their expanded security prowl.

***

Marsch awoke to a dim and quiet room. Glancing at the time, he groaned: *only one hour and forty-seven minutes sleep?* He groaned again and peeked across the room to where Kidahin's bunk should have been and blinked.

Where did she go?

Marsch felt it suddenly. Someone waited at his back, close. Pulling a buried combat knife from the mattress, he rolled into the figure curled next to him and brushed the twitching tuft of tail pointing at the ceiling.

Damn her!

The touch roused Kidahin wide awake. She spun from her bunk, pulled her curved flint knife, and turned large glowing amber eyes on him.

"What are you doing in my bed?" he demanded.

Kidahin glared at him and scanned the room before concluding that he was safe. He had a long knife in his hand. Would he take it with him on the morning prowl, or would he take the curved sword? He must have brushed her on waking. If he prepared to leave, then she had better get ready, too.

She gave him a bewildered look. "You slept alone. I helped you sleep better," she said.

"Oh," he said. Her explanation made no sense. "What if you had rolled into me? What if someone saw us in bed together? How could I explain that? How could you explain that?"

"Explain what?" *Males were strange.* "Why would anyone care?"

"Kidahin, someone might think we had sex!"

"Sex? Oh, you mean reproduction. No worries. I told you. I am not in my season. I do not understand this preoccupation with mating. Females choose their mates when they come into season, and males mate only with females who are in season. Simple and plain."

"What if someone thought I forced you into bed, uh, to mate with me?" he asked.

She laughed in his face.

Marsch watched her shake in amusement, her tail wrapping around her waist, her laugh a trilling, fluting sound. When she regained her composure, she explained.

"A male cannot force a female to mate. Mating requires a mutual pheromone-empathy connection. No empathic tie, no pleasure feelings for anyone. If one does not want to entwine tails, then neither experiences the pleasure feelings. Besides, mating is not necessary for Eyloni to share the same pleasure feelings. Entwining tails produces the same empathic sharing with or without physical mating. We entwine tails with other females or males when we feel the need for shared companionship. Physical mating is for reproduction only."

Marsch struggled to find an analogy he could understand. If humans had Eyloni mating habits, then a man and a woman would enjoy sexual pleasure just by cuddling, but only if they agreed to do so through a mutual empathic link. If intercourse by itself offered no pleasure, and pleasure came through an embrace and shared feelings, then Eyloni society should have no history of sexual assault crime.

Kidahin grew curious. "Human females cannot have pleasure feelings unless they mate? Is it because you have no tail?"

"Never mind. We'll discuss it later. We must get ready for the morning security briefing. I need to shave, use the head, and take a shower before breakfast. Do you want to come along, or should I pick you up on the way back?"

"Shave?" That meant cutting something close. Did he mean whittling? Precision cutting?

"Yep, remove the hair from my face," he said.

Kidahin's eyes narrowed. She examined his face in the window's dim light. She reached out, touched his cheek, and caressed the rough, short hairs. They felt alien.

"Oh, I feel it. You cut it off with your knife?" She wanted to watch him do that.

"No, I use a gel that loosens the hair, so I can wipe it away."

"Oh. Can I watch?"

Kidahin wanted to know how to care for him if the need ever arose. Females always took care of the males they associated with. Eventually, males needed females to save them, protect them, or care for them.

"I suppose so. Come on, get your gear and get going." Marsch shook his head, relieved he had distracted her from a discussion on sex. If watching him shave made her forget about it, then he'd let her watch him apply the gel and wash the hair away. He grabbed clean clothes, his equipment, and shower kit, while she made up her bunk and put her personal items back into her waist pack.

They walked along the path to the showers. At the sinks, Kidahin watched him apply the cream and wipe the stubble away. She rubbed his unnaturally smooth skin and nodded her approval. He walked her over to a shower and reminded her how to set the temperature and pressure controls. He turned to point out the modesty curtain and heard the shower spray on. Turning around, he found her under the spray, scrubbing away.

"Kidahin! Aren't you the least bit shy?" True, she wore little even when fully clothed, and she scowled at him in perplexed annoyance.

He crossed to the next shower cubicle, pulled the curtain, and gave himself a quick wash and rinse.

Afterwards, they walked to the mess hall. There, Marsch picked ham and eggs, apple juice, milk, and coffee.

Kidahin looked the offerings on the buffet table over with distaste. She glared at the eggs and wrinkled her nose in disgust at the bacon and ham. She fled to another table and, once there, filled a large bowl with apples, white grapes, grapefruit, oranges, and mixed nuts. She filled a large glass with water and poured a hot cup of coffee.

Marsch watched her give the animal food products a wide berth and remembered: *Eyloni were vegetarians!*

Marsch threw the ham and eggs into a waste chute, sighed, and wondered how a warrior culture could arise from a race of strict vegetarians. He sipped his coffee and asked her about it.

"Fight to protect males!" she said. "Food plentiful on Elleio. Even in ancient times it was, except when rare fires, pests, or droughts occurred. In the past, females fought each other for land or scare resources before the Tribal Compact and technology made intertribal wars wasteful and unnecessary, but even back then the only real reason for becoming a warrior people was—and still is—to protect and defend males." She paused and added, "Males need females."

They finished breakfast and walked to base security. Marsch relieved the night watch duty NCO and received updated status reports.

"We've been tracking some significant movement in Compact forces all night, Sir," Petty Officer 1/c Darrough reported.

"Any info from them, Petty Officer?" Marsch asked.

"No, Sir. They've extended their patrols all the way to the perimeter's edge, turned parallel to a predetermined tangent point, and continued awhile before stopping. They move about at irregular intervals, but they're not trying to hide from us, Sir. They haven't bothered to mask their body heat signatures. They're real jumpy about something, Sir," he said, and nodded to the Eyloni Hunter waiting patiently next to Marsch.

"What do you think they want, Kidahin?" Marsch asked.

"Strange it is...," she drifted off as the heat signature scan sped through a replay of the night's perimeter movement up on the panoramic wall display. "Maybe they heard us singing."

"No way," Marsch said, giving the security personnel a mean-mug look that halted their wide smiles and wagging eyebrows. "I shielded my quarters with a sonic screen. Nobody heard us."

"I thought standing orders said no singing around the Eyloni, Sir," Darrough said.

"Not if they want you to, Petty Officer, not if they want you to," Marsch muttered.

"What is the shielding technology, Del?" Kidahin asked.

"An audio inverter. It samples a sound, inverts the signal, and replays it. The inverted sound and its original cancel out, but the delay between the two signals causes noise artifacts that you can't hear to leak through the shield. I switched it on before I started drumming."

"It cancels sound in the human hearing range only?"

"Of course. Why worry about frequencies and harmonics you can't... Oh, yeah, I know what you're getting at," he said.

Kidahin nodded. "They heard me, maybe heard you, too. It does not matter. They know I would not sing with Kalinn dead unless a male sang," she said with a smile of impish delight. Her society now knew that Marsch sang.

"Well, I suppose we ought to hike out there and find out what provoked them into increasing their sweep range. Bet they're angry because I sang with you. I better go out and try to explain."

"Not angry," she countered. "Excited. Pleased. They will ask you to sing with them."

Great. It goes from bad to worse, Marsch thought.

The morning began beautiful, bright, and with no rain, thankfully. Marsch and Kidahin made good time through the forest. Clear turquoise filled the sky with nary a cloud in sight. They pushed through scrub brush and small trees and passed beneath tall trees. Marsch walked through shade peppered with sunlight for a few minutes and then headed for the larger trees, wove through more shade and brush, and turned toward the waiting Eyloni positions.

Kidahin took off and ran out ahead of Marsch before turning into her own prowl through the forest. Quiet, she slipped through perpetual shade. When she reached the thorny brush, she swam through the forest undergrowth, weaving in graceful spiral patterns until she smelled what she expected to find: female pheromones wafting around her on the cool damp air. She knew they watched her from the strange dead-green trees. By now they should smell her scent, too.

They remained in place, and she prowled through their irregular watch positions. Their comforting scent sang verses filled with mounting concern for her and the sire cairn.

Marsch hunkered down and waited to see if he could catch an Eyloni sneaking up on him. He doubted it. They had already pre-scouted the area, and they maintained an alert presence. He'd need help to catch them off-guard.

The hair on his neck bristled. Someone stalked him. He felt it in the same way he had felt Kidahin stalking him, knew it in the same way he knew where she waited in the forest even now.

An Eyloni patrolling her sweep, no doubt, and not one that sat in place, either. He was certain it wasn't an animal. Animals in the field gave off a cunning vibe when they stalked. People reeked with intelligence. A rational tracker's pattern betrayed itself with hesitations, stops, and starts every time she reassessed her progress. A stalking animal lacked the faint rational hesitating presence. That gave him an idea. He changed bearings and closed on the target. As he crept in silence across the leaf litter, he felt imaginary cobwebs brushing his face. He stopped, listened to the breezes rustling through the trees, and felt strong feelings of ownership and curiosity fill his head from out of nowhere.

Kidahin had seemed certain that her people heard her singing and would want to talk to him about his music, but they wouldn't want to interfere with the oath he made. If they wanted an excuse to meet, then he'd oblige them. Why not turn their curiosity into a training exercise for Kidahin? He hoped she paid attention and would catch on by watching his movements. He swung out and away from the stalking female, moving through the forest to put her between himself and Kidahin. If she followed his progress, then she should reason out his intent, turn, and close with him on their mutual target.

Melkorka watched Marsch flank her. His scent all but masked by Kidahin's. The huluhar had more thoroughly marked him with her scent than the co-ambassadors had.

What had possessed her to do that?

Melkorka stayed put and watched Marsch swing around her. He sought to catch her unprepared like he had done with Kidahin. She had no doubts that he knew where she hid.

Phelindra and her Hunters held their positions and watched Marsch and Kidahin stalk the erstwhile Mistress of the Ship. Phelindra knew that a Hunter's stealth outmatched a Warrior's, but Warriors had their skills, too. Melkorka should be able to pass within a few ells of a human unobserved, but Marsch, a sire cairn, made all her expectations uncertain.

Melkorka crouched in a tall patch of grasses and grumbled. Kalinn never told her anything about human sire cairns. He would have approved of Marsch, she thought. She remembered his music and drifted off into the Eyloni female obsession with all things male.

Minutes later, she froze. The sire cairn and the huluhar came at her together. Melkorka smiled and set herself to meet them. Suddenly, she sensed something rushing up on her exposed rear. Instinct and cultural imperatives drove her to defend the male. She turned and crouched to take the assault. Teeth bared, and ears flattened against her head, she hissed a warning.

At Kidahin?

The huluhar froze in surprise at the Mistress of the Ship's challenge. Kidahin's surprise appearance gave Marsch the time he needed to reach Melkorka's back and tweak her tail tuft.

"Tag! You're it."

Melkorka spun as he pinched her pons and bit back her temper. At a time like this, they played with her! He had used the huluhar to distract her. She would not have fallen for the ploy had she not forgotten that Kidahin had scent-marked him, making them appear to advance as one. That she had been tailchasing ideas about him made her both furious and embarrassed at the same time. She gave them a critical appraisal, Kidahin stood at the ready, holding a defensive, warning posture.

They turned toward the sound of Phelindra dragging her bare feet through the grass, intentionally noisy. Melkorka's eyes narrowed at the mild insult, and she snapped her ears back at the Eldest Huntress's bemused expression.

Spirits, but if she laughs, I will tell her what I think of her, so help me I will! She already had much to consider and was not in the mood for trading Warrior and Hunter jibes.

"Good morning, Melkorka. No one changes patrol patterns this much unless provoked. What's happening?" Marsch asked.

He knows, Melkorka thought, pleased. His presence dispelled her rising anger.

"Yes. Warship scans detect neutrino spray. It came through the atmosphere, in the night. We increase prowling range," she sang, "You find same spray?"

"No, not in significant amounts and not in the atmosphere." He didn't like it. Red alerts flashed in his head and a tingling came over him like ants crawling on his skin. "Dammit, that sounds like a Lizard scout ship, maybe even a shuttle or some small proxy vehicle. Alert all personnel: enemy vehicle in local space. Atmospheric-capable craft probable. Prepare for surface combat. Scan for atmospheric combat probes. Reinforce the security perimeter. Recall all solitary recon parties and make irregular timed sweeps in force."

"By your command," the Mistress of the Ship replied and flicked her ear to activate her comm gear.

Kidahin watched them, surprise reflecting from her face.

"Warleader," she said, awed.

"What?" Marsch said over his shoulder.

"Warleader," she repeated.

"I don't think we need to bother Anlann. It's just a feeling I have, but my gut is telling me that something is up."

Kidahin dwelled on what she had just heard. The response 'by your command' acknowledged a Warleader's order. Melkorka's lapse highlighted the stress they all continued to suffer since Kalinn's death.

The group walked together under alien green trees.

"We sorrow on the deaths of the battle dead. We sing them good-bye to the spirits. The leader of Death Songs is always male. You sing with us to the spirits," Melkorka said.

"You want me to sing for your dead? Are you sure? Don't you need an Eyloni male for this?" he asked.

"No. Tradition demands any male of our choice. We will not wait on a strange male. We already know you. Will you do this for us?" Melkorka asked.

She insisted. More than insisted, she came as close to pleading as possible and yet maintain her dignity. He looked over her shoulder.

Eyloni females surrounded him, a hundred or more. They had planned this encounter. Without a doubt they didn't understand Melkorka's pidgin Coalition standard, but their expressions told him that they already knew what she had asked.

They wanted him to sing funeral songs—mourning songs—to the memory of their dead. How could he accomplish that in any meaningful way?

Maybe he should ask Anlann about it. He was a Warleader after all.

Or maybe he shouldn't. Anlann held the rank of Warleader and commanded a Compact ship. He and Seralin had spoken at length about warship autonomy. The crew of *Hunter's Moon* would not allow outside interference in their ship's business.

Marsch looked at the Eyloni gathering among the trees. He met their eyes, gave them a curt nod, and turned back to Melkorka.

"When?"

"Tomorrow?" she asked in hushed hope. "Just before dusk. Many songs are better," she added.

"Who else comes?" he asked, thinking about the Eyloni working in the Forward Operations Base.

"You, Kidahin, and all of us," she said.

"All of you?" That couldn't be possible. They wouldn't teleport the entire crew to the surface—over twenty-eight hundred Eyloni—would they?

"Are you sure? Wouldn't you rather wait for the male coming here to take command of your ship to sing for you?"

Melkorka bridled at the offensive question and bit back her explosive, violent retort. "Not 'take command'. *Chosen.* Chosen from *Fearless'* supercargo of males," She paused, "We may not know any of them. We know you. We want you."

Melkorka sounded nearly hysterical. He glanced at the faces watching from the trees. Haggard expressions and drooping ears betrayed the mask of grief they had suppressed since the battle. They needed an outlet, and from what he understood the ceremony sounded more like a wake than a funeral procession.

He sighed. That was good at least. Funerals had religious overtones, and he knew nothing about Eyloni religious thought. No amount of coaching from Kidahin could prepare him for a religious service taking place in little more than a standard day.

Kidahin and Phelindra jabbed fingers at one another, signing in a heated argument. Quite aggressive they argued, too. He smiled as Kidahin punctuated her remarks with another savage jerk, the older Hunter growing more incredulous with each jab. He had no idea what drove their frantic discussion, but he bet they argued about him. Judging from the glances the older female and the others gave him.

Even Melkorka's shocked expression fell on him.

They growled in that rhythmic whistling hiss of theirs. They didn't like something Kidahin had signed. Whatever it was, it didn't seem to involve him; they vented their hostility on her. Well, nobody likes the bearer of bad news. And it didn't seem to diminish their insistence on him giving them a musical eulogy for their dead crewmembers. In fact, he felt a powerful sense of inclusion that he couldn't explain.

"I shall sing for your dead," he promised. "I have duties to perform at dusk tomorrow that I must delegate to my staff. Captain Winters may refuse me his permission to participate in an official Compact function. You must understand that Ambassador Harrison and Captain Winters have diplomatic concerns, and they will object to any contact between Compact and Coalition personnel that they think might endanger their diplomatic mission."

"Warleader Anlann and Seralin his Protectress are the Compact co-ambassadors, yes?" Melkorka said. She walked through the situation as she understood it in her own mind. Anlann was a warleader, but he could not interfere, would not interfere in matters not concerning his ship or his society. Even if he agreed to help, her society would resent his direct involvement because he did not belong to them. But, as Compact co-ambassador, he had limited leeway in matters touching on human events. He could pressure the human warleader on Marsch's behalf and, as the spirits live, the problem would vanish. Mindful of the rules of both warship and male autonomy, she could only make a brief suggestion.

"See Warleader Anlann."

Surprised, Marsch thought her curt suggestion over. It might work. Anlann could apply diplomatic pressure on Harrison. After the tirade the ambassador had performed in the captain's office, it was clear he wouldn't appreciate being bullied into accepting another agreement between the warship's crew and him. Winters would understand. He encouraged and fostered good relationships whenever possible. Unfortunately, Harrison had the latent authority to exercise command orders if, in his opinion, the occasion warranted extraordinary intervention to preserve mission integrity.

Anlann might agree to give him the diplomatic cover he needed to participate in the memorial service, but he couldn't stop the swift and sure official sanction coming down from on-high. A vindictive Harrison would play up Marsch's part in the ceremony as endangering a critical mission.

To hell with Harrison. I like the Eyloni. Marsch's stubborn resolve reasserted itself. Eyloni culture made sense to him, what little of it he'd experienced so far. They needed him to save them from their grief. He understood that, too. Besides, it was the right thing to do. He nodded in agreement.

"I will speak to Anlann. I should give him a head's up, so he can prepare for any problems that might affect his mission." Marsch paused. "I shall sing to the spirits in any event. Should I come to your base?"

Relieved, Melkorka shook her head. "No, the place is along the sky-placement direction of the mountain and along the winter ice valley filled with melt water. Face the mountain overlooking the runoff. A large clearing opens into a low singing place behind it. Come there before dark, tomorrow."

"It sounds like a good place to sing good-bye. Now then, tell me more about the neutrino emission you've detected. My ship registered a momentary trace only."

Melkorka described the Compact warship's scans, and Marsch considered their significance. Neutrino traces didn't always signal a warning. They happened all the time. Stellar fusion and nuclear power systems accounted for the ubiquitous clouds of particles. Ship's sensors determined the origin of most neutrino emission sources with ease. One artificial source emitted neutrinos with a theta-13 mixing angle of zero, which gave away the antihydrogen-hydrogen fusion artifact of FTL propulsion. The Lizard drive shed them as its warp bubble brushed against the dimensional 'sides' of a multidimensional manifold while in subspace, much like a bobsled sprayed shaved ice with its runners as it raced down a hill. When the neutrinos entered normal space, they emitted Cherenkov radiation along with a slew of decay particles. Marsch considered the neutrinos and his instincts screamed Lizards. But even a Lizard ship of frigate class or greater left more than a negligible neutrino trace.

Still, they might have an FTL scout snooping about. A scout carried no more than three or four crew. They would code and transmit everything they scanned here to a capital ship somewhere outside the system's heliopause.

ANLANN'S ADVICE

Marsch thought about the neutrino problem all the way back to the Compact FOB. Kidahin and Phelindra waggled their fingers at each other the whole time, ignoring him. Other Eyloni brushed their tails against him often. They came from the forest depths, caressed him shyly, and melted back into the jungle. He stopped counting after the two hundredth coy touch.

He couldn't remember seeing any Hunters older than Phelindra. Had the Hunters surrounded them like a cloud of persistent mosquitoes for that reason? Kidahin was a Hunter, too. Maybe they just wanted to know what he'd been putting their youngest Hunter through.

A few hundred Warriors joined them. The Hunters wiggled fingers at them. The Warriors waggled their fingers back. They studied him, considered Kidahin's body language, their fingers twitching. They turned to each other, eyes seeking specific individuals. Eyloni female hierarchical standings reaffirmed, they flicked tails, pricked ears forward, jabbed more fingers at one another, and nodded in curt agreement: each had her own important task to complete.

Melkorka asked for a repair update. The Mistress of Fortifications would have to divert construction teams from repair duties and have them prepare the Place of Mourning. Warleader Anlann's help posed a problem for warship autonomy. She needed an indirect action, a feint. She settled on asking the Coalition warship's Mistress of Communications to relay a message to Anlann, telling her that Marsch needed to speak with him as soon as possible. Anlann would then seek out the sire cairn on his own. *Perfect*, she thought. *That is how you set a plan in motion without interfering with anyone's dignity and autonomy. Hunters may have an edge on stealth, but Warriors were tacticians at heart.*

Phelindra deployed her Hunters. They scattered, surefooted and certain, intent on their mission: shadow Marsch and Kidahin. She told them to stalk the pair without being discovered. She reminded them that they tracked a sire cairn and risked detection, and she described what she knew of his abilities to stress the point.

Females shadowed males by nature. Males, the spirits knew, flaunted risky behavior and put on airs suggesting that they did not need their help. Males were strange and, Phelindra smiled, respected, loved, cherished, and looked after like errant infants.

She told them that Marsch must not smell their clandestine surveillance for his own good. Oh, he might tell them to back off if he found them shadowing him, but they would merely nod in absolute agreement and then disregard his order. Females listened to males always, but they ignored them when they had their best interests at heart. When males did not know their own need, and they usually did not, females kept them safe. Only when females fought did a male's direct order command unquestioned attention.

Much later that day, Kidahin inhaled the crisp evening air and sighed. Marsch had spent the morning sending extended random security prowls deeper into the forest. He either worried about a potential ground force assault, or else he only wanted to run the Hunters tailing him ragged. She smiled. They waited out there, watching from distant trees. She never caught their scent, never saw them, but she knew that they hid out there all the same. Marsch seemed preoccupied with the neutrino update. Touched by his concern, she knew he drove himself to make sure that they came to no harm.

By this moon's incredibly swift high sun's arrival, they had hiked several thousand ells through the jungle. On their return to the Coalition base, they found a secluded meadow covered with green reeds tinted blue and surrounded by large bushy trees. A broad swath had been beaten down in its center. Marsch told her the flattened reeds reminded him of herds sheltering in tall grass. She agreed. She knew that herbivores did the same thing on her homeworld, but they also left signs of their passing, and she told him so. She saw no tracks or trails leading there, she smelled no evidence of them, either. Together, they paced one hundred ells in a tight crescent shape. Kidahin dropped to the ground and pushed the downed reeds aside to feel the soil. She fingered the hard clay. More compact than the surrounding soil, the reedy meadow grasses had wilted, dried, and died, yet the nearby standing ones flourished in all their contradictory greenery.

Marsch decided to conduct a training exercise in the unfamiliar area. He briefed his ARTs about an unexplained neutrino source detected from orbit. He divided them into pairs and sent them on a search-and-destroy mission into the dense jungle. Kidahin participated too, helping them locate the exercise's target, a neutrino packet communications transponder.

When they arrived back in the human base, Marsch led her into the mess hall. There, he tried to entice her with something called a 'cream stick'. She took a cautious nibble and declined, explaining to him that its refined sugars would upset her stomach. She settled on a bowl of raw vegetables from the salad bar, two large glasses of water, and a cup of hot black coffee. She found she had acquired a taste for the bitter stuff.

Now she waited, gazing into the evening sky and twitching her ears in quiet humor. No doubt their earlier delay in the meadow had the Hunters tailing them perplexed, and she imagined them trying to reason out why the sire cairn had invested so much time there.

Kidahin reviewed the afternoon's training mission while she waited. She glanced up into the evening sky and craned her neck about, taking in the flaring auroras. What kept him? How much time did a human need in the necessary, anyway? Humans seemed to make frequent use of the sanitary facilities, and she wondered if that had anything to do with them needing paper when they eliminated. She tailchased the idea for several minutes before he finally returned.

"I stopped by Administration, and the Duty Officer passed me a message queue from the ship. It says that Melkorka contacted the ship earlier and asked me to deliver a message to Anlann. The DO thought it odd that your ship wanted me to courier a message easier sent by commlink. The DO also said that Melkorka sounded both cryptic and insistent. Do you think she's changed her mind about the Death Song ceremony?"

Kidahin's large eyes narrowed. She flipped her ears to the sides of her head, gave her tail a snap, and shook her head. "No. She made sure that you must speak with Warleader Anlann now."

"Dammit Kidahin, she didn't have to contact the ship! Anlann and Seralin have VIP quarters down here. We just walk over and visit them."

"Melkorka helpful. She requests that you meet with him. She gave you the cover you need to meet with him. You do not speak to him on a normal basis, do you?" she asked.

"No, I don't. You're right. And I can't fault Melkorka for taking the initiative. I had hoped to grab a brief moment of Anlann's time later today."

"Take you more than a brief time," Kidahin said. "Death Song ceremony is significant. All of *Hunter's Moon*'s society shall come, and it will last a long time, longer than when we sang together last night! You must tell Captain Winters about the ceremony's significance. He must also know that only Eyloni females are permitted to attend. Except for you, no one else is allowed near the Place of Mourning, not even Anlann and Seralin. You must speak with Captain Winters before you begin the ritual. Melkorka made sure that you and Anlann must meet soon," she said.

Marsch found no fault in her logic. It made sense, too. He had an official reason for intruding on the co-ambassador's time. He hoped the communications officer hadn't forwarded a notice to Captain Winters. Regulations required her to log the request and note it in her report.

No doubt Harrison would claim Winters should have found it strange that a message between two Eyloni required a human courier, and why did that courier have to be Delwyn Marsch?

Marsch knocked on the co-ambassador's door.

It opened to a polite Anlann, his ever-alert Protectress close behind him, Marsch wondered how he'd feel always shadowed by an overprotective personal bodyguard twenty-four and seven.

"Greetings, Del! Ki Kidahin. Come in, come in and be welcome. We have wanted to speak at length with you again," Anlann said. "I know you have duties that keep you busy, and you have even more responsibilities now that you give Kidahin intense training."

Anlann thanked the spirits that it was Marsch and not Harrison standing in the doorway. Anlann had been considering poking his tail into the business of the Compact Counsel for some time now. He had dictated a communiqué, but had not sent it yet, suggesting the Counsel demand that Captain Winters be made the Coalition Ambassador in accordance with Warpact conventions. It confounded him that Harrison could impose his will over the human warleader. Anlann understood Warpacts. A male could have precedence, but a male's honor required that he relinquish Warpact command if he lacked the skills necessary to complete the mission. Harrison had never experienced combat!

Anlann beckoned Marsch to a chair. He sat down on a bed corner across from the sire cairn. Neither male paid attention to the drama unfolding around them that reflected the nuances of Eyloni female life. Kidahin and Seralin glared challenges at each other. Seralin flaunted her higher military rank, her tribal standing, her Hunter's social standing, and her duties as a warleader's Protectress. Kidahin paraded her status as an elite class warship's huluhar, as an elite status Hunter, as a member of an elite warship's society, and as an associate of a sire cairn. Pheromones flew about the room as ears twitched and tails flexed in the dance of status and rank.

Marsch remained blithely ignorant of their posturing. Anlann ignored them. He had no complex ranking system to contend with. He had only to respect Eyloni social manners, clan and tribal laws, fellow males, and Compact Counsel Decrees. Males followed a single rule: *first on-scene precedence*. First on-scene precedence gave the first male respondent arriving at a scene of conflict the supreme and absolute command over subsequent male arrivals. First male on-scene precedence applied to the first incidental male arrival as well, but he almost always surrendered it.

The first arrival's rank or ability did not matter. Custom assumed, rightly so, that the females associating with him would take umbrage if another male dared to undermine their male. Social custom required the late arrivals to surrender their autonomy to the first arrival by joining with him in Warpact. The Warpact leader enjoyed absolute command over the later arrivals and their assets, but his command did not extend into the internal affairs of the individual males' teams, units, forces, or warships.

Simply put, no strange male dared to order the females who associated with another male. They, and his own female association, would not tolerate the territorial intrusion. Of course, honor demanded that the first incidental or respondent arrival surrender his command to a subsequent arrival if he lacked the skill to continue as Warpact leader.

Anlann nodded at the two females, "Do not worry about them, Del. They have their own tails to twist," he grinned at their reproachful stares.

"See? What did I tell you? They will ignore us and tell each other unflattering stories and other juicy, gossipy tales about us. I do not know about you humans, but I think all females do is spend their time talking about males!" Anlann smiled and punctuated his comment with a snap of his tail.

Both females paused, gave the males dirty looks, and continued their signing. Marsch tried to follow Kidahin's hand movements, only to earn himself a glare from Seralin.

"I don't know about Eyloni females, Anlann, but I think it's clear they sure do blather about everything."

Kidahin narrowed her eyes and snapped her tail at him.

Anlann grew curious. "I have wanted to ask you so many things about human command chain issues. How do you organize males under your command? Are they joined to you in Warpact?" He fired off several questions at Marsch, giving him little time to answer before following up with more questions.

Marsch asked his own questions. How did a warleader, or a sire cairn, exercise command over his crew or combat teams? How far did that command extend? Just how much would they take from him before they refused to obey? They traded questions and answers until Marsch got around to the point of his visit.

"Anlann, I came here because I have a message from Melkorka to give you."

"A message from the Mistress of the Ship?" Anlann leaned back, perplexed.

"Yes. Here, read it for yourself," Marsch said and passed the encrypted omni to the Eyloni.

The Warleader accepted the device, but hesitated. He indulged himself in a moment of whimsy. Marsch's character smelled beyond reproach. His voice, his pheromones, his posture, and his ease radiated confidence and compassion. He commanded respect and high honor. The possessive, territorial stance and scent of a youthful, impatient Kidahin solidified his good opinion of the human battle leader. The warship's females attested to his character through her presence. Their scent on him proclaimed his suitability as a leader. Anlann believed that he could, without reservation, enter into Warpact with him if the need arose.

Leaving scent on another was personal. Eyloni females brushed their pons against family, friends, associates, and others with whom they felt affection. A warship's society marked their warleader often. The act was, Anlann knew, a misdirected defense mechanism, just as a smile was. In ancient times, the smile cleared the lips from the teeth for ritual threat displays and for biting. Scenting served a prehistoric need, too: mate preselection. To replenish and grow a general population that possessed few males, mating females had to share the rare male by necessity. Exclusive male-female pairings did not exist in Eyloni society and never had.

Compatible females made voluntary associations with a single male. Over millennia, custom gave males unfettered freedom of travel, which spread their genes and extended Eyloni genetic diversity. In those ancient times, females rubbed their pheromone-laden pons on the male they preferred. Over time, it became a gesture of warmth among associates. But when stressful or combative incidents threatened, instinct prompted females to mark able and trustworthy males. The younger the female, the stronger the pheromonal signature. Eyloni evolutionary biology being what it was, the more possessive, the more protective, the more proprietary the females associating with a male, the more they acted in his defense. Infants sensed male suitability and, counter-intuitively, drew adult females to their males. Which, Anlann laughed, was why the huluhar and Seralin postured their aggression to each other.

He chuckled, shook his head, and tried not to laugh, but he knew his scent would give them notice of his amusement.

He held the human's omni to his eye for a retinal scan.

"Verify and accept," he told the device.

One line of pictographs scrolled down the device's tiny screen: a modest, cryptic, and respectful suggestion.

"Meet with Sire Cairn Del."

Anlann blinked and reread the line.

That was it? Melkorka sent this?

Marsch turned to the two females. They gave him irritated looks for some reason. No doubt Kidahin had already told Seralin about the upcoming memorial service. They fixated on something. Kidahin fidgeted. Seralin measured him; judged him, weighed him. Her attitude had changed. He couldn't tell how, but the feeling persisted.

Anlann's perplexed expression caught their notice as though he had grown a second tail.

"Strange, but Melkorka has asked me to contact you. An odd request. Do you know what she has on her mind, Kidahin?" he asked.

Kidahin glanced at Seralin, and they both gave him curt nods.

They are in this together. Anlann sighed his annoyance. *Females are strange.*

"Ah, I know what that message is about, Anlann. She just wants to make sure that you and I have a chance to speak. She may not have known that I could reach you in such a casual manner."

"She wanted us to meet? Why?" Anlann realized that something important had happened. By the way the two females had been jabbering in their finger-wagging and by their now sudden feigned innocent expressions, he knew something critical was happening.

"Melkorka thought I should speak with you about Eyloni customs. I want to know about singing songs dedicated to the fallen in battle."

"Why?" Anlann asked. He knew it. He knew it! Marsch had gotten those females fixated on something, something having to do with Death Songs.

Oh, spirits! "They want you to sing their dead to the spirits, do they not?" Anlann should have known. They trusted him, and even if they had not heard him singing, Kidahin would have told them about it by now. He understood their desire to send their battle dead into the spirit world. It should have been done soon after their deaths. The warleader led the Death Song ceremony, but with Kalinn numbered among the dead, his eventual replacement would perform the duty. The ritual helped solidify the empathy between a warship's society and their chosen warleader.

When a warleader died in battle, his warship returned to Elleio. There, the crew searched for suitable males to choose a new warleader from. However, with her ship's FTL drive inoperative and days away from even minimal realignment and testing, Melkorka had no choice but to signal the

Compact Counsel and ask that a group of qualified males from the La'huaset tribe be brought here.

The new warleader would not appreciate another male's involvement in what he would consider his duty, but he had no say in the matter, of course. What a warship's crew did prior to the choice of a new warleader concerned them alone, and never him.

Nor did it matter that Marsch was human. The rite originated, as did most of Eyloni law and custom, thousands of years ago, when intertribal conflicts raged. It did not matter what tribe or clan he belonged to, since males had near unlimited autonomy. Custom and tradition demanded only that the singer be a male associated with them.

Marsch held the title of battle leader. He had no Eyloni female society attached to him. That meant they must have chosen him as their sire cairn. That gave him command over all Eyloni on the surface. The warship's crew wanted him to sing their dead to the spirits so much that Melkorka, very indirectly, had interfered to bring them together.

"Del, do you intend to sing the Death Songs for them?"

"Yes, I do," Marsch said.

"Good."

Anlann turned to the two Hunters and sang to them at length. They took turns arguing with him.

Spirits! Females will argue over which way the wind blows a leaf. No matter how hard a male tried, he could never get his point across without explaining even the minute details. And still they argued. The huluhar lent her support to Seralin, but he knew she did so only to remain near Marsch.

He let them have their say—a male always let females have their say— before he snapped his tail and insisted on his way. He told them to leave. His bland suggestion that they go to the mess hall and eat some fruit met stiff resistance.

Both females stood tense with their hands at their sides, sending identical unequivocal messages: they had no intentions of going anywhere.

Kidahin refused. She argued, and Anlann held firm. She sang her vehemence at Marsch until she smelled his baffled amusement.

"Anlann says Seralin and I must leave. I am not leaving you!" She shook with fury. Her violent presence would have caused the average human to cringe in fear.

Seralin adopted the huluhar's strategy, switched to Coalition standard, and glared at Anlann.

"I am not leaving you to your own devices! I am your Protectress, and I will not allow you to face even a hint of danger alone!"

Oh sure, a warleader went off by himself at times. Many times he wandered off thinking he had left his Protectress behind, when in fact she stalked him at a distance and made sure he did not get into trouble. Males tended to do just that. Sometimes, like now, a male had to put his tail up and insist his Protectress leave, and to the spirits with her subsequent ill mood.

Seralin understood that as well as any female did, but she did not have to accept it, or be happy about it, either. She growled, whipped her tail in agitated loops, and tried to glare sense into the lovable fool's thick head by force of will.

"I am not alone, Sera." He crooned her natal syllables to soften his point. "Del is with me, and we can handle any threat. Go. Go on, both of you! We must discuss male things. Go now," Anlann said, making shooing motions with his tail.

Kidahin and Seralin appealed to Marsch with long looks, to no avail.

He shook his head and waved them to the door.

"It's all right, Kidahin. We'll be fine."

Kidahin's impulsive leap caught Marsch off-guard. She wrapped her arms and tail around him in abrupt fierceness before stepping back just as quick. Seralin managed a somewhat more dignified brush of her pons against Anlann's bare side in wistful banter before rejoining the huluhar. Seralin glared at Marsch.

"All males are tiresome!" she proclaimed in an aggrieved voice.

When the door closed, Anlann turned to Marsch.

"We do not have much time. They enjoy testing. It is their favorite thing to do. They never tire of it, and they do not think we can be left on our own for long without their company. What Melkorka has asked of you is serious, deadly serious. She would never have dreamed of asking you without first obtaining unanimous support from her society, and I do mean unanimous consent. What they ask of you is rare, but within their rights."

"I understand the seriousness of the matter, Anlann, but I need to know more about the rite itself, so I don't offend them. I need a general outline. What do I wear? How do I enter the area? How should I begin?

How do I conclude the rite? Do I make a speech? Must I mention the dead by name? Things like that," Marsch fired off.

Anlann sat idly examining the point of his adulthood knife. This event touched on female hierarchy business, and he had always said that he did not care what females did, so long as they kept their tails out of male autonomy.

Anlann sighed. "Please understand. I am constrained by custom and tradition in this matter. We Eyloni males take a dim view of interfering in another male's territory. More important, Eyloni males never interfere in the affairs of females who do not associate with them. Anything I tell you, beyond simple basics, will infuriate them because they will see it as unwanted meddling in their affairs, and it matters not that Melkorka initiated this meeting. I can suggest, *suggest* mind you, in the most circumspect way I can manage. Do you understand that I have cultural limits as to how far I can advise you before they will see my tail in the mix and feel their privacy pealed back for outsiders to see?"

"I think so," Marsch allowed. Who was he kidding? Melkorka and Kidahin had somehow involved him in a ritual that needed a priest and a grief counsellor, not a soldier.

"Good," Anlann said. "First, approach the rite like a male walking into single combat. You have rules of engagement and an objective. The objective, simply put, is to dispel their grief. If you sing well, then all you can do has been done. I *suggest* these rules of engagement: they will lead you into a central place that opens out onto some awesome, inspiring natural phenomenon, such as the mountain range here. They will flank you close about when you face the phenomenon. You then turn to look, as best as possible, at each female. Understand so far?"

"So far, so good," Marsch said.

"Excellent. Now, the rite itself follows a simple pattern. I *suggest* you begin it with a song that is profoundly personal to you, one that deals with death and loss, and let it build up to a triumph of the spirits over death. Do you know a song that calls forth vivid imagery of death and loss, the sorrow connected with that loss, and the joy of knowing that the dead join with the spirits?"

"Yes, Anlann, I know a song like that," Marsch deadpanned.

Concerned, Anlann hesitated a moment before giving an absentminded nod. "Next, I *suggest* you sing many songs that pick up on the themes of death and battle. Weave those themes into ideas of death and the spirits, and then continue into an expression of victory and triumph. I warn you now that you cannot give them adequate release with just a few songs. I do not know how your music will affect them. Except for Kidahin and Melkorka, no one understands your tongue. They will follow your rhythms, compare them to your scent, and make the empathic links that will translate your meaning. You may have to sing longer than an Eyloni male would to give them time to acclimate to you. I hope you have many songs," he said, raising an ear in inquiry.

"I do. I'm considering a few of them now," Marsch said.

Crap! This could take hours, and he could screw it up at any time, but he'd already promised them.

He was committed.

Anlann drifted, deep in thought, his ears twitching. He held the low ground here. Those females considered Marsch their sire cairn. Dealing with his own female association, his crew, *Surefooted*'s society, did not compare with poking his tail into another warship's society.

It could even prove fatal.

Not for Marsch, but for him!

Males do not intervene in the affairs of other female societies, he chastised himself again before continuing.

"When you believe that you are ready to conclude the rite, sing one last song. That song must somehow link them to you. The song must give them a subtle familial link. After you finish, salute the natural phenomenon Melkorka selected for the focus and then walk with slow dignity back out the same way you came. They will follow you out in social rank order. The rite is completed when the last one of them exits the ritual area," Anlann concluded. "Do you grasp the battle plan?"

"I think I got it."

Marsch wondered how much longer they had before the two Hunters returned.

"With respect, Anlann, I have an—uh—logistical problem."

The co-ambassador leaned forward and nodded. "Go on."

"I have duties to perform at the same time the rite is scheduled. From what you say, it'll take longer than an hour or so for me to complete it."

"Yes, it will take much longer than that," Anlann agreed. "Remember, begin with a serious song about death, then expand the idea through triumph and victory, and conclude with a song that ties them to you."

Seralin put her lemur-like face in at the door. For all their respect of privacy, Eyloni did not seem to understand knocking when it came to males.

"The two busybodies have returned, Del!" Anlann joked in a loud voice as Seralin and Kidahin entered the room. They grimaced and gave both males irritated looks.

Anlann turned back to Marsch and added, "As to your duties, I can help you there. The way I see it, the request made by Melkorka is a personal one involving her warship. An offense against a Compact warship is a stab at the heart of honor and an insult to the Compact Counsel and the Ten Tribes of Elleio that it represents. We take serious interest in personal honor issues. The Compact Counsel will see any hindrance you may suffer while acting on Melkorka's behalf as an action meant to contradict honor. Also, Compact interests are represented by Seralin and me, and we will consider it a grave insult to the honor of the dead if anyone stops you from singing the rite."

"Aren't you playing up the seriousness of the matter a bit?" Marsch asked.

"Not at all. That is why I said I will help you. Custom and tradition prevent me from taking direct action in matters affecting the interests of another warship. I can, however, maintain the honor of the Compact and the warship that represents it. I am not feigning insult, Del."

He's serious, Marsch realized. Anlann seemed pleased with his assessment, but Marsch frowned. Another problem, the diplomatic standing order, stood in his way.

"Anlann, Harrison ordered the crew of *Henri Edda* not to sing or play music while you and Seralin remained aboard."

The sudden chill in the room filled Marsch with dread.

"Why?" Anlann demanded. In his culture, refusing musical empathy violated the rules of hospitality.

Seralin jumped at the intensity of her Warleader's vehemence. She set herself for an attack directed against him. Kidahin slipped herself between the Protectress and Marsch. Both females glared at each other in challenge a few minutes before it dawned on them that no hostility manifested itself.

They glowered at the males before their eyes met.

Males, their gazes spoke in perfect agreement, *always find ways to annoy females!*

"Del, that is the most outrageous thing I have ever heard! The Compact Counsel thinks you humans may suffer from amusia or some social defect, some mental instability! Seralin and I wondered how you humans have meaningful social relationships without the unifying phenomenon of music. On Elleio, people who have amusia are schizophrenic at best or sociopathic at worst! Seralin is my Protectress, but that is not the reason why she is also co-ambassador here. Aboard *Surefooted*, she is my Mistress of Inner Strength. She heals through counseling the health problems that result from traumatic brain injury. The Counsel has grave misgivings about human sanity."

Seralin's noisily whistling warning notes penetrated Anlann's thoughts, reminding him that he had just blurted out sensitive Counsel information. He snapped his tail-wagging mouth shut but glared back at her in reproof. He thought it was dishonorable to keep secrets from a friend. It did not matter in any event: humans had musical ability. Marsch proved it, Kidahin proved it, and the request from Melkorka proved it. Besides, he felt an affinity for Marsch he could not ignore.

Anlann knew what caused that, too. Recent casual contact accounted for part of it, but most of it came from the feel he had on an instinctive and cultural level. His instinct assured him of Marsch's sanity and trustworthiness. Males read the truthful content of another male's character through the pheromonal empathy link they made when they smelled the scent of the females who associated with that male. Female scent flaunted their male's competency and sociability. Their empathy reflected his integrity like a mirror reflected his image.

Anlann watched the huluhar whenever the opportunity arose. She had been selected by her society for her extreme juvenile sensitivity to males. Her opinion of a potential warleader figured highly in her society's ultimate choice. She would choose Marsch if she could. Why, he would wager his warship that Melkorka felt the same.

Anlann mulled the idea over. Marsch's humanity did not prevent her choice: he lacked familial clan and tribal ties. His status as ni'zakhon—beyond the tribal law; clanless—prevented him from being a lawful choice.

Marsch's voice recalled him from his tailchasing.

"Well, Harrison thought, or the Coalition Diplomatic Corps thought, that you would find offense in an improper or inappropriate song or melody." Marsch felt no insult from Anlann's disclosure. Diplomats fixated on issues that did not relate. Still, unless every diplomat suffered from the same blind ambition that Harrison seemed to, they should have explored the Eyloni cultural importance of music rather than shrugging it off as superstitious nonsense. That said, he also understood why the diplomats might choose not to pursue the matter. Both Kidahin and Melkorka had made casual references to spirits, music, and cultural continuity. Diplomats would avoid religious matters: one false assumption and negotiations crumbled. And yet, they could have made a tactful, polite inquiry, and by doing so avoid the Eyloni fear of human psychopaths.

Anlann shook his head. "Offense might occur, but it would have been attributed to misunderstanding and allowances would have been made." He sighed, relieved he had not offended Marsch with insulting references to his species' state of mental health. Nobody made unsubstantiated accusations against an Eyloni's mental status without great personal risk. Mental defect, except for physical trauma to the brain, occurred rarely in males, Hunters, and Warriors. The Comara had not a single instance of mental defect in the historical memory of the past several thousand years.

"I sang with Kidahin, Anlann. I violated Harrison's posted general order, and he's going to make an issue about it when he finds out."

"I do not see it that way. The order prevents you from singing while Seralin and I remain aboard your ship. You sang with Kidahin here, on the surface of this moon."

The two females nodded in vigorous agreement.

Marsch watched Kidahin's animated nodding and snapping tail and spoke his doubts.

"I don't think Ambassador Harrison will see it in quite that way, and he has the power to put Captain Winters in a bind. He's going to have a screaming fit over this. You remember how he was in the Captain's office?"

"Let him. He has no Warpact over you, and I will explain the significance of the rite to Captain Winters. We," Anlann indicated his Protectress, "can then help Ambassador Harrison understand, too. Remember, you also have the full backing of a Compact warship. His crew's wishes will draw the notice and support of the Compact Counsel."

Marsch was moved. "Thank you, Anlann. I'm in your debt."

The co-ambassador waved the words aside.

"No. It is I who am in your debt. You have shown me that you have both integrity and musical ability, and that helps me deal with your people. Melkorka will contact Captain Winters about it herself when she arranges security provisions with him. Also, we males must stick together. I think it is a universal constant that females think we cannot do anything!"

Both females scowled at them before returning to their signing.

"Security provisions?" Marsch echoed, mystified. What security presence needed arranging for a wake?

"Of course," Anlann said. "They shall abandon *Hunter's Moon*, placing him on automatic for however long it takes you to complete the rite. Everyone shall come to the Place of Mourning to hear you sing the dead to the spirits. None will remain aboard him. In the event of attack or orbital incident, Melkorka will ask Captain Winters to maintain Battle Status until they return to their ship. And he will do it, I am certain. He is honorable and will balance the needs of his ship and your Coalition against the wishes of Ambassador Harrison. His actions will solidify the good opinion of the warship's society, Seralin, myself, and the Compact Counsel. Much honor will come from his actions when the Compact Counsel sees that he guards the exposed tail of a Compact warship."

"Wait, Anlann, Melkorka said they would all attend, but you're saying that not one of them will remain aboard their ship during the rite?"

"Of course, Del. As I said, the rite and the honor they do you is important to them. We do not take trivial stands on things like these."

Marsch looked at the two Hunters and knew that what Anlann said was solid truth. Their serious expressions, their twitching tails, their perked ears drove the importance of the matter home.

Nobody allowed a combat vessel to remain on full automatic unmanned. Even in dry dock, security personnel remained aboard, and a skeleton crew manned key stations in the event that the ship had to make an emergency exit. While in orbit and free to navigate, a ship lacked the controlled environment that a dry dock provided. The ship maintained full power, rather than running on the dock's umbilical power. Worse, the Compact ship had suffered battle damage and remained at Condition-1. The Lizards could return in force at any time, and with the entire crew on the surface, they would become easy targets of opportunity that Winters would have to defend until they could teleport aboard their ship and get to action stations.

Have mercy on me, Marsch prayed into the night.

9

SINGING WITH THE INVISIBLE DEAD

"He's what?" Harrison screamed, his voice echoing off the walls in Winters's office.

"Del has been invited to participate in a ceremony dedicated to the memory of *Hunter's Moon*'s dead," Anlann repeated.

"Like hell he has! He's no diplomat. He's not even a commissioned officer. I forbid it! Winters, confine Marsch to his quarters. I shall go in his place, say a few consoling words, and make a few remarks on the benefits that an economic and military alliance with the Coalition of Earth Colonies will provide," Harrison said.

"Mr. Ambassador, perhaps you should let Marsch participate in the memorial as a sign of goodwill. Dammit man, he's not negotiating a treaty," Winters said.

"That's quite enough, Captain! I've made my decision. You inform Melkorka that I will attend the ceremony scheduled for local sunset tonight, and..."

"No!" Anlann interrupted, "Melkorka did not invite you! She exercises her rights under Compact law and custom. As the Warleader of a Compact warship and as the Compact Counsel Co-Ambassador plenipotentiary, I insist Del sing the Death Songs for her warship's society. If you refuse, I shall suspend diplomatic talks between our two governments."

Seralin hissed a rhythmic warning. She watched the humans for body language clues. Human scents and human words did not always match human intent, but the body never lied. She shifted her bare feet, tail twisting, and checked her balance and footing. The human ambassador's pale bald head had turned the color of *maltha* berries. Checking her balance again, she wondered if the ambassador's reddening scalp signified a threat display. She flattened her ears and curved her tail around Anlann. Her pons hovering just above and away from his right shoulder in warning. Her body quivered, tense, ready. She glared at Harrison, bared her gleaming white teeth, and hummed a whispering growl.

He stared back at her, challenging her! She pulled back her deep red lips, revealing deep red gums and a deep red tongue that made her bright white upper canines look longer than they were. She sang another hissing warning.

"Ambassadors!" Winters thundered, "I've had enough! Marsch is under my command. He shall participate in Melkorka's ceremony, is that clear?"

"Of course, Captain," Anlann said,

"Yes, Captain," Seralin said.

"No, Captain. I command the diplomatic mission. You retain tactical command relative to all military matters, but I have operational command of this mission. Didn't you hear a word Ambassador Anlann just said? Melkorka wants Marsch to sing to them! He could insult or offend them at any time during the ceremony. That is why Marsch is under diplomatic orders not to sing near an Eyloni, and I will not rescind that order!"

"Excuse me, Ambassador," Anlann interrupted, "But you ordered Del not to sing while aboard your ship?"

"Yes. No. That is not quite correct."

As a diplomat, Harrison knew how to spot weasel words. He considered Anlann's question and parsed each word until he thought he found the co-ambassador's misunderstanding.

"No, Ambassador Anlann, I posted written standing orders prohibiting the crew from expressing music in any form. The order's purpose is to shield you and Ambassador Seralin from offense or insult during your stay with us."

Anlann was no diplomat by occupation. Properly speaking, no such thing existed in Eyloni culture, but a warleader had to manage the various female hierarchies and the numerous clan and tribal squabbles that arose among several thousand Warriors and Hunters. He also had to exercise subtle restraint during Warpacts. A warleader should know his limitations and know when to yield Warpact command to the more qualified male. Likewise, he also had to show restraint when he joined in Warpact with a male whom he felt less qualified.

"Excellent!" Anlann said. Pleased surprise reflected from Harrison's face, but Anlann would not give him the chance to gain the high ground. "Del will not sing aboard your ship, will not sing anywhere near us, and will not insult us in any event."

"I agree," Winters said. "Therefore, I hereby state for the record, and upon my personal authority as Captain of the Coalition of Earth Colonies carrier *Henri Edda*, that Senior Chief Warrant Officer Delwyn Wyrnette Marsch is ordered to proceed at his discretion in all matters pertaining to the request made of him by Melkorka, Mistress of the Compact warship *Hunter's Moon*, for the next twenty-four hours."

"You can't do that, Captain!" Harrison barked. "He's got to have supervision! Marsch has no diplomatic training. You may have the authority to order him to act on his discretion during a military mission, but you can't give him that kind of latitude on a diplomatic one. As such, and in accordance with the contingency powers granted me by the Coalition Government, I invoke diplomatic override and exercise mission priority. To facilitate that override, I hereby impress Warrant Officer Marsch into the Diplomatic Corps as my aide. He shall accompany me to the memorial ceremony."

"You try that!" Seralin trilled. "Del sings to their dead and to comfort their society. Melkorka warned you that no human but Del is invited!" She gestured to Anlann. "Even we cannot impose upon their grief. They would kill you before you could reach the Place of Mourning," Seralin did not know about Melkorka, but she knew what she would do to anyone trespassing on her grief if Anlann or a number of her warship's society had died.

Winters interrupted, "Mr. Ambassador, he's only singing a song or two. He's not talking to them let alone negotiating with them. Perhaps we should remain close by, but outside a perimeter set by Melkorka. From there, you could monitor the event."

Harrison mulled the idea over, looking for any traps and pitfalls that might snatch away the victory he wanted too much.

"Well, yes," he mumbled. "If I directed this great event by commlink and made sure Marsch didn't make any binding agreements, it might work. I would give official approval for the event. I will make a record to preserve this diplomatic triumph. I think I should review the list of songs Marsch knows, so I can make the proper selections. I can't have him singing anything too radical, you know. Oh, and tell him I'll have a condolence speech for him to memorize. Better he delivers it from memory than reads it from his omni, but if he can't memorize five or six hundred words— better make it a thousand—make sure he understands he'll have to read it without sounding like he's reading it, if you know what I mean."

Magnanimous now, Harrison beamed charm from his cherubic face. He nodded to the seething co-ambassadors. "Please forgive my excitable enthusiasm, but you must understand that the Coalition Government considers our talks crucial. They would find it disturbing if I allowed Marsch to conduct an official ceremony without proper diplomatic guidance and support."

Winters rolled his eyes for Anlann's benefit. He understood the Eyloni's fury. Harrison sought to undermine the wishes of a Compact warship's Mistress. Vested with command authority, Melkorka had the freedom to conduct a memorial to her fallen shipmates and the freedom to choose whomever she pleased to sing at their memorial. The ceremony was a private affair between her and her crew and Marsch. Besides, the Iota Horologii star system fell within Compact jurisdiction.

Tension filled the room. By sheer luck and misdirection, Winters maneuvered his way between Harrison and the co-ambassadors. How long would their restraint hold out? Harrison had all but declared his intent to commandeer a spiritual event to advance a diplomatic goal. The two Eyloni stared speechless at him, and Winters wondered if Harrison even realized that he was firing torpedoes into his own mission.

Winters hesitated. Now wait a damn minute! That gave him an idea. He thought he had an answer, something having to do with regulations and mission priority. He needed time to recall the specific regulation from memory.

Anlann doubted the human ambassador's sanity: he dared dictate terms to Eyloni females! He listened to his Protectress' soft high-pitched growling. He knew that she did not care for Harrison yanking her by the tail into the jaws of another warship's business. This was why, Anlann concluded, you did not allow the unskilled to make strategic or tactical agreements. Warleaders or sire cairns discussed terms and made alliances because such talks tended toward verbal combat.

"No, Mr. Ambassador," Winters said. "You pointed out yourself that I command all tactical military operations. We are in Compact space in response to a distress call from a Compact ship that has suffered severe battle damage. We are in a potential combat zone."

Harrison gaped in dawning horror as Winters continued. "It is my command opinion that the threat of a Lizard attack exists for as long as we remain in this system. That being the case, I declare our present circumstances a continuing military action. Further, Melkorka's request for close orbital support while her crew is on the surface argues for a continued military state of readiness. Therefore, under Coalition Naval Regulations Chapter Three, Section Two, Paragraph One, I relieve you of mission operational command authority until such time as the Compact warship is free to navigate and we leave Compact space."

"But the diplomatic mission, Captain! My mission concerns the Lizard threat as well! A military alliance is needed to counter the growing Lizard threat!"

Harrison realized that he'd overplayed his hand. He was a diplomat, a political appointee, and an attorney. He understood the limits of his authority. Winters had him in a legal box so long as they remained a support vessel for the Compact ship. It was a certain fact that the warship's FTL drive wouldn't be repaired before tonight. Even if the ship's jump drive had been working, the Eyloni weren't going anywhere until a new warleader arrived.

He had to maneuver them into letting him observe the memorial ceremony. At least he would know what happened as it happened and not after the fact, when it was too late to fix any misunderstandings.

"Very well, Captain. However, I cannot perform my duties unless I watch the event."

Seralin growled again, audible to human ears this time.

"I don't mean that I have to attend the memorial, but I must somehow observe and hear it." Smiling his best diplomat's smile at an angry Seralin, he added hastily, "I intend no disrespect to Melkorka or her crew, but I must see the event as it unfolds and note any cultural misunderstandings that might arise. I am content to watch from the same place as you and Ambassador Anlann."

Seralin gave him a curt nod.

Anlann agreed. He understood. The Coalition Fleet relied on a diversified command structure with overlapping zones of influence. Harrison commanded in nonmilitary matters, and Winters commanded in military matters. Here, their commands overlapped. Of course, military missions superseded nonmilitary ones. That let Captain Winters exercise his authority as military commander. Anlann did not doubt that once they left the system, Harrison would regain diplomatic command. Anlann explained the strange dual command concept to his fed-up Protectress.

Why did they not just say so? Seralin fumed as she nursed a grudge against all things male. She glanced at them one at a time, Harrison first, then Winters for an instant, and then she glared daggers at Anlann.

Seralin calmed herself by thinking of Marsch. What would he sing? She thought about his music all the way back to their VIP quarters.

❖❖❖

"Incoming message from the Compact Counsel, Mistress," the Mistress of Communications reported.

"Transfer it to my console," Melkorka said.

"Affirm, acting."

Melkorka watched the hyperlink's artificial intelligence packet form the sender's communications avatar on her command console's holodisplay.

Even FTL communications could not make instantaneous connections over interstellar distances. Hyperlink signals traveled barely a few cees faster than twice a warship's maximum jump rate, but even that phenomenal rate could not support bidirectional communication in real time. Standard FTL comm packets sent their messages with an embedded

AI avatar of the sender. The AI gave the avatar the sender's personality so it could deliver the message and discuss its content with the recipient.

"Ki, Melkorka. I, Thelindrallin, extend to you the greetings of the Compact Counsel."

Melkorka appraised the elderly Hunter's image and nodded, ears perked forward in respect.

"Greetings Mistress Thelindrallin. To what honor do I owe your words?"

"I am saddened, as we all are, to hear of your loss. We extend our sympathy. We knew Kalinn well, and we sing songs in his memory. As a male's loss is cataclysmic to a warship's females, we sing strength to you. We have scoured the La'huaset tribal continent's clans that built *Hunter's Moon* for qualified males. Kalinn cannot be replaced, but you shall pick a male to succeed him."

Melkorka nodded, daggers tearing at her heart.

"I can confirm for you that the current contingency warship *Fearless* is already en route to Nikkiolo with ten combat experienced males. By the time you receive this message, he will be 33.4 Tyreniioroneo Standard days into his journey. Warleader Phalalin shall contact you prior to his final FTL jump into the Nikkiolo system. He has agreed to scan for your hyperlink comm codes between jumps, should you desire to communicate."

The Mistress of Tactics nodded to Melkorka, confirming the Counsel Mistress's estimate.

"With respect, Mistress Melkorka, I ask that you instruct your Mistress of Saga to transmit updated warship, combat, and personal logs. The Counsel also desires an updated damage control assessment of your warship and a summary of his battle readiness."

Melkorka ground her teeth. The request bordered on an intrusion into warship autonomy. She could refuse. It would take almost 40 TST days for the return hyperlink transmission to reach Elleio. *Fearless* would arrive in 43 TST days. That was a bit over 20 Coalition standard days, but Marsch would put the number closer to 10 days as his people counted. *Why would a sentient species use the fingers of both hands as a basis for their number system? Why not use fingers and toes for that matter?* Her thoughts returned to *Fearless*. At the rate reported, he would have to jump once every 1.12 TST days. They were 31 jumps away by now. No doubt they were in a hurry to complete the mission and rid themselves of their male passengers.

The Counsel's request for ship's logs was standard procedure. The warship's historian treated them like her own infants. She sent all ship combat, operations, and personal logs to Elleio for archival purposes on a regular basis. Others would study the records, including crew observations, warship performance data, and battle tactics. They studied how a particular ship, warleader, society, or individual fought in any given battle to exhaustion. Even personal notes and opinions might hold key revelations. Of course, the Compact Counsel placed all personal logs under privacy seal and never pulled them from the archives unless the individual played a crucial role in the event under study. Melkorka understood and agreed with the reasoning behind that part of the request, too. But asking after a warship's battle readiness hinted at a nosiness best ignored.

The males would arrive soon. She could well imagine what *Fearless'* society thought about them and grimaced. No female wanted more than one male aboard her ship. Multiple males threatened the safety of the ship because females would divide their attention among them to make sure they remained safe. Besides, you could not have a Warpact of males aboard the same ship. While aboard Phalalin's ship, they would remain secluded in separate, lavish quarters on a sealed deck.

They were quarantined.

Only one rallying point existed aboard a warship, on a battlefield, or under any circumstances where a solitary male's presence triggered the instinct that drove females to optimal combat performance.

Melkorka grimaced again. Yes, the females aboard Phalalin's ship could not wait until they rid themselves of their male passengers. They had to courier all of them here, and then they had to take all but the one chosen back to Elleio.

Thinking about males aboard a warship forced her mind back on Marsch.

What would he sing? Kidahin had been ecstatic about his acceptance, but she was all but tail-twined to him. Melkorka smiled. Now, if only the huluhar responded to one of the males aboard *Fearless* like she did to Marsch!

✦✦✦

Marsch listened as Kidahin lectured him on Eyloni customs.

"Tribes are divided into clans and societies. A great many female hierarchies weave them all together into a living oyya web. The Ten Tribes have thousands of clans and societies tied together by hundreds of female hierarchies. Each clan has its own customs that it adds to its tribe's traditions. Societies number in the thousands because a typical Eyloni belongs to many different societies at the same time. There are societies for gender, clan, tribe, general occupation, and specific specialty, among many others. For example, a warship's crew is a society, all crews of all warships together make up a single society, and all Hunters are a society.

"Each tribe has its own continent on Elleio. I, and everyone aboard our warship, belong to the La'huaset Tribe. La'huaset means the Land of Mountains. I am of the Uahua'asee'a Clan. Uahua'asee'a means the Land, the Sea, and the Sky. Tribes and clans no longer fight among one another, but they do form alliances, a leftover from ancient times. Today, outright battle among tribes and clans is theoretical, but rivalry and dissent remain a part of certain tribes' and clans' histories. Members of the same society do not compete against one another even if their clans or tribes do so. This structure, this web, kept communication lines open among clans and tribes, even during open warfare. The Compact Counsel embodies the web of societies and hierarchies into a check against intertribe and interclan warfare. The Compact is ancient, having formed several thousand years before the rise of industrial technology.

"Ritual is part of social life. Every ritual has its own Mistress of Fire, Mistress of Legend, Mistress of Songs, Mistress of Names, Gracious Mistress of the Singing People…"

Marsch's omni chimed, interrupting the social studies lesson.

He pulled the device from his belt, tapped it, acknowledging the signal, and read the change of orders scrolling down the holographic display. Kidahin hovered at his side and watched him squint at the patterns flashing before his eyes.

Marsch smiled. The Hunter stuck close to him now. She used to wander off several dozen meters at a time before returning. Now, if he didn't know better, he'd have thought she considered herself his Protectress. She pestered him no end by suggesting some of the songs they had sung together. She told him what to wear, what weapon to take, not to take a commlink that could interrupt like his omni had just now, and other fussy tidbits as they came to her.

"I've been given twenty-four hours leave from regular duties. That should give us more than enough time to prepare for tonight's ritual and have a rest afterward. I guess Anlann got them to agree."

"Good. Warleader Anlann did his best, but Melkorka made the request. Without her, he could do nothing."

"Orders say I'm not to discuss the rite with Ambassador Harrison until tomorrow, and if I don't want to discuss it, I don't have to. Hmmm. The Captain must anticipate some problems with him. I bet that was some tense meeting."

"It does not matter," Kidahin said. "The rite is Melkorka's concern. Our concern. Now we can prepare without disturbances," she added.

He laughed and agreed with her. "We can. Want to see how the area is coming along?"

"No! Place is being prepared for you. You may not go there until the Mistress of Names summons you. This means we can sing now, yes?" she badgered.

"Yes, we can," he relented.

Marsch knew that preparing for the memorial was problematic. The enormity of it all threatened to overwhelm him. He didn't need practice. He knew the words, and he knew the music. Anlann told him to give them a commanding male presence, sure of himself and of his place with them. He must radiate confidence and put their minds at ease. He must help them express their grief as they sang with him.

And just how, Marsch asked himself, *do I do that?*

✦✦✦

Allinha, the Mistress of Fortifications, oversaw the construction crews at work landscaping the Place of Mourning. The area they developed included a large natural oval depression in the exposed bedrock several thousand ells from the repair base. From here, at sundown, they would see the sunset reflecting from the icy peaks. The vapor rising from the melting ice would produce prismatic effects in the sky as it refroze high above the mountains, dazzling them as the sun sank below the horizon. The light from the rising gas giant and that planet's effect on the atmosphere would produce glitter and auroras that would flash above the mountain range. The Mistress of Knowledge assured her that the evening sky would remain clear.

The visual effects would persist and move everyone watching, regardless of the moon's extremely swift sunset.

The work crews altered the depression into an outdoor amphitheater. It waited there, a wide, shallow bowl of rock, and Allinha planned to bevel the sloping sides into tiers narrow enough to accommodate the entire seated crew. Her construction teams cleared away the scrub growth and sand from the bowl's floor that runoff had left behind. At its deepest end, an access had already been cut into the stone to give the sire cairn an isolated path into the bowl and on up to the inclined rocky ledge. Flowing out from and behind him, they would sit, from highest rank nearest him to descending rank as they filled up the terraced sides.

It shall look beautiful, she murmured with awe. Here, before the spirits, they would sing of their dead. Marsch would lead them in song as they sang good-bye, just as a male should.

Allinha strove to preserve the continuity of the natural environment. All Eyloni constructions took environmental friendliness and ecological balance into account. Except for the brush, brambles, and the material removed to create the terraced seating, the area would keep its rugged, natural look. After the Death Song ritual, the construction teams would return the area to its natural state.

It shall look beautiful, she sighed again.

Later that afternoon, Winters looked down into the ceremonial grounds from a distant stand along a line of trees. They stood a fair distance away: he could blot the place out with his thumb held at arm's length.

"I can't see a thing from here even in broad daylight, let alone when it gets dark," Harrison complained.

"Count yourself fortunate, Ambassador," Anlann volunteered. "It is their rite, and they could have insisted upon no witnesses at all. The reason Melkorka agreed to let us watch from here, I suspect, is one of gratitude for your ship's sentry duty during the time that they must remain on the surface."

Anlann watched. The construction crews had wrought wonderfully. They carved tiered seating along the edge of, and down into, the lopsided rocky oval. He looked down along a shallow angle onto the Singer's Place. The females would sit around and behind Marsch, from the oval's rim all the way down to the bottom and then back up to within touching distance of him. The oval's low side edge opened out toward the distant mountains.

A tongue of stone leaned over the edge and above the murmuring runoff water below, pointed in a shallow incline toward the mountain peaks. His voice would ring out from the bowl and echo back to them, along with his massed female accompaniment.

Anlann satisfied himself by knowing that he covered Marsch's tail, least Ambassador Harrison wander too close and unleash the anger of the warship's crew.

Seralin stood near Anlann. Custom and respect prevented them from singing along with the warship's society, but it did not prevent her from stopping anyone from trying to interfere with the ritual.

They murmured back and forth as they watched the warship's crew enter the terraced bowl and mill about.

Winters glanced at the time. It wouldn't be long now. *I hope Harrison behaves himself.*

Marsch watched the colorful, iridescent avian reptiles wheel in the early evening sky. They always flew when the huge gas giant rose over their roosting places before dropping into the treetops as the glowing agate disk climbed above their trees.

It was time.

Anlann's advice had been to visualize the rite as a combat mission.

Like any combat mission, Marsch geared up with an intensity that excluded all but his ARTS members. For this mission, he had at first thought of Kidahin as his solitary team member until he remembered that it was the warship's crew that formed his team. For this mission, he led them into action. They looked to him for guidance during the ceremony.

He dressed simply, in keeping with Eyloni custom. He wore tan shorts, no shirt, a necklace, a large combat knife, and the old saber. He chose the piano for the ceremony. It gave him greater flexibility and offered him an easier instrument to sing along with for the time expected that the ceremony would last.

Marsch and Kidahin waited until Anlann and Seralin came for them. The co-ambassadors had agreed to escort them to the Compact FOB. Silent and empty, it reminded Marsch that the warship orbited bereft of his crew. By now, they had all come to the surface and were waiting for him.

Melkorka met them, nodded to the co-ambassadors—a dismissal— and escorted them to the ritual area, the Place of Mourning. By now, *Henri*

Edda would have taken up station near the Compact warship and would remain there until the Eyloni returned to their vessel.

The setting sun approached. He had to be in position and singing by the time the sunset hit the distant mountain peaks.

They walked down a gentle slope and up a rise that had a notch cut into it, allowing him access into the bowl without having to climb down its terraced sides. Around him, he saw Warriors and Hunters perched along the terraced oval bowl. They filled the thing from its edge down to the bottom, leaving the shallow end facing the mountain somewhat open.

Melkorka, the ritual's Mistress of Names, stepped aside and beckoned him to continue across the bottom and up to the outstretched stone finger pointing to the mountain's heights.

Marsch marched past the hundreds seated around him and stepped out onto the rocky spire. Kidahin stopped just short of it.

The setting sun's prismatic rays reflected from distant icy peaks, throwing a peacock's tail of kaleidoscopic colors above the tiered bowl. Marsch slipped the piano roll from its belt pouch and unrolled it across the stone pillar set there to hold the instrument. He began to play as the refracted light from the mountains combined with the sunset's colors. The simple beauty overwhelmed him.

He heightened the melancholy tune, building up emotional intensity. He watched in awe as rainbows flashed before him. The setting GO star bathed the peaks in yellow light. The clear turquoise sky formed a smooth background that framed the wavering rainbow shimmers bouncing across distant peaks. As the sun continued its relentless descent into the dark night, the sky faded into pale blue dusk. A false aurora of rippling rainbow colors fanned out into a curtain that seemed to collide with the sky's true green and yellow auroras. A wavy orange wedge surrounded by luminescent blues and greens crossed the summit's glittering face. The sparkling, yet dying sunlight fell from the summit down into the shallow valley before him. The colors shimmered in a riot up and down the mountain side as the sun fell farther into eternal night.

Kidahin turned her back on Marsch and the colorful display and gazed into her society's eyes. They let her break rank order and stand near him tonight because her superior command of his language let her interpret his words for them. She flexed her fingers and signed Battle Language to the crowd. Standing on a level ridge between him and Phelindra—the Mistress of Songs for tonight—she adjusted her stance. Kidahin would sign the Battle Language meaning his words sang so they could better participate in the rite. His scent might not carry to everyone seated around him. She followed the introductory beat and prepared herself for the all-important first song, the song that would set the mood and tone for the rite.

He did not fail her. He played, and his voice sang a low, heavy beat that traveled out from behind her and washed up the bowl's terraced sides. The dirge-like resonance mesmerized them. The beat shifted. Marsch sang, and Kidahin flinched so hard she stumbled back, catching her bare heel against the uneven rock, and stepped on her pons. She bit back a momentary shriek and fell.

I know this song!

She stood up and looked out at the gathering. She saw flashes of displeasure ripple across their faces. She saw it in the set of tails, in the pitch of ears, and she knew what they were thinking: her youth and inexperience made her ill-prepared to hold such an exalted and honored title in the rite as the Gracious Mistress of the Singing People.

She had to explain. She did so not to excuse her clumsiness, but to refocus their attention on Marsch. She signed the meaning of the song as she sang with him.

"This is the Death Song of his three infant females!" she signed to them. She told them how they had died even as she translated the words themselves.

Her society understood her shock. They felt it, too. The sire cairn saw in them a worthiness great enough to warrant their inclusion in his sorrow. He did not impose upon their grief; instead, he shared in their pain on a personal level. Her people held family matters and privacy in high regard. A male offering such a sharing also implied a willingness to share pain and hazard.

Marsch listened to Kidahin's voice. She knew this song, heard him sing it once before. The dying rainbows met with the true evening auroras. As they shifted and wavered across the night sky, he began a second verse of the first song.

And nearly three thousand voices singing, not in vocals but in instrumental strains, joined with him.

They sang with an intensity heart-wrenching to hear. It shocked him. Marsch remembered Kidahin's triple singing voice and should have been prepared for their combined effect.

He hadn't been, not even close.

They sang notes that put musical instruments to shame. They sang their pain and their grief. They sang their sorrow; they sang along with him; they sang through him. They sang their anguish at being bereft of the company of their crew, their friends, and their loved ones. They sang away the agony of their loss, and they sang away his loss as well.

Seralin kept a careful watch. The Death Song rite began as shattered rainbows glittering from mountain ice. Rippling auroras danced across the sky. Sparks of life at the veil. Spirits condensed from light. Marsch's deep resonate voice brought back the reality of the ritual: people had died. A male had died! The beat changed, and she saw Kidahin fall.

Anlann groaned beside her.

"Youthful clumsiness or bad omen?" Seralin whispered.

The huluhar stood and resumed her Battle Language monologue.

Seralin's eyes followed the signing and rocked backward on her heels. She sucked air through her teeth, and Anlann gave her an ear-flick of inquiry.

"Del sings of his dead infant females," she whispered.

Anlann blinked in surprise.

"Has anything happened?" Winters asked.

"No. Kidahin stumbled is all," Anlann replied.

It definitely is not all! Seralin muttered to herself. She gazed into the deepening night. There, she saw sentries keeping a wary watch over them. Their glowing amber eyes looked up in a tacit warning not to interfere.

Marsch completed his first song, the one about sharp knives cutting short lives, and began a rhythmic bridge that would link the previous song with the next one, one about the living singing with their invisible dead.

Ibeetu's short evening raced toward midnight. The fractured rainbows of light faded into the darkening yellows, greens, and maroons of aurora-filled night. His next songs picked up on the themes of the invisible dead and linked them with victory. The dead Eyloni became victorious invisible spirits. Marsch sang of promised victory, and those left behind sang of victory and freedom. They would sing on the graves of their enemies, and they would sing to the dead in that victory.

The notes rang through the night air; Melkorka felt them wisp across her face and into her breasts. She felt the notes enter her and settle deep in her bones.

Marsch looked out across the tiered bowl. Remnants of light from the rising gas giant and the multiple auroras glinted off the snowy mountain slopes, causing Eyloni eyes to blaze back at him. Eyes wide open, their irises reflected, depending on the individual, sparks that ran from deep orange, to amber, to dark yellow. They focused on him to the exclusion of all else.

Well, him and Kidahin, as she signed his words.

She had told him that her language was one never spoken but sung. The same words sung with different notes and tempo up and down the scale could have many different meanings. The name for her people, the Ey-lo-ni, meant people: the living or dead, the unborn, and the spirits. The chord *ey* meant a physical power that animated, be it a person, an animal, a storm, or an earthquake. *Lo* meant a space reserved for someone in the present time, but the chord *ni* was its opposite because it referred to all possibilities that did not yet exist in the present. She explained the principles surrounding the chord *ki*. Ki remained unrealized until touched by Oyya. Oyya embodied the forces of nature that made things what they were. The song and the web come from the mouth, not the breath but the melody heard, the weave of the music and the Oyya of the spirits. She had told him once that it was dangerous to make a mistake with Ki. If you sang the wrong song into an Oyya web, you could make a knife sing. Marsch knew her people sang in metaphysical terms. Their music led them to the spirits, and their spirits led them to the patterns discovered by their science. For her people, physics described the action of spirits.

The warship's crew paid him strict attention, an attention any concert musician could only dream of. They didn't look away, didn't talk, didn't eat or drink, and didn't stand or wander about.

Marsch's next song built on the themes he dreamed up earlier in the day. He joined spirits and victory to triumph and joy. Martial songs carried the rhythm of triumph as the interwoven Eyloni melodies followed him. They poured out their communal grief. He sang songs of joy, of life, of living, and the joy of being with the spirits. They followed his rhythm with melodies weaving and winding about his voice. They took the lead, and he chased their melodies, rapping keys in pursuit of their expression of exultation and joy.

Kidahin recognized the Battle Song that had sent her into combat readiness. Marsch had modified the tempo to prevent the assembly from rising to a call of battle. Unfettered by the song, she listened to the words, compared them with his scent, and signed their meaning. Well into the song, she wondered about her empathic link with his scent and if she properly signed his meaning: could a water-creature's body substitute for an artillery piece? By the looks they gave her, her society found it hard to believe a projectile forced down its throat and explosives rammed up its rear-end could substitute for an effective cannon.

Before Marsch knew it, early morning had come. Anlann told him to conclude the ceremony with a song that linked himself to the rite, to them, and to the final expression of victory.

And here he ran into a problem. Every song he had sung so far fit into the ritual expression he wanted the rite to convey: salute the dead, revere the spirits, and console the living. He grappled with the final requirement: how to link himself to them. He knew only one song that wove his identity into an expression of triumph. It honored his dead ancestors, their past, considered the present, and implied a future together. A spotty family tree, it honored those of his family who had served military duty. It named them, their rank, and the battles they had fought. As the last of his line, he added a verse about himself, describing the 'battle' he fought as being here in support of the Eyloni while they repaired their ship.

Marsch pounded on the keyboard, and the females sang high, haunting tunes like moaning whistles. Harrison and Winters listened to the music. Neither cared much for Marsch's singing, but the eerie sound of massed Eyloni voices surprised them. The voices sounded so weird that it took some time for them to realize that they mimicked the sounds of mournful animal calls, the winds, hymns, instrumental music, rushing water, rustling leaves; they sat in place as they sang, but every so often they would raise their cupped hands and wave them in the air in some odd pattern.

"I don't understand how the Diplomatic Corps misjudged the place of music in Eyloni life," Harrison said. "Thank God Marsch didn't sing anything political. If he can wind this thing down without saying something stupid, then we can safely assume that a diplomatic crisis has been averted."

Winters shook his head and turned back to watch. He saw little that told him people sat down there in the dark. He heard them, of course, but at least the co-ambassadors could see them. Sentries stood around the ritual area. Throughout the night he saw sparks of orange flashing like fireflies. The co-ambassadors excited musical murmurs drew his attention again. They had been doing that all night.

"What is it, Ambassador Anlann? Ambassador Seralin?" Harrison asked. He'd been listening to the words of the song rather than the Eyloni musical accompaniment. Anxious, he ran Marsch's words through a mental sieve and strained to connect the words with a negotiating point that either helped, or hindered, his mission.

Marsch is singing about his family's military service. Good, Harrison sighed. No Eyloni cares about that.

Seralin stammered in shock and could not get her tongue to work. She resorted to the infantile expression of wringing her tail like a wet rag.

Anlann relaxed. What Marsch sang did not surprise him one bit. He could do what he wanted. He had the right of male autonomy and unattached status to link his family history and clan status with the warship's society. By doing so, he announced a willingness to accept full responsibility for them. If Marsch wanted to be their warleader, well, that was none of his business, either.

Seralin regained enough of her voice to squeak out, "Did Del just do what I think he did?" Stunned and discomforted, she leaned against him for support.

"What do you think they will do?" he asked her.

Seralin wrapped her tail around him and said, "They are not tearing him to pieces."

Anlann nodded. "Then they either consider it a serious overture, or else they think Kidahin misstated his intent. I think they will interpret his words as a misstatement, unless he gives them reason to think otherwise. In any event, we shall know for certain if they respond to us with the same proprietary possessive intensity that Kidahin already exhibits around him. If they do, then I am not sticking my tail anywhere near them! Besides, do you think they would choose a human?"

Seralin turned and smiled at him. "Females choose whoever we want, *as you well know*. Nothing in Compact law forbids us the choice of any male. The right is very ancient. I think they have no difficulty with Del as sire cairn here on the surface, but he lacks familial standing with a tribal clan. I think the lack of standing would either make it almost impossible for him to mediate the hierarchical disputes always present in any society, or it would make him the ideal neutral choice. But even if they ignored his clan status, the Compact Counsel will still find him outside the tribal law. They could even declare the entire crew outlaw for choosing him. Although

Kidahin knows we have the absolute right of choice, tribal law is a bludgeon that would make them think twice about it. I think they will assume she misstated his intent. Besides, we are reading too much into his words. He meant to sing about his status as a male here on this moon while guarding them in the face of a Ni'zakhonii threat."

Kidahin thanked the spirits she did not trip over her tail this time. Her sire cairn began the Death Song ritual with a song that tied their grief to his, an intimate sharing that spoke of the intense regard he felt for them. The rite had been flawless, and everyone had experienced the release of grief and pain and the elevation from aching despair to joy. None of them, she knew, had ever thought of singing with the invisible ones as singing with both their dead and with the spirits themselves.

But that last song, the song of male familial pedigree, had been excessive. Marsch had linked her society with his clan. As the last strains died away, he touched the piano just so, and rolled it back up into its bundle, stuck it back into its pouch, and walked down the stone spar, past her, and through the others.

They were *supposed to* give way for him to pass, and then follow him in rank order.

10

Eyloni came up to Marsch. They brushed their pons against him momentarily as he ducked and dodged his way out of the Place of Mourning.

Kidahin shot off after him, evading them like a leaf dancing on the wind. They smiled at her persistent effort to regain her place at his side. The return trip to the repair base would take some time, thanks to Marsch's frequent stops. He paused often, offering encouraging words to those who came up to him.

Anlann watched them leave the ritual area.

"Well, they are not tearing him apart," he stage-whispered to his Protectress.

Seralin glared at him for stating the obvious.

"Why would they, Ambassador Anlann?" Winters asked.

"Well, Captain, the rite ends with the male exiting the area by himself and…"

"*Henri Edda* to Captain Winters, come in Captain."

Winters sighed and tapped his omni. "Winters."

"Captain, Rodgers here. Sir, Combat Information Center has detected another neutrino burst. This time it was accompanied by a Cherenkov radiation spike. CIC has detected enough signal for an analysis."

"Put the CIC Command Duty Officer on, Exec," Winters said.

"Aye, Captain. Patching in. CDO Cabrera is in the loop, Sir."

"Very well. Report, Commander Cabrera."

"Aye Captain. Sir, Lieutenant Vincent has classified this contact as a Lizard FTL probe's drive artifact. He says the neutrino emission delta between the angle of incidence and the angle of refraction matches the Lizard subspace bubble parameter for an object decelerating from Lizard R-band velocity to just under Mach 1."

"Can you predict the target's mass?" Winters asked.

"Somewhere around fifty metric tons, Sir," the CDO replied.

"Did you obtain a tracking solution, Commander?"

"Working on it, Sir," Cabrera replied. "Lieutenant Vincent, switch pickup. Sir, Lieutenant Vincent is in the loop now."

"Very well. Report, Lieutenant," Winters said.

"Aye, Captain. Sir, when a Lizard ship strikes the subspace manifold, neutrinos scatter into normal space at specific angles to the strike, depending on the vessel's velocity band. Once in normal space, those neutrinos resemble the ones that come from cosmic ray decay as they strike photons. Such collisions create neutrinos, pions, muons, electrons, antielectrons, antineutrinos, and gamma rays. The electron-antielectron pairs annihilate and produce Cherenkov radiation."

"I know that, Lieutenant. Continue."

"Yes, Sir. Sorry, Captain. Without knowing the mixing angle of the neutrinos, the trace could amount to nothing more than spurious cosmic ray collisions in the upper atmosphere that happen to coincide with a velocity band scattering angle. With all the high energy activity in Ibeetu's upper atmosphere, we couldn't confirm that the Cherenkov radiation spike came from a Lizard FTL drive until we isolated neutrinos with a theta-13 mixing angle of zero. The artificial mixing angle and the emission angle delta together allows us to predict with high confidence that these neutrino emissions come from a Lizard probe operating in the R-band FTL velocity range," Vincent said.

"Can you reconstruct its trajectory?" Winters asked.

"Yes, Sir. The subspace bubble surrounding a Lizard ship affects neutrinos like a water droplet affects photons. The analogy matches so well that we name the seven Lizard FTL velocity bands for the rainbow colors they're analogous to. The emissions exit subspace perpendicular to the line of flight that the ship travels in FTL. As subspace is a continuum of discrete arcs, we can calculate a relative trajectory, but we can't determine the target's entry or exit point along the displacement arc with any accuracy. For this target's mass, the plot accuracy will be off by tens of kilometers."

"Understood, Lieutenant. Good job. Commander Cabrera, I don't like coincidences, or apparent coincidences either. Assuming the trace is not leakage from our own or the Compact ship's reactors at coincidental delta emissions, or a Lizard vessel's transient emissions as it passes through this system's subspace domain, plot the signal's most probable inbound trajectory."

"Working on it, Sir. Stand-by."

"Problem, Captain?" Ambassador Harrison asked. He couldn't decide which he wanted to do more, rush the warship's crew and learn what impressions Marsch had left them with, or find out what all the important physics talk was all about.

"I'm not sure. CIC thinks they have a bogy operating in the area. I'm awaiting a plot assessment as we speak."

"A bogy?" Anlann said. "And a bogy is a what?"

Winters smiled at the co-Ambassador's query. "A bogy is an unidentified vessel. Navigation, Plot, and Tactical analysts on the bridge and down in CIC think they've found a Lizard probe signature in the atmosphere."

"We should warn Melkorka," Seralin interrupted.

Before anyone could reply, she sang out a sharp, haunting series of five notes after the departing Eyloni. She repeated it a second time, for certainty's sake.

A reply came back at once, and seconds later irregular phosphorescent ripples betrayed mass quantum translations in progress.

"Captain, Rodgers here."

"Go ahead, Exec."

"Sir, Tactical Ops agrees with Plotting on a probable fix. Tracking suggests that, after accounting for anomalies, a probe popped into normal space in the upper atmosphere 126 kilometers beneath the ship and descended along a diagonal that overflies the mountain range north, northeast of your position."

Winters tensed. "Did it reenter subspace?"

"Inclusive, Sir," Rodgers said.

Winters swore. A Lizard ship's subspace wake entered normal space as a trail of neutrino pulses that betrayed its passage. They may have even detected a slow Lizard assault force passing through the system's subspace analogue. They scanned for an R-band delta emission and a few FTL-generated neutrinos in a sea of stellar and artificial ones. The normal space entry angle and low mass made identifying and plotting the target difficult. The preliminary classification of 'probe' came from the signal's R-band velocity signature and its presumed low mass entry angle. A larger target, or one exiting subspace faster than Mach 1, would leave an ionization wake in the atmosphere obvious to the sensors aboard both warships.

"Judith, could the probe have soft-landed?" Winters asked. Now that was all he needed. If he was a Lizard, he'd want to know what the construction activity on the surface was all about. They couldn't know the incidental and temporary nature of the work. Joke on them or not, they just might send a ship here to investigate. It was bad enough having a probe keeping tabs on them as it was.

"I don't think so, Sir," Rodgers said. "To get a useful scan from the ground, a surface probe would have to land this side of the mountain range to sweep an optimal scanning field. We would have detected its orbit-to-surface entry track in the atmosphere."

Yeah, Winters thought. They'd have seen its ionization wake disturb the auroras during the memorial, while every Eyloni eye on the moon faced the mountain range.

"Understood. Sound general quarters. Set Condition-2. Commence full power surface scans. Inform Mistress Melkorka of your results and suspicions. Relay to Teleportation that the ambassadors and I are returning to the ship."

"Aye, Sir."

Melkorka ordered the retrieval of all but essential personnel from the surface. She had not taken Seralin's keening cry of *"enemy presence probable"* as a spurious or trivial warning. Kidahin remained near Marsch, of course.

Marsch knew the moment he heard the melodic trill that something was wrong. The Eyloni had reacted at once. Melkorka warbled a reply, flicked her ear, and sang demands into the air. Within seconds, people vanished in rapid succession.

It must be an alert, he thought. He saw nothing in the darkness. He didn't have a combat scanner. He didn't even have his omni. Frustrated by the lack of actionable intel, he yelled into the whispering night.

"Sitrep!"

Marsch paused in the quiet but tense darkness, waiting for a report. None came. He felt a sense of confusion around him and wondered why until it dawned on him that they had never been exposed to the security term before.

"Situation report!" he demanded.

"*Henri Edda* advises possible Ni'zakhonii probe in the atmosphere," Melkorka said. "They cannot establish whether or not the probe is a fly-by asset or a surface operator."

"Assume that contact is a surface operating probe." Marsch considered options. A surface probe would spy out both bases. A Coalition carrier and a Compact warship operating in the same area would have the look of a joint military venture.

Melkorka waited for the sire cairn to continue. She knew by his changed expression and scent that he was evaluating the situation and that more orders would follow.

"I have to contact my Special Operations Group and get a sitrep. Melkorka, may I contact them from here?"

"Of course, Del. Ask Kidahin. She knows where the spare personal communications devices are stored. We must secure our warship and evaluate conditions," she said. They walked into the Compact base's security hub. Melkorka scanned orbital tracking reports on the security monitor. She thought her grasp of his tongue had improved over the past few hours, and she found it much easier to make empathic ties with him now. "I must resume my place," she added.

It surprised Melkorka that a stubborn and persistent Phelindra, a small group of her Hunters, and a group of equally persistent Warriors remained close. She concurred. The Warriors belonged to the warship's boarding party assault forces, and the group of Hunters came from the planetary force recon group. The current situation justified keeping them on the surface. She could spare them from their Battle Status stations aboard ship,

"I think Phelindra and a few others must remain here and hold the repair facility," Melkorka said, wincing at her evasive hyperbole. She employed a technicality; she meant them to safeguard Marsch and not to hold the repair facility, and they knew it.

They walked farther into the active security center. The wall holographic screens displayed several views of the Compact base perimeter, the Coalition SOB, and several tactical orbital plots filled with telemetry from *Hunter's Moon*. Marsch watched the displays and their scrolling pictographic legends. He saw a Warrior pass something to Kidahin.

Interested, Marsch stared at the device in her hand. The thing looked like a dull orange silk square close to a fingerprint in size with fine whisker-like feelers. It reminded him of a removable tattoo, a decal. She tried several times to affix the device to his ear. Frustrated, she pressed it against his left temple and ran the contact feelers to his eyebrow. She touched the decal, pushed on his eyebrow a few times, and sang to the device. Another minute passed before she told him he could contact his teams.

Doubtful, he spoke into the air, "Marsch to Sog Ops. Comm check, Sog Ops."

Marsch felt idiotic talking to the decal on his temple. Seconds later though, a vision of SOB Security Ops popped up in holographic clarity before his eyes.

"Senior Chief Marsch, is that you?"

"Yes, Lance Corporal. Report!"

"Aye, Commander. The Captain has ordered the ship to general quarters, Condition-2. The SOB is on Red Alert. All nonessential personnel have been recalled. The Captain and the ambassadors have returned to the ship as well. Base security has locked down all buildings and is standing-by. All first response ARTs teams have teleported to the surface and are combat ready. Sir, the Exec says we may have a possible Lizard probe operating in local space. Command, Control, Countermeasures, and Intelligence C^3I data from CIC suggests that a probe may have soft-landed near the mountains. Confidence is high. The Exec says she's not sure of that determination and that you are to exercise full discretion and take the initiative concerning any surface action. What are your orders, Commander?"

"Set Condition Alpha-1. Go EM-silent after advising the ship as well. Begin deep-field passive EM-sweeps. Inform XO Cummings that he's to have one of the light transports, one of the beta fortresses, sent down for team insertion. Find Master Chief Deering and tell her to muster a recon-in-force team for Ibeetu dawn deployment. They are to proceed to an LZ six klicks into grid reference B-3-Alpha and rendezvous with me and a Compact assault force. Copy that, Daniels?"

"Yes, Sir. Relaying, closing down, and going EM-silent, aye, aye, Sir," Lance Corporal Daniels said.

The Compact commlink impressed Marsch. Rather than project an image up from an omni's surface, this device projected a panoramic 3d image of incoming video onto his corneas. It also let him set a transparency value to the streaming video. He fiddled with the controls by wagging his eyebrows and found a setting that made the data stream turn as transparent as a ghost or as solid as a wall.

"Melkorka, I think this probe is mobile, one that lands, scans an area, moves some distance, and takes another scan. It can't transmit to a nearby Lizard ship without being detected from orbit and blown to atoms. I think it stores sensor data and then couriers it back to some small ship, certainly nothing much larger than a cutter or a frigate. Assume it has already pre-sighted the two surface operating bases for a land assault and is now gathering useful intel on our equipment and personnel. I want to reconnoiter in force along the probe's projected baseline course, try to find it on the ground, and destroy it. I'm going to meet up with my ARTs teams on this side of the mountains. We'll cross the rock slides and peel pairs off at regular intervals along its baseline entry track, while another, stealthier force moves in strength parallel to that baseline."

Marsch paused, looked into her large, bright amber eyes. "I want you to assemble that force and have it move out with me on that objective."

"By your command," Melkorka said. Marsch planned a surface action as sire cairn. In the absence of a warleader, a battle leader organized combat operations and provided the necessary male focus.

She pricked her ears and flicked her pons at Phelindra, and the Eldest Huntress strutted off to recruit more bodies for Marsch's reconnaissance force.

Marsch stared at his feet and swore. He had worn little to the Death Song rite. He wore sandals, of all things! He hoped the ARTs remembered to have his equipment sent down on the beta.

Phelindra called out to him. She brought twenty with her, a mix of Hunters and Warriors. He recognized more of them now. He matched names to them by using their tribal colors and skin patterns as reminders. It was easy, even for him, to tell the difference between Hunters and Warriors. There were body mass distribution differences between the two female phenotypes, and they had distinctive facial differences, too. A Hunter's nasal bones formed a broad and short, flat muzzle that sloped up and fused into her forehead, and her skull was more oval, like a blunted football. A Warrior's skull was rounder, and her nasal structures narrower, more humanlike, giving her eyes a recessed, almost masklike quality. Some of the Eyloni, however, had skin patterns and tribal colors that were nearly identical to him, and that made it harder to keep their identities straight in his head. Marsch knew that their clothing and color schemes, and the knot patterns across their breasts, had rank significance that he could only guess at. If he included Phelindra and Kidahin, he had a total of thirteen Hunters and nine Warriors.

"We are ready to participate in surface stealth operations!" Phelindra reported. To him, surprisingly, and not to Melkorka.

Marsch nodded to the Eldest Huntress. He walked up to her, and they formed a circle around him. Each brushed her tail against him. Many clumsy caresses groped behind him, expecting to brush a tail. They crowded him, and Kidahin snarled at them, twisting past bodies to regain her place near him.

Marsch watched her glare at them, and him. He thought her reaction to them seemed odd. He clasped her bare shoulders a moment before turning to inspect the group Phelindra had brought.

The Hunters wore narrow flint knives curved below their left breasts as all Eyloni females did, but they also wore large daggers that hung from leather sheaths laced to their thighs. Each wore her webbed rank earring and the decal commlink in her left ear. Marsch noticed that for the first time they wore wooden shoes. They looked like sculpted clogs milled from polished fine black wood. Each wore a small pouch diagonally from shoulder to waist.

And they carried bows and arrows.

The Warriors wore similar items, but they also carried short, broad bladed, dull black ceramic swords that reminded him of Roman short swords. They wore bracers on their forearms. Two of them even wore bucklers, small shields the size of a large dinner plate. No Warrior carried the simple recurve bows and bow quivers the Hunters carried, although the bundle of spears carried by one Warrior would make excellent pikes.

Swords and knives Marsch understood. Never underestimate the utility of a good blade, but pikes and bows? They must be ceremonial. Perplexed, he asked Melkorka about the Eyloni's nostalgic interest in archaic weaponry.

Melkorka gave him a crash course in Compact battle doctrine. They used EM emitters to fry enemy weapon electronics before charging into battle in either open field or set piece deployment.

Marsch nodded. The Eyloni viewed battle as a personal matter, an individual's exercise of valor, bravery, and honor. Kidahin had already given him an idea of a female's ready response to a male singing voice, and Marsch realized he would have to decline the SOG standard weapons his ARTs would certainly bring to the rendezvous site. He would not insult Eyloni customs, and he didn't want to look incompetent or weak in their eyes.

"You do know," he pointed out, "that my ARTs team members use modern weapons, don't you?"

"Of course," Melkorka's voice sang from the other side of the room. "Our standard briefings on Coalition combat tactics stressed your use of such weapons. We do understand that you have your own battle doctrines just as honorable as ours. But you are sire cairn. You carry many blades yourself, and you lead an elite combat force. You do not fear personal close combat. You have never carried an energy weapon in all the times you came to us."

Great, Marsch griped to himself. He was no coward, but dammit, why risk your life in melee combat when you could blow the enemy's head off from seventy meters away? He was a pragmatic combat veteran, and he consistently applied the practical lessons of his family's folklore. Those stories said that the gods and goddesses never disposed of guile if it won them the victory in the end.

The Eyloni needed him to fulfill the role of male battle leader. Under battle conditions, his presence would allow them to access the instinct that drove them to deadly combativeness, and he would care for them while they fought locked in single-minded obsession over his safety. He thought of them as his unit, but the worry he felt for them did not manifest in the usual posttraumatic stress symptoms that gripped him at times like these. Those symptoms hadn't bothered him for the past few training exercises, either.

They searched for a probe, a mechanism, and not a ground force. Both the Eyloni and his ARTs teams had enough firepower to shoot down a probe. When they found it, they could even paint it with targeting lasers. Either ship could then lock onto and destroy it with their energy weapons, since the probe lacked the mass to mount EM Faraday countermeasures sufficient to deflect a particle beam fired from a combat vessel.

"You do plan to take appropriate arms to shoot down a probe, don't you? I don't see anything honorable in personal combat with a device," Marsch told Phelindra.

Battle Language flashed among the Eyloni. Some spared a moment to fire glares at him, disapproving ones. Fingers flashed with greater fury. Phelindra gave him a bewildered look and then recited a list of equipment she planned to issue, the mobile platform weapons they would take, who would operate them, and the qualifications each had in the weapons issued. By the time she finished, Marsch had committed the list of assets to memory and was considering how he might integrate them into his plans.

Odd, but that was the longest speech he'd ever heard from Phelindra. He never had the need to speak with her at length before, but it sounded to him like her standard was almost as good as Kidahin's.

Funny, but Melkorka's words sounded as good as Kidahin's did, now.

Nah, I've just gotten used to them.

Marsch no longer paid much attention to the imaginary cobwebs brushing his face.

Kidahin found herself in a dilemma. She belonged with Phelindra's stealth striking group, but she also wanted to remain with Marsch. She knew he had to lead his own elite combat forces. She went everywhere with him, but she knew the difference between training and deployment.

Marsch planned a combat action, and she already had a standing combat assignment. Aboard her warship and during Battle Status, she was the backup command center navigator and the Mistress of Pathwalking's second. On surface deployments, she was a stealth strike team member under Phelindra's command. She must report to the Eldest Huntress, and only the sire cairn could countermand that assignment.

Marsch played out deployment options in his head. He glanced at the Eyloni gathering nearby and froze. Possessed, he had the sudden wild urge to reach out and touch them. He ran a hand across Phelindra's shoulder and down her bare, burnt orange and crimson red muscular back to her tail, tracing her yellow variegations with his finger. Her skin felt like fine velour left to warm in the sun, soft and warm over hard muscle. She turned into the caress, brought her tail up, and coiled it around his forearm.

He read her touch as a 'no' gesture and tried to pull back. Her puzzled expression distracted him long enough for the others to act. They arrayed themselves around him and insisted he touch them in a set order, Kidahin last.

The fussy display of precedence gave Marsch an idea of how each female's hierarchical rank in the group meshed. Strange as it was, the intricacy of webbing in their earrings didn't always match their place in line.

"All right Phelindra, break out the equipment and have everyone get what they need. I want to move out and meet up with the ARTs teams at dawn. Grab some carbohydrates and water and return."

"By your command," Phelindra said. She turned and led her team from the base security center.

Kidahin held back and gave Marsch a forlorn appeal. Phelindra paused and snapped at her, a suggestion wrapped around the core of a command.

Kidahin had no choice. Marsch was sire cairn over all Eyloni females on the surface. He gave Phelindra an order she had acknowledged in the formal ritual manner. He had made no special provisions for her.

She turned to follow, and Marsch reached out to hug her. She wrapped her tail around him. Breaking the embrace, he looked into her eyes, and she nodded.

She was to accompany Phelindra.

Kidahin flipped her ears in assent and joined an impatient Eldest, who gave her a brief, soft scold for distracting the sire cairn during battle planning.

Fifteen minutes later, they left the Compact FOB and headed into the predawn forest. Sunrise would break over the horizon in about thirty-five minutes, and Marsch wanted to cover as much ground as possible: he had a mission to complete. He reviewed what they knew: an enemy probe lurked nearby. It couldn't snoop from orbit or local space without risking detection. That meant covert surface scans. The probe would likely use passive sensors, otherwise either ship could pinpoint its first active scan and relay its exact location.

He didn't like it.

A bogy this small spied on places like naval yards or surface emplacements and not here, of all places. A smart probe should have noticed the absence of permanent garrisons, naval bases, orbital shipyards, or planetary defense systems. If a small enemy vessel, say a frigate, lingered within the system, then a probe mission was inefficient. Better the enemy ship jumps into normal space behind the gas giant and below the arc of sensor sweeps, takes active readings using its more powerful scanners, and jumps back into subspace at the end of its sweep before either warship could acquire a firing solution and destroy it. And why scan the moon's surface, anyway? The tactician in Marsch would have been far more interested in the combat effectiveness of a battle-damaged Compact warship and an undamaged Coalition carrier.

No, pissing around on the surface made no strategic sense. *Could there be a tactical reason?*

The rising sun in mostly clear turquoise skies reminded Marsch of dawns on Earth, minus the green tints. The two groups met at the prearranged rendezvous point. Shadows retreated up the mountains as the joint combat force swept along the ground, following the probe's estimated overhead flight path.

Marsch told Phelindra to make the projected flight path her baseline and move out below it in a scattered parallel formation. He and his ARTs would follow them, pairs peeling off at regular perpendicular intervals in their wake.

His teams brought him an ARTs pack and Type-II uniform, six throwing knives and bandolier, and an additional two combat knives. He declined the M-414 particle weapon, the M-88 rifle, the 9mm, and the omni, preferring to use the Eyloni commlink.

He dropped the rolled piano keyboard into the pack along with a field combat scanner. Called a combat omnipad, or 'pad for short, it was a soldier's best friend and a necessity. Slightly larger than an omni, it could scan and analyze data in battlefield situations. It lacked the omni's commlink, but it outperformed an omni when it came down to scanning and computation. It was a need item, not a want item like the piano. That he could leave behind, but the idea of playing for the Compact force when he reached the Failsafe rendezvous point appealed to him.

Shadows vanished as the sun sped over the mountains. Different trees grew along the search path. They had low branches covered with oval, marine green, rough leathery leaves with silvery undersides. The bark curled from the trunks like birch did, resembling stiff burlap. The trees' roosting avian reptiles complained like scolding squirrels as they passed beneath their territory. Vines resembling holly covered the forest floor. Their leaves spanned both hands put together, the twelve points on each leaf gave them their holly-like resemblance.

And like jungle terrain everywhere, the low branches, large leaves, and twisting vines made travel on foot difficult. They intertwined, making natural fences and snares, or they ran along the ground like gnarled fingers, making footing uncomfortable, slippery, and uncertain. Marsch gazed after the Compact Light Armored Vehicle with a bit of envy.

The Compact LAV reminded him of a black robotic carpenter ant. Six-legged, possessing mandibles and bug eyes, the comparison was uncanny. A driver and a gunner rode in the thing's head, and the Eyloni operating mobile weapons platforms, door gunners, and point gunners rode in and above the LAV's thorax. A few others, Hunters, scouted around and ahead of the vehicle while his ARTs team pairs peeled off one at a time from the main group and followed their preassigned lissajous search patterns. Marsch's team buddy, Private First-Class Serena Nadine Butcher, a nineteen-year-old volunteer from the United Earth Army, took point and moved out. He watched her for a time before turning back to reconsider the vines.

Time passed and still no probe. He doubted it would be flying much with two warships blanketing the area with active scans. It dare not transmit, and flight risked discovery. That should make this about the easiest search and destroy mission Marsch ever had. Eventually they'd find it. Unless it had already fled into subspace. *No. Sensors would have detected a Cherenkov spike. What if it could navigate the forest floor?*

Marsch spat. That was all he needed. A mobile probe. They'd have to get close enough to detect its power source EM emissions.

Marsch hated the amount of time the search was eating up. Too bad *Henri Edda* couldn't vector them in from orbit. They couldn't, of course. A target this small operated at low power and was shielded for stealth operations. It could elude scanners so long as it didn't expend too much power or call attention to itself.

It took some time for Marsch and Butcher to reach the outside edge of their search pattern. They scanned the length of a spiraling outer loop that would swing them back around to the baseline some two klicks from the Compact Failsafe point. What little mountain shade that remained had vanished in the noon sun, and yellow light fell across the forest, striking large, scattered trees. Among them, the holly vines thrived in the ample sunlight. The farmer in Marsch wondered if the soil retarded the tree growth here, or if the numerous large rocks below the surface prevented good root growth. He leaned over and poked at the dirt, and saw Butcher hesitate.

"Private?" Marsch inquired, alert.

"Commander, something just registered for a second on my 'pad, but I've lost it, I'm not picking up anything now, not even normal background radiation!"

Marsch checked his own 'pad.

He cursed. The scanner didn't even register the sunlight. "Did you get a directional fix?"

"Yes, Sir. Surface contact, bearing 103 degrees, 2,960 meters, stationary object massing 56 metric tons."

"Roger that," Marsch said, "We've stepped into a nullification field. That means no commlink or scanner transmission or reception."

He backed up a few meters and tried a second scan. "No joy. The null field must have just activated."

Proximity activation? It had to be. A scan would have registered on Serena's 'pad before it died. That meant it had to be close.

"Move out, Private. Let's see if we can take this sucker out," Marsch said.

"Yes, Sir!" she said. She moved, rifle at the ready. Cautious, they worked their way through a kilometer of thinning forest without incident.

"Commander!" Butcher yelled. "My 'pad's back up and registering a strong continuous transmission being beamed into space!"

Marsch activated the comm device on his temple and called his ARTs. "Break EM-silence. Surface contact! Target that transmission and fire!"

"By your command!"

Wait. *Melkorka?*

Oh, dammit! The Compact comm gear. Melkorka must have reset it to the Compact tactical frequency by remote command.

***

Melkorka turned to the command fire control station.

"Mistress of Tactics, lock forward primary weapons onto that transmission source and fire when target acquired!"

"Affirm, acting!" Hlinlodyn replied. She pinpointed the hot transmitter's location and fired particle weapons designed to tear a shielded warship apart.

Melkorka watched the salvo punch through the moon's atmosphere and rake the surface. Intense satisfaction passed through her as the twelve-ell-wide beam plowed a furrow into the jungle floor.

If anyone in the warship's command center felt it odd that they had obeyed an order to direct offensive action against a target from a male not their warleader, none voiced it aloud.

***

"Captain! Tight-beam transmission from the surface directed into deep space detected, Sir!" Lieutenant Romaine reported.

"The probe?" Winters asked.

"Can't be anything else, Sir," Romaine said.

"Exec, prepare to fire on that transmission source!"

"Aye, Captain. Fire Control, bridge…"

"Sir," Romaine interrupted, "Message from the surface, Compact surface-to-ship commlink."

"On speakers, Lieutenant!" Winters ordered.

"Aye, Sir."

"…tact. Target that transmission and fire!"

"What the hell?" Winters muttered.

"Del!" the co-ambassadors sang out together.

"I wonder why…" Anlann began.

"Captain, the Compact ship is powering up her primary weapons!" Rodgers reported.

"Anlann?" Winters asked, glancing at the co-ambassador.

"Sir! The Compact ship is firing on the signal source."

"On screen!" Winters demanded.

"Aye, Captain."

They watched as *Hunter's Moon*'s offensive armament struck the moon's surface. The 6.6 petajoule-per-second bursts would vaporize everything that was not at least moderately shielded.

Melkorka's swift action impressed Winters. Marsch, now that was quite a different story. If the Senior Chief wanted to order up a fire mission, he should have made the request to him and not to Melkorka.

Seralin could not believe it. Marsch had ordered a Compact warship to take offensive action. Not the surface action party, but the warship himself. No male gave an order to a warship unless he was his warleader. That Melkorka had obeyed the order shocked her. That the Mistress of Tactics had carried it out boggled her mind.

Anlann blinked, looked around the human warship's command center, and shrugged. He deemed the action appropriate. Marsch ordered the warship to engage in offensive fire, and the crew had carried out that order. He could well imagine Melkorka's understandably trigger-happy feelings in the wake of the deaths they had suffered. Marsch had sounded insistent. He was the first male on-scene, and he was the sire cairn. Melkorka weighed the risky delay in relaying the request to Winters rather than fire on the target herself. She made a tactical decision that saved time. That made so much sense to him, and he explained his theory to Seralin.

Seralin ignored the activity around her and fought to make sense of Anlann's words. Yes, it was true that Marsch had ordered immediate fire support; yes, it was true that Melkorka needed no formal order to fire on a suspected Ni'zakhonii probe; yes, it was true that the time taken to transfer the request to Winters would have delayed the fire mission; and yes, it was true that Marsch was in command of the surface action as sire cairn. But he did not command the warship. Even a sire cairn had to ask, and Marsch had *ordered*.

11

RESIGNATION

Phelindra watched the pale beam pierce the turquoise sky, heard its deafening percussive clap. It struck the jungle floor not far from where Marsch prowled his search loop. They had heard him transmit the fire order over their comm gear. As sire cairn, Marsch had the authority to request fire support from their warship. He had first male on-scene precedence, and so he had Warpact command over both the surface mission and any vessel that supported the surface mission. Marsch's order, and Melkorka's response to it, followed her people's laws and customs. *Sort of.* Her warship had no warleader to join with him in Warpact, no male for Marsch to give the fire order to.

She sang a command to her assault force and as they moved out from Failsafe, her LAV took incoming fire.

Marsch listened to the strike's fading rumble as an anxious voice replaced it.

"Del? Melkorka. Acknowledge."

"Go ahead, Melkorka."

"Can you confirm target destroyed?"

"Negative. I'm moving in to check out the strike zone now. Put a teleport trace on us just in case."

"By your command," she said and relayed the trace order to the Mistress of Conveyance.

"Keep your comm open, Del," Melkorka commanded.

"Copy that. Proceeding with caution."

"Winters to Marsch, come in, Senior Chief!" Winters's voice snarled over the Compact tactical channel.

"Marsch here, go ahead Captain."

"Kindly make your report to me, Senior Chief, and not to Mistress Melkorka!"

"Aye, aye, Captain. Sir, we're approaching the target area. The ground's been pretty well chewed…"

Thump!

Marsch felt more than heard the muffled concussion. His skin tingled with prickly heat sensations.

"Marsch to Winters, come in, Captain."

No response. Static crackled and hummed over the open channel.

Marsch pulled out his 'pad and scanned the area. The 'pad registered an ionization field in the immediate area. He smelled damp iron, a whiff of ozone, probably a by-product of the warship's strike.

No, that wasn't all. The 'pad's combat analyzer reported that the blast wake alone could not account for the residual electromagnetic interference. The weapon strike had been northwest of him, but the weak pulsed EM field came out of the southwest, about where Phelindra waited for his staggered ARTs recon pairs to arrive—the Failsafe rallying point.

"Come on, Butcher, we gotta get to Failsafe!"

"Yes, Sir!"

Failsafe designated their baseline's terminal end. Each ARTs pair's search lobe ended up there. The Compact force both held it and served as a reserve force just in case an ARTs pair found something too big to handle. When Marsch had sent his ARTs off on their separate lissajous search patterns, he staggered their deployment so that the first pair sent would arrive last, and the last pair—he and Butcher—would arrive at Failsafe first. If a critical situation developed, standard operating procedure demanded that the ARTs pairs break off their individual search loops and proceed directly to Failsafe for a mission update unless ordered to do otherwise. He and Butcher had the shortest search lobe and were the closest pair to the Compact force.

"Commander? My skin tingles like I just laid in fireweed," Butcher said.

Damn! That was the initial warning sign of an antipersonnel EM pulse! Marsch imagined a straight line back to Failsafe and knew that the Compact force had taken the brunt of an AP strike.

Kidahin!

He had to save his daughters!

✦✦✦

"Captain," Commander Rodgers said, "CIC has analyzed the probe's signal."

"Report, Exec," Winters said.

"Aye, Sir. Captain, signal analysis has failed to detect any data in the transmission. The probe sent a continuous stream of white noise."

"White noise?" Winters echoed.

"Yes, Sir. Signal processing algorithms analyzing the transmission found only a powerful carrier containing a broadband random static signal at maximum peak power. Signal scrubbers found no information pattern or encryption telltales. Data analysis suggests there are similarities between this signal and the pulse modulated transmissions some distress beacons use, but this transmission didn't even pulse the carrier."

Winters digested her report. Why would the probe give itself away by signaling at best that it had been discovered or at worst dared them to shoot it down?

A decoy? It had to be!

"Marsch, data analysis suggests a decoy. Marsch? Senior Chief, acknowledge!" Winters said.

"Negative contact, Captain," Lieutenant Romaine said.

"An artifact of the weapon strike?" Rodgers asked.

"Unknown, but I don't think so, Ma'am."

"Captain, this EM field scatters comm signals. It is fading, but it will take another twenty minutes or so before intelligible ship-to-surface comm traffic can get through," Romaine said.

"Understood, Lieutenant."

Winters knew he'd have actionable intel from the surface soon, but he didn't like it. He wanted information now, not several minutes from now. Guessing was both a bad habit and a poor way to drive combat operations. Why would a decoy probe break comm silence? Marsch must have somehow prompted the device to transmit. That led directly to Marsch ordering a fire mission before the thing could complete its transmission.

"Judith? Could the Eyloni have destroyed the probe before it began transmitting data?"

"You think the white noise alerts the Lizards to an incoming data stream?" she asked.

"I do. If so, then it's possible that no data transmission took place, but it is also possible that the signal lasted long enough to alert them to an incoming transmission. What does the signal path tell us?"

"Lieutenant Romaine?" Rodgers asked, yielding to the communications officer's expertise.

"Yes, Ma'am," Romaine said. "As you know, Sir, the Lizards lack hyperlink communications technology. They're stuck using courier ships. I cross-checked Lieutenant Carstairs's navigation data and projected the signal path out of the system. An on-station courier ship receiving the signal would likely run for the closest system, Chi Eridani, seven light-years away. The system is part of a frontier group of stars situated between Compact and Lizard territories, but this close to Compact space, the Lizards can't have much there. Chi Eridani's likely the staging area used by the destroyers that attacked *Hunter's Moon*. They probably have a communications intelligence asset based there. They either sent the probe directly from there, or they could even have sent a frigate here to operate the probe in real time tasking. If it were me, I'd hide my surveillance asset somewhere in this system's heliopause and wait for the probe's signal and then courier the intel back to Chi Eridani for combat analysis. A Lizard ship under V-band FTL velocity could travel from here to there and back again in about four days, including the time it would take the signal to reach the courier ship from here."

She paused, "Captain? The Compact warship is hailing us."

"Ship-to-ship, Lieutenant."

"Aye, Sir. Channel open."

Winters looked up as Melkorka's severe features formed on the main viewscreen.

"This is Captain Winters. How may I help you, Mistress Melkorka?"

"Captain, we have detected an EMP ionization anomaly on the surface near the destroyed probe that hinders tactical comm traffic. Have you been able to contact Del or the others?"

"No, Mistress," Winters said. "I'm waiting for the ionization wake to clear. I've a mind to send down a beta fortress with fighter escort and have it fly over the area and pull out Senior Chief Marsch and his ARTs teams. I'll pull your people out too, so long as they don't mind crowding up a bit. I shall do so if I can't establish communications in the next twenty minutes."

Winters didn't want to send the beta in yet. A beta fortress might give away the ARTs teams and create a hot LZ if a Lizard ship got a trace on it.

✦✦✦

Marsch and Butcher sprinted through the jungle toward Failsafe and the Compact assault force. They wound through the exhausting heavy forest coverage for several minutes before Butcher saw movement.

"*Sir!* Lizard at your seven o'clock!" she hissed and grunted as she dove for cover under the knee high, broadleaf holly-like vines.

Marsch followed her lead and scrambled under leafy cover, busting his knees on the knobby vines. He looked between pointy leaves and thought that they'd make ideal sniper cover.

"Commander! Eleven o'clock! What is that?"

Marsch tore his eyes from the patrolling Lizards, looked where she pointed, and froze.

A ship squatted in the aquamarine field. It was about the size of a Light Attack Craft. Marsch peered out from under the vines and studied the ship's lines. It looked as if two mottled green and maroon pitcher plants had been fused at their base and bent into a bulbous horseshoe. The two pitcher's liplike openings flared forward, suggesting a double bow design. It rested in slight profile, and the starboard side and aft view gave him enough perspective to guess that it was about 25 meters tall, 60 meters long, and had a 30-meter average beam.

Butcher watched the Lizards while he made notes as best his obscured vantage point allowed. The aft area resembled a bladder made from two bulbous casings fused into a single oblong oval. It reminded him of someone bent over a desk, mooning him. Atop the aft section, three domed blisters sat like boils, one at the top of each cheek, and a larger one sat in the center, on the tail bone. The center blister was easily twice the size of the other two combined.

I bet the center dome is probably the ship's bridge, Marsch speculated.

The LAC sat on the ground. He could see no landing gear or other support struts. It just sat there, pressing reeds into the hard soil. Now he knew what had pressed the tight crescent into the forest meadow's reeds. A large bay hatch stood open to the ground. The bay door resembled a huge iris about where a grafted pitcher plant's roots would attach. Puckered wrinkles and ridges radiated away from the opening like the stripes on a gourd radiated away from its blossom end. The bottom edge met the ground, forming a wrinkled exit ramp.

Lizards were carrying Eyloni bodies into the ship.

Where was the Eyloni LAV?

"Butcher, they got the drop on the Eyloni somehow. I don't see any evidence of a firefight. I think the antipersonnel EMP blast took 'em out."

"Looks that way to me too, Commander," she agreed. "I think we got here just in time to see them take the last of them aboard, Sir. They might still have a few more coming in from a field recon sweep. I don't see the Eyloni's antlike LAV. You'd think it would be shielded against antipersonnel EMP. The Lizards must have taken it out."

Marsch looked out from false holly leaves and nodded. The Eyloni couldn't be dead, except for maybe the LAV's driver and gunner. Lizards ate their prey alive, not dead, not even fresh dead.

He had an idea.

"Butcher, back up forty meters and then swing out in a flanking arc to our seven o'clock. I want one of them!"

"Yes, Sir!"

He had to save Kidahin. She was a Hunter. As a stalker, she wouldn't have been in the LAV. She was his responsibility. He had given his word to Melkorka. He was responsible for all of them!

But first he had to kill a Lizard quietly and get aboard the LAC before they sealed the bay.

Marsch and Butcher backed off under the vines as fast as possible before ranging out into the most probable return path that an enemy patrol would take.

Ten minutes later, Butcher saw one.

"Straggler, Commander, bearing 220 degrees true, about 60 meters."

"I see it. Good eyes, Butcher. Okay, assume it has a working comm and a ranged weapon. You stay here and keep watch for its buddies. Don't fire on it! This close, the LAC's proximity scanners will detect the discharge and target you with AP fire. If we're lucky, it's the last one reporting in. Just sit tight."

"Yes, Sir."

Now it gets dicey. He had to take the Lizard out before it got too close to its ship, put on its equipment, and get aboard before the bay door closed. He couldn't enter the ship once it had sealed. He didn't know the hatch codes, or even if the iris opened from the outside. Ship's security argued against that option. He didn't dare pantomime a bad comm unit to gain entry, either. He didn't know where to face to signal the bay officer, and he didn't want that kind of attention anyway.

Marsch closed on his target. He assessed the Lizard and its equipment. It wore a flexible field suit made from monofilament carbon nanotube graphine bundled into course threads and wove into a pliable auxetic material. It would resist punctures and would not cut. The enemy wore boots and gloves made from the same mottled green material. A hood of the same stuff formed a cowl over the Lizard's head, resembling a broad, shallow snorkel with pleated necklines. A visor covered its eyes. Marsch saw a hideous knife at its side that reminded him of an old-fashioned clothes iron. The iron's base flared out into a blade like a sharp pack shovel. The Lizard held a particle weapon sidearm at the ready.

How was he to get a kill shot on the armored Lizard using the old saber he carried?

He was running out of time. Bay security would see the returning Lizard in seconds.

How do I hit it?

The Lizard stood almost as tall as a man, but bulkier. The one vulnerable spot he could see, the unprotected open mouth, drew his attention.

Yep, that's the sweet spot. The Lizard had a round head, like a large bowling ball, with a wide jaw running from earhole to earhole. The jaw unhinged, allowing it to bite off chunks like a small shark. At full extension, it would look as if someone had cut a quarter slice from a large cantaloupe and peeled it down. The seed ball at the center marked the gullet. Just remove the slice's flesh and replace it with shark teeth. The open lower jaw would stretch the pleated neck of the field suit, which told him about how far the Lizard could open its mouth.

The Lizard paralleled him now, and that meant Marsch would have to throw his knives perpendicular to its direction of travel. He thought he could plant at least one heavy throwing knife in the back of its throat as soon as it turned to face him. He would bury the blade into its gullet and hope that he hit either the spinal cord or a major artery.

If it opens its jaw wide enough!

Marsch closed the distance. He had less than thirty seconds before they crossed into an unobstructed view of the ship. Pulling two knives from the bandolier, he turned and rushed the Lizard, clicking his tongue as he ran.

The Lizard snapped around, its sidearm swinging up, its mouth opening in reptilian reflex. It closed on Marsch faster than he thought possible. He stopped, stood there, heart pounding, as the Lizard charged. He imagined the smell of rotten flesh in its mouth, the sweetish smell of blood, the sickening stench of the carnivore. This thing stood between him and his daughters! He threw the first and, then an instant later, the second heavy knife.

They tumbled through the air before arrowing into the Lizard's gaping mouth. Barely clearing the creature's shark-like teeth, they buried themselves halfway to their hilts in the back of its throat. Knife blades nearly a forearm in length stabbed, one below the other, through the base of the creature's skull, severing its spinal cord in two places.

The Lizard dropped as though an off switch had been thrown. Marsch jumped onto it and shoved both blades through the back of the Lizard's neck and yanked them savagely apart before pulling them free.

Marsch waved Butcher over and set about inspecting the alien field suit. The fabric mesh looked like standard field issue for an average Lizard soldier. He saw no plates or hard surfaces fastened to it. The field suit itself bent at odd angles and snapped together using magnetic fasteners. The Lizard's sidearm had a multi-claw trigger that made it impossible for human or Eyloni fingers to fire, assuming the weapon had no biometric safety device to prevent its unauthorized use. The field suit was about his size, but built to accommodate the gait, posture, and upper body musculature of a bipedal reptile.

Marsch removed the suit's cowl and visor. The Lizard's hide glistened like a gleaming apricot in the sun. A short bony crest jutted from the top of its head. The hornlike thing looked about the size of a man's fist. It had been smoothed into a short-tapered end like a polished unicorn horn's stump, and he wondered if it had been a part of some rite. The Lizard had heavy brow and eye socket ridges filled with red, unlidded compound eyes—bug-eyed bug eyes—the size of tennis balls. It had no snout and no nose, just two vertical slits for air holes. Its chest jutted out; its sternum pointed away from the torso like the apex of a triangular prism, making its chest appear wedge-like.

"Hurry up and help me strip this suit!" Marsch demanded.

Butcher unsnapped magnetic fasteners and helped him pull the coverall garment from the Lizard. She tried not to be a wimp in the company of the Special Operations Group commander, but more than enough adrenaline pumped through her veins at the moment. It made her jumpy, and that made her testy.

"What are you going to do, Commander?"

Time was Marsch's enemy now. He had to pass himself off as a late returnee, but he couldn't arrive so late that he'd invite either a challenge from the bay officer, or a reprimand from a superior.

"I'm going after them," Marsch snarled.

"*You?* How? Are you going insane?" Butcher asked.

"No, I'm going in disguise," he said and nodded at the Lizard's field suit.

"In *that* thing?" Butcher swore. "You're crazy! It won't fit. This Lizard is thicker than you and has an inverted V-shaped breastbone. You'd never pass for one on close inspection."

"I don't have time to argue, Private."

Marsch swore under his breath and stripped to his tan shorts.

"Here, shove my Type-IIs and field pack around me here, here, and here. Fill the damn thing out. Now, strap the helmet to my rear to fill in where its stumpy tail goes. Pull the piano from its pouch and activate it. Mute the sound system. Good. Now, stick it on its edge along the suit's chest V-slot and strap it to me. No, no, set it against my chest so it gives the illusion that my sternum juts out more forward. That's it, good," he encouraged.

"You can't do it, Commander. You're Coalition military. You're going to try and take over a Lizard military asset. That's an act of war! The Compact is not an ally of the Coalition."

Her ridiculous retort caught him off guard.

And she was right. The Compact wasn't a formal Coalition ally. Yet. If he attacked the Lizard ship while serving in the Coalition Fleet, he'd commit an act of war in its name.

"You are absolutely right, Private Butcher. Give me a piece of paper and your grease pencil."

"Yes, Sir."

"I'm issuing you written orders. Private First-Class Butcher, you will get out of jamming range and contact the ship. Report my actions to Captain Winters and tell him that I hereby resign from Coalition Fleet service. Tell him that I ordered you to tell the Compact co-ambassadors that I'm going after Kidahin and the others, and I'll bring them back. Tell the Captain that I have ordered you to report to Melkorka in person and give her my saber as both proof of my words and as confirmation of my actions. Do you understand?"

"Yes, Sir. Resign, Sir?"

"Yes, Serena, I resign, effective immediately. Now get going. Make your report so Melkorka will know what's happened to her crew. Go on now, I have to save my daughters!"

"Yes, Sir," Butcher said doubtfully. *Daughters?* But the look in Marsch's eyes made further comment unnecessary and warnings of the consequences of her failure superfluous. She stood, dazed, and watched her former commander shuffle off toward the enemy ship's open bay.

Marsch hurried as best he could and wondered just how far behind the last returning Lizard he was. He tried putting on more speed and still walk with the pelvis-twisting gait of a fellow Lizard. It was tough going. The Lizard's field suit stank of snake musk. It made him want to gag. The visor threw off his depth perception, and the compound eye focal lengths blurred his field of view. He had at best another forty meters to go.

Marsch spotted the pile of flint Eyloni knives on his left, the curved ones they always wore beneath their breasts, out of the corner of his eye. Luck had blessed him. Butcher's M-414 would have been more of a comfort, but the LAC's internal security sensors would detect the first particle discharge and pinpoint his location within the ship. The same would apply to her 9mm's loud report. He veered aside and managed a passable casual walk toward the pile, crossed his fingers, and bent over. He grabbed the bundle in a single swoop, opened a magnetic catch in the field suit, and stuffed them into its gaping voids.

Maybe the Lizards watching would think he wanted trophies. The knives remained sheathed and their attached neckwear had tangled them all into a ball. Even so, some of them jabbed and poked at him while others ground between him and the suit.

He turned back to the open bay and saw no one waiting.

The bay door looked more like a mooning man's backside than the mechanical shuttered irises Marsch was familiar with.

He cleared the puckered opening. It formed a seal behind him that looked like a crystal plate made from light green ice marbled with maroon veins. He walked further into the dim compartment. Lights glowed on the walls and on panels throughout the small, sealed bay. Indicators sparkled like rubies, sapphires, emeralds, and diamonds burning with internal fire.

Ahead, the last Lizard and its Eyloni burden stepped through a smaller iris and on into the ship.

Of course! Marsch realized. *I'm in an airlock. I have to go through the inner door to enter the ship.*

He followed. The Lizard would lead him to where they held the others.

The inside hatch started forming crystal layers, closing. Marsch hurried the best he could. Too late! The hatch was sealing before he got there. Lacking options, he shoved his arm through the narrowing aperture and held his breath.

The hatch stopped at once and reopened, re-absorbing the crystal iris back into its frame.

Good, he sighed, *safety override*. Unless in vacuum or under battle conditions, the hatch should open whenever a crewmember passed close enough to the sensor.

He stepped through the interior airlock hatch and planned his next move. Intelligence drove operations. That said, he had no actionable intelligence. Strategy, he knew, was an art and not a science. He had stressed to his ARTs on many occasions that there was no secret formula for victory. The key, he told them, was not to manipulate the enemy. The key was to create circumstances that favored the mission. Whatever circumstances he created here, the odds didn't favor this mission. He likely couldn't deliver on the promise he'd made to Melkorka.

Marsch followed the Lizard from a distance, cautious. He could barely see. The corridor stifled him. It was a warm, damp tunnel that intersected other dim, damp tunnels. The walls glowed here and there with the same crystals he saw in the airlock.

Wet, stale humidity hung in the air, a sauna for snakes. It sapped his strength and magnified the effort it took for him to lug the unwieldy field suit forward. He'd have to ditch it soon. The material didn't breathe, and he couldn't pop the magnetic catches without collapsing the suit's shaky integrity. Only the snorkel opening kept him from suffocating. The dead Lizard's drool and blood masked his human scent some, and he hoped that the spicy yet comforting musky Eyloni scent wafting down the burrow would help.

Burrow, that was it. He lunged his way through a creepy burrow. The ship's interior reminded him of the ropy, seedy insides of a pumpkin, a light green pulp and maroon veined pumpkin. He once read a story to his daughters about a mouse that lived in a discarded jack-o'-lantern. Only here, his daughters weren't mice, he wasn't Mouskin, and this house wasn't golden.

The burrows ran through the ship like grub trails. Glowing multicolored crystal pumpkin seeds lined the walls, shrouded in damp, stringy green pumpkin gore. He reminded himself that the ship used crystals, not plant life, in its structure. Interior iris hatches formed and deformed in rapid crystalline layers, giving them a fleshy, puckered look.

Marsch passed more glowing seed-like jewels without meeting another Lizard. *Where was the crew?* He couldn't stop to examine the crystal controls for fear of losing the Lizard and his Eyloni prisoner.

How long would the Eyloni remain unconscious? He couldn't take the ship by himself. He needed them. The longer he waited for them to regain consciousness, the better his chance of discovery.

Marsch ran through what he remembered of brig procedures. Aboard Coalition ships, a stunned prisoner was taken to the brig, where the stunning agent was neutralized once security locked the prisoner in a holding cell to increase the capture's psychological effect. He hoped the Lizards operated their brig in the same manner.

Deeper and deeper into the maze of tunnels he scrabbled, mindlessly following the clueless Lizard. Marsch felt like a termite following another termite along a chewed-out path. How many Lizards manned this ship, anyway?

If his guessed dimensions were right, then the LAC had a volume of 45,000 cubic meters and a mass of 20,000 metric tons. It shouldn't have more than forty Lizards aboard.

He felt punchy. The air reeked of ripe fruit, a hint of rotting flesh, and snake musk. He cursed and snapped his mind back on task.

Marsch saw the prisoner's dappled orange and red arm twitch. *She's coming out of it!* If she revived soon, then the others should, too.

He picked up speed and closed on the Lizard.

The creature stopped, turned, and faced a closed iris hatch. It touched a blue gem set into the hatch frame. The iris cycled open to admit the Lizard and its prisoner, and Marsch caught the Eyloni in profile as the creature passed through the hatch.

Kidahin!

Deprived of exposure to Eyloni scent for hours now, Marsch suddenly felt the old, familiar, hyperarousal surge within him as adrenaline rushed him toward jumpy awareness. His heart rate doubled, and he fell into a guarded paranoid mentality. The burrow around him took on the dreamy look of Valhalla's open plains. In blind panic, he put on speed and rushed after the Lizard.

Marsch slipped through the hatch and behind the Lizard before it could close. He smelled his daughters. Their strong, combined spicy scents cleared his head and focused his mind. Marsch found himself back on the LAC again. He looked around in momentary confusion, recognizing the ship's brig by its obvious features. Two Lizards stood in a pod on his left, operating the brig's security systems. The control pod and main deck stood five meters above a small bay and its holding cells. The Lizard carrying Kidahin stepped down into the bay, where sixteen others already waited. Those sixteen had removed their field suits and stood there waiting on Kidahin's captor.

He counted nineteen Lizards in total. He bet that over half of the crew stood there waiting for him to kill them.

He glanced into the pod. The two Lizards and their control consoles stood less than ten meters away. Each monitored a table filled with a multicolored matrix of flat, hand-sized crystals. Right now, the Lizards were watching the activity in the cell bay more than they watched their controls.

They paid him even less mind.

Marsch looked down into the cell bay as Kidahin broke free of her reptilian captor.

He glanced again into the pod. Like the Lizards down in the brig bay, they wore no field suits, but they did wear red woven smocks that slipped over their heads like women's nightgowns.

They watched, engrossed, almost hypnotized by the activity below and gave him little more than a second cursory glance.

He turned back in time to watch a Lizard knock Kidahin across the floor. Like a mouse to a cat, she was live food for them, and they intended to make sport of her before devouring her alive.

He heard Eyloni shouts of encouragement echo up from the cells below.

Marsch muttered a prayer to the Giver of Victory, turned to face the two pod guards, his right shoulder in line with Kidahin below, and popped the field suit's magnetic catches.

He pulled two heavy knives from the bandolier and threw one at each Lizard, killing both.

The sudden movement in Kidahin's peripheral vision caught her eye. She threw a distracted glance over the Ni'zakhonii's head and into the pod's wide window.

She could not believe what she saw.

###

United Earth Army Private First-Class Serena Nadine Butcher ran.

Marsch had ordered her to contact the ship ASAP. It didn't matter that he had resigned his warrant. His orders came before he had resigned. Regulations made it clear that his orders remained in effect until countermanded by either SOG XO Cummings or the ship's command staff. Absent new orders, she would do her best to carry out his last.

She wanted to swing left in a half circle and run all the way to the SOB. She knew that the instinct to run toward reinforcements was wrong. That thinking would keep her within the communications blackout zone. She had her orders. She must get clear of the interference and make her report to Captain Winters and the Compact ship's Mistress.

She ran a parallel course heading along the SOB's northwest flank and put the enemy ship and any lingering enemy ground forces to her back.

Minutes passed, and Butcher patted herself on the back for pacing her stride. Distance mattered. Unlike EMP nullification fields, an AP EM-pulse dissipated over a brief time. It also lost strength the farther you got from its emission point. Standard procedure recommended twenty minutes before trying the comm, but the field strength might have faded enough to justify an attempt at contacting the ship.

A low, deep chime reverberated behind her. Butcher turned in time to see a ripple of light from the Lizard ship's jump into FTL.

Impossible! That ship just jumped into FTL from the surface of a planet! If a Coalition ship had tried that, it would enter hyperspace in the same manner a child slung a large bucket of bolts across a garage floor.

"Butcher to *Henri Edda*, Butcher to *Henri Edda*, Buster-99! Buster-99! Buster-99!"

Static whistled and popped back at her.

Butcher pulled her 'pad and scanned the area.

Residual interference from the AP detonation still blanketed the area, but her 'pad reported rapid improvement in the signal-to-noise ratio. Ship-to-surface transmission should be possible soon.

Butcher ran another two minutes and tried the comm again. "Butcher to *Henri Edda*, Butcher to *Henri Edda*, Buster-99! Buster-99! Buster-99!" She spoke the code meaning that she had contacted enemy forces and that her Charlie Oscar—her Commanding Officer—had been lost.

"*Henri Edda*," Winters here. "Repeat, Butcher!"

"Yes, Sir! PFC Butcher confirming Buster-99. Captain, Lizard LAC and surface party on the ground. Sir, Senior Chief Marsch and the Eyloni are aboard the LAC, Sir."

"Relay that ship's coordinates, Butcher!"

Butcher did so, adding, "Captain, the Lizard ship jumped into FTL just above the treetops. It's gone, Sir. Also, Senior Chief Marsch gave me written orders to brief you, the ambassadors, and the Compact warship's Mistress on the current situation before he stowed aboard the enemy vessel, Sir."

"Private Butcher, are you telling me that Senior Chief Marsch was not captured with the Eyloni?"

"Yes, Captain. Sir, he killed a straggler and put on its field equipment as a disguise. I saw him enter the ship before bugging out per his orders to reach a clear transmission site and make my report."

Butcher heard dead air on the open channel as Winters muted the comm.

He came back on the blower a few minutes later and ordered her to stand-by for immediate teleport.

Ten minutes later, PFC Butcher found herself in the SOG briefing room with XO Cummings, Master Chief Deering, TAC Ops Commander Millford, the Exec, Captain Winters, Ambassador Harrison, and the two Compact co-ambassadors.

Time passed very slowly after that, and Butcher wondered whether the better part of valor would have been to accompany Marsch on his rescue foray. From the moment the debriefing began, Ambassador Harrison hadn't stopped screaming about the Senior Chief's blatant act of war. SOG Acting XO Deering took the ambassador's side. The charge also brought SOG Acting Commander Cummings and TOC Millford to Marsch's defense. They screamed at one another until Mistress Melkorka arrived.

Melkorka entered in her usual manner, which meant she poked her head into the room, flexed her ears in inquiry, and walked on in. Anlann and Seralin stepped up to her, while Captain Winters and Commander Rodgers threatened to have Ambassador Harrison removed and restricted to quarters.

"Warleader Anlann says you have a message from Del for me?" an imposing Mistress of the Ship asked her.

Butcher squirmed under her intense, scrutinizing glare and nodded. She couldn't break her eyes away from the alien woman's gaze.

"Yes, Ma'am," she stammered, more scared of her than the Lizards.

"Captain, do I have permission to report?"

"Carry out Senior Chief Marsch's orders, Private Butcher," Winters said.

"Yes, Sir. Mistress, before Senior Chief Marsch entered the Lizard ship, he ordered me to tell you he went after Kidahin and the others and would return with them. He also told me to give you this sword too, Ma'am," she finished and held the sheathed saber out to her.

Numb, Melkorka stared at the weapon.

Voices erupted around her once again, but Melkorka ignored them. She stared in dumbfounded amazement at Marsch's sword, aware of the co-ambassadors' riveted gazes and perked ears.

The male's sword carried by a Mistress of the Ship certified her rank and symbolized her authority. A warship's mistress always carried the sword while engaged in either her warleader's or her warship's business. When Melkorka sat in her command chair, she had lain Kalinn's sword across her thighs, tail curled around its exposed blade. If she returned holding Marsch's sword, her crew would assume that she, on her own and without their consent, had accepted him as their warleader.

She could not do it.

Every female had to agree to accept Marsch as warleader, and that was not possible because those aboard the Ni'zakhonii ship could not choose. Compact law demanded that a warleader have no prior obligation and not be subject to outlawry. Marsch owed an obligation to the Coalition and his warship. Her people's concept of outlawry applied to him as well. Not in the sense of criminal guilt, but because he had no familial ties to a clan. Without a familial stake in Eyloni culture, he lacked the ties that bound an individual to the people.

Melkorka sadly looked into the young human female's eyes and told her why she must not accept Marsch's sword.

Butcher's face fell, and Anlann intervened on her behalf.

"Melkorka, Del stepped back from Coalition military obligation. Humans choose their obligations and may remove themselves from them with all due honor under special circumstances. Del is no longer attached to this society and is free from obligation."

Melkorka turned wide-eyed to Winters.

"This is truth?" she asked him.

"It is, Mistress. If Marsch commandeers the Lizard ship while in Coalition Fleet service, he commits an act of war against the Lizards. By resigning his rank and duties, the Coalition can renounce his actions as interstellar piracy."

"*Piracy?*" she spat. Snarling in black rage, Melkorka snatched the proffered sword from the human female's grasp and turned toward the closed hatch.

"I am leaving now!" Her voice snapped the deadly command. It could not have been confused with a request. She stalked out, doors closing quietly behind her.

"Well, that certainly went well," Winters commented to the shocked room. Had the deck not been covered with soft graphine plating, Winters was certain that he'd hear the Eyloni's bare feet stomp all the way back to the amidships teleport station.

Seralin sent a worried look at Anlann.

She did not doubt that Melkorka would have much explaining to do when she returned with that sword.

Melkorka thought about her options as she returned to her warship. She did not dare unsheathe the weapon. She must not carry it about, either. She would have to stress she held it in safe keeping until Marsch's eventual return.

Marsch had placed the sword in her care while he rescued members of the warship's society. By sending her the sword, he had clearly declared that he assumed responsibility for the missing females, but not for the warship's society at large. If he returned, she would give his sword back to him at her earliest opportunity.

Del was their sire cairn, after all.

12

EXPEDIENT ACTIONS

Melkorka stalked off the warship's translation platform, heart racing. Her mood had not improved one bit by leaving the Coalition ship.

Piracy! She snarled under her breath. They dared accuse Del of piracy!

The Mistress of Conveyance glared at the curved alien sword in her hand.

Let her! Melkorka sneered.

She stalked onto the command center, demanded a security update, and laid the sword across her command chair's raised armrests. When all mistresses had reported in, she opened the combat address system and told her ship's society what Marsch had done for them. She told them about the Coalition's piracy charge. She told them Marsch had transferred his sword to her through a human female for safekeeping until he returned with their missing females to reclaim it. She told them that Marsch had honorably removed himself from Coalition obligation and engaged the Ni'zakhonii in combat on their behalf.

Melkorka's tail twisted and her ears twitched as she spoke. Her understandable anger drew sympathetic rhythmic growls and hisses from the command center crew. The force of her empathic rage struck them like a fist, further baiting their combative ire.

She slapped a control on her command console.

"Mistress of Saga, transmit log entries concerning this incident to the Compact Counsel."

"Affirm, acting," the chronicler's filtered voice sang over the intercom. It sounded muffled, as though she spoke through clenched teeth.

"Status?" Melkorka demanded.

"We remain at Battle Status. I show a green light on the quantum singularity gravity lensing system," the Mistress of Tactics replied.

"Estimated time until the jump drive is online?"

"Power Systems and Propulsion estimates thirty-two days, Mistress.

Melkorka punched another control and shouted into the address system's pickup.

"Mistress of Sails?"

"Yes, Mistress?" the primary engineer's voice echoed from her command station in Power Systems and Propulsion.

"Jump drive repair has battle priority. Revise your estimate for earliest armature spooling and FTL emergency restart."

Anailiatha paused, considering what repairs could be halted and what effort could be redirected to the jump drive, before she replied. "Twenty-two days, Mistress. We are not waiting for *Fearless*?"

Melkorka ignored the pointed inquiry.

"Implement!"

"Affirm, acting."

"I intend to go after Del," Melkorka told her society.

"Mistress, transit time to the Surutia system is almost eleven days," the Mistress of Pathwalking said.

"I know that, Trebithia! When Del drops the Ni'zakhonii ship out of FTL—probably about halfway there, maybe even less—we must stand ready to jump to that location at a moment's notice."

Melkorka paced the command center, her impatient fury mounting. They were stuck tailchasing here for at least twenty-two TST days, a bit over ten human days, and Marsch needed them in less than three.

Piracy! Her mind grated on the word like a dull knife on gristle.

Marsch's going after Kidahin and the others honored and deeply moved her. He was displaying typical male behavior. That Winters deemed Marsch's selfless act piracy insulted her society, declared them unworthy of a male's attention, and implied his sacrifice worthless.

Marsch had the combat skills of a surface striking force, led by Phelindra, to help him take the enemy ship. Once they took it for him, he need only drop the vessel out of FTL and wait for them to come and get him.

A long fourteen TST day wait for them, a long four Coalition standard day wait for Marsch, adjusting for his longer day and his odd way of counting.

"Mistress of Tactics, once long-range FTL scanning capability is restored, commence sensor sweeps of that ship's most probable course. When Del drops the ship out of FTL, lock onto the radiation spike from the velocity dump and transfer the data to the navigation console."

"Affirm."

"Mistress of Pathwalking, no matter how long it takes, once you receive jump coordinates from the Mistress of Tactics, plot a jump point and prepare to jump us the instant the drive is online."

"Affirm."

♦♦♦

"Lieutenant Romaine, please transmit this message to the Coalition Government," Ambassador Harrison said.

"I'm sorry, Mr. Ambassador," she said, "but any transmission during Condition-2 requires the Captain's authorization."

"Captain Winters!" Harrison shouted.

"Mr. Ambassador?" Winters hedged. *Now what?*

"Order Lieutenant Romaine to transmit this message to the Coalition Government."

"What is the message's purpose and content?" Winters asked.

"Nothing you need concern yourself with, Captain. It's just the usual diplomatic chatter."

"Pursuant to General Order Four 'there shall be no non-military traffic transmitted during battle conditions' Mr. Ambassador. You know that."

"My message *is* military related, Captain!"

"You just said it was a diplomatic message, Mr. Ambassador. Under General Order Four, I have the authority to examine any message and determine whether or not it meets the conditions stipulated in the Order."

"Fine," Harrison said. With bad grace he handed the message omni over to Captain Winters.

Winters read partway through the scrolling text. He stopped, backed the file up to the beginning, and reread it again.

"This…this is…You can't be serious!" Winters thundered while thrusting the omni back at Harrison in disbelief.

"I am absolutely serious, Captain."

"You're advising the Coalition Government to file interstellar piracy charges against Marsch with the Justice Directorate? The charges are baseless, and you know it!"

"Does that matter? I'm trying to find a way to insulate the Coalition from Marsch's illegal military alliance with the Eyloni and his unauthorized assault on a Lizard military asset. I'm not going to risk everything on this 'resignation' of his. I wouldn't believe that story if I were a Lizard. If there is a chance that Marsch's misguided attempt could precipitate open warfare, then I want a diversion that I can dangle in front of them. Better to extradite Marsch to Psi Serpentis as a delaying action until we are ready to fight a war we are not yet ready for."

"We should have already been at war with them, Mr. Ambassador. They've raided our frontier systems seventeen times in the past nine years."

"Occasional terrorist attacks do not warrant hasty declarations of war, Captain!" Harrison said, flicking his hand in dismissal.

"Capturing and eating people alive is not terrorism, Mr. Ambassador. It's obscene!"

"Whatever, Captain. Transmit my message. Now!"

"Permission denied, Mr. Ambassador."

"I insist, Captain."

"I said no, Mr. Ambassador. Get off my bridge."

"You can't order *me* off the bridge, Winters. As the Coalition ambassador, I have free access to the bridge during all ship conditions but Condition-1. Only then can you restrict noncombatants from the bridge."

Seralin and Anlann spun their tails in twists and jabs; their ears were dropping ever lower as they listened to the heated exchange. Marsch had spoken truth: The Coalition did not avenge aggression against its own people. How could the Compact Counsel know if the Coalition would help them avenge an assault on Compact territory?

The co-ambassadors stared dumbfounded at one another before coming to the same unspoken, obvious conclusion: they misunderstood. Ambassador Harrison caused their misunderstanding. He behaved disgracefully and seemed incapable to simple honesty.

They had heard enough.

"I have a suggestion, Ambassador," Anlann offered.

"Oh?" Surprised by the unexpected offer, Harrison smiled. "Go on."

"On behalf of the Compact Counsel, I hereby withdraw the Compact from any diplomatic talks that include your presence."

Harrison, for once at a loss for words, blinked in confusion, stunned.

Anlann turned to Winters and continued in a more cheerful tone. "Captain Winters, once Del captures the Ni'zakhonii ship, the females with him shall declare him the ship's warleader. When he arrives here, he shall have first male on-scene precedence and will hold superior rank to me. He shall hold it because he is the first warleader with his ship and with his female association on site at a military incident. The females with him shall enforce it, and so will the females aboard *Hunter's Moon*. I will surrender my precedence to him, and those females will advise him to accept me into Warpact. From that point on, I am constrained to obey any order Del decides to issue. He will seek my counsel, and when he does, I shall tell him to take *Henri Edda* into Warpact and designate you as the Coalition representative empowered to negotiate with me, captain to Warleader."

Sweating, Winters tried to follow the Eyloni's reasoning. Anlann spoke like a man explaining the obvious. How could a small group of Eyloni females confer upon Delwyn Marsch, a human, the military rank of warleader in the Compact Fleet just because he helped them capture a Lizard ship?

"What are you saying, Anlann? I don't understand. Marsch is a human. Besides, even if he captures the ship—and that's a long if—then he does so with the aid of Compact military personnel," Winters said.

Seralin shook her head and explained.

"Captain, once Del frees those females, and they capture the Ni'zakhonii ship for him, then he is the only male aboard a ship with a female society. They will associate with him and make him warleader because it is natural for them to designate a male combat focal point. In their eyes, and in the eyes of the Compact Counsel, he is the warleader of a Compact vessel."

She paused for effect before continuing.

"Of course, had Del not withdrawn from Coalition obligation, the vessel would then have Coalition jurisdiction with Del as captain. His written message to Melkorka stated that he voluntarily withdrew from Coalition obligation specifically to prevent the Ni'zakhonii from concluding that the ship's capture had been ordered by your government."

Anlann picked up where Seralin left off.

"Captain, once Del enters this system, he becomes the only warleader on-scene with a ship and his society. Under both Eyloni tradition and Compact law, Del's arrival grants him Warpact command over any Compact force and personnel here because Melkorka has no warleader and I am unwilling to assume Warpact command. Precedence places Melkorka and her society, Seralin, and me under Del's command. If *Fearless* arrives here after Del does, then Warleader Phalalin also comes into Warpact and is subject to any order Del may choose to give him."

"How can an interstellar government maintain a cohesive naval force and command structure that way?" Harrison demanded. "It sounds to me as if you're saying that the Compact Counsel simply issues letters of marque and reprisal to privateer vessels, and the first captain to arrive at a naval battle takes command of the task force."

"Marque and reprisal?" Seralin's ears twitched. "What is that, a declaration of revenge?"

Uh-oh, Winters thought. "A letter of marque and reprisal is a warrant issued by a government to a ship's captain, authorizing him to fight on its behalf and seize its enemy's war materiel. Such a warrant prevents the ship and crew from being accused of piracy while in the act of engaging that government's enemies."

Anlann nodded. "Yes, Captain, that sounds right. Individual tribes, tribal alliances within the Ten Tribes, or clans within a tribe finance and build their own warships. The Compact Counsel gives them the authority to fight in its name. If a warship engages the enemy, then his warleader knows the tactical situation better than any late arrivals. Subsequent arrivals, more powerful warships or a more experienced warleader, remain obliged to obey the first male on-scene until the event that fostered the need for a

Warpact ends, unless the first on-scene male surrenders Warpact command to the experienced warleader. That is the essence of a Warpact."

Harrison opened his mouth, but Winters steamrolled him before he could get a word out.

"Let me see if I got this straight. You're saying that although Marsch is not an Eyloni and is not a member of the Compact Fleet, he will still hold this Warpact command over any other Compact vessel in the system?"

"Of course, Captain," Seralin interrupted, puzzled that he did not comprehend. "Del is a single male aboard a ship having a female society. They will associate with him because he is their sire cairn. The doctrine of precedence is a simple concept, and its implied Warpact obligation is binding."

"You see, Captain?" Harrison bullied his way back into the discussion. Political appointees never tolerated being ignored. "Every warship in the Compact Fleet is a privateer vessel. If Marsch captures the Lizard ship. Then it becomes a privateer vessel operating under an implied Counsel letter of marque and reprisal."

Anlann shook his head. "No, Ambassador, Compact warships are owned by their female societies. They are not private vessels. When Del captures the Ni'zakhonii ship, he becomes the property of the females fighting with Del specifically and the property of the females aboard *Hunter's Moon* in a general sense. As warleader, Del may retain the ship for as long as he has need of him, but by custom, Del should release the ship to Melkorka and allow her to take the ship back to Elleio for military analysis and as proof of female fighting prowess. Del will gain much honor and respect in doing so. The Compact Counsel and the tribe and clans represented by the females aboard *Hunter's Moon* will owe him significant obligation."

"*Privateer* does not mean a private vessel Ambassador Anlann. It means a pirate vessel, a ship owned by pirates and used for piracy. You just told us that Compact Fleet structure is nothing more than a group of independent pirate vessels! How can you possibly coordinate a naval engagement when the flagship of your task force might be a garbage scow?" Harrison sneered.

Oh, no! Not again! Winters thought as Seralin and Anlann both flushed a furious deep red and started singing those high-pitched growls of theirs.

Later that evening, ship's time, Master Chief Alannah Deering looked carefully around, making sure no one was in sight before she opened a maintenance hatch. Ambassador Harrison had insisted she come to the evening diplomatic staff meeting, but why make her sneak through the between-hulls catwalks rather than simply come to the diplomatic suite? Light streamed onto the dark 'tween-hulls catwalk an instant before she turned and manually dogged the hatch, shutting out the light and the heavy thrumming noises emanating from the carrier's engineering spaces. She hurried down the four-hundred-meter-long narrow path suspended between the inner and outer hulls. If the ship were hulled now, she'd be sucked into the vacuum of space. The macabre thought quickened her pace and she flew past several hatches before stopping at one marked with a white chalk check mark.

From the other side came a muffled voice, one she recognized.

She opened the hatch and was challenged.

"What kept you?" Cultural Attaché Parakh demanded.

"I'm busy, that's what kept me. I'm the acting SOG XO, and I've been reassigning personnel. What am I doing here, anyway?"

"Helping us decide what to do about your commander, Marsch," Parakh said.

"What? Why? He's gone, probably dead by now!"

"He'd better be. If he comes back now, he'll wreck everything."

"Oh, don't be so dramatic. He's no threat now. Might as well consider him KIA," Deering said.

"No," Harrison interrupted, "I got a good look at him when he first brought that Eyloni woman into the SOB. He's dangerous, single-minded, and resourceful. I shouldn't have to tell you not to let his intense, easygoing mannerisms fool you. He may be a grunt, but he thinks. The man is sharp. Once something triggers him, he doesn't let go. He probably will fly that Lizard LAC right back here."

"So?" Deering prompted.

"Anlann told me that if Marsch returns in command of that ship, he will return with the rank of a Compact warleader. Anlann wants to negotiate with Winters of all people! Anlann made it perfectly clear that he's going to suggest to a *Warleader* Marsch that he should recommend to the Compact Counsel that they demand the Coalition Government make Winters the acting ambassador plenipotentiary in my place!"

"So this is actually all about you?"

"No, it is not just all about me, Deering! Winters is no diplomat. Hell, I don't trust Marsch either. He's cast his lot with the Eyloni. It's as if they've infected him somehow. We have to discredit him before he comes back or kill him somehow if he does come back and prevent him from asking Melkorka to contact the Compact Counsel on Winters's behalf," Harrison said.

"But Marsch hates the Lizards!" Deering objected. "They ate his family alive. He's a natural ally, and we need an alliance with the Eyloni. Marsch's ties to Melkorka and his friendship with the co-ambassadors would help smooth over any lingering concerns the Compact Counsel might have."

"No!" Parakh cut her off. "For the good of the Coalition, we must carry out Coalition policy. That policy is exquisitely simple. Don't provoke a war and recruit an ally that has experience in fighting the Lizards. The Compact jump drive allows their ships to teleport anywhere within a little over two light-years. Their FTL technology makes them an ideal border force. Place enough of their ships near strategic Coalition defense points, and you can stop further attacks before they start. Look, Deering, the Eyloni are honor bound to their word. If Marsch and Winters are allowed to negotiate, they will make a deal that gives the Compact too many concessions. I want the Eyloni locked into a defense treaty their honor won't let them easily escape. The Lizards have already staged several marauding task forces, and if Marsch captures a Lizard ship, and they somehow get word of his involvement, that's war now and not some hypothetical later, when we can count on the Eyloni as honor bound, reliable proxy forces."

"Yes," Harrison agreed. "Marsch has to go. If he's not killed aboard that Lizard ship, then we either have to remove him from the picture or destroy his reputation with the Compact Counsel."

"How are you going to do that? I'm not all that certain he's out of the picture. As you said, he'd resourceful. Besides, his reputation with the Eyloni is secure. I saw how that female, Kidahin, watched over him. She acted like she owned him," Deering said, a hint of disgust in her voice.

"That's why we have to tie into the ship's hyperlink communications network. A Compact warship makes instantaneous FTL jumps once every fourteen hours, fifty-one minutes, and six seconds, but it cruises in normal space between jumps. We're going to contact that ship's warleader and advise him of the situation here. We'll play up Marsch's bad character, his deceitful attempt to trick Melkorka, his dishonorable acts of piracy. We're going to make sure Marsch cannot recommend to the Compact Counsel that Winters replace me in any negotiations," Harrison said.

"Mr. Ambassador, are you certain such a radical step is necessary? There is no way the Eyloni would let Marsch arbitrate for them or let him make demands in their stead. I still don't believe Anlann seriously suggested that Marsch would be made an honorary Compact warleader," Edwin James, Harrison's senior aide, offered.

"I was there, Edwin, and believe me when I tell you that Anlann spoke with sincerity. He's serious. And you weren't with me back on Earth at the closed-session Security Counsel briefing, either. The Coalition Defense Directorate plans to cordon off Lizard territory using the Compact Fleet as the primary blockading force. It's not common knowledge, but the Lizards are starving, some kind of ecological disaster. The Eyloni either don't know or don't care because they've been hit harder by them than we have. The Coalition Government will do anything to gain an alliance with the Ten Tribes of Elleio. That guarantees they'll listen to any demand Marsch may make on the Compact's behalf if he does come back, and I won't allow that."

"Mr. Ambassador, I don't understand why you've invited me into this little cabal of yours. Why don't you just..." Deering began.

"No. No. *No!* Use your head. The success of this mission depends on you, Master Chief. Think only of the greater good. Marsch has resigned. He's no longer your commander. But if he does return, Anlann will manipulate him into making recommendations disastrous for the Coalition. That's what I would do. We need Marsch's influence neutered. You get back down to Special Operations and monitor the hyperlink from SOG communications. If *Fearless* signals Melkorka, I want to know about it. If we can get that ship's warleader with us, then he can order Melkorka to stand down until he arrives. He might even be persuaded to force Melkorka to arrest Marsch if he does return with that Lizard ship. That would be enough to keep him away from Winters and the co-ambassadors. Then he'll be in no position to recommend anything to anybody."

Turning to his aide, Harrison smiled. "Edwin, you can pass for a hyperlink communications repair technician, can't you?"

Several hours later, Herald "the angel" Edward Deeren sat in the SOG Tactical Operations Center manning a quiescent hyperlink communications hub. A hunting and fishing enthusiast, he dreamed of fishing and deer hunting trips. He had a month's leave saved up, and he couldn't help planning his Lake Michigan fishing trip repeatedly in his mind. This little diversion into Compact space added to his wait, and he hoped they'd be leaving soon.

He glanced at the mission clock. 12h23. He sighed. Another hour and thirty-seven minutes before the end of alpha shift.

He heard the relief comm NCO singing up another tirade and moseyed across the room.

"What's the matter, Alan? Slop coffee into the communications panels again?"

"No, Ed. Some guy came in here earlier and fixed the TAC comm systems again. See him? Short, middle aged, oily black hair, chews his tongue all the time...?"

"And looks like he just pulled himself out of a grease pit? That's the new Spec 4. He's been down here a couple of times over the past few hours."

"Yeah, that's him. He bothers me. I can't put my finger on it, but something's not right about him. He came to fix the TACC CMDCC interface."

"So? What's the matter?" Deeren asked.

"The TACC CMDCC interface has never given us problems before, and now it's on the fritz? How would anyone know that? Nobody in the TOC is directing combat ops over the hyperlink!"

Right then Senior Chief Petty Officer Six crossed the room and into the communications hub, spied Deeren and his relief leaning over the open communications panel. Her eyes narrowed, and she watched the scanner in the relief NCO's hand trace a line on a holographic schematic.

"You should have reported this!" she exploded.

"Reported what, Senior Chief?" Deeren asked, bewildered.

"Reported to me that the TACC interface has been firing communication sprites through the CMDCC." Her face turned red. "Some Spec 4 told me that this crap has been happening on and off for the past few hours. Maintenance requests go through me, Petty Officer. That means you follow the chain of command, and that means you don't send for a technician on your own. What if it had come to the attention of Acting Commander Cummings, and he asks me about it, and I don't know what the hell he's talking about?"

Six ignored their objections, too pissed to pay them any attention.

***

Winters glanced at the bridge chronometer. 14h19. Nineteen minutes into beta shift and no Harrison yet. He considered evasion tactics. Maybe he should call the ship to Condition-1 for the duration and…

The ship shuddered. Seconds later a vibration rumbled up from below decks.

"What was that? Report!" Winters ordered.

"Impact off the starboard beam, just aft of the Tower. Low-ram kinetic impact or minimal-yield explosion," Lieutenant Carstairs replied.

"Ordnance?" Winters asked.

"Unlikely, Sir. Preliminary analysis suggests a low-mass natural object impact."

Winters sighed. Translation: space stuff.

"Damage report," he ordered.

"Comm CMDCC shows a red light. It must have hit the SOGCC hyperlink relay," Lieutenant Romaine said.

"What? That must have been some rock!"

"Stand-by, Sir. Wait. Wait. Uh, Captain, CMDCC now shows green. A stray fifty kilo asteroid gave the Special Ops independent communications hyperlink emitter quite a smack, but a repair tech happened to be there to shut down and reset the TACC emitter."

"Damage control assessment?"

"The Spec 4 reports that damage control is not necessary. CMDCC hyperlink monitor systems show go-green across the board," Romaine relayed.

13

A PRINCESS COMES

Kidahin fought down the instinct to perk her ears at Marsch. The gesture might tip the Ni'zakhonii off to his presence.

She goaded them, distracting them.

One of them backhanded her, smacking her to the deck. Rolling to her feet, she dodged another stunning blow. Waggling her fingers subtly, she watched Marsch. A third Ni'zakhonii swiped at her, but she held her ground.

Phelindra beat her fists against the cramped cell's invisible force field and growled. Enraged. The enemy had surrounded the huluhar and were taking turns slamming her to the deck. She sang a second warning to Kidahin. She fought poorly, like an infant, but even an infant gave an enemy no obvious openings. What in the spirits was she doing?

The huluhar's fast fingers drew Phelindra's notice, and her jaw dropped.

Kidahin slammed into the deck again, rolled to her feet, and resumed her seemingly aimless circling, edging toward the raised deck and the pod window.

Marsch, watching the young Hunter drift closer, yanked knives from the pod security guards' bodies and cut their throats, making sure that they were dead. Pulling the wad of Eyloni knives from the collapsed field suit, he ran for the ledge and jumped. Landing on a Lizard's back, he used his momentum to drive the two combat knives into its spine. Marsch felt something snap near his tailbone as he hit. The shock flashed all the way up his spine, exploding in his skull. *Dizzy! Fight it! Ignore it!* He couldn't afford to lose the element of surprise. He had to kill them all before one of them sounded the alarm.

Fear filled Marsch, threatening to crush him, but stimulated by an intense autonomic arousal, strength filled him as he smelled his daughters, alive and close. Their sweet scent filled his nose, singing subtle messages to the protective, loving father in him, and he gave himself over to it.

Phelindra heard bone snapping and tore her gaze from Kidahin in time to see Marsch roll off a dead Ni'zakhonii's shoulders. He threw a twisted bundle at her; it bounced off the force field hatch: their adulthood knives and neckwear, waiting for them.

A battle cry rang out from the cells around her.

Kidahin limped to Marsch's kill and with effort pulled the two battle knives from between its shoulders, swinging one of them up over her shoulder and behind, tracing a diagonal line across her tormentor's throat, biting deep into its windpipe. Pivoting, she charged the three enemies closing on Marsch's flank. Graceful wiry strength made her combination of backswings, foreswings, and tumbling attacks a string of deadly blows. Parrying, evading, blocking, and striking with the inborn frenzy of an Eyloni female protecting a male from harm, she alternated smashing fists with slashing knives.

Marsch pivoted on his right foot. Stepping back and spinning left, he sliced a Lizard's neck. Sidestepping a slashing claw, he dropped back and twisted his knife across a second's throat.

Flipping the two knives into the air, Marsch caught them by their tips and hurled them toward a third and a fourth target. Tumbling across the bay they drove into Lizard flesh, putting them down forever.

Pulling two more knives from his bandolier, Marsch charged a fifth enemy. Swinging both knives down, around, up and across, the left-hand blade slashed an available neck while the right-hand backswing caught the Lizard across the abdomen, disemboweling it in mid-lunge. Death claimed another prize.

The deadly dance was just getting started. Sliding into a new position Marsch caught a sixth foe with a left-hand backswing across it stomach, while a right-hand move slashed its jugular.

Charging across the bay, Marsch swung around a seventh opponent and a spinning right-handed foreswing across its gut combined with a left-hand knife drawing a bloody line along its jaw from earhole to earhole put another on the deck.

Three long strides away waited an eighth Lizard. Scissoring his blades, twisting in a feint, Marsch dodged a clawing defensive parry. Swinging his outstretched blades up and around in a wide arc he separated the head from its body.

Two Lizards crossed from opposite sides. One charged him, intending to overbear and drive him to the deck, while the other ran for a purple crystal on the wall. One knife throw ended the ninth's charge and the other throw made sure number ten never made it to the crystal.

Pulling his last two knives from the bandolier, Marsch headed toward an eleventh target. Slashing its throat with a left foreswing, a left backswing, and a pivot to its left side allowed a final slash from earhole to collarbone.

Kidahin extended her arms wide and spun on her bare feet, slashing the throat and abdomen of the last standing enemy.

Phelindra blinked, shocked and not quite believing what she had just witnessed. Eyloni males fought with deadly cunning intensity, but she had never seen anything like this! Their sire cairn had killed twenty-one enemy in forty-three seconds!

Marsch, turning, began closing in on Kidahin. Bright, pink blood drenched him as if he had tumbled through the killing floor of a slaughterhouse. His knives dripped pink. Kidahin's body odor snapped him to his senses even as it chained his hyperaroused fight response.

"Kidahin? Come on! We have to get them free while there's still time!"

They ran to Phelindra's cell. A blue gem beckoned within its green, pumpkin gore shroud mounted in the cell portal.

A control crystal, Marsch figured, that was either a simple switch, or a biometric code key.

He reached out, restraining an impetuous Kidahin.

"Don't touch it! Wait here."

Marsch limped up the stairs and into the overhead control pod, There, he hacked off a claw and shuffled back down to her.

"Phelindra, we don't have time to waste. Step back."

Marsch put his hand over the reptilian claw and touched the gem with it. The flat blue crystal flashed white and then glowed with black light.

Nothing else happened, and he waved the Eldest out.

She stalked through the force field threshold, confident. Marsch handed her the severed claw.

"Get everyone else out using this."

"By your command."

Marsch hobbled back up into the pod and a minute later returned.

He gave Kidahin a second grisly prize.

She twitched her pons at the corpses littering the bay and asked, "Why not take one of these?"

"They're regular crew, but the guards in the pod are brig security. If the cell controls scan for biometric data, then the crystal will read their genetic profiles."

Phelindra and Kidahin set about releasing the others. Marsch grabbed the tangled Eyloni knives lying on the deck. Only after he began untangling the mess and trying to match each item to its owner did he realize that two of the females were missing.

The LAV driver and gunner.

Where were they? In another part of the ship? Still in the jungle? Dead? He couldn't think about them now and shook his head to clear it. He sorted the flint knives and tried to return them.

They accepted the neckwear in quiet dignity, but they refused the flint knives. Like Kidahin had done once before, they insisted he tie them on himself. He grumbled at them about the waste of time, but they remained adamant and unyielding.

A few minutes later, Marsch led them up the steps and into the pod. There, he cleared away a flat surface between the two consoles. Glowing flat crystals hummed in each device. The matrix tables reminded him of a sandbox in both size and depth but was filled with black glittering wet-looking sand. Slots had been molded into the rough hard stuff to hold the multicolored crystals.

The Eyloni surrounded him as he pulled out a grease pencil and began drawing lines on the station's shelf. A few of them at a time paused long enough to examine the drawing and move aside for the next few to get a look. Hunters and Warriors wrapped their tails around him and took turns brushing at his arms, legs, and waist. Their individual scents lingered on him, and he daydreamed of them as he drew.

He sketched the ship's general outline and added a stick figure next to it for perspective. The overhead view showed them where he entered the ship and his approximate path to where he believed they were now. He drew two sets of dashed lines with arrows. One line traced a path to the blisters atop the vessel, and the other line led to the presumed engineering spaces opposite the airlock.

"We take engineering and the bridge. If we take the bridge only, then engineering starves our power and life support. If we take engineering only, then the bridge cuts off our life support before we can figure out how to override the environmental control system. Break up into two strike teams. One, led by me, will take the bridge, the other, led by Phelindra, will take engineering."

The Eldest grumbled but twitched her tail in acknowledgment. "I should go with you." She made the comment a sullen whisper and flattened her ears before adding a belated, "By your command."

Marsch passed a long, heavy throwing knife over to her. "Take this. There's no telling when you may need a heavy blade."

He faced the group. "Each team must have members best capable of operating bridge or engineering stations. Phelindra will decide."

He gave up the floor to her with a warning. "Hurry, we haven't much time!"

The Eldest looped her tail tight around the long knife's blade and focused on the task the Warleader had set for her. He had just declared her the Mistress of the Ship, but she had already declared herself his Protectress. She snapped her tail in spitting fury that she could not be in two places at once. She knew it was impossible, but she viewed it as a failing anyway.

She distracted herself by assigning team members. She divided the Warriors into two assault groups. Their endurance made them better fighters in pitched battles. Most of them belonged to her ship's combat boarding teams, but two served in the surface combat teams. Marsch needed the heavier females to help him take the enemy's command center, but he needed qualified command center personnel, too. With two Warriors missing and presumed dead, she assigned two with auxiliary control experience, one with life support systems training, one from Fire Control, and one from Damage Control to Marsch. She assigned the last two Warriors to her strike force. Next, she doled out her Hunters. She assigned Kidahin to him because she was a navigator, one from tactical analysis, one from communications, two from combat analysis, and she put the remainder in her charge. Satisfied, she returned to his side and wrapped her tail around his upper arm.

Nodding an absentminded acknowledgment, Marsch briefed the two strike teams. When they had committed their missions to memory, he added a cautionary reminder. "Don't let the enemy touch a control crystal. Navigation, propulsion, and communications will bother us no end as it is without trying to figure out scrambled control settings."

Marsch checked the time. A half hour gone. They had to hurry. He guessed enemy numbers near forty, and they had killed half that already.

"Phelindra, engineering should have a crew of four, maybe one or two more at most. A ship this size should also have two pairs—or four individuals—held in reserve for security. It goes without saying, kill them quietly."

She looked at him as if he had told her that water was wet.

"Right," he muttered. "When you take engineering, contact me. Otherwise, maintain EM-silence."

They stared at him, ears twitching. He smelled what could only be described as bitter defeat.

It took him some effort, but he grasped the tentative empathic link. It drew his eyes to their ears. None wore their webbed rank earrings. Their comm decals had been torn away as well.

Marsch understood. The comm gear meant nothing, but by referring to it he reminded them of their lost status symbols. That loss had a profound effect on them. It wounded their hierarchical standings in ways he couldn't imagine.

He passed his borrowed comm gear to Phelindra and told her to contact him through his 'pad, but not to expect a reply.

"Let's go!" he ordered.

He touched the Lizard's severed claw to the brig hatch control.

The gem pulsed blue and the hatch retracted. Phelindra twisted past him, looking down the dim burrow. She made sure, blocking his way with her body before nodding an all-clear. She snarled a comment at the Warriors before taking her group and backtracking along the path Marsch had traced. The unnaturalness of leaving him behind gnawed at her. Minutes later, they passed the main airlock and began prowling blindly toward the inside edge of the ship's bulbous curved shape.

Marsch took his strike team and continued his original course up the burrow. The Hunters with him rotated through a set stalking order. As solitary scouts they ranged ahead, and fell behind, at irregular intervals, giving each a continuous change of vantage point. The Warriors stayed close to him. Support bulkheads crisscrossed the burrow at infrequent intervals. They reminded him of old Wild West mineshaft supports cast from sparkling fine black slag. The material glittered like new snow in the moonlight. Dim fluorescing gems as big as Type-II helmets gave off cold, pale light. The burrow leveled out and opened into a compartment, some kind of common access deck. Several hatches lined the low, cavernous chamber. Marsch jumped as Kidahin's tail brushed his cheek. She held up three fingers and pointed ahead.

He nodded, calm and ready.

A minute or two passed before she gave him the all-clear. They moved out of the chamber. Rounding a bend in the burrow, they came across three dead enemy and four self-satisfied Hunters. Marsch glared at them, certain they had conspired to shield him from combat.

Grumbling, he pointed at a nearby hatch. "We need to stow these bodies somewhere out of sight. I'll open the hatch. Get ready!" He jammed the severed claw against a blue gem and watched the iris melt into its frame.

The room was empty.

They barely finished hiding the bodies when Zalzadrin poked her head into the room.

"Del? A hand approaches," she said.

Marsch smiled. A hand meant five to him, but it was written 10 as the Eyloni counted, an Eyloni ten. The common deck's dim and uneven features made it the ideal ambush site, much better than being caught out here in the narrow burrow.

"Kill them," he told her.

Zalzadrin's curt nod told him he ordered the obvious.

The Warriors retreated through the chamber, pulling a resisting Marsch along with them. They wanted to fight, but Phelindra had been quite clear. That did not diminish their desire to show him just how lethal they were.

Zalzadrin twitched her ears at the withdrawing Warriors, sending an empathic pheromonal message down the burrow after them. A not so subtle brag, she yanked their tails with a mental picture that sang of Hunter superiority. She had bright orange hair and was short for a Hunter, and it grated on her that almost every Warrior stood above her. She took her team of Hunters and melted into the chamber's rough walls, hiding in plain sight as the enemy entered. Unaware of the silent death lurking within, the Ni'zakhonii advanced into the chamber.

The Hunters returned soon enough.

"Forward! Hurry! We're out of time!" Marsch ordered.

Zalzadrin clutched her arm against her side. Wary, Marsch turned on her. She turned with him, keeping her left profile out of sight.

"Zalzadrin, come here."

Reluctant, she complied.

Marsch saw the long bloody gash running down her left side from just beneath her breast to well past her hip.

"Come here! Don't argue!" he hissed. He pulled the medikit from his pack, opened it, and took out the wound stapler and liquid bandage. The stapler closed most flesh wounds and would serve until she could report to a sickbay, but it hurt like hell until the anesthetic liquid bandage hardened and took the pain with it. That, and it left a nasty scar.

"Not bad. Not bad," Zalzadrin protested as he bent down to her wound.

"Quiet!" Marsch hissed and set about stapling the lips of the gaping wound closed. She clenched her jaw, enduring his painful treatment of her. He smeared the liquid bandage over the stapled wound and watched it harden on contact with living skin. The battlefield treatment burned through ninety seconds they couldn't afford to lose.

"*I'll* take point, Zalzadrin. Don't argue. Move out!"

Ten minutes later, Marsch considered three closed puckered hatches set at equidistant points along the ship's interior curved bulkhead. The distance between them roughly matched where he figured the dorsal blisters waited.

†††

Phelindra and her assault force made slow, steady, and undiscovered progress toward the power systems and propulsion center. Heavy vapor reminding her of sublimating dry ice pooled low in the burrow, obscuring their feet.

The heavy vapor vented from a frost shrouded insulated housing. No environmental engineer, Phelindra wondered if this equipment was part of the life support atmosphere gas exchange system. If so, then she knew they were near their goal.

Alien voices whispered from a large closed nearby hatch, sounding like lisping hisses. The hatch's size and placement looked about right for a power plant's blast doors.

She palmed the hatch's control gem with the severed claw, and it opened. Light streamed into the burrow, followed by the heavy thrumming sounds of the ship's power plant and drive.

Without mercy, the Eyloni fell upon the ship's engineering crew.

†††

"Get ready!" Marsch whispered.

Hard muscles and intoxicating spices crowded him. Zalzadrin shoved her way up to the sealed hatch. Silent, she waited, her face contorting into a vision of dark rage.

He pressed the dismembered claw against the shining blue gem.

The crystalline hatch melted silently back into its frame. Five Lizards, backs to them, wearing the same sunset orange smocks, sat at obvious bridge stations.

Marsch threw two knives, one after the other, while the Eyloni jumped the other three with bloody savagery. One of his knives hit, but the other flew wide off its mark, inflicting a mortal but not a drop-dead fatal wound. The Lizard pulled its sidearm and aimed, not at Marsch, but at the matrix table and its crystal controls.

Marsch threw a snapshot at the creature and then rushed it. The knife pierced the side of its neck, drove through its throat, and came out below and behind an earhole as its sidearm fired wide.

He grappled the Lizard. Still not embracing death, it twisted like an alligator in water, knocking him aside and into a dark sparkling matrix table.

His collarbone snapped, and he grunted.

The muted sigh drew swift looks. Four females detached from their melee, and running up to him, helped him stand.

"I'm okay! I'm okay! It's just a broken bone!"

Marsch cursed his sloppiness. The break grated, bone on bone. He had to bind it, get it out of his way, and ignore the pain. Plasticast set small breaks—fingers, hands, wrists, and the like. It wasn't for setting large areas.

His upper arm hurt. It burned, burned like he'd been stabbed with a dull, red hot spike.

A projectile? It had shot him. Marsch knew from experience that if the slug exited, then it would hurt, of course; but if it didn't exit, then it would both hurt and burn—like it did now.

He'd have to watch for signs of shock, dammit.

"The command center is secured, Del," Zalzadrin reported. She paused at the sight of a bloody hole in his arm big enough to put her finger into.

Horrified, the pain in her side melted away.

Her heart raced, her body preparing her for species survival combat.

"Good. Well done. Send a pair out to find Phelindra. Report back for support if you see a Lizard," Marsch said. He swayed on his feet, feeling a little nauseous, and fumbled for the medikit and its antishock meds.

Impatient and demanding, Zalzadrin waved the others over to look at his wounds.

"By your command," Zalzadrin said, ignoring his order, and continuing her careful examination.

Irked, Marsch started feeling put upon about five minutes into their doctoring. He explained, using short clipped words, how to use the plasticast. He vented, trading verbal jabs with them as they set his collarbone and cleaned the gunshot wound—they could not remove the slug. All eight of them held him down while the temporary cast hardened.

Marsch bellowed at them in protest. For one, it didn't take all eight of them to do the job, and two, an enemy counterattack could come at any moment.

And he told them so…because yelling made him feel better!

Obedient to Eyloni culture and instinct, they ignored him and continued their care. Marsch wasted his breath arguing with the inconvincible. They, smiling and twitching ears, sent pheromones to one another that formed empathic images conveying the same universal idea: males always needed females to care for them.

Marsch chafed, waiting for them to finish. Several more minutes passed. He calmed down and relaxed, his mind doodling, trying to connect feelings to what he thought he smelled.

His 'pad bleeped, dragging him from their pheromonal otherworldliness.

He pulled the scanner from his belt and played back the recorded message.

"Del? Phelindra," the Eldest Huntress's filtered sing-song voice warbled. "We have taken Power Systems and Propulsion. Four enemy are no more. None had a chance to damage the equipment. I have three with minor injuries. One is in a serious condition. Raelindra comes to you. She waits at the ship's security confinement area and will lead you back to us."

Marsch swore under his breath. Just what did a *serious condition* mean?

He glared at the 'pad, blaming it. The battlefield scanner detected combat hazards, but it made a crappy emergency receiver. A utility scanner, it could scan an extremely wide EM bandwidth, analyze the signals it found, and report the results in seconds. It could transmit active scanning fields or narrow beams and receive passive wideband signals, but it couldn't transmit audio and visual communications data. Programming it to receive the Compact commlink audio had been like trying to tune a primitive crystal radio to a distant AM station on a stormy night.

"Kidahin, continue working on the helm controls. Everyone else keep trying to access the drive and navigation systems. Maintain alert for a possible counterattack against the bridge. Zalzadrin, come with me."

His orders made them unhappy. They considered themselves his protectors and hadn't let him out of their sight since taking the command center. Ears twitching concern, they obeyed, waggling insistent fingers at the passing Zalzadrin.

The wounded Hunter arched her long, beautiful brick red, burnt orange, golden highlighted tail in a huff and followed him.

Zalzadrin, ever watchful and hyperalert, escorted Marsch to the brig, There, Raelindra led them to the vessel's engineering spaces. Zalzadrin fell back a short distance, loath to leave Marsch, and guarded his rear.

Raelindra stepped through the large crystal iris and into the ship's power and propulsion spaces, Marsch on her tail. Inside, the engineering bay followed the interior lines of a bloated horseshoe curve. The compartment resembled a pitcher plant from the inside, too. Marsch stood where the insects drowned. The walls lost their ropy green pumpkin guts look and took on a smooth maroon and green sheen. On the curved walls above him, bristles the size of sickle blades hung like upside-down eyelashes, reminding him of the hairs inside pitcher plants that kept the bugs from escaping. Bladder-like machinery grew out of the deck. Some of the equipment resembled puffballs and shelf fungus, but they were grown from the same sparkling dark slag as the ship's bulkheads. Control crystals flashed psychedelic patterns in tables attached to various machines. Large clear crystals punctured the green tints and maroon shades filling the chamber, giving off cold, dim light.

His eyes drifted away from the odd machinery to Phelindra and the others. They crouched around an injured female lying on the deck. Waistwear removed, legs hitched up and apart, her uncomfortable repose jogged memories. She squirmed and gasped in a torrent of shallow pants.

Oh, no! She's in labor!

Phelindra waved him over.

Marsch stood next to her and tried to radiate calm amid a storm of conflicting emotions. Memories of shock, remembrance, joy, pain, and death engulfed him, threatening to trigger his PTSD, but the scent of Eyloni females banished the symptoms and his mind cleared.

The pregnant female had fixated on him from the moment he cleared the equipment. When he reached her side, her focus intensified.

"She is pregnant, and a blow has caused premature labor to begin," Phelindra explained.

Marsch met the pregnant female's eyes. Her features, her skin colors, her build marked her as a Hunter. The others caressed and petted her, while her tail whipped about in rhythmic sympathy with her contractions. He bent over to get a closer look.

His jaw dropped. He had been briefed, but briefings—like all intelligence—never conveyed the reality. A single opening stared back at him, a cloaca, slightly distended and dripping clear fluid.

Marsch glanced at her stomach. She didn't look pregnant. She had a slight bulge around her navel, but it looked like the normal minimal abdominal body fat common to many women. Eyloni bodies favored lean builds. Both the lithe Hunters and the muscular Warriors lacked obvious body fat. Her belly made him think that she was pushing her stomach muscles to give it a slightly rounded look.

Acting on impulse, he squatted before the panting Hunter.

Amber eyes larger than his followed him. He shifted his feet for better balance and leaned forward. Her warm, velour-like soft tail wrapped him fast, binding him to her as tight as a float to its lifeline.

"Can you help her?" he asked Phelindra.

"She cannot push with those rib injuries, and she is one hundred twenty days premature," she said, shaking her head.

Marsch did some quick mental math. An Eyloni 120 converted to his 35, but two Elleio Standard days together ran about 23 Coalition standard hours long. That gave a total time of what, somewhere between 15 and 17 Earth days?

"Only sixteen days until a full-term birth? She doesn't look that pregnant."

"Really?" Phelindra eyed him curiously. "She is obviously with child. See the swell of her stomach?"

"So, we can help her deliver it, right?"

"Yes. The infant must come out," She whispered.

Why was Phelindra so sad?

Marsch watched the pregnant Hunter struggle. Her nipples dripped milk. Below the orange patterned red skin bloomed severe, terrible bruises across her chest, along her upper abdomen, and down her side.

Her bruises looked nothing like a human's yellow, blue, or purple ones. She had blended yellow and green, brown, brown and red, and brick red bruises, depending on which skin colors the bruises spread under.

Marsch put a hand on her heaving stomach and felt her abdomen ripple low into her waistline. He remembered helping his dad with animal births on the farm. He had helped his wife with natural childbirth, too. He knew how to shift babies in the womb, had done it before. It took intuitive feeling and intuition, something he had within him that was at odds with his combat skills.

"I'll guide the baby, and you help her push."

The laboring Hunter had calmed since his arrival, and she had calmed even more since embracing him with her tail. She watched him, eyes and ears following his every move.

Marsch sucked air through his teeth and winced, the sudden movement sending his collarbone to aching. He nodded, ready. The others rubbed her stomach in rhythmic circles, singing soft songs to her. The Hunter did not join them in song but remained focused on him alone.

He needed to wash the Lizard blood from his hands and arms. The medikit lacked surgical scrub supplies. He tried stepping away from the Hunter, but she panicked, refusing to slacken her tail. He stepped sideways, griping as he pissed on his forearms and hands, scrubbing away the vile pink blood. The corpsman's manual recommended this as a last resort for wound irrigation because a healthy person's urine was sterile.

A concert of ears climbed into ringlet hairlines, then flipped forward in curiosity. The Eyloni fixated on his urine stream. His reproductive structure dwarfed an Eyloni male's nipple-like organ.

Eyloni males did not expel water through it, either.

Ideas finger-waggled back and forth before they settled on a theory: humans stored water in an internal bladder for later use. Their homeworld must be a desert.

Marsch patted the Hunter around the puckered slit and gently probed inside.

Minutes later, he swore.

A breech!

Human babies twisted, he knew, as they passed down into the birth canal. Eyloni births must work the same way. The strike to her chest must have dropped the baby into the birth canal before its turning maneuver. He had to turn it around before they could help her push.

He felt the narrow canal's rhythmic contractions ripple down from her stomach in time with their singing. Her hips, like all Eyloni, betrayed a pelvis smaller than that of a similarly built human woman.

Marsch used his fingers and cautious external pushing to gain headway.

It took him an hour's cramped stooping to turn the baby around and down.

He nodded once again and pulled; the others kneading her abdomen in time to his pulling.

The laboring Hunter gave the final agonizing push herself, and the baby fell into his open hand.

It was female, in keeping with the Eyloni tendency to bear females.

And she was small, like a doll.

Her pale-yellow skin felt like a horse's wet nose. She lacked her mother's colorful autumn camouflage. Marsch guessed that she was about a fifth as tall as her mother, about thirty-five centimeters, with a tail just as long. Dark red hair in tiny, tight ringlets covered her head and the last thumbnail length of her tail. Unlike human babies, she resembled her mother in miniature. Arms, legs, hips, and chest matched the adult Hunter in all but size.

Marsch laid the baby over the mother's shoulder so she could suckle without aggravating her bruised chest and ribs.

The mother kept Marsch in a firm tail grip, her eyes begging him. The females surrounding her remained as concerned now as they had been when he first arrived.

Why? *Premature?* He doubted that sixteen days early made her that premature. Then again, he didn't know how long it took an Eyloni to reach full term, either. Her small size plagued him with memories of congenital birth defects associated with low birth weight. She looked normal enough: two arms, two legs, fingers and toes okay, a tail, two twitching ears, and two large pale tan eyes.

Marsch was tired. Crouching in an awkward stance, held there by the Hunter's tail, he swayed. His collarbone hurt. The gunshot wound hurt. The pinching temporary cast hurt. His broken tailbone hurt.

His eyes drifted back to the baby again. She looked fine to him. He never saw a newborn more alert and mobile. She sought something. Her round eyes and flexing ears roved the chamber with escalating despair. She smelled…frantic to him.

Marsch studied her ear movements, mystified, and figured she listened for something. She ignored the voices around her, turning her head about with growing anxiety.

Was she born deaf?

Did she hear something he couldn't? He knew from watching Kidahin in the field that Eyloni had sensitive ears.

No, the others didn't cast their ears about, killing that theory.

She listened for something specific.

But what? The hums and clicks of alien machinery?

Marsch decided that he didn't much care. Stuffing the used gauze packs back into their empty wrappings, he sighed, turned, and reassured the new mother.

"It's all right. It's over now. You can let go."

A sharp, musical note rang out from the newborn. The insistent high pitch and empathic thrust startled him with memories of babies and baby daughters. He rocked backward and would have fallen on his back but for the grip of the mother's tail.

Marsch leaned forward and looked at the baby. She stared back at him, intent; her ears flexed wide open, their pointed tips thrust forward and quivering. He had no doubt that she heard him.

Not deaf then. So much for guessing. It *was* nice to be wrong sometimes.

But the infant's musical squeal shocked Phelindra. Caught off guard and unprepared, the others had flinched at the demanding note. They watched the infant swipe at her mother, scrabble across her bruised chest and abdomen, crawl down her thigh, and jump across the small gap between her knee and Marsch's thigh. Hopeful, they watched her crawl up his waist, wrap her tail around his arm, look into his face, and flute an insistent plea.

Marsch put his free hand behind the baby and took a closer look at her.

Ears flexing and eyes squinting, she sniffed over and over in a desperate effort to catch his scent.

She somehow knew these pheromones.

Male!

Her nose wrinkled again, and she fluted a demanding, complex musical score at him.

Marsch held her close. She reminded him so much of his daughters' dolls and their gowns and tiaras.

"Princess. Yeah, princess. You're a little princess," he told her.

Hervorallin unwound her tail the moment Marsch had spoken to her daughter. From her vantage point on the deck, she saw the shock playing out on the faces above her. Her daughter heard the sire cairn's voice! Newborn Eyloni females could hear only the bass component of a male's voice. And her daughter smelled his faint male pheromones and received empathic images from him.

She listened as her society sang the natal syllables Marsch had given to her daughter. A few of them, herself included, struggled with the musically awkward chords. It took a minute of Phelindra's patient coaching before they could mimic the notes he intended.

Princess.

Hunters and Warriors embraced. Expressing their relief and excitement, they caressed one another and entwined tails. Princess tightened her tail around Marsch's upper arm, scrubbed her nose and cheeks against his face, and called to him in musical ecstasy while they watched and waited.

The baby's agility and strength surprised Marsch. Her long tail held her secure against his right arm, and her thumbs and toes clenched at his side and shoulder.

The adrenaline thrill fading fast, an exhausted Marsch felt the need for rest yammering at him, but first he had to inspect the ship, and he could do neither with a baby clutching at and singing to him.

Maybe if he sang her a lullaby, then she'd go to sleep? He thought of his daughters and started humming "Brahm's Lullaby."

Princess halted her demanding melody the moment *her male* sang the first note.

She clutched there, listening. Relying on instinct, her newborn mind grappled with his sound and smell. Together they wove an awareness of an identity other than herself, an identity vastly more important than herself, more important even than the vague omniscient idea of 'mother'.

When Marsch reached the end of the lullaby and started to repeat, Princess joined him. Her triple fluting notes wove around his simple melody. Together they sang her first song over and over.

He was her male.

She knew him by the unique signature of his scent. She knew him by the sound of his voice.

She knew this song now and forever.

The others sighed in relief and followed the melody, listening as Marsch and his near-daughter sang their repeating duet.

Princess watched her male with territorial possessiveness and flashed suspicious glares at the shadowy female scents surrounding her. Until her male made proper introductions, she had to keep watch over him herself.

The females smiled knowing smiles. Eyloni infants depended on pheromonal signaling and, but for growling or singing, were not verbal communicators. They did not make baby noises, did not cry, but they did make their feelings known through empathic imagery. The infant, too young, did not know and did not care that her scent reflected exactly what she thought of them.

Her mother's contented unconcern shocked Marsch. With undisguised joy, she let him handle her baby. He knew Eyloni viewed everything though a territorial lens, but she didn't seem to care. Baffled, he asked Phelindra about it.

"You are a male, and you are known to us," she said.

"Oh?" he asked, mystified.

Princess growled a warning.

Phelindra held her hands out to the hissing infant, and Marsch passed Princess over to her.

The infant complained but sniffed the Eldest Huntress in spite of herself. She thought about it and sighed, satisfied. She chirped a note at Phelindra and then reached back for him.

"What was that all about?" Marsch asked.

"You must introduce us to her before she will let us near you."

"Why is she so interested in me?"

Phelindra shot him a startled look, smelling his clear bafflement. He was not Eyloni. He did not know.

"That is how it is with us. In times past, no male presence at a birth meant no males in a clan, and that females on the move were either engaging in desperate warfare or living in areas suffering from plague or drought. Female infants developed the need to form subtle empathic links with any adult male, the indicator of a stable clan. Infant females who find no male presence refuse to eat, become lethargic, and die within a day or two."

"Why just females? I'd think such an instinct would apply to males as well."

"No. Male births are exceedingly rare. Eyloni evolution considers male biological fitness, the ability to reproduce, a higher priority."

"So males have no need to form empathic bonds?"

"No, infant males do not, but adult males share emotional bonds with the females who associate with them."

"And this continues into modern times?"

"Yes. You see how Princess responds to you. The instinctive need to form an empathic bond still expresses itself. You saved her life. You did for her what Kalinn would have done if he were here."

"What about her family, or her clan? Shouldn't the father or a male relative have bonded with her?" Marsch asked.

"Relative? Father? Oh, you mean the male who mated with Hervorallin? No. We have no monogamous mating unions. Mating produces infants. It is the bond that creates familial ties and not the mating. Males belong to their mother's clan until their adulthood ceremony. Adult males join clans though the empathic links they make with their near-daughters, not through the infants they sire."

Marsch had difficulty squaring that with Kidahin's social studies lessons. She had told him that a male enjoyed near total freedom of action across all strata of society. That made no sense if clan membership depended on a male's near-daughter connection. He asked her about the idea of male autonomy.

"Males hold places of honor and clans seek their opinions. Females in counsel cajole, beg, and argue with males at times, but they *never* alienate them," Phelindra said.

Her response answered nothing, and yet something about it nagged at him, but he shrugged it off.

Marsch thought about the infant clinging to his shoulders. She had hummed herself to sleep. As near as he could tell, she couldn't see far, not much farther than her tail. She had doll hands and tiny four-knuckled fingers. Her pencil tip black nails had hardened. Razor sharp they were, too. She held onto him with special care not to slice or puncture him by accident. He thought of them as her baby nails, like kids had milk teeth, and wondered when she would grow into her deep red adult ones.

Hervorallin joined Phelindra and him. As she reached for her daughter, Princess roused from sleep. She smelled her mother's pheromones and made an empathic link with her on a primitive want-need level. She let go of Marsch with a reluctant sigh, but when she smelled the Eldest Huntress too close to him, she snapped wide awake, leaned against him, and slashed at her with fingers cupped into a V-shape, hissing through pure white teeth in tiny fury.

Marsch blinked in confusion. They smiled, flexed ears, and chatted among themselves the whole time Princess trilled warnings from under his chin.

"Familial bond," Phelindra told Hervorallin, thrilled.

"Familial bond?" Marsch echoed. "What does that mean?" They ignored him.

Princess hummed her lullaby and crossed over to her mother's breast. He watched her nurse, noticing as she did so that Phelindra's nipples dripped milk. He craned his neck around and looked at the group surrounding him. They all were dripping milk, too.

Sympathetic empathy? Were all Eyloni females natural wet nurses?

Much later, several females came to Phelindra and conferred. She sought Marsch.

"Del, there are no enemy aboard. The bodies have been taken to the airlock and jettisoned."

"Excellent. The ship is yours. When you gain access to the engine systems, drop us out of FTL."

"By your command."

Marsch relaxed. Phelindra could command the ship. He was a combat specialist, not a ship's captain.

He wandered through the ship, tired but not sleepy. Suddenly, out of nowhere, two females strolled by, unconcerned. Their gazes, cool, penetrating, intelligent, took in every feature. They had the eyes of Warriors ready to kill without regret, and yet they gave him delighted smiles, coyly flitting ears, and caresses with their tail tufts before resuming their stalking.

They were strange, his Eyloni crew. They prowled the ship in pairs all the time, like animals prowling their territory. Well, the ship did belong to them now. He thought of wolves and the need for social creatures to make something theirs by attaching territorial ties to it.

Marsch returned to the bridge and found Phelindra and Kidahin studying the crystal matrix tables set into the helm and navigation consoles. The rest of the bridge crew looked up as if they were expecting him. No doubt the two Warriors he met in the burrow had tattled on him.

"Del," the Eldest Huntress greeted him. She crossed the bridge and arched her tail behind and around him. "The crystals not only work like switches when touched, but they also control the energy flow by the pattern they occupy in the matrix table. Changing the pattern is a control setting in itself.”

“Have you figured out how to change our course and velocity?”

“Of course not. I shall tell you when we do,” was her miffed reply.

Marsch glared at his Mistress of the Ship. She had led the others to him about an hour after he gave her command of the ship. One at a time, each stood before him, put a woven rank earring in his hand, and waited for him to pierce her ear. He had to trim away the torn tissue and stitch the edges together first. They sat though his corpsman treatment without complaint, while a curious Princess crawled all over him and watched. Indeed, they seemed relieved to have the rank symbols back in place.

They had made a big deal out of it, too. Each told him, using precise words, what each web, color, bead, and knot in the dreamcatcher-like earring meant. They felt it important that he hang the earrings himself, after each female recounted her acts of bravery, her accomplishments, her missions, her clan, her societies, and her tribe by pointing to a web, a bead, or a knot. His acceptance of their word, the piercing, and attaching the web to the earring completed the ritual. He couldn’t tell how the gold hoop attached to the fine gold braids they used for earrings, so he tied them together with gold wire, using the same knots he tied when tying flies for fishing.

For reasons Marsch attributed to his own ignorance, he thought Kidahin should show some jealousy whenever the other females rubbed against him at every opportunity, like Princess did. He played with her whenever she wandered from her mother to him and at other times when she wasn’t nursing from someone or taking her apparently normal five to fifteen-minute naps. When she slept, she hung on someone’s back like a baby lemur. He sat back, favoring his tailbone and hip, enjoying Princess’ snuggles, feeling her questing mind send him empathic love-protect babble, and watching the others work together.

The Eyloni observed rank constantly and were conscious of it always. Phelindra held the superior rank, both as Eldest Huntress and as the nominal leader of his improvised crew. He had somehow reinforced her rank in some way by giving her the throwing knife. Zalzadrin was the apparent executive officer. And yet, they all worked together as equals. They debated issues and alternatives, and no one lacked an opportunity to be heard. They encouraged sharing, but once Phelindra snapped her tail, the matter ended at once.

Unless he intervened in some blundering way. On those occasions when he asked for a simplified account or wanted to hear another person's point of view in depth, then the female offering the account or contrary point voiced her opinion without fear of reprisal from the higher ranked females or the group. Regardless of rank, they all expected unconditional access to him, and none tolerated limited access to him under any circumstances.

Kidahin held the lowest rank, and yet she participated on an equal footing with them. Even so, Marsch picked up on an ever so slight and testy deference she gave the others.

Princess, however, apparently hadn't received the notice on Eyloni female hierarchy yet. She had her own ideas about rank: she had it and no other did. She watched after him with the certainty of a hyper-jealous girlfriend. She had made herself clear early on with agile and savage nail slashes. Only after he had introduced her to the others did she deign to tolerate them near him.

Barely.

The Eyloni thought her possessive displays hilarious and reassuring. A relieved Phelindra reassured him that Princess's premature birth hadn't affected her instincts. They apparently found her antics as besotting as any mother found a toddler's.

Princess's interest in him was endless. She rubbed her face along his cheek and neck, scenting him and leaving her scent on him. She rubbed her ringleted tail tuft, her pons, all over his exposed skin. She always did so after someone touched him, usually quite furious with the toucher, too. She spent some time glaring at the plasticast on his collarbone. It bothered her, and Marsch guessed it was because it prevented direct physical contact. It didn't take long for her to notice that she could sink her nails into it and keep a secure hold there without harming him.

Over the next few hours Princess's pale-yellow skin began developing its own unique fall leaf color patterns. Her soulful, pea-sized pale tan eyes changed as well, giving over to a dark amber. She practiced focusing, her pupils contracting and dilating in dramatic fashion, changing from pin pricks to black depths; she made it clear that her eyesight worked just fine. As far as he could tell, her hearing remained about the same, and she responded only to his voice and to the occasional bass noises the ship made. She crawled about with extreme agility and confidence and could walk on two legs for short distances, but she did so by leaning far over and letting her tail counterbalance her. An arboreal creature, she preferred climbing and climbed up anything, including his legs. Marsch thought of kittens, but Princess never used her nails on him, preferring to grip him with her opposable thumbs, big toes, and tail. He thought her climbing normal because the others didn't seem too concerned about it.

That is, not after they all but sterilized the bridge deck plates.

The bridge and engineering controls diverted everyone's attention from Princess for lengthy periods at a time. Hervorallin stayed near Marsch. Although she had several cracked and bruised ribs, she clenched her teeth, bound her sides, and shuffled her way around the ship's control center until she found the bridge engineering station.

They were on a combat mission after all.

Marsch, ship's figurehead and baby-sitter, had little else to do, and he envied the others as they delved into the alien vessel's secrets.

He felt useless.

He joined Hervorallin at her station, and they talked about the ship's control systems while Princess slept clamped across his shoulders. Talking with her reminded him of talking with Melkorka all over again. The new mother's poor standard made her words sound strange. She told him they felt frustrated by the lack of proper diagnostic tools necessary to probe the unfamiliar alien technology.

Her wishes gave Marsch an idea.

His 'pad could perform analyses on energy flows. He'd used it earlier to check the bridge for combat hazards and to find basic power distribution nodes. He was no engineer. He had no idea how to interpret the data the device reported, or what to do with it even if he tried.

He pulled the 'pad from his belt and explained how the device worked and its limitations to Hervorallin.

Together, they worked out a system. She told him what to scan for, where to scan, and he entered the parameters, scanned the crystals, and read the results back to her. Several minutes later, Phelindra's curiosity overwhelmed her, and she wandered over to listen. It took her a minute to grasp the device's usefulness, and after watching them work together, she called the others.

Marsch scanned the presumptive engineer's station again and showed them how to perform different analyses on the data. Their voices rose in animated discussion, rousing Princess to ire once she felt too much of their focus on her male, and gave them a sleepy, annoyed growl that had them all sneaking indulgent smiles at her.

A newborn trumped rank as far as they were concerned, too. The Eyloni held another group meeting and discussed how best to use the device.

Marsch needed to stretch his legs again. Happy for a chance to get in more solitary exploring, he walked out the bridge portal. Phelindra darted after him into the dim tunnel. She did so not because of the sleeping infant, but because as his Protectress, she had determined that he would never go anywhere by himself ever again.

The ship's design revealed thinking in simple austerity. Burrows connected rooms, chambers, and compartments throughout the ship. The crew quarters didn't look that much better than the brig cells. Each had a single large crystal for light and a small matrix table filled with four different colored crystals controlling unknown devices in the cabin. The ship's sanitary facilities were functional and utilitarian, and they were clean. Pools filled with hot clay replaced bathtubs and showers. They found no sinks or mirrors.

The mess hall, on the other hand, made his hair stand on end, produced a hissing fit from Princess, and had Phelindra darting her eyes everywhere. Princess tugged at him with the strength of a two-year-old child, her tiny grip biting into his leg, her insistent yanking and empathic sendings making it clear that he must not remain here.

The mess reminded Marsch of a cross between a butcher shop and a morgue. Cafeteria lines ran along the front of alcoves fitted with clear crystal doors. A stasis field had held living creatures immobile. A Lizard would go to an alcove, select a living meal, drag it to the common mess area, and devour it. The feeding area had tables but no seats. They looked like narrow pool tables, even down to the raised sides and pockets in the corners. Nothing remained in the shallow tables now. They had foot toggles. When he stepped on one, water sprayed from under the raised sides, flushing like old toilets. The water ran across the table and into the corner pockets, following grinding noises and gurgling sounds echoing from each pocket's disposal unit.

The alcoves appeared empty.

There was no kitchen equipment. They found no ovens, no kettles, no fryers, no cutlery, no utensils, and no foodstuffs, spices, or any ingredients at all. Phelindra found water and a beverage resembling liquefied blood pudding.

"The crew can't have been living off this congealed blood drink and water. They must have been starving," Marsch said.

"That explains their frenzied behavior in the security area. They fixated on Kidahin at first and then on the both of you during the battle."

"I'm surprised they didn't devour you right after they stunned you."

"They knew you came for us. They dared not risk you ordering Melkorka to fire on them. If she had not destroyed the probe, they would have."

They left the mess and headed for engineering, to Princess' obvious relief. There, Marsch made a few vague encouraging comments to the engineering crew and left them to their work.

They returned to the bridge, where Marsch pried a protesting Princess from him and passed her back to Hervorallin.

Weakness swamped him. The bridge crew looked frustrated, but they did their best to mask it for his sake.

Marsch watched Kidahin work and a memory surfaced. He retrieved his scratched but still working piano, set it across his thighs, and played a soft gentle song. Soon, he had them singing while they worked.

Curious, he watched them react to the music. They became less tired and more focused as they sang.

He upped the rhythm to a subdued martial beat and just as Kidahin had, they responded to the militant beat, becoming even more focused and attentive.

But the beat also put Princess into a vicious rage. The rhythm triggered instincts that told her to protect her male. She wasted no time issuing combative challenges. Her demands in turn forced the others to rally their focus on her.

It didn't take her long to have them all ready to stomp off and kill something.

14

ABOARD THE NI' ZAKHONII LIGHT ATTACK CRAFT

Hours passed and although Marsch knew that playing cadence rhythms for the Eyloni was reckless, they must have produced results given Phelindra's apparent good humor.

"Del, we have reached the point where we must begin experimenting with the equipment," she said.

"Good. Anything in particular you want to try first?"

"Yes. We have traced the helm and navigation controls, but we still cannot gain access to the navigation computer."

"Then how are you going to navigate? Manual control?"

He hoped not! Manual navigation errors even over short distances grew to several hundred million-kilometer misses. Flying by the seat of the pants was fine for fighters, orbital maneuvering, or most interplanetary travel where a ship had the power to squander on repeated course adjustments, but manual interstellar navigation at FTL velocities was foolhardy.

"Yes. Kidahin thinks she can manually plot a return arc into the Nikkiolo system without the navigation computer. Once in the system, she will pilot the ship back into stable orbit around the moon. As a last resort, *Hunter's Moon* can tow us into orbit."

Marsch nodded. The plan sounded good, and it gave them a goal to shoot for.

"What about engineering?" he asked.

"We have discovered that FTL propulsion is powered by two integrated hydrogen-antihydrogen fusion reactors. One powers the helm and trim fields and the other generates the subspace warp field. Everything within that field phase shifts into a dimensional state where the speed of light changes scale the farther into the subspace dimensional domain the ship drops. Shut down that reactor and the field collapses, and we jump back into normal space at scaled down velocities relative to those we were moving at in subspace. When that happens, *Hunter's Moon*'s FTL scanners will not miss the significant neutrino emission and deceleration shockwave the ship will produce when we enter normal space."

Marsch frowned. "If we're travelling in the V-band, then we're moving at nearly fourteen hundred times the speed of light. When we cut power to the dimensional warp, we'll drop from 1,400 cee to a relativistic velocity of what? About 0.59 cee? At that speed interstellar hydrogen, dust, and Cherenkov radiation will light us up like a supernova. If the LAC's shields fail, we'll be fried by all that radiation."

"True, but we still do not know our current velocity, and we cannot calculate the normal space velocity dump without knowing the current FTL velocity band in which the ship travels. We assume the ship is traveling at its maximum speed, the V-band, and we will make a 0.22 of light velocity dump when we jump into normal space."

Marsch converted the Eyloni 0.22 base-five number in his head and came up with 0.54 cee. That was still awfully fast, and it would take them about seven minutes to come to a full stop at maximum reverse thrust.

"If our suppositions hold true," Phelindra continued, "then we should automatically decelerate to some nominal cruise velocity. The navigation computer may even initiate automatic braking. We are confident that, at minimum, the ship will reenter normal space and maintain some constant velocity. We also think the ship's proximity sensors will prevent him from jumping into occupied space. It is doubtful that we will hit a massive body."

Oh, really? Marsch didn't care about their exit velocity. It wasn't velocity that worried him so much as it was the vanishingly small chance of hitting anything of real mass. They dared not jump blindly into something too massive for the navigation shields to handle. Generally speaking, LACs weren't known for their heavy shields. *Sigh.*

"Fine," he conceded. "I have confidence in your abilities. Prepare to jump the ship to normal space."

"By your command," Phelindra snapped.

Twenty minutes later they all filed into the bridge and waited. Kidahin swapped glowing crystals in the navigation station's matrix table. When ready, she nodded, and propulsion technician Gruntilha grabbed the presumed warp field control crystal and pulled it from its slot in the FTL drive systems matrix table.

A receding, droning whine filled the bridge. The ship fell into normal space with a staggering shudder. The forward viewscreen snapped on, displaying familiar white stars on a black background.

Marsch sighed, relieved that they hadn't slammed into a rogue asteroid or something.

They appeared to have exited on a stable course. The viewscreen displayed a constant velocity-shifted star pattern. The lack of a tumbling view meant that the attitude control systems had engaged.

"Status?" Marsch asked.

"We have reentered normal space at some constant velocity relative to our current heading," Kidahin reported.

The crystal Gruntilha held started buzzing like a fistful of angry hornets. She looked at the pulsing white crystal and then at them in helpless confusion.

Mistress of Sails Rathrinda knew at once what was wrong, and she shouted over the rising din, "The crystals perform different tasks by the patterns they make in the matrix. You must replace the crystal in your hand with another crystal!"

They had to hurry. The thing rasped harsh grinding noises, an alert tone no doubt, that warned the operator of an open circuit or one that had not been shut down in the proper sequence.

"Gruntilha, you have to swap the crystal in your hand with the appropriate FTL drive shutdown crystal in the table. The system uses double redundancy controls. Look for a null crystal, one resembling the one in your hand," Rathrinda yelled.

"Affirm, acting!"

The crystals in the drive matrix flashed in sympathy with the missing crystal. The flashing patterns signaled a system overload and an imminent failure of the bridge drive control system.

After several frantic seconds of searching, Gruntilha found the required crystal and swapped it into the drive crystal slot at the same time she dropped the scalding hot drive crystal into the former crystal's space.

The rasping buzz ceased at once, and the crystal matrix stopped flashing alert patterns and resumed the normal brightness and colors it had displayed prior to the drive shutdown maneuver.

Marsch checked the time. It had taken them over twelve hours just to figure out how to shut down the FTL drive.

Days later Kidahin stood at the Command Center navigation station, chest heaving. Thwarted by the equipment and stymied at what to try next, her outrage fed into itself and grew as the minutes passed. It had taken her hours to trace and access the attitude and reaction control systems. She could pitch, yaw, and roll the ship using the manual maneuvering crystals in the navigation matrix. She spent several more hours picking through crystals and placing them in the matrix—almost blowing her hand off and then nearly melting the table to slag—before she was able to put the LAC through its paces by setting circular, elliptical, parabolic, and hyperbolic courses and using the RCS to drive the ship several hundred-thousand ells. While the reaction control system could propel the ship forward, it was no substitute for the sublight drive. She needed the engine systems active, and by day's end she still had not succeeded in tying the fusion engine into the manual piloting system or into the navigation plot matrix.

"It is not fair!" she screamed. She glared at the navigation station and flexed her long fingers into balled fists, ready to smash every multicolored gem into glittering dust, grind the dust into its component atoms, and pour them down the necessary.

Kidahin's impulsive anger walked tails entwined with her youth. An adult by tribal decree, she still had many instinctive tendencies more in common with the infant Princess. Kidahin reverted to them when under stress. It made her the ideal huluhar because she retained the same bonding instincts that drove the infant to form an empathic bond with Marsch, but it also made her by far the most impatient and rash adult aboard.

She jumped back from the helm controls and screamed in abject fury.

For far too many times now, her society agreed.

Among the rank-conscious, her lack of control did not endear them to her.

Marsch happened to return from engineering in time to find her growling and snarling at the navigation station.

Except for Kidahin, the others stared at him. Their scents passed ethereal suggestions as waves of patient tolerance—*do something!*—echoed in his head. They empathized with Kidahin, but her immature displays distracted them from their work.

It dawned on him what they wanted, what they hinted at without voicing it aloud. In their culture this was one of the reasons for having a male warleader. As the only male aboard, his presence should reassure Kidahin. And them. How, he wasn't quite certain. He didn't understand how just being there could inspire confidence in anyone.

An empathic Princess chose that moment to fidget at Hervorallin's breast, causing her mother to wince as her bruised ribs started aching again.

Marsch crossed over to them and rubbed Princess's back and shoulders with his index and middle fingers. His touch quieted her and produced a rewarding smile from her mother.

They smelled…contented. He felt simple pleasure from Princess, but Hervorallin's feelings gave him a convoluted vision of satisfaction.

He turned to Kidahin and made the connection.

Physical contact!

Eyloni females always expressed a need for casual physical contact, and it had increased since Princess's birth. Marsch remembered other times when they had made coy, fleeting contact with him. No matter what occupied them at any given time, they always paused to brush an arm, shoulder, hip, or tail against him. More than once he had responded in kind—a strange reflex hard to resist—before he knew what he was doing.

He stood there, watching the young Hunter whip her tail. Inspired, he wandered up behind her. She turned, wrapped her tail around his waist, and gave him a miserable look.

Touching her face, Marsch caressed her cheeks and forehead before reaching behind her to rub her back and shoulders.

Her scent filed his awareness, banishing what little remained of his wary paranoia.

Her relief washed through him in waves.

His touch calmed her. Leaning deeper into him and drawing him closer, she hummed in musical delight.

"Anything I can help you with?" he murmured.

"It is nothing, Del. This box of junk makes no sense. Attitude control and reaction control routes through the manual piloting subsystems in the normal space navigation system, but the sublight drive does not interface with the normal space navigation system."

"What about the FTL? Maybe the sublight drive and FTL drive control systems share crystals."

"Do you not think that I have already thought of that?" She turned, glaring vengeance at the humming, glowing matrix. Hate and vicious fury reeked from her scent, and the mental image Marsch felt made him cringe. The bloodthirsty revenant in his mind bore slight resemblance to the petite Hunter's personality.

Do all Eyloni have Jekyll and Hyde personalities?

Kidahin wanted so much to kill the navigation console. Marsch's stabilizing influence stood between her anger and the mocking baubles. His touch focusing her mind back on task, his scent calming her.

"The FTL drive and navigation control crystals occupy the upper right and lower left corners of this table. Manual flight, RCS, and ACS systems are controlled by manipulating the crystals in the upper left corner. By simple logic, the lower right corner crystals must control the sublight drive system, but no combination of crystals in both corners tie the normal space piloting and navigation systems into the fusion drive control system," she said.

Marsch weighed her analysis. The helm and navigation station included two glowing matrix tables and a fishbowl navigation display set between them. One crystal matrix plotted navigation data and accessed the navigation computer. The other set of crystals controlled the FTL drive, FTL navigation, the sublight drive, and the manual flight ACS and RCS systems. Kidahin could not find the interface linking the manual flight control crystals or the navigation plot with the sublight drive.

"The matrix table on the right controls the drive and helm systems?" Marsch asked.

"Yes. The ship's subspace FTL controls I understand. I think I can plot a subspace arc on the left matrix against this display using the crystals in the lower left corner of the right table. Engaging the FTL should be a simple swap of the drive control crystal into the navigation matrix. Using a different crystal from the upper right corner changes the current FTL velocity band."

"That makes sense. RCS and piloting controls close together makes sense, too."

"Why?"

"Well, you said the manual piloting, ACS, and RCS are controlled by the upper left corner crystals in the right matrix table. It makes sense because the RCS and ACS are in constant use during manual flight for either slow-and-close docking maneuvers, or for fast combat closure and evasion maneuvers."

Marsch rubbed her back as she thought about it.

His presence calmed her, cleared her mind, and helped her focus on the problem. "Wait, you are saying that the upper left corner crystals are dedicated to the manual flight ACS, RCS, and piloting controls?"

"Yep. Anything beyond manual piloting in normal space is slaved to the navigation computer for the long haul."

"No, Del. That cannot be correct. The lower right corner crystals are dedicated to the fusion drive. Signal analysis shows these crystals routing control signals to the sublight drive interface in the engine bay. An interface between the fusion drive and the navigation plot matrix should connect them."

Well, so much for his help. He was tired, but the longer he caressed Kidahin, the more his strength returned. It comforted him to be in physical contact with her. He shook his head to clear it and swayed on his feet.

Marsch's stumbling didn't seem to bother Kidahin, but it did attract Phelindra's attention.

"You need sleep!" she scolded.

"Later, I feel better now," he lied. "We're trying to puzzle out how the Lizards plot a course through normal space and transfer navigation data to the sublight drive."

Phelindra glared at Kidahin. "I thought you solved this problem when we spent all that time spinning around on thrusters."

"No," Kidahin grumbled. "Those crystals are dedicated to manual piloting only. They do not interface into the sublight drive control system."

"What about the FTL navigation system?" Phelindra demanded.

"What about them? They would not work for normal space navigation. Those crystals plot courses as a series of arcs. Ni'zakhonii physics maps subspace as a continuum of multidimensional arcs."

Phelindra wondered about that. Much older than Kidahin, the Eldest Huntress had more practical experience solving navigation problems. She could visualize a ship's course plotted as a series of arc lengths. Orbital mechanics and gravity wells guaranteed no straight-line plots in interplanetary space.

"Maybe they navigate through normal space in the same way they do while in FTL. A shallow enough arc is a straight line, after all."

Kidahin growled at her stupidity and moved crystals back and forth between the FTL navigation quadrant and the sublight drive quadrant. As they flashed a series of prismatic colors, Marsch's 'pad displayed a schematic that flashed an active signal pathway.

"Del, I show normal space engine systems active," Kidahin spat.

"Outstanding. Plot a short distance course and engage the fusion engine."

"By your command. Course plotted and ready to engage."

"Do it."

"By your command."

Kidahin pulled out the sublight drive crystal and swapped it into the FTL navigation quadrant and plugged the FTL quadrant crystal into the drive crystal's slot.

A deep reverberating drone filled the bridge as the LAC accelerated along a shallow arc, Marsch used his 'pad to record the star field on the forward viewscreen. He knew enough physics to calculate a Doppler shift from the starlight while under acceleration. With the data, he hoped he could make a crude velocity estimate.

The ship continued its constant acceleration for about ten minutes before the engine shut down. Once the maneuver had executed and the engine ceased its rumbling, the drive crystal pulsed a black light strobe.

Kidahin yanked the flashing crystal out and swapped it with its previous occupant.

Marsch consulted his 'pad. "I show our velocity at 0.55 plus or minus 0.04 cee and maintaining. Kidahin, you'll have to find a way to null our velocity. We don't want to slam into anything the navigation shields can't deal with."

"By your command."

"Good job Kidahin, Phelindra."

They preened and wrapped their tails about him in affectionate play, sandwiching him between them.

"I think the best way to null our forward velocity is to plot a reverse course over zero time," Kidahin mused.

"Won't that set the drive for maximum braking power instead of a gradual deceleration?" Marsch asked.

"Of course."

"Well, try it. I hope the inertial dampening and structural integrity fields can handle a dead stop from 0.55 cee."

"By your command. Ready to apply maximum braking power."

"All stop!"

"By your command."

Kidahin shuffled crystals around in the slotted table and slammed the final crystal home. The crystal matrix flashed a color pattern three times before a screeching, rending sound roared up from below and behind them as a sudden lurch threw them all to the deck.

Kidahin leapt back to the navigation station before the rumbling faded. Her eyes swept over its crystals.

Two no longer sparkled with internal fire. They were dead, burned out.

She reported the unhappy news to Phelindra.

"You should find replacements in ship's stores. They must have a complete set here or down in Power Systems and Propulsion. You must find a better way to dump velocity, otherwise we cannot decelerate the ship in normal space more than once or twice more without burning through the reserve navigation crystal inventory."

"Affirm," she said,

Phelindra turned to Marsch. "I have an idea about our reference difficulty for FTL navigation."

"Reference difficulty?" he mumbled.

"Yes, how to determine our velocity for FTL navigation. When you used your scanner to determine the ship's sublight velocity, you scanned the degree the starlight wavelength shortened toward the violet. If you scanned the star field before we jump through a known arc and then take another scan, you can calculate our displacement arc and velocity in known units."

Marsch turned to Kidahin. "Would that work?"

She thought about it, twitched her tail, and nodded for his benefit. "Yes, but accuracy will depend on the instrument's scanning resolution. The results will be rough, but it would give me enough rudimentary data for plotting a course back to Nikkiolo. Scanning errors introduce calculation errors over increasing distances. The viewscreen's display accuracy will compound the error."

Phelindra hissed a scold and shook her head. "You need only mathematically filter the errors introduced by Del's scanner and any navigation display nonlinearity."

"Yes, Mistress," Kidahin sulked, "I know that. But I cannot account for the display's spatial accuracy. The viewscreen is a visual aide, not a navigation aide. It may use scaling factors that present data more pleasing to the Ni'zakhonii eye, and we have no Ni'zakhonii eyes aboard that we can scan."

"Why don't you scan one of the field suit visors?" Marsch suggested. "You can use it as a model to reverse-engineer Lizard eye optics and normalize the viewscreen image."

Both Hunters gaped at him, shocked.

Marsch caught their amazed looks and snapped at them. "What? I'm not just a soldier. I have a degree in agricultural science."

Their astonishment followed him as he disentangled himself from their tails and stomped across the bridge. It didn't take long for the adrenaline surge from the navigation maneuver to wear off. His broken collarbone hadn't been too fond of the sudden stop either, let alone the stomping he now regretted.

The thin plasticast had cracked, allowing just enough movement for the bone to grate along its fracture point. The slug in his arm burned like it'd been punched over and over before being stabbed again with a red-hot ice pick. He should take another dose of pain killer. Both he and Hervorallin shared what little of the drug he had. She used little of it and not very often, either. Marsch wondered how much her refusal was feigned stoicism and how much was fear that it would get into her breast milk. He sat down next to her and talked himself to sleep.

Hervorallin smiled as Marsch's voice mumbled into silence. *It was good that the Warleader rested.* She shifted her nursing daughter so she could watch him.

A disturbing noise soon started rasping from his throat.

The soft snarling sound drew concerned ears, and inquiring eyes sought Kidahin.

Smelling their worry, feeling their pointed gazes, she shrugged the odd noise off.

The huluhar smelled unconcerned, so they returned to their work.

The growling did not escape Princess's notice, either. She swiveled her tiny ears and listened, considering the sound. Her male needed her. Jumping from her mother's breast to the deck, she crawled into his lap. Stretching to her full height, she stood there, leaning against his chest, sniffing him and listening to the noises he made. Eyes closed, considering, she weighed his sounds against his scent. Satisfied that her male had taken no hurt and made no warning growls, she settled under his neck, wound her tail around his upper arm, and set her tiny pons erect and quivering,

She was still hungry, and she was tired but she stayed with him.

Just in case.

Hervorallin's amused lilting notes caused the others to look first at her and then to where her ears pointed.

They watched the infant set her territorial warning stance. Looking at his face, Princess hummed their first song. The others returned to work smiling, but their collective discussions centered on more important matters.

Marsch spent the next few hours in blissful sleep.

"Del?"

"Mmm-hmm?" Marsch groaned, batting a hand at the voice, feeling cramped and sore from sleeping on the hard deck.

"We are ready to try an FTL reference flight," a kneeling Phelindra said.

Marsch came wide awake on hearing the warning growls of a displeased Princess posturing herself in the cutest threat display.

Phelindra stood up and stepped back. Marsch didn't blame her, either. He remembered how well Princess could swipe her sharp nails.

"Tell me how you want to proceed," he said.

"First, we must determine our FTL velocity to some degree of accuracy. Kidahin and I agree that we should jump the ship over three unequal time intervals and in three different directions. By doing so we can confirm or eliminate any nonlinearity in either the acceleration rate, or the distance traveled. Once Kidahin has FTL displacement and velocity references, she will plot a series of three return jumps using the reference flight data."

"I take it we can't use the original plot in reverse because we didn't reach the programmed destination."

"No. If we use the same arc with the same drive crystals, we will overshoot the Nikkiolo system by a displacement equal to the distance between our current position and the ship's original destination," Phelindra explained.

"Okay. Any progress with communications?"

"Some. Gaundellin and Herallin discovered that the ship's sensors and communications are routed through two matrix tables. They tell me that the Ni'zakhonii employ a broadband multiplexed EM emitter. There is no obvious way to know if we are transmitting a communications signal or activating a scanner. So far, they have isolated the subspace navigation sensors. They can generalize to some extent and guess where in the spectrum the normal space sensor probes, navigation beams, and communication channels probably are, but they do not know how the information is carried on any specific channel. The Ni'zakhonii may use any one of several possible modulation techniques," Phelindra said.

"Can you isolate the frequency ranges used by Compact or Coalition communication channels?"

Phelindra glanced at Gaundellin and sighed relief when she nodded but sucked her breath back as the Mistress of Communications added a caveat.

"I can activate the matrix and set it to transmit on a wide band. I cannot cover the entire range at once because the ship was not designed to operate all active sensors and communication channels at once. Different settings require the same crystals, but some crystals are incompatible with certain settings. I think this fact does not reflect a technical limitation so much as it does an engineering acknowledgment of design economy. The ship would require twenty tables to carry out simultaneous transmissions on all scan and comm bands."

"Can you program the device to rotate through the entire broadband range?" Phelindra asked.

"No, Mistress, not yet anyway. I can it turn on and off, but I am not able to program the system. Neither am I able to record a message for broadcast. We must transmit from the command center communications station at full power and nonstop. We cannot receive a specific incoming signal, either. I might receive any signal, a navigation sweep, a sensor sweep, a weapon scan, a tractor field, or an incoming message."

Gaundellin's disappointment showed in her flattening ears and drooping tail. Marsch remembered Kidahin's similar behavior when he had taken her knife from her. He reached out to the Hunter and touched her cheek before caressing her shoulder, and her ears perked forward.

"I think that's wonderful news, Gaundellin. Use your best-guess slice of bandwidth and key the emitters open when we jump back into the Iota Horologii system. Transmit for a minute or two and then reset the matrix for the next slice and repeat. If you somehow detect a response, isolate the bandwidth and report," Marsch said.

"By your command," she said, relieved.

"Phelindra, have Kidahin plot her FTL reference test flight and advise me when you're ready to implement it."

"By your command."

He missed something. The test he understood. They had to somehow quantify velocity and displacement before Kidahin could plot their return path along a flatter, shorter arc.

Marsch stood there, lost in thought. Princess reached up and grasped his cheek with her tiny velour kitten-like hand. He looked down in response to the tender caress and gazed into her eyes.

Princess knew her male's feelings, and any changes in them alerted her. She struggled to understand his scent and emotions. The other females irritated her so much when they took up all his time, but her empathic link with him was certain. She learned more about his moods and feelings the more he sang with her and held her.

She made an instinctive empathic link with his anger over something lost, a stab of pain to his side, and a deep tone she had once heard. She patted his face and warbled an octave-dropping rhythm.

Marsch hummed back to her. She acted like a princess, and he loved the demanding little monarch. He carried her everywhere, to Hervorallin's obvious and enthusiastic joy. He watched her ears swivel from him to Phelindra. Then she patted his cheek again and sang out a loud note that dropped in both volume and pitch.

Then she hissed at the deck.

Princess stared at Marsch. Her scent made him think 'remember', but her musical pitch reminded him of the ship when it…Oh, of course, the sudden stop.

"Kidahin, have you come up with a way to dump velocity when we jump back into normal space?"

"Maybe. The best I can do is change our exit angle. The dump in normal space arises from the arc plotting in the navigation matrix. When the ship exits subspace at right angles to the arc course's edge, he nulls forward momentum by bleeding the excess energy off as particle emissions. If we exit along the arc course's edge, we continue on at relativistic speeds and must decelerate using more conventional means."

"Oh. Sounds good. Proceed."

"By your command."

Marsch sighed. At least they wouldn't burn out any more crystals. He turned around and stumbled over five females sleeping on the deck, close to where he had been sleeping. They curled up and cuddled together around him like puppies on a blanket.

He shrugged, alternating between wishing he was sleeping with them and watching Kidahin and Phelindra remove and replace glowing crystals.

Shouldn't be long now.

15

Melkorka awoke from a fitful night's sleep, sighing, feeling helpless. For several days now, she had been expressing her annoyance as she prowled pathways, giving everyone she met empathic tail yanks. She had made no friends in Power Systems and Propulsion, either. The drive technicians and engineers crammed into the FTL armature spaces threw empathic daggers at her until she apologized and left them to their work. Now rested, she hoped to quell her inherent aggression, an aggression all Warriors suffered when battle had not gone their way.

She left her quarters for the command center. On her way there she opened the comm while admiring the pathway's holographic beauty.

"Anailiatha?"

"Yes, Mistress?" came the Mistress of Sails' prompt reply. Melkorka paused, gave a silent hopeful sigh to the spirits, and asked the same question she had been asking for days now.

"How long until our jump drive is online?"

"Between two and three days, maybe less, Mistress," came the better than expected but still disappointing reply.

"Do you have any good news for me, Anailiatha? I need some."

"Yes, Mistress. I can report at this time that, but for the jump drive, all damage has been repaired or bypassed and the ship is at maximum readiness."

Good, Melkorka hissed, *we can fight.*

An idea came to her.

"Anailiatha, will it hamper jump drive repairs if I call upon maximum sublight velocity?"

"No, Mistress. We are tuning the drive armature coils and will soon begin spooling simulations. The gravity lensing system is back to full operational status. Long range FTL scanning capability has been restored. Combat maneuvering will not affect testing and drive simulations. Why do you ask?"

"I am considering options. If one looks promising, I shall brief you before I commit to it," Melkorka said.

She prowled through the simulated rain forest terrain admiring the orange and golden grasses and called out again.

"Hlinlodyn?"

"Mistress?" the Mistress of Tactics replied.

"What is the status of the Coalition warship?"

"Mistress, the Coalition ship maintains position and continues launching and recovering fighters."

"Have they found anything?" Melkorka asked.

"Unknown, Mistress. We are tracking two sorties now. One group of twenty-four is flying reconnaissance sweeps in local space. The second sortie, a group of two, is following the destroyed probe's projected transmission path out of the system to where we engaged the Ni'zakhonii. This second sortie is the eleventh they have sent to the battle site. Mistress, the Coalition vessel's hyperdrive coils have been powered up since the sorties began."

"Acknowledged. Maintain vigilance."

She thought about Hlinlodyn's report as she hiked through simulated jungle terrain.

Melkorka arrived in the command center and slipped into her chair. She absentmindedly unsheathed Marsch's sword, placing it across her legs just above her knees and curling her tail around its blade before realizing what she was doing. Looking about guiltily, she sheathed the weapon and returned it to its place across the chair's raised armrests, thanking the spirits that nobody saw her lapse. Leaning back, all businesslike now, she asked the Mistress of Communications to open a channel to the Coalition ship.

✳✳✳

"Deep Probe-6 flight of two calling Stone Temple, come in please," Lieutenant James Caplain transmitted. He banked his Dart fighter to port and pitched down twenty degrees. "We have arrived at the Eyloni battle site."

He waited the eighty second delay it took even hyperlink comm traffic to travel thirty-five billion kilometers and back.

"Stone Temple copies, Deep Probe-6. Begin high resolution scanning of the debris field per your orders."

"Copy that. Commencing scan."

Caplain and his wingman swept along the leading edge of the debris field. There wasn't much left of the three Lizard destroyers. The field had expanded and grown more diffuse since the battle. What little remained amounted to metal filings, pieces of scorched metal, and twisted bulkheads not much larger than maybe twice his fighter.

Most people thought wreckage in space just floated there. A common misunderstanding, but like space battles themselves, wreckage was anything but stationary. Sir Isaac Newton had said that a moving object continues moving in a straight line unless something else acts upon it. During space battles, ships exploded. When they did, they became a confusion of pulverized fragments and twisted metal; sometimes significant parts of a ship went tumbling off in random directions. He and his wingman were searching for those significant parts and marking them for later retrieval.

They had been sent to find junk, an inglorious salvage run.

The routine scanning was boring. Pitching over into their seventh sweep, Caplain daydreamed about dogfights and fancy maneuvering, taking off during an alert, firewalling the three Thrush T0-220 hydrogen-antihydrogen microfusion engines, gripping the stick, rolling into attack formation, ignoring incoming fire, blasting enemy ships, targeting enemy fighters, closing on them, firing intercepts and countermeasures, banking down hard and left in evasive…

"Caplain! Wake up! Check your scan! What's that EM field signature mean?" Lieutenant (jg) Terry Shantz, his wingman, screamed.

Caplain shook his head and blinked, focusing his eyes on the scan summary. The scanners had locked onto some powered device as massive as his fighter.

He sighed. No enemy with guns blazing. It was just another piece of alien scrap.

"Stone Temple, Deep Probe-6. We've found a cluster of intact instrumentation. I think it might be a…"

"Deep Probe-6, Deep Probe-6, this is Stone Temple. I didn't copy that last. Say again, Deep Probe-6."

✦✦✦

"Problem, AOC?" Air Group Commander William F. Guthrey asked Air Operations Controller Justine Renee Burrell.

"Contact lost with Deep Probe-6, CAG."

"Did Caplain report anything, Petty Officer?"

"Yes, Sir. He said he thought he found intact instrumentation. He was about to scan it again when his transmission and telemetry cut off."

"Damn! Did he transmit any sensor data on what he found?"

"Negative, Sir."

"All right. Keep trying to raise them. Divert Blue Squadron from their local space survey mission to Deep Probe-6's last known position. Advise them that they're heading into a hot zone. They are to evaluate the situation, rescue or recover if possible, and complete Deep Probe-6's mission."

"Aye, CAG."

Guthrey reached up and grabbed the bridge direct line comm handset.

"Bridge, Flight Operations."

"Bridge, aye," Winters said, "Go ahead, CAG."

"Captain, I've lost contact with Deep Probe-6 flight of two at the Eyloni battle site. I'm retasking Blue Squadron to investigate, but I'd feel a lot better with Red Squadron launched and flying fighter cover."

"So ordered. What's your assessment, CAG? I want to give Melkorka a head's up."

"Sir, after what happened to Senior Chief Marsch and those Eyloni with him, I've got a bad feeling that I just lost two men. I recommend we adopt a defensive posture and prepare for incoming, Captain."

"I concur. Launch Red Squadron with orders to provide fighter cover for us and the Compact warship. We're going to Condition-1 CAG."

"Aye, aye, Captain. Flight Operations, out."

"Action Stations, Mr. Carstairs. Set Condition-1."

"Aye, Sir," Carstairs said. He toggled the bosun's whistle, the alert klaxon, the shipwide address system, and spoke in clipped, measured words.

"Action Stations, Action Stations. Set Condition-1 throughout the ship. Action Stations, Action Stations. Set Condition-1 throughout the ship."

✸✸✸

Blue Squadron arrived at Deep Probe-6's last known position an hour and forty-three minutes later. The FTL flight took them a mere eighty-two seconds, but sublight flight from *Henri Edda* to the hyperlimit and from hyperspace exit to the target area accounted for the remaining time. Short jumps always resulted in overshoots which took time to correct.

Coalition hyperdrive jump reliability increased over distance. Jumping from star to star made navigation calculations easy because hyperdrive was meant for interstellar travel, not interplanetary trips. Shorter hyperdrive jumps, those under thirty or forty billion kilometers, pressed even a capital ship's navigation computer and overtaxed a fighter's flight system. A fighter's bare bones hyperdrive was meant only for long range launch and return to its carrier or for bugging out if overwhelmed by enemy forces.

"Blue Flight Leader, Blue Flight-2."

"Go, Blue Flight-2."

"Blue Flight Leader, I'm reading an energy signature inside the debris field."

"Type and source, Blue Flight-2?"

"EM chatter mostly from something small and stationary at -18 degrees, 10 o'clock low, range 784,340 klicks, Ma'am,"

"I got it on my scope now, Blue Flight-2. Blue Squadron, break left and close."

Blue Squadron dove into the debris field. No sign of Deep Probe-6 yet, but the signal ahead superseded search and recovery operations.

Suddenly, Cherenkov radiation spiked on their scanners. The intensity and duration of the contact screamed that it was a ship. No theta-13 neutrino mixing angle emissions detected, but then again fighter FTL scanners were meant for plotting hyperdrive jumps, not combat tracking.

Blue Squadron Commander Ilyce Ison ordered her fighters to break off, get clear of the debris field, resume formation, and orbit above the field's leading edge in a five-thousand-kilometer circle.

"Blue Flight Leader to Stone Temple, come in Stone Temple."

"Stone Temple copies. Go ahead Blue Flight Leader," AOC Burrell said.

"Stone Temple, we have detected an energy pattern within the debris field coinciding with a Cherenkov radiation spike at extreme range."

"Did you get a fix on that spike, Blue Flight Leader?" Guthrey interrupted.

"Affirmative, CAG. It tracks as a pulsed shock wave spiking along a rough arc that comes close to intersecting the probe's transmission path. FTL scan puts the pulse at 1.19 light-years distant. That means the pulse occurred seven hours ago, real time. At V-band velocity, it will arrive here in another 3.58 hours, Sir."

"Standby, Blue Flight Leader."

✦✦✦

Guthrey reached for the red bridge direct comm handset.

"Bridge, Flight Operations."

"Bridge, aye. Winters here, go ahead CAG."

"Sir, Blue Squadron reports two contacts. One, a distinct radiation spike apparently incoming along the probe's transmission path some 1.19 light-years distant and 3.58 hours out. The second contact is an apparent stationary powered device operating within the debris field."

Winters hesitated. The Cherenkov spike hinted at an FTL-capable ship popping in and out of normal space, but that made no sense. The signal in the wreckage, while important, was less critical at this moment.

"CAG, do you think the distant contact is more than one ship?"

"No, Sir," came the prompt, certain reply, "An analysis of Blue Squadron's sensor telemetry predicts a single ship."

"What do you make of it, then? Why would they give themselves away? Why give us over three hours to prepare for them? Better for them to have jumped directly from Chi Eridani. Hell, they could have jumped from any direction outside of FTL scanning range. What about the power signature floating in the junk?"

"Sir, telemetry analysis suggests some kind of marker beacon. Captain, I think the Lizards placed a drone there, so they could come back with a vessel and recover or destroy any surviving tech before the Eyloni could mount a salvage mission."

"You think the inbound is the same vessel that shadowed the Compact warship and followed it into this system?"

"Yes, Captain. That ship lagged several hours behind the Compact ship and arrived long after the battle ended. They must have planted it there after we arrived."

"CAG, could that beacon have fired on Deep Probe-6?"

Guthrey thought about it. Beacons didn't mount weaponry, but an automated drone now, that was something different.

"Yes, Captain. I would guess it has a defensive radius, and Deep Probe-6 entered its defense perimeter. If Blue Squadron stays beyond its threat assessment range, they can ignore it until you decide whether to blow it up or send in a demolition team to disarm and recover it."

"Good to hear, CAG. Keep Blue Squadron there and assume for now that the FTL signature points to a patrol ship homing in on that beacon."

"Aye, Sir."

"Bridge, out."

"Flight Operations, out," Guthrey said.

✦✦✦

Warleader Phalalin of the Compact warship *Fearless* stood on the Warleader's Watch, shaking his head.

"Verikaralee, replay the human's message again."

"By your command," his Mistress of the Ship sang.

Phalalin watched the human's body language. The body never lied. He could not smell him of course, but the human male's posture betrayed a lurking deception.

This human played at verbal battle.

"Phalalin, we have identified this human. He is the Coalition counsel-speaker, the one meeting with Warleader Anlann," Verikaralee said.

"Can you make any sense out of what he says?"

"Nothing he says makes sense! He warns us that a human ni'zakhon has committed piracy by seizing a Ni'zakhonii ship holding several Eyloni females prisoner. He claims that this outlaw intends to use them to mislead Anlann and make demands on the Compact Counsel, demands that will destroy Anlann's mission. He wants you to order—*order!*—Melkorka to arrest him."

"Are you certain of this?" Phalalin asked, his scent reeking doubt.

"No, I am not certain of this! His claims are ridiculous!"

Phalalin turned his back on Verikaralee, smiling at her impatient, testy tone. Her words and scent worked their way into the minds of the command center crew, and now they took turns growling at the implied insult to society and warship autonomy. He smelled their anger fermenting and knew it would take little time before they became an unpleasant lot.

And for their own good reasons, too. This Harrison must be quite the fireside taleteller at male gatherings.

Why would not Anlann advise them of the problem himself, if there really was a problem? And why did Harrison think that the capture of a Ni'zakhonii ship was such a terrible thing? Was that not Kalinn's mission? And what about Melkorka? If this alleged outlaw human returned to Nikkiolo with an enemy ship and returned captured Eyloni females to her, then in the eyes of the Compact Counsel his honor would be unassailable and…

…and he would be warleader!

"Battle Status," he ordered. "The final jump into Nikkiolo will be a combat jump."

✦✦✦

"Incoming message from the Coalition warship, Mistress," Hlindredreda said.

"Accept," Melkorka said.

"Mistress Melkorka," Winters began, "We've picked up potential Lizard FTL signatures 1.07 light-years out. Assuming a ship travels under V-band velocity and jumps here, it will arrive in 3.21 hours. I have lost two fighters operating near where you destroyed the Lizard ships. Tell me, did you plant a demolition probe there in the event a Lizard ship came investigating?"

"No, Captain, we did not. Consider that target an enemy device. Please transmit your FTL scan data to us for analysis," Melkorka demanded and cut communications.

"What is your opinion of these scans?" Melkorka asked Hlinlodyn.

"It is not an optimal approach for any Ni'zakhonii vessel or combat tactic of theirs that we know of. This maneuver negates surprise."

Melkorka ordered the long-range scanners retasked to the coordinates indicated by the Coalition fighter data.

Fourteen hours later, Hlinlodyn detected a second FTL shock wave. She reported that scanners had found the telltale neutrinos that confirmed an FTL-capable ship. He followed an erratic course along the probe's signal path. The maneuver was inconsistent with any sane approach strategy. The ship had jumped twice now, skipping like a flat stone across calm water toward them.

The maneuver offered no tactical or strategic advantage Melkorka could see, either. A single direct jump improved the chances of a surprise attack. Why linger outside the system flashing bow shock radiation like a signal mirror? The Ni'zakhonii had—or wanted them to think they had-drive problems. But why? Compact battle doctrine dictated the destruction of any enemy vessel as standard procedure. The Ni'zakhonii knew that.

Navigation error? Perhaps. Stuttering along like that demonstrated an utter lack of navigation skill and suggested they had a junior navigator on her first training mission.

That sounded wrong in her ears, too. Nikkiolo was Compact territory. The Ni'zakhonii would not conduct training in enemy space. They would remain near the Surutia system.

Insistent intuition sang in her mind, and she froze.

Not a trainee, but maybe someone unfamiliar with the ship's drive and helm controls?

"Trebithia, how long before the Ni'zakhonii ship reaches his heliopause intercept point?"

"One and one-half hours, Mistress."

"Anailiatha, I need the jump drive now!"

"Mistress, quantum singularity programming is in simulation. I cannot abort it without losing the energy buildup. Even then, we must test the jump spooling sequence in simulation," the Mistress of Sails objected.

"We will test it in battle! Advise when the jump drive has spooled up!"

Melkorka pounced on her primary navigator.

"Mistress of Pathwalking, prepare to break orbit. Plot to intercept the Coalition fighter group at the apparent intercept point of the inbound enemy vessel. Maximum sublight velocity!"

"Affirm, acting," Trebithia replied and poured over her navigation console, plotting a course that would assist a quantum jump when the FTL drive came online. "Orbital departure plotted and transferred to helm. Sublight drive is online and ready for interplanetary maneuvering. Jump drive plot is on standby."

"Break orbit!"

"Affirm, acting."

A red light flashed on Carstairs's orbital traffic monitor.

"Captain Winters?"

"Yes, Mr. Carstairs?"

"Sir, the Compact ship is breaking orbit at high acceleration."

"What? Lieutenant Romaine, open a channel to them!"

"Aye, Sir. Channel open, Captain."

"Mistress Melkorka, explain your actions. Why are you breaking orbit?"

Melkorka's image appeared on the bridge main viewscreen. "Captain, that incoming Ni'zakhonii ship is commanded by Del."

Winters gaped at her.

Was she serious?

Winters slowly shook his head. "No, Mistress. That's not possible. Senior Chief Warrant Officer Marsch and your missing crew are dead by now. There is no way a single man could free twenty-two Eyloni and take control of that ship no matter how good a tactician he was.

"And Mistress, I've lost two fighters already. I'm not going to lose any more. I have ordered a fighter squadron to destroy any Lizard vessel that crosses the heliopause into the system."

Melkorka shook her head, ears flat, tail snapping, "Captain. I remind you that you are a guest in Compact territory. If you fire on a Compact-captured enemy ship, you will very much come to regret it. Other than in self-defense, if a Coalition asset fires on any vessel without my authorization, I shall fire on that asset with the intention of destroying it. You are warned, Captain."

"Transmission terminated, Captain," Romaine reported.

"Call the co-ambassadors to the bridge, Lieutenant Romaine!"

"Aye, Sir."

"Helm, plot a pursuit course, maximum sublight velocity!"

"Aye, Sir," Carstairs said.

Winters resisted the urge to find something to throw across the bridge. She *was* serious!

Melkorka's judgment must have been rattled by the loss of her warleader and his boarding party. The loss of twenty-two more must have pushed her over the edge. Now she was charging off on some insane hope that Marsch and her lost crew were on that ship.

And those damn Lizards left a weapon platform in the debris field that had destroyed two of his fighters. He bet a month's pay that thing would squawk combat telemetry to the inbound ship, providing firing solutions against Blue Squadron.

"Captain, the Compact ship's high delta-vee is outpacing us by a significant margin. I can't believe that ship's acceleration rate. They're maintaining $492km/s^2$ to our maximum $339km/s^2$. We're never going to catch them, Sir," Carstairs said.

Anlann and Seralin entered the bridge, both glancing at the active departure plot.

"He is at his maximum emergency sublight acceleration," Anlann said. Seralin nodded and glided up behind him; her eyes following the fleeing warship.

"What has happened that causes Melkorka to break orbit?" Seralin asked.

"We detected activity in the Lizard debris field and lost contact with two fighters. Then a Lizard ship jumped in and out of normal space twice at extreme range. I ordered a squadron to investigate. They are to intercept the ship and destroy it if it enters the system. When I advised Melkorka of the contact and my precautions, she lost her head and broke orbit. She's suffering under some delusion that Marsch commands the enemy ship, poor woman."

"What makes you so certain that the vessel is not under Del's command?" Seralin demanded.

"You, too? Come now, Ambassador Seralin, Delwyn Marsch was a damn fine strategist, but even he could not, by himself, sneak aboard an enemy vessel, rescue its prisoners, take over the ship, and master its systems well enough to navigate."

"Why not?" Anlann asked.

Winters gaped at him in open-mouthed disbelief. *Eyloni humor*, Winters decided, manifested at the most inopportune of times—or their wild hopes did, anyway. Maybe that was how they dealt with worry. He understood their desire to keep hope alive, but he had to deal with reality. As a ship's commander, Anlann should know better.

✦✦✦

"The third FTL jump has been completed, Del," Kidahin said.

Marsch looked up from the kakuro number crossword puzzle he'd been working through on his 'pad and nodded.

Time to take another reading.

Fantastic.

His 'pad processed the before and after scans and moments later spit out the latest jump's approximate velocity and displacement data. The course back to Iota Horologii, the system his crew called Nikkiolo, hadn't been optimal. He passed the data over to Kidahin and Phelindra for their latest course corrections, glanced around the bridge, and nodded.

"Kidahin, plot a course that places us just inside Nikkiolo's heliopause. We don't want to hit any space junk on entry into normal space. Use the sublight drive to take us into Ibeetu orbit. Let me know when you're ready to make the final jump."

"By your command."

"Del," Phelindra interrupted. "The drive crystals cannot take the continued punishment of hard delta-vee dumps as we drop back into normal space. We might lose the FTL drive matrix altogether on the next jump. If we lose the wrong crystals, we shall lose the sublight drive as well."

"I know. Kidahin, plot a gradual FTL deceleration before jumping into normal space. Hopefully, we can save our sublight drive if nothing else."

"Del, I know we are traveling at V-band velocity, and I know the other crystals select the slower bands, but I do not know which crystals swap which bands, and experimenting will only guarantee burning out more crystals. Without further trials, I have no raw velocity data for them, either. Without velocity data, I cannot plot a variable-speed course."

Marsch cursed, pacing the bridge. They would have to chance it using what little knowledge they had already pieced together.

"Okay. Okay. Let's hope we got someone's attention with our bow shock spikes. They should have picked up our last two jumps by now. If so, then they have had at least a few hours' notice of our coming. Kidahin, plot for Iota Hor…Nikkiolo's heliopause as close to our outbound arc as possible. We know there are no massive bodies along that path."

Marsch pulled the piano out of its pouch and activated it. His crew needed the energy and focus that his music provided. He crossed over to the bridge's main viewscreen. There, an ecstatic Princess crawled up his back, wrapped her tail around his neck, and straddled his shoulders. Her tiny hands flew to his head, gripping his hair in their tiny grasp.

"Ready to implement the final jump," Kidahin reported, snapping her tail.

"Take us into the Nikkiolo system."

"By your command."

They fell into subspace and traveled through the final 0.11 light-year displacement arc before jumping back into normal space ahead of the debris field's leading edge and well within Blue Squadron's scanning range.

"Stone Temple, this is Blue Squadron Leader. We have a Lizard light attack craft on our scanners. Repeat: we have a Lizard LAC on our scanners. Vessel is between us and the debris field and heading across our flight path in a wide flanking maneuver."

"Blue Squadron Leader, Stone Temple copies your last. Stand-by," AOC Burrell replied.

The CAG grabbed his red handset.

"Bridge, Flight Ops."

"Bridge, aye. Winters."

"Captain, Blue Squadron reports contact with a Lizard LAC."

"CAG, order Commander Ison to hold position one hundred klicks off that ship's beam."

"Captain?"

"You heard me, CAG. Tell her to observe only. They are to take no offensive action or otherwise engage that ship."

"Aye, aye, Captain Sir."

"Observe, hell!" Guthrey growled down Burrell's neckline. "Tell 'em AOC."

"Blue Flight Leader, Stone Temple. Adjust to parallel course one hundred klicks off that ship's beam and observe only," AOC Burrell said.

"Copy that, Stone Temple," Ison acknowledged.

"Observe?" Lieutenant Commander Ison spat, clenching her teeth so hard that she cracked a tooth.

❋❋❋

Commander Guthrey heard Ison's open comm curse and looked down. Burrell sat beside him in the crowded Flight Operations Center, her gray eyes cool and still in the open visor of her battle armor. A pulsed particle sidearm hung from her hip.

"Blue Squadron flight status, AOC?" Guthrey asked her.

"CAG, Commander Ison reports that they have matched velocities and are running parallel to the inbound ship at one hundred klicks. Their weapons and shields are hot and combat ready. They're ready to engage if necessary."

"Very good, Petty Officer," Guthrey muttered, thankful that Ison's last assignment had been with the heavy task force patrolling the Mu Arae system.

"Patch me in to her on TAC-2 hyperlink, AOC."

"Aye, CAG."

Seconds later, a tone beeped in Guthrey's handset.

"Commander Ison, this is Guthrey. Do you copy?"

"Yes, Sir. I copy you," the voice in his handset replied. "I have the squadron maintaining position one hundred klicks off the enemy ship's beam. No hostile action so far."

"Copy that, Commander. Disengage the LAC but keep an eye on it. I think the Captain hopes Marsch is aboard. You can't take that chance. If it twitches, or you get a bad feeling, blast it!"

"Aye, CAG. Copy that. Beginning our first pass."

❋❋❋

The Ni'zakhonii demolition probe drifted in space, mimicking the debris surrounding it. It lurked in the floating junk and awaited the arrival of investigating Compact vessels. Its mission: survey enemy ships, pinpoint high-value targets, attach fusion mines to their hulls, and remote-detonate them.

The probe's scanners detected the return of its service vessel and, per standard programming, overrode its mission directive and retasked itself for recovery. Its computer noted a discrepancy in the service vessel's approach vector and flagged the deviation. Hostile fighters in the area necessitated an on-the-fly recovery. It plotted an intercept course and engaged engines.

"Commander Guthrey!"

Guthrey whirled at the insubordinate shout. Burrell jabbed her finger at the mission plot, and Guthrey swallowed down the dread all commanders feared. A small craft had detached from floating debris and closed on Blue Squadron. Ison's talkback telemetry was screaming weapon lock warnings.

The demolition probe gathered speed and evaded drifting junk with radical sharp turns, pursuing the Coalition fighters even as they withdrew from its service vessel.

"That's no simple probe! It's going after Blue Squadron," Guthrey snapped.

Closing on its service vessel, the Lizard probe's threat assessment scanners painted several craft matching the profile of the non-allied fighters it had destroyed earlier. Legitimate targets, it disengaged safeties, acquired the nearest one, and fired.

"Blue Flight Leader, this is Blue Flight-5. Bogy closing fast on my nine o'clock. Its shields are hot, and I'm getting a weapon lock warning! It's firing on me! It's firing on me! Oh God, someone help me!"

"Blue Squadron, Break! Break! Break! Fire at will!" Ison ordered as Blue Flight-5 vanished like the morning frost in the dawn's brilliance.

Ison pulled out of attack formation, kicked in full military power, went evasive, glanced at her scanner, and swore. "We're coming up on the LAC intercept point. Even flights, stay on my six to the IP. Odd flights, engage the probe." She flipped her safeties off. A moment later, the targeting system status light turned red. Changing her grip on the stick, she rested her thumb on the trigger.

"Fire at will! Fire at will!" she barked.

Fifty gigajoule bursts rippled through space like tracer fire, chasing after the Lizard probe as the Dart fighters closed on it, scoring several hits before it veered off, heavily damaged, and made a run straight for the Lizard ship.

Ison scanned the enemy ship. Composition readings pegged the hull as a type of carbon-iridium crystal. Mass: about 18,327 metric tons. Maximum drive output: 9.4 terajoules per second. Maximum sublight velocity: 0.59 cee. Maximum normal space acceleration: $396.3km/s^2$, Maximum FTL velocity: Lizard V-band 1,339.25 cee. Armament: a single free electron x-ray laser capable of delivering eight terajoule per second bursts plus four torpedo launchers. Eight-point defense clusters and four torpedo intercept launchers peppered the hull, Ison scanned its sophisticated electronic warfare and countermeasures and its heavy overlapping multiphased particle defense shields. It was a hardened target. That was unusual. Light attack craft were fragile and ran under minimal shields.

And it reminded her of two fused half-ripe tomatoes with two green and pink daffodil horns curved forward.

❋❋❋

"Captain!" Executive Officer Rodgers yelled, "Flight Operations reports Blue Squadron taking fire from a mobile weapons platform exiting the debris field. They're taking casualties, Sir!"

"Time until we reach the heavy-mass hyperlimit?" an impatient Winters asked Carstairs.

"Twelve minutes, twenty-four seconds, Sir. Captain, even if we jump, recharge the hyperdrive, and jump back, we will overshoot the Combat Zone by millions of kilometers! It'll take at least another nine minutes to arrive at the CZ, Sir."

Winters glanced at the navigation plot, noted the changing delta-vee, and did the math. He shook his head and swore. A lot could happen in twenty-one minutes.

"We will overshoot the CZ. Can't help that. Plot a minimum possible distance hyperspace jump at dead slow. Jump us back as soon as the hyperdrive coils recharge."

"Aye, Captain. Minimal jump into and out of hyperspace plotted. Hyperdrive is on standby. Time to hyperlimit, ten minutes. Mark!" Carstairs said.

"Contact Melkorka. Warn her of enemy fire ahead and tell her so much for Marsch's return, dammit!"

"Aye, Captain. Channel open, hailing," Romaine said.

Aboard the Compact warship, Melkorka was studying battle formations streaming in from Combat Analysis. She ignored the Coalition warship's hail, preferring to pace back and forth in and out of the three-dimensional maneuvering plot. She had been studying it ever since they picked up the Coalition fighter transmission reporting enemy fire. Her eyes followed the incoming Ni'zakhonii ship's projected plot. He had not fired on the fighters. Nor had he changed course to take advantage of the armed probe's covering fire

Puzzling.

***

The demolition probe closed on its support vessel, signaling for auto-docking protocols. The LAC's asset recovery bay outer hatch cycled open and transmitted recognition and guidance data for recovery under battle conditions. As recovery commenced, the probe reported hostile craft to the LAC's threat assessment system. That system scanned the closing fighters, compared vessel profiles, and sent a priority alert to the bridge.

Phelindra looked first at the flashing pattern in the console's crystal matrix and then at the activated tactical display next to her station.

"Del, some object approaches from behind. A probe, I think."

"Where? What's it doing?"

"It has matched our course and speed," she said. Several crystals blazed in another matrix table. "I think it is attempting to dock with us," she said.

"Object is aft and closing," Kidahin reported. "Its approach vector suggests it has lined up with our stern. It is trying to access a probe recovery hatch near the main airlock. I think it... Wait! Incoming fire! Incoming fire!" she yelled.

"From the probe?" Marsch asked.

"No. Aft sensors report several fighter craft. Visual contact. Silhouettes match those of Coalition fighters, Del."

Marsch jockeyed around Kidahin's station and squinted at the screen.

"Yep," Marsch grunted. "Dart fighters. A squadron of them at least. Captain Winters must have sent them out after that thing, and they've chased it into us. I bet it's like the one Melkorka destroyed. Communications status?"

"Cycling through all bandwidths using the command center combat address system. No response."

Krump. Krump… Krump… Krump…

Mild concussive impacts shook them. Field harmonics induced a rumbling vibration through the ship as the shields distributed the striking energy across the hull.

"We are taking fire from the lead fighter. No damage," Phelindra reported, surprised.

"Understood," Marsch said. "They think we're a courier ship coming in to retrieve this probe. Phelindra, watch the tactical scan. Kidahin, take manual control and go evasive. Maybe we can jinx around long enough for someone to copy our transmissions."

"By your command."

He forced himself to return to his piano playing. The bridge crew joined him in song.

Marsch played for their morale and to help them concentrate. The Eyloni reminded him so much of his daughters. The aching wound that was their deaths was gone. He hadn't forgotten them. He still missed them horribly, but the Eyloni occupied a place beside them. Princess was his daughter somehow, too.

Playing for them here was like playing for his daughters and wife back home on Valhalla. The anxiety, the hyperarousal, the nightmares had left him. The dread was gone, fettered by the Eyloni somehow.

Unless he started worrying about them.

There were two others he couldn't save.

Their scent—the LAV driver and gunner—nagged at him.

He felt them here, on the ship.

But where?

Mesmerized, he thought of them.

Del?

An alert Princess shrieked at the females surrounding her.

Listen, her pheromones told them.

The infant's scent drew arrows pointing at faint pherornonal signatures.

Kidahin, her youthful instinct drawing her to the infant Hunter, was the first to stop singing. They had an unspoken understanding, a shared affinity, and a common interest.

Marsch lacked the olfactory structures necessary for making sense of the faint scent, but his PTSD sensitivity to Eyloni pheromones drew Princess, Kidahin, and then the others' notice. A feeling, something like déjà vu, sent Marsch on a mission, and the Eyloni following close behind.

They returned to the ship's galley and its autopsy table dining areas.

✦✦✦

Hunter's Moon crawled toward the edge of the star system under maximum sublight acceleration, pulling farther and farther away from the Coalition carrier. Melkorka planned her attack: Captain Winters intended to jump to the heliopause and then plot a return course back to the Action Zone at maximum sublight velocity. She had no doubts that they would emerge close to the AZ. She glanced at the command center's chronometer and hoped Anailiatha's estimate matched her skill.

Real time battle assessments crept across the tactical plot. Coalition fighters gave chase to the probe as it closed on the enemy ship.

"Mistress of Tactics, plot firing solutions against the Coalition fighters," Melkorka ordered.

Anlann's mission notwithstanding, no one would harm an association's male.

"Mistress!" the Mistress of Pathwalking interrupted, "I am receiving modulated signals over my FTL navigation scans!"

"Modulated signals? Do you mean comm signals?"

"Yes, Mistress. The pattern is consistent with audio and visual data harmonizing with the scan return."

"Hlindredreda, acquire that signal and transfer it to the Warleader's display!"

"Affirm, acting," the Mistress of Communications said. She tied her communications equipment into Trebithia's navigation sensors and transferred the signal.

The image warped at the edges and puckered circular distortions filled it, only the centers of each circle showed clear visual pictures, and those in the middle of the holographic display were much clearer than those along the edges. Audio shifted in and out: a kietl's melody, Marsch's deep singing voice, and female accompaniment sang to them.

Melkorka counted their distinctive singing voices. Two were missing, but the rallying pitch of an infant female sang with him, too. Hervorallin had given birth early? The screen cleared, and she watched the possessive infant Hunter grip Marsch with her tail, her strident melody urging the others to help her defend him moved her in ways no call to battle ever could.

"Hlindredreda, open a channel to Captain Winters. Advise him we have visual confirmation that Del is aboard and in command of the enemy vessel," Melkorka ordered.

"Affirm, acting. No reply, Mistress. The Coalition ship has reached his minimum safe jump distance for his mass."

Melkorka watched as a hazy violet portal swallowed the carrier. She turned to the tactical chronometer and timed the jump.

One minute. Two minutes. Three minutes…

"Mistress, the Coalition warship has emerged from hyperspace 2.432 light-minutes from the AZ and is correcting for overshoot and decelerating. He will reach firing range in 14.1 minutes," Hlinlodyn reported.

16

LOGISTICS

"Mistress! The jump drive is online!" the Mistress of Sails sang from her station in Power Systems and Propulsion.

"Bless the spirits!" Melkorka said. "Mistress of Pathwalking, plot an FTL jump 40,000 ells off the fighter group's left flank and match velocities. Mistress of Tactics, load torpedo bays with EM pulse torpedoes and prepare to fire upon jump exit."

"Affirm, acting," both Mistresses replied.

"Prepare for combat jump!" Melkorka said.

"Jump plotted. Vectors set. Ready to jump!" Trebithia said.

"EM pulse torpedoes set for maximum spread, minimum yield. Ready to fire!" Hlinlodyn reported.

"Jump!" Melkorka ordered.

The Compact warship quantum translated them to the Action Zone in almost no time at all, slamming into existence 5.3 kilometers off the fighter group's left flank.

"Fire torpedoes!" Melkorka said.

Hlinlodyn targeted the fighter group and fired.

A stream of shimmering plasma balls belched from one of the warship's starboard broadside torpedo bays and streaked into the Coalition squadron.

Blue Flight Leader and Blue Flight-3 had just completed their closure maneuvers and were streaking inbound under full power and taking up their attack positions. The remaining odd numbered fighters were lining up behind them for multiple strafing runs when multiple threat vector alerts flashed on their scopes. Ison screamed a warning, too late, as incoming fire streaked into them.

Multiple starburst patterns erupted all around them, not concussive or flak ordnance either. Ison frowned.

Their fighters bristled and shimmered, bathed in energy. Ison watched as pyrotechnics more at home in Dr. Frankenstein's lab flashed across her fighter's skin for several seconds before her power systems—including battery backups—failed.

Her fighter dead in space, Ison looked out her transparent canopy into the cold dark vacuum and glared at a massive *Hunter's Moon* looming off her squadron's flank.

Compact EM pulse weapons technology made fighters all but obsolete against a Compact warship. All Blue Squadron fighters lost internal power and continued adrift. Only vessels large enough to mount Faraday cages could shunt EMP away from critical systems. The Dart fighter, basically a pilot's seat strapped to three microfusion engines, had no defense against EMP ordnance designed to weaken heavy warships.

♦♦♦

Melkorka studied the impotent fighters, satisfied. Their fusion systems scrammed when their control systems had fried. Flight suits and bottled emergency oxygen would keep their pilots alive long enough for Captain Winters to mount multiple rescue and recovery missions.

"Mistress, Del's ship is maintaining his present course and velocity," Hlinlodyn said.

"Have you tried contacting him?" Melkorka asked the Mistress of Communications.

"Of course, Mistress," Hlindredreda snapped. "The vessel cycles through all active scan and comm bands. I think Del has ordered them to sweep all frequencies to increase their chances of being detected."

Melkorka nodded. She wondered what secrets the enemy ship held. What little enemy tech the Compact Fleet had managed to find so far had been useless battlefield junk. The capture of an intact enemy vessel would make an impressive display.

"Mistress, I have a perimeter alert. The Coalition warship has entered the AZ. There is priority comm traffic for you from the human warleader. He is not pleased," Hlindredreda said.

"Of that I have no doubt," Melkorka said, smiling in wicked humor.

***

"Del! Jump signature! *Hunter's Moon* has jumped in behind us and is flanking the attacking fighters," Raelindra reported.

Marsch nodded but continued singing. Only their singing was keeping him alert now. If he stopped, he was certain he'd lose his edge.

"*Hunter's Moon* is firing on the fighter group. Visual effects suggest an EM pulse torpedo spread," Phelindra said.

Marsch hoped Melkorka wouldn't have to destroy the squadron to save them.

"Kidahin," he gasped to the busy Hunter in the pilot's seat, "Prepare to shut down the drive and assume station-keeping off *Hunter's Moon*'s beam."

"By your command."

The tactical display showed fighters adrift and tumbling. With their flight avionics burned out, they couldn't null out the fractional thrust the EMP ordnance had imparted to them. No doubt a few pilots were already hurling into their helmets by now.

"Del, we are decelerating, and Melkorka is matching velocities and adjusting to parallel our course," Kidahin said.

"Sounds good. All stop. Hold us relative to them," Marsch said.

"By your command. All stop. Melkorka is reducing velocity to all stop and is holding station several thousand ells off our flank."

"Does anyone have an idea how Melkorka can talk to us?" Marsch asked.

They looked at one another in speculative confusion for several minutes before a bruised Hervorallin spoke up.

"We have a visual on them. Ask Melkorka to flash an optical device at us."

Marsch thought about it, wondering why she didn't ask Melkorka herself, and nodded. He played a repetitive rhythm and sang the idea over and over again to Melkorka.

✦✦✦

Melkorka listened to the modulated deflector return, humming along with the music, and thinking about his communications suggestions. Marsch had not found a way to activate the enemy ship's communications systems, except to transmit across large segments of bandwidth at a time. He could not receive her calls, not even the ones Hlindredreda had tried to send on the navigation deflector harmonic.

Marsch changed tempo, and Melkorka considered his list of several optical signaling alternatives. Optical lasers or running lights might work. The laser needed an optical pickup. Running lights would work if Marsch knew how to magnify and focus his viewscreen. No. She stamped her bare feet on the simulated jungle floor. Too many unknowns. Better for her to flash the ship's shields in the visual spectrum and send messages in Drum Language.

In ages past, her people used large bass drums mounted in tall trees for sending distant messages. A drummer beat a series of notes that identified sender, recipient, urgency, and the message itself. When technology made distance drumming obsolete, her people refused to allow the language to fall out of use. Many times, a warleader beat commands while on the battlefield. Prudence argued that the ancient language be taught for times when technology failed, was insufficient to the need, or was not available. An optical strobe could not replace the music, but the language itself was a shifting series of notes embedded in a song. To decode the message, the recipient played a cipher song and listened for the beat frequency notes that coded the true massage.

All Eyloni knew Drum Language. The radiological defense shields would fluoresce an electric blue when ionized. If she flashed the language beats off the shields, then anyone watching could interpret it for him.

✦✦✦

"Comm status, Phelindra?" Marsch asked.

"We have narrowed our transmissions to a scanning frequency harmonic used by Compact navigation deflector beams. This ship's transmitter is modulating a return sweep's harmonic image." she explained.

"Oh," Marsch grunted. He pictured a radar signal reflected by some nearby navigation obstacle. Their transmissions were modulating the return echo. It surprised him that Melkorka could get enough signal from the return to reconstruct their live broadcast. That said a lot about Compact signal processing capabilities.

"If they sent a message by modulating their navigation shield, could you transfer it to the viewscreen?"

"No." She shook her head and rubbed her pons against his side. "I cannot access the Ni'zakhonii navigation deflector array for the same reason I cannot access ship-to-ship channels. It comes down to the total crystals in the matrix table and all the combinations possible using those crystals. It would take me years to exhaust every possible grouping. Without extensive technical analysis of the comm system, one sequence is no better than the next. Imagine an ancient radio that uses piezoelectric crystals to tune in a channel. If the radio is this console, then the piezoelectric crystals are these control crystals. Now imagine that my ancient radio works only when I select all these crystals in the proper order. How many ways do you think they can be grouped?"

"About twenty-one trillion," Marsch muttered.

✦✦✦

"Mistress, the Coalition ship is demanding that we open communications," Hlindredreda interrupted.

I cannot ignore him forever, Melkorka sighed. She had already made him wait a quarter of a Coalition standard hour.

"Accept."

The tactical data ghosted as Winters's face solidified in the holodisplay.

"You fired on my fighters!" Winters bellowed.

Melkorka gazed at the human a moment before replying.

"Yes, Captain?"

"You had no right to fire on my fighters! Blue Squadron posed no threat to your ship. I demand an explanation and an apology for your actions!"

"Captain, you are in Compact territory. I gave you clear warning not to engage in offensive conduct while in our territory but for self-defense. While I grant you had probable cause for engaging the enemy probe, you did not have cause for firing on the captured Ni'zakhonii ship. I was well within my rights and freedom of action to fire offensive ordnance into your fighters. Consider yourself fortunate that I chose pumping the area with electromagnetic pulses and destroying electronics over shooting down your fighters."

Winters bit back a retort. She did have a point. He had been warned, but he resisted conceding the point that Blue Squadron lacked cause to fire on the LAC. But he'd gotten off easy. All the intelligence briefings had warned of Eyloni deadliness when defending their territory. Realizing he'd not get far by pushing the argument, he changed tactics.

"Have you confirmed that Marsch commands the Lizard ship, Mistress?"

"Yes, Captain. We are receiving Del's transmissions on a harmonic of our navigation deflector. We cannot transmit to him because he has no fine control over the ship's comm systems, but I am in constant contact with him by optical means. He has made his orders quite clear to me, Captain."

"His *orders* to her?" Anlann whispered to Seralin.

She batted at him with her tail, trying to listen.

"Mute," Winters said.

"Transmission muted, Sir." Romaine said.

"Lieutenant, can you tie into their navigation sweeps and pick up that signal? I want visual proof Marsch is in command of that ship!"

"Yes, Sir. It'll take a few minutes, but I'm sure I can tap into it," Romaine said.

"Do it."

"Aye, Captain."

"Open, Lieutenant," Winters said.

"Aye, Sir. Channel open."

"Mistress, have you tried teleporting Marsch and the Eyloni aboard your ship?" Winters asked, stalling.

"Yes, Captain," Melkorka said. "Something about the ship's hull makes quantum translation impossible. We do not know why. He is a stealth vessel. I am considering alternatives."

"I have the signal, Captain," Romaine said.

Winters nodded. "Transfer it to my station screen and record."

"Aye, Sir."

"Mistress, we're going to try locking our teleport systems onto Marsch and bring him aboard our ship. As Marsch is still a Coalition officer, the captured Lizard ship has been, and is, under Coalition control. We will tow it into our flight deck for study. Once we have secured the vessel, I'll have your crewmembers teleported to your ship."

Winters thumbed a switch. "Chief Kidwell? Lock onto Marsch and bring him aboard."

"Aye, Captain," the teleport chief replied. She paused. "Captain. I can't get a lock on him. The Mobius interface point isn't stable. It just reflects off the hull. It's some kind of scattering effect, Sir."

"Can you compensate?" Winters asked.

"I think so, Sir, given enough time."

"Do it and contact me when you have Marsch aboard. Winters out."

Melkorka and both co-ambassadors began yelling at once.

"Captain," Anlann overrode the infuriated Mistress only by his physical presence, otherwise the spluttering Warrior would have kept Winters at the viewscreen. "Del removed himself from Coalition obligation and does not act on its behalf. I told you that if Del returns in command of that ship, then he also holds the rank of a Compact warleader."

"But that was hypothetical, Anlann," Winters objected. "This isn't the time for hypothetical musing. Marsch hasn't exercised command since his arrival. He hasn't transmitted any Warpact command orders to you or Melkorka. Correct, Mistress?"

The fuming Warrior glared at Winters. "Del does not assume Warpact command by lording it over us, Captain. He holds it because he is the first on-site male with a combat asset. He does not declare a Warpact; we presume it because a female society under the direct command of a warleader of the O'un Tu Clan of the La'huaset Tribe captured that ship."

O'un Tu? Anlann's tail dropped to the deck in astonishment. Forgetting Melkorka's technical misstatement of Warpact protocol, he turned to Seralin.

The Fire River Clan? his pheromones asked her.

How in the spirits was that possible? The O'un Tu Clan elders and its people would have had to first adopt Marsch in a ceremony on clan territory, back on Elleio. Away from the homeworld and home territory, mating with an O'un Tu female gave a male provisional standing in the clan until she gave birth. That standing then vanished, and his membership reverted to his mother's clan unless he bonded with that infant female. Marsch could not have done that either, even granting that an Eyloni-human mating could occur and carry to full term.

"Birth bonding," Seralin whispered. Her voice took on a soft, meaningful tone.

"Birth bonding? No. A female would have had to give birth in his presence for that to…Oh!" his ears pointed at her as understanding dawned.

Winters hated to admit to it, but Anlann was right. Marsch had resigned from the Coalition Fleet. He couldn't undo that fact.

"Mistress, it pains me to admit it, but you are correct. I concede to your claim on the Lizard ship. Compact personnel captured it while in Compact space and therefore, it belongs to the Compact Counsel. However, you must return Marsch to me. Ambassador Harrison has filed a formal complaint charging him with interstellar piracy. It is beyond my authority to order the Ambassador to withdraw his criminal complaint."

"That is unacceptable, Captain!" Melkorka shouted and broke contact.

"Ambassador Harrison?"

Harrison sat up in his bed, stretched, and reached for the nightstand's comm.

"Master Chief Deering?"

"*Swan Lake*, sir."

"Switch to your omni, channel TAC-B, and scramble."

"Yes, Sir."

Harrison dug his omni out of a desk drawer and waited. Marsch and those damn Eyloni, it had to be! What the hell had happened? Dammit, that insane Marsch must have flown that Lizard ship back here.

Oh, no! Anlann had said he would cede his authority to Marsch if he returned in command of that ship. Marsch would hold Compact command authority over all Eyloni in the system.

Harrison cringed, remembering what else Anlann had said. He would ask Marsch to recommend to the Compact Counsel that Winters be considered the Coalition negotiator, and any future talks would then proceed between Anlann and Winters.

His omni bleeped.

"Report, Master Chief!"

"Mr. Ambassador, Marsch has captured and returned in command of the Lizard LAC. Melkorka doesn't seem in much of a hurry to take any action at all."

"Has Warleader Phalalin made further contact?"

"No, Mr. Ambassador, not after advising us that he intends to jump into the system ready for battle."

"That sounds to me like he bought it! How long before they jump into the system?"

"Not long, Sir. I ran the numbers while I was in the TOC. They should arrive in about ten minutes, but they programmed their jump for Ibeetu orbit. We're between thirty and forty billion klicks from there. It would take them about forty-eight hours to get here at their maximum sublight velocity. It'd be faster for them to wait fifteen hours in Ibeetu orbit while their jump engines recharge and then jump here," Deering said.

"Fifteen hours? Well, that doesn't matter now, does it? Ten minutes! Phalalin is almost in the system now. That makes him the on-site warleader with his warship. He's not going to let some human in a dinky Lizard LAC tell him what to do, and he's certainly not going to let a human dictate Compact policy. Phalalin has no reason to make any diplomatic changes, and by the code of Eyloni male autonomy, he can't interfere with Anlann's mission on his own. We must keep Marsch from talking. I'll force Winters to press for his extradition to Coalition custody."

"Mr. Ambassador, Captain Winters already tried to teleport Marsch off the LAC. It's shielded."

"Can a shuttle dock with it?"

"I don't think so, Sir."

"Well, Marsch can't set foot aboard Melkorka's ship without getting himself killed. He can't stay on the LAC like it's some *Flying Dutchman*, either. I'll insist that Winters tow it onto the flight deck."

"That won't work either, Mr. Ambassador. Captain Winters has already conceded ownership of the LAC to the Compact."

"That fool. I swear Winters has no backbone at all. It's no matter. Marsch can't get off that Lizard ship until Phalalin arrives. When he gets here, he can order Melkorka to board that ship, put Marsch in restraints, and once they get him clear of that ship, we'll teleport him here."

***

Phelindra continued analyzing the ship's crystal technology. Kidahin translated Drum Language flashes from the warship's shields. Marsch passed the time playing with Princess.

She kept his mind off the two Warriors they'd found in critical condition in the mess stasis alcoves. Missing limbs, their extensive injuries made him quail at the sight of them.

And yet those two worried more about how their injuries were unsettling him!

He murmured vague baby-talk, and Princess sent him another rhythmic scold. This time for calling her by baby names. She made it quite clear repeatedly that she knew her name. She objected with feelings of loss whenever he called her by any term of endearment. She made him feel her hurt and lost, as if he had forgotten her. The emotions she projected through her pheromonal link into his head made him feel like a two-year-old lost in a department store.

She had a routine: sleep for between three and fifteen minutes, nurse from one of the females for a few seconds, nurse from her mother for about a minute, play with him like a spunky, smart kitten, and fall back asleep.

Princess didn't cry like human babies. She sent strong empathic impressions at him. His mental impressions of her and his daughters, their importance in his life, were blurring, merging. The overlapping family ties felt strongest with Princess. Kidahin came in at a close second, somewhere between the awareness of an infant and an adult daughter. The other Eyloni were merging into his fatherly instinct too, but as if they were his daughters grown into womanhood.

It felt uncanny to him. The Eyloni didn't swamp the emotional memories he had for his daughters. They complemented them, as if he now had many living daughters. Every time he thought he understood the complex undercurrent of feelings, they vanished like fleeting intuition.

Marsch could not know that he suffered a biological handicap from an Eyloni point of view. He lacked half of the sensory organs needed for understanding their pheromonal signaling. Eyloni pheromonal empathy depended on both a vomeronasal organ and a large olfactory epithelium in their sinuses. Humans lacked the vomeronasal organ—a pheromone control center—but pure genetic luck had given Marsch a larger than normal olfactory epithelium and reinforced neural ties between it and his brain's olfactory bulb, medial amygdala, hypothalamus, and cerebrum. The lucky net result allowed him to smell their feelings and perceive them as intuitive impressions. That had made him sensitive to babies, animals, and his surroundings, giving him a natural situational awareness.

The type of PTSD Marsch suffered affected his olfactory, amygdala, and hypothalamus pathways. Eyloni pheromones chemically altered those pathways, modulating his symptoms as they modulated Eyloni male aggression. The Eyloni could not know that he was missing the pheromonal language interpretation, receiving only hints and ghostly suggestions. They did not know the details he missed, and they assumed he read more from their scent than he was capable of understanding.

Princess's humming and Kidahin's body movements nabbed Marsch's wits. Adrift, his mind cruised along the edge of consciousness. After some interminable period, his bliss shattered into a storm of angry growls and challenging hisses.

Marsch opened bleary eyes and looked around. The first thing he noticed was a crowd facing the main viewscreen pickup. The second thing he noticed was that they had all crowded into the bridge. Their tails whipping, ears twitching, and hands gesturing, they punctuated serious words in that sign language of theirs.

Princess somehow took an active part, too. She did not understand their waggling fingers, but she had picked up on their intense group pheromones, and her fierce snarls were goading them along.

Something had made them angry. He'd never seen them so angry before, not even when they had discovered the two critically wounded Warriors—*who they had carried here for this argument*—in the mess.

They stopped signing and started speaking in their sing-song melodic tongue.

They weren't arguing. They were debating.

Phelindra trilled an expletive, snapped her tail, and sang a lilting inquiry.

To Marsch, they seemed to have come to a consensus.

Except for Princess, they turned and faced the main viewscreen. Making a short statement to Melkorka, each sang the same musical score.

Marsch stood next to Kidahin and tried to find out what had made them so agitated.

"What's going on here?"

She ignored him.

Melkorka watched Marsch's females. When they had finished declaring their intent, she addressed her society over the interactive mode combat address system.

"Are we in complete agreement?" she asked her society.

Everyone aboard the warship alternated between listening to Melkorka's persuasive plea and watching the images streaming from the LAC command center, listening to Marsch's females argue their case, watching their huluhar constantly wrapping and unwrapping her tail around his waist, watching in anguish the two suffering Warriors make their stand, watching with humorous curiosity as Hervorallin's infant kept snapping her tail at Kidahin in annoyance, smiling at her possessive complaint. They remembered after all these years the scent of their bonding males and their welcoming songs. The familial bond between male and newborn female was unforgettable and permanent.

Time passed.

No one aboard the warship objected.

Melkorka gave a wistful sigh.

She was about to do the unheard of. She would bring a male aboard a Compact warship, one not his warleader, violating all custom and tradition.

"Mistress of Tactics Hlinlodyn," Melkorka said most formally and with deliberate specificity, "lock tractor fields onto Del's ship and prepare to tow him into the main troop staging area of the combat deployment bay."

✦✦✦

"Captain! The Compact warship has locked a tractor field onto the LAC. I think they mean to tow it into their troop transport bay, Sir!" Rodgers said.

"Does Teleport Control have a lock on Marsch yet?"

"Negative, Sir. The LAC's hull still scatters the lock-on signal."

Coalition teleport technology opened a Mobius transfer conduit between two physical points. Because the transfer conduit existed outside of normal space, no shielding technology could prevent a teleport from one point to another. But heavy shielding could disrupt a target lock. The teleportation system had to acquire a stable lock, otherwise the teleporter would randomly project the transfer conduit at some point within a proximity radius of the target and teleport anything that could fit onto a receiving pad.

Even a piece of hull plating.

***

Fearless erupted into the gas giant's local space.

"Jump completed, Phalalin," Verikaralee said.

"Where are they?" Phalalin asked.

Neither the looming gas giant nor its habitable moon hosted the two warships he had expected to find.

"Scanning," his Mistress of Tactics said. "Phalalin, I am detecting drive signatures in local space. Scan indicates an exit vector heading out of the system."

"Extend scan out from the moon's orbit. Coalition ships must put some distance between them and a star's gravity well before jumping into FTL."

"No! Really? I would not have thought of that without your helpful insight! No wonder we chose you as our Warleader!" his Mistress of Tactics snarked, hating having the obvious dangled before her.

Pheromonal snickers surrounded Phalalin, and he sighed, shaking his head in mock seriousness. "Fine. I shall keep my mouth shut all the way back home!"

Denials assailed him in empathic waves, but he waited a minute or two longer before yielding to them, least he hurt their feelings.

"I found them, Phalalin. They are at the outer heliopause shell," his Mistress of Tactics said.

"Mistress of Communications, establish privacy channel with Melkorka and send her our respectful greetings."

"By your command."

Phalalin knew he must prowl carefully here, else he find himself ensnared in another warship's business.

"Phalalin, the warship gives the automated response of *sahagan*!" his Mistress of Communications said, thunderstruck.

Phalalin thought about that for a moment.

"I think we will remain in orbit around this moon. Resume Action Ready Status but keep scanners on those two warships."

Do not disturb!

♦♦♦

The LAC shook.

Marsch looked up at the main bridge viewscreen. The stars rotated as they were pulled around and behind the Compact ship.

"Del, Melkorka has locked a tractor field onto us. She reports that Captain Winters has made a claim against you for the crime of interstellar piracy. He says he has no choice. Ambassador Harrison made the claim of ni'zakhon, outlawry, and you must be returned to him," Phelindra snarled. Her voice, twisting tail, and twitching ears telegraphing her mounting fury. She paused to look at the others on the command center before sweeping her tail around him in an inclusive hook.

"He has been trying to get a translation lock on you ever since Melkorka disabled the fighter group. We will not allow that. You are sire cairn, a battle leader of Compact forces. We name you Warleader of this vessel, a Compact rank, bestowed by us in accordance with Compact law and custom. We have agreed, and everyone aboard *Hunter's Moon* has agreed, to bring you aboard our ship and prevent Captain Winters from taking you from our care," she said. She had to stop talking and bring her anger in check again.

Marsch grinned without humor. "That will infuriate Ambassador Harrison. I bet he's running around Winters's ankles, nipping at his heels like an old bald Chihuahua."

They looked at him, mystified. Phelindra frowned. Marsch constantly missed the subtle cues given off by their body language and pheromones. They struggled to work around his differences. It was a failing on their part because females always cared for males. Marsch was handicapped by his physiology, yet not handicapped. He was a male, and Eyloni females never gave the physical challenges of others a second look. They worked around them. Concentrating on the fleeting image that his pheromones drew in her mind's eye, she finally burst out in a trilling laugh.

"A good joke, Del. Harrison sings oyya deceptively, and his adulthood knife flies from his hip and runs around his feet, stabbing at his ankles!"

Grins and rhythmic trillings spread from Phelindra to the others. Zalzadrin, the second-eldest Hunter aboard, slapped her rippled stomach and winced. Hervorallin hid her smirks by clenching her teeth, trying to save her ribs from convulsive laughter. Raelindra bounced on the balls of her feet, while Kidahin doubled over in outright laughter. Marsch didn't get their view of his insult; he usually got their plain meanings, but their humor always evaded him.

"Knife? What knife? A Chihuahua is a small animal, a dog."

"What is a dog?" Zalzadrin asked.

"A domesticated animal that a human allows to live with him."

"An *animal*? Why would a human form an empathic link with an animal?" Phelindra asked. Without exception, animals were fearsome creatures on Elleio.

"For companionship, company."

"You shall never do that, Del. You have us!" Kidahin said.

"Yes, Del, you are our animal!" Zalzadrin quipped.

Marsch glared at her, not sure he liked being considered their pet. They had a knack for snide remarks when they felt he had ignored their good advice, and he wondered if they were pulling his leg or not. Eyloni had an odd sense of humor, but Hunters' humor had a mock seriousness that invited second guessing.

He ignored their yucks at his expense and turned back to the viewscreen. He watched as they continued to close on the Compact warship. His Eyloni crew crowded him, seeking the casual contact that reassured their empathic possessive natures. Even Princess joined in the communal act, until she decided that too many were focusing too much on him and warned them off.

Hervorallin, bruised ribs complaining from her infant's jerking about, smiled in wonder. Her ears perking forward and her tail curling high, she brushed her pons against Marsch's cheek and let her daughter climb back onto his back. Once there, she coiled her tail and took to humming.

Marsch shook his head as Princess played with his hair. He glanced up at the screen. Compact tractor tech was impressive. He had to squint to see the twin beams. Their incandescent shimmer reminded him of heat waves rising off asphalt and warping summer landscapes. The beams worked in tandem, pushing and pulling them forward, shifting them underneath the huge vessel's engineering hull. They were approaching the ship's two octagonal hydrogen-antihydrogen sublight engine ports. He saw the two parallel FTL jump drive armature housings mounted into the dorsal engineering hull drop out of sight as they were pulled under the warship.

Dive! Dive! Dive! Marsch shouted in his head, an order he had heard from an old submarine warfare movie he always wanted to give.

This close, Marsch could see detailed artistry in the warship's hull plates. The exterior plates looked like gray stucco sheets with golf balls pressed into them. Superimposed antique gold leaf patterns climbed along the entire length but only about a quarter of the width of the pebbly hull, like vines growing up the side of an old stone chimney. Huge castings outlined the bottom rear of the engineering hull. No doubt they housed the antihydrogen fuel cells and cooling system for the warship's sublight drive.

Marsch whistled at the sight, distracting his crew with the expressive musical note. He guessed that the Compact warship was between 700 and 800 meters long. The engineering hull itself was about 200 meters long, 160 meters wide, and 80 meters stern to keel. He worked on his 'pad and calculated the ship's volume at somewhere between 6,000,000 and 7,000,000 cubic meters. Total mass worked out to a range of somewhere between 7,000,000 and 9,000,000 metric tons. That meant Melkorka's ship was about half his carrier's length, a third her volume, and a third her mass. The Coalition carrier resembled a woodsman's axe—long and narrow. By comparison, the Compact ship was short and wide. The combat bow reminded him of an upside-down shovel blade that was attached to a shoe box command hull that in turn was connected to a square engineering hull. Two outrigger hulls hung from the command hull, giving the ship a catamaran-like wide 250-meter maximum beam.

He whistled again. The technology used to build such ships boggled the mind. Here, together, were three FTL-capable ships. Each relied on different physics to drive them as close as possible to the absolute maximum apparent FTL velocity of 1,460 cee that matter could achieve. Unified physics made that possible.

Unified physics considered the universe a probability construct. The universe is the way it is because it is most probable for it to be that way. In general, the universe rested in a probability equilibrium, and its physical laws likewise manifested as most probable likelihoods.

Tremendous energy production allowed physicists to change extremely local probabilities.

Marsch knew enough physics to get though the math and science his agricultural degree required. Coalition and Compact technologies might share some probability commonality because they shared similar physical laws, but they were so different from a physicist's point of view that the science behind them was mutually-exclusive *to the physicist*, but not to the universe at large. The Coalition and Compact physicists were like high priests of their respective religions of technology. They were hidebound to any physics but their own and didn't yet understand how different probability references could work even when confronted with working examples.

Human science couldn't calculate a probability function that allowed quantum black holes to teleport a Compact ship up to 2.332 light-years in an instant every fifteen hours. Eyloni physicists couldn't calculate a probability function that allowed hyperspace to carry a material object anywhere. Neither Coalition nor Compact scientists knew how the Lizards calculated their n-dimensional subspace FTL drive probabilities.

Probability physics made Marsch's head hurt. Thankfully, his all-female crew understood the science much better than he did.

The tractor field pulled them underneath the engineering hull. The warship's yellow-filled rectangular combat deployment bay filled the aft lower ventral decks of the command hull up ahead.

Forward motion stopped.

They hung stationary below the huge warship for a few long minutes before forward motion resumed.

Marsch thought he understood why. The tractor field operator had to jiggle them about. The large open bay loomed before them, but the LAC stood much taller than any of the troop transports or heavy combat vehicles that normally exited the bay. The LAC's dorsal hull might even scrape against the emitters of the force field that kept the atmosphere from escaping the open bay hatch and into the vacuum of space if the tractor pilot wasn't careful.

Marsch stared into the bay portal. There, the features of several large objects were resolving into familiar assets within the well-lit bay. The staging deck itself reminded him of a beach covered with yellow sand the color of baby chicks.

The LAC stopped less than ten meters from the open bay hatch. Marsch's eyes followed the lines of several vehicles parked in service alcoves marching along both the port and starboard sides of the bay. The center staging area itself spanned an area wide enough for several companies to form up and board the heavy troop transports parked further forward.

The LAC hovered there motionless, and Marsch sweated. The Lizard ship was as tall as the interior hatch. The tractor field operator would have to shift them around with some precision to get the proper alignment.

He hoped she got it right the first time. The LAC would take up so much room in the bay, making using the reaction control system to move hazardous.

The LAC shuddered again as the tractors disengaged.

Marsch cringed, hoping that they didn't expect his crew to fly the ship into the bay manually. They lacked fine thruster control and the helm fields would tear the bay apart, and the waiting made him sweat.

Another beam, a pilot tractor field, locked onto them from inside the bay itself. An oblong pod mounted in the bay's ceiling withdrew into the bay, pulling them along with it. The main viewscreen flared as coruscating energies flashed across the LAC's hull.

Field dynamics, Marsch guessed. The pilot tractor field was interacting with the force field that soft-sealed the open bay, producing the bright green Saint-Elmo's-fire effect.

Ahead, several hundred Eyloni gathered, waiting. Clothed in usual ship's wear, they milled about as if skipping along in ritual dance. Around them the troop transports stood like stage scenery in a play. Each of the eight transports were easily large enough to carry one of the alcove-housed combat vehicles or at least a hundred men. All along the port side, antlike LAVs and beetle-like light hovertanks rested in charging niches built into the bay's bulkheads. The starboard niches held heavy tanks and artillery pieces that waited until they were needed.

This was one mean assault vessel, Marsch thought with envy.

He ripped his gaze from the surface combat assets. Ahead, the Eyloni moved further into the forward staging area. They were settling down, organizing themselves into a shallow semicircular arc on the bright yellow deck, like human troops standing at parade rest.

Marsch rocked sideways. The ceiling towing pod had released them, and the warship's artificial gravity pulled them into the sandy deck. By his estimate, the LAC would fill the last third of the bay, take up half its width, and just miss the ceiling. That meant the bay measured about 150 meters long, 70 meters wide, and 40 meters deck to ceiling.

The crowd grew. Marsch could make out individual faces on the screen now, if he squinted into the fishbowl display hard enough, long enough. Melkorka stood out in front, looking severe and imposing. The others appeared more curious than anything else.

I'd be more than curious if this thing was sitting inside my ship!

But not the Eyloni. A warrior people, they watched and waited.

"Del, we must leave," Phelindra said, breaking into his thoughts. "They wait for us."

Marsch stared at the main viewscreen. The warship's crew stood around the thickening semicircle. They waited for the rest of their own to join them. His ship, his first and last command, belonged to them now. It was destined for extensive military analysis, meaning they'd cut it into pieces. It would never fly again.

He sighed. *They're leaving me.*

"Del, we must leave," Phelindra repeated.

Numb, he nodded.

More Eyloni gathered up ahead.

They waited.

He sighed again.

Emotions brushed across his forehead, flutterings that grew stronger by the second.

The feelings they recalled made him sob.

He waved the cobwebby flutterings aside.

They refused to leave him.

He watched Melkorka step forward a pace and stop, ears cocked, waiting.

He stared hard at her.

A whirlwind of impressions stormed through him.

They withdrew, trickling away from him like beads of water after a shower, but did not vanish.

Behind him, Princess sang out a challenge, her eyes darting everywhere at once.

Hervorallin laughed a measure of notes at her daughter. Princess glared unamused suspicion back at her mother.

"Del?"

Marsch nodded, a curt wooden jerk of chin.

He turned to face Phelindra. Behind her, the others had drawn around him in a semicircle of their own. The obvious agony of the critically injured Warriors tore at his heart.

His daughters!

They had all removed their neckwear and curved breast knives and were holding them out to him.

Ears perked forward, twitching tails held high, they stared at him with a fierce intensity.

Even Princess glared at him, quiet and still for once.

"Del, you must take our adulthood knives and hold them for us. We will exit the ship first. You must wait and accompany Kidahin last. Go to Melkorka with Kidahin at your side. When you get there, tie my adulthood knife on first. Then you must tie everyone else's adulthood knives back on her neckwear in rank order, Kidahin last of course. If the rest of our society removes their adulthood knives and places them on the deck, you must tie them back onto their neckwear. No matter how long it takes, you must complete the ritual. They will send strength to you."

Marsch let that last comment pass in favor of an apparent contradiction.

"Phelindra, I can't step onto the deck of your ship. Anlann made it clear to me that only a warleader can stand on the deck of a Compact vessel."

"Yes, that is so," Phelindra nodded. "*Hunter's Moon* is ours. We choose who may board him. We also choose the male allowed to walk his pathways and trails. We have all agreed to permit you this. No offense will arise from your acceptance of us and the honor we bestow upon you. We implore you to come with us."

Winters watched on Romaine's tap, riveted to the sight of two Warriors. One missing her arm and tail, the other missing both legs. Listening to Phelindra's casual tone, he shook his head and turned to face Anlann.

"Another ceremony? Even when they have critically wounded casualties?"

"Yes, Captain."

"What are they celebrating now?" Ambassador Harrison interrupted, "the return of their kidnapped crew, or the capture of the Lizard ship?"

"Neither, Ambassador," Seralin said, refusing to elaborate further. She did not want to miss even a single word. The Eldest Huntress of the Ship was telling Marsch how he must exit the enemy ship and step onto their warship, a historical event in the making. *Their Mistress of Saga must be dancing with her tail by now.*

Absent orders from their warleader, and even then very rarely, no Eyloni female ever permitted another male aboard their ship. It was their territory. *Female* territory. Seralin caught sight of a smirk wrinkling across Anlann's face.

Huh. He is so smug. She sighed, exasperated. Males were stranger than fireside stories.

"Then what's this celebration for?" Harrison asked. What an annoying people these Eyloni were. They had a ritual for everything. It was this ritualism that made diplomatic relations with them impossible. One minute, music was offensive; the next minute, music was sacred.

"This ritual is for Del, Ambassador," Seralin offered after a moment's pause.

"For them, too, Ambassador," Anlann added. "As you know, no male but a warleader is permitted aboard a Compact ship absent his strict orders to the contrary. This ritual gives Del the right of free movement aboard their warship."

"Oh. Then the males sent here by the Compact Counsel had to go through this ritual before they could board *Fearless*?" Harrison asked, mystified.

"No, Ambassador. *Fearless* has a warleader."

Harrison rubbed his hands together with glee. Phalalin had come through! Once Melkorka tricked Marsch out of that LAC, she would arrest him and have him sent here, where the brig awaited. Once there, Deering would fix it so Parakh could get to Marsch and put him out of the picture permanently.

"If you'll pardon me, Anlann, but this ceremony looks a lot like a side party piping a visiting captain aboard," Winters mused aloud.

"No, Captain. A warleader rarely ever visits another warship. Let me try to explain using your Coalition Fleet as an example.

"You, as captain, have the command, the honor, and the respect due you from your crew. If you were warleader here, then the moment you stepped aboard another Fleet vessel, his crew considers you a usurper trying to take command of their ship from the lawful authority of their warleader, and their mere tolerance of your presence constitutes an intent to make a mutiny and install you as warleader of their vessel.

"At the same time, your presence aboard their ship is seen as willful abandonment by your ship and crew in favor of them. Given those circumstances, without special permission granted by the second warleader for the visit, both crews are obliged to kill you. Your crew's obligation stems from your abandonment of them, and the second crew's obligation comes from your mere presence."

Winters gaped at him in disbelief, at a loss for words.

"But, Melkorka has no warleader. Why conduct a ritual at all when no warleader is present for Marsch to supplant?" Harrison asked.

The viewscreen went dark and silent.

"Captain? Marsch's transmissions have stopped," Romaine reported.

"Blocked by the warship's hull?" he asked.

"Negative, Sir. I think Marsch may have shut down the transmitter."

"Makes sense. He's about to disembark. There's no need to keep transmitting, and continued comm chatter for no reason is a breach of security."

"Captain?" Romaine interrupted, "I'm receiving transmissions from the warship now. I don't understand it, Sir, but they're transmitting on both ship-to-ship and on the Compact Green Channel."

"On screen, Lieutenant."

"Aye, Captain."

The main viewscreen lit up with a panoramic view of the warship's bright yellow combat staging area. Winters' eyes were drawn to the crowd standing in front of the Lizard ship. He guessed their numbers at somewhere in the high two-thousands.

Winters's heart skipped a beat. Had they put their ship on automatic again? How could they run a battleship that way? Or a fleet? Or the entire Compact Fleet for that matter? Harrison might well have a legitimate point about his worries concerning the state of the Compact Fleet.

"The Green channel is the Compact Fleet priority hyperlink communications channel! Anlann, how can Melkorka justify tying up the emergency channel just to broadcast some ritual?"

Silence.

"Anlann?" Winters repeated.

No reply.

Winters frowned. Something damn peculiar was going on here. The co-ambassadors' demeanor had changed.

They looked awed.

No, Winters amended. They were downright reverent.

He watched the warship's 'priority' transmission, watched Melkorka stand there patiently waiting.

The predatory gleam in her eyes made Winters suddenly uncomfortable.

17

SETTLING ACCOUNTS

Melkorka growled. Phelindra was tailchasing the time away. Yes, she had to get to the ship's airlock; yes, she had to exit the ship; and yes, she had to walk around the ship.

Holding her impatience in check, Melkorka waited.

Her society did a much better job of it than she. Most of them were leaf-chasing the time away by pretending interest in the enemy vessel. Others were sneaking glances aft, hoping to catch a glimpse of Marsch and his crew.

Del. Soon it would be inappropriate to call him by his natal chord.

Delwyn was his formal adult male name.

Thoughts of him made her eyes wander over the nearby troop transport's flank and the sheathed sword resting on it.

Would he know what to do? Custom and law made no allowances for ritual ignorance.

Under the law, no one could tell him what to do once the ritual began. Phelindra should have already told him how to proceed without injuring their honor. Insults such as refusing to participate could have dire consequences.

Spirits, I hope I have not killed him, a soprano plea rang through her mind.

Melkorka's critical gaze appraised her society again. Each female had found her place in the rough semicircle as befitting of her rank. Tails and ears betrayed an excitement their feigned indifference could not hide. Their pheromones told another story. Their empathic sendings filled her with foreboding. Doubt and fear mingled with confidence and hope spread out from them; their wide amber and yellow eyes kept wandering back to the rear of the captured vessel.

Their soft, sweet-sounding sighs suddenly engulfed her, and she braced herself.

It begins.

Phelindra led her group around the Ni'zakhonii ship. She walked with a slow stiff dignity, flaunting the makeshift Protectress' sigil above her rank earring. She had embroidered the three superimposed down-pointing triangles into her upper earfold herself using a length of fine gold wire from her rank earring. She would never remove it no matter what Melkorka had to say about it.

She stopped one tail's length from the Mistress of the Ship. Melkorka weighed the Eldest's presence. Phelindra wore no adulthood knife. Melkorka's eyes narrowed. Phelindra had chosen the formal mode. Formal mode was safer for Del, but the wait would prolong the two injured Warrior's agony.

"I welcome you back to your society, your family, your home, and your people. My loved one, my daughter, my sister, my friend, we rejoice in your return, but I see that you have returned weaponless. Do you come to us as a child, or have you placed your unarmed trust in another?" Melkorka sang in ritual cant.

"I rejoice in that I am found, I am protected, and I am returned to you, my lovers, my daughters, my sisters, my friends. I have found the one upon whom my trust is absolute," Phelindra sang back in the same cant.

Melkorka flicked her ears. The Eldest's pheromones wove patterns in her mind confirming the truthfulness of her reply. Phelindra's scent further flaunted the improvised Protectress symbol, a challenge and a warning to them all. One wrong move and lover, sister, and friend notwithstanding, the old Huntress would die here protecting Del from their wrath. Her endorsement should satisfy the Hunters of their society, but Hunters stood in the minority. The ritual could still go so wrong.

They had to proceed. They could not turn back now. The ship's hyperlink transmitter broadcasted the ceremony to the Compact Counsel. They participated indirectly through the transmission, as they did in all significant events. The Death Song rite had been sent to Elleio, as a part of the updated warship chronicles, but now the Counsel would witness this ritual along with *Henri Edda*'s crew, co-Ambassadors Anlann and Seralin, plus everyone aboard *Fearless*. They would all watch it unfold in the ancient manner.

Melkorka nodded a curt acceptance. "Sit Eldest Huntress and remain seated until I am satisfied you have not been declared a child."

"Yes, Mistress."

Zalzadrin, the next Hunter in rank, stepped forward and answered the same ritual questions in the same ritual manner. Melkorka dwelled on the injured Hunter's responses. Concerned, she paused to inspect the Hunter's stapled wound under its clear hard covering. Melkorka's eyes wandered back to Zalzadrin's face. Compassion filled her heart, and she wrapped her tail around the Hunter. While doing so, she saw the pair of stitches in Zalzadrin's earfold and froze.

Like all Eyloni females, Melkorka knew the military and hierarchical rank of everyone aboard. She knew every knot, every bead, and every web in a female's military rank weave perfectly. In a culture that prized social standing and hierarchical status, a female compared her rank earring with another's as naturally as she defended a male. Melkorka stepped back and made a melodramatic show of examining the odd new honor knot she found on the Hunter's earring.

"Zalzadrin, who has advanced you in rank, and what was the justification for your advancement?" she demanded.

Zalzadrin stepped into Melkorka's personal space and glared into her eyes.

"Del, of the O'un Tu Clan, of the La'huaset Tribe, Warleader of the Compact vessel standing behind me, advanced me in rank at his pleasure and for his own reasons, Mistress."

Melkorka heard a storm of sighs whisper around her.

Everyone knew by now that Hervorallin's infant was Del's near-daughter, but that he had conferred rank was news to them.

She turned to the sitting Phelindra.

The Eldest Huntress had likewise been advanced in rank. Melkorka thought she knew why. Del had pierced their ears and hung the new rank earrings for them. While joining the rank weaves to their earrings, he tied honor knots, advancing them in rank for their instrumental assistance in the ship's capture.

The Compact Counsel would no doubt recognize the new rank. Females owned their warships and chose their warleaders, but males conferred military rank, or withdrew it for that matter. They did so without favor or for arbitrary reasons, too, otherwise the various female hierarchies would confront them on an issue of honor.

Melkorka shook herself, gave the ritual response to Zalzadrin, and ordered her to sit with the Eldest.

Hervorallin came forward next with her daughter. She wore her severe bruises like a rank weave and ignored torn ligaments and cracked ribs. Princess clutched at her, trying to decide between investigating the strange females and crawling over her mother's shoulder to look back at the alien ship. Hervorallin stopped. The infant Hunter whipped around and growled menace at the gathering.

Everyone smiled and hummed comfort to her.

Princess would have none of it. They had not been introduced to her. She saw them as potential rivals and regarded them as such. She doubled her threat displays and sang a demand that her male come at once.

The infant's musical summons put their concerns at rest. Relieved nods and tail brushings filled the bay.

It took Melkorka little time to work her way through them. All but one sat on the deck, weaponless, in a semicircle facing their society. Each had been advanced in rank for her part in the vessel's capture, Melkorka felt certain. Males never gave rank away. Rank had to be earned, otherwise it soured in the stomach, worthless.

A warleader always told a female why he advanced her. Almost always. However, events arose when the reason, while known, was never admitted, so the female had no cause to brag about a particular bead, knot, or web. Secret missions and other classified reasons justified a warleader's silence on the matter. Del must have considered the ship's capture a strategic victory classified under Compact Seal.

Scents in the air projected images into Melkorka's mind, and she knew they had all come to the same conclusion: the vessel's capture reflected Compact Classified Knowledge status.

A hush fell over the gathering. Del stepped from behind the vessel, flanked by Kidahin, their huluhar. She pulled him along, wrapped in her tail, in protective custody, and marched him up to Melkorka.

Ignoring him, Melkorka concluded the initial ritual routine with Kidahin and ordered her to sit on the deck with her peers.

Melkorka's gaze measured the human male. He, too, had taken injury during the ship's capture.

He needed a stay in Health Center and rest.

Marsch returned her stare. He smelled hints of potpourri in the air. Not the Eyloni, they smelled of musky spice. The bay was hot and humid, but its lighter gravity was a welcome relief to his fatigued muscles.

"Melkorka," Marsch rushed, "I don't think Warriors and Hunters should sit around without their adulthood knives, do you?"

He stood before his LAC crew. If he hurried, then Melkorka could have the two injured Warriors taken to sickbay. He began with Phelindra, tying her adulthood knife onto the flimsy strings of knots, cinching it against the chest wall under her left breast. He crossed to Zalzadrin, tied her knife to her, and then continued to Hervorallin and the others in the same order that Melkorka had spoken to them. Completed, the formal act declared before witnesses that he did not consider them children.

Melkorka and the others watched with special interest as Kidahin, her adulthood knife once again in its proper place, wound her tail around him and pulled him to her, humming with musical pride.

Princess's trilling echoed the huluhar's pleasure.

The moment their huluhar chose Marsch, Melkorka and the others sat on the deck. Each untied her adulthood knife and placed it before her. Eyes on him, they flexed their ears forward, drew their tails along their left or right thighs, and twitched their pons against their neighbor's knees.

Marsch stood with his former crew and faced them.

Phelindra, for the first time in her life truly scared of anything, locked eyes with Melkorka and knew by her scent that she was just as worried.

Now what? Marsch asked himself. He looked the warship's crew over. They hadn't taken the wounded Warriors for medical attention yet, so he wasn't done.

His concern for them distracted him, and he forgot what to do next.

Princess chose that moment to sing a melodic protest. She would have nothing to do with these females, but if her male met with them, then she had to meet them too.

He was her territory.

Hervorallin let Princess climb onto Del's back, where she leaned over the top of his head, gripped his hair, and glared at them.

Marsch sighed in relief as Princess's pheromonal joy swamped him. She must have picked up on his doubt and linked its cause to them. She didn't seem to care that there were many of them, and he wondered how long Eyloni females let infants ignore social rank.

Rank. Marsch grabbed at that straw. Eyloni always observed rank. Even when he introduced Princess to the others, she had been passed to Phelindra, then Zalzadrin, and on down to Kidahin. He should introduce Princess to them in rank order, otherwise she'd never let them get close to him.

Marsch knew that Melkorka held the highest rank aboard, but her rank was a special case, a remnant of Kalinn's choice. How was he to figure out the rank order of over 2,500 Eyloni? Many of their dreamcatcher weaves looked so alike to him that he couldn't tell fine distinctions between them,

He glanced helplessly at Phelindra. She ignored him. He'd get no further help from her, or from the others for that matter. An Eyloni male would know what to do and could recognize the weave patterns or maybe even smell how a female perceived her rank.

A storm of intuitive images flooded his head: Princess's inklings of the females before her that she shared with him through their empathic link.

Patterns filled his head like fall leaves blowing across grass.

Waitaminute. Phelindra and her group sat in a peculiar order. He knew their rank order. They had made issues of it all the time. They insisted he touch them in that order. They described their rank weaves to him in that order. He pierced their ears in that order. He introduced Princess to them in that order. They left the LAC in that order. Melkorka had spoken to them in that order. And now they sat in that same order. Although they sat in a semicircle, they touched certain others with their tail tufts, their pons. If he followed their tails, the twenty-two made a branching pattern that reflected their rank order.

He faced the larger gathering.

They sat in a layered semicircle that matched the seating order they had taken during the Death Song ceremony. They touched each other in a similar branching pattern, but on a much larger and more complex scale than his twenty-two females could match.

He introduced Princess to Melkorka.

The infant Hunter, scowling objections, sniffed the rigid Mistress of the Ship for his sake, considered her for a moment, chirped a note at her, and accepted her as a part of her male's association.

That gave Marsch the time he needed to remember his ritual purpose here. He knelt to retrieve Melkorka's sheathed flint knife and tied it under the swell of her left breast.

A collective sibilant sigh filled the staging area. Marsch stepped over to the next female in the pattern, Mistress of Tactics Hlinlodyn, introduced Princess to her, and tied the adulthood knife to Hlinlodyn's neckwear.

Thank the spirits! Seralin sighed as Marsch shuffled to a third female.

Harrison grew increasingly impatient by the minute. Why show a baby to everyone, one person at a time? Why did they take their knives off just to have Marsch tie them back on? And why did they wait until Marsch had gone through ten of them before those ten took the two injured Warriors out of the bay?

He yawned. When would Melkorka arrest Marsch? This ceremony would delay it for some time to come. Why go on with this charade anyway? Why give him freedom of movement just to arrest him?

Of course! No male could step on the deck of a warship except the warleader. Marsch wasn't a warleader, so they couldn't drag him off the LAC without violating their taboos. Did that mean Melkorka couldn't arrest him until he showed the little creature to the entire crew, one at a time? At the rate he was going, it would take hours!

But that was good news. Marsch couldn't say anything to Anlann while he was stuck in this ceremony.

Harrison wondered why the Eyloni insisted on transmitting this farce back to Elleio. Was it some extradition formality? That had to be it. The Coalition and the Compact had no treaty, no formal way to surrender fugitives.

They wanted a record.

Harrison smiled. Anlann was about to lose his human ally, and the diplomatic mission would remain in his hands and not in some inexperienced interloper's.

Winters watched Marsch inspect another crewmember. Something about it jogged his memory. "Anlann, this ceremony reminds me of a crew review."

Anlann heard Winters's musing comment but kept his own counsel, loathing his apparent lack of courtesy. This rite was as specific as to form as it was to the proper conduct of witnesses. He and Seralin were forbidden to speak once it had begun in earnest, least any word somehow alter the rite and spoil the ritual. Many hours from now, when the Compact Counsel received the transmission, they too would watch in silence, in keeping with custom. When this ceremony was rebroadcasted by the Counsel to the tribes and clans represented by *Hunter's Moon*, they would likewise watch in absolute silence, lest they attract the spirits' ire.

A few hours into the rearming rite Marsch realized that it would take him hours to complete it. Princess had fallen into an odd sleep routine. He spent over two minutes with each female. During that time, Princess would sniff her, chirp an okay, and fall asleep while he tied the adulthood knife back in place. When he stepped to the next person in the pattern, she awoke and let herself be introduced again, giving her about a hundred second nap for every thirty second introduction—unless she took a snack from a weeping breast.

Marsch started wondering why pain and exhaustion hadn't claimed him yet. As he advanced through the living pattern, he felt Eyloni minds, their empathy. They drove him onward with an intensity that reminded him of PTSD hyperalertness. Eyloni scent replaced those awful smells from that day on Valhalla, but their body odor didn't shatter his nerves.

They directed him toward a sane goal. He didn't re-experience traumatic past events, but he had the same physical responses: sweating, rapid heartbeat. He lost interest in food, water, sleep, and the passage of time.

Ten hours into the ritual, Winters headed back to his quarters with orders to wake him if new developments arose.

Ambassador Harrison left with Winters, all but running for his quarters.

There, he set his omni to the day's TAC channel and selected the scrambler option.

"Deering, this is Harrison."

No response.

"Deering, this is Ambassador Harrison. Answer me, damn you!"

"Mr. Ambassador?" a sleepy voice quavered.

"Yes, dammit! Report!"

"Yes, Sir. *Fearless* maintains orbit around Ibeetu. Phalalin is not responding to any hails. We did intercept a transmission from him to Melkorka, but we couldn't decipher its content. Melkorka's response was curt, brief, and abrupt."

"That sounds to me like a captain not caring for her orders. Phalalin must have ordered her to arrest Marsch."

"Then what's taking her so long, Sir?"

"Some Eyloni ritual. We can't teleport Marsch from the LAC, and he can't step on Melkorka's ship without completing this ritual. At the rate he's going, it'll take him over three days."

"That's bad, isn't it, Sir?"

"Absolutely not! It's boring, but not bad. Marsch can't exercise Warpact rank while he's stuck in the ritual. Soon Phalalin will arrive here, ready to act."

Sixty-eight hours! Winters sighed. How could Marsch keep it up?

Indeed, Marsch moved from one Eyloni to the next with the same vigor he had when he first approached Melkorka three days ago!

And the co-ambassadors had stood on the bridge and watched him the entire time. They moved aside for people but wouldn't speak to anyone.

Harrison. Now there was a strange bird. The old fart danced around like a kid on his birthday. He came to the bridge, watched Marsch go from one Eyloni to the next, gave the co-ambassadors a veiled smirk, checked tactical for an update on *Fearless* and ran back to his quarters.

He'd been doing that every waking hour once every ninety minutes.

Suspicious, Winters thumbed a switch on his command chair armrest.

"Security, this is the Captain. I want a round-the-clock watch placed on the diplomatic party until further notice. Ambassador Harrison is not to know about it. Winters out."

Phalalin watched the ceremony along with his crew. Attentive and silent, they waited. He held his breath several times now. If this Delwyn was not careful, then he was one dead human.

The Huntress Verikaralee was drawn to the infant Hunter. Clearly the infant had made an empathic bond with the human male. Hervorallin was an O'un Tu Clan female. Her daughter was an O'un Tu Clan infant. That made Delwyn an O'un Tu Clan male by familial bond.

Verikaralee was also an O'un Tu Clan female, and she watched the screen closely, committing the faces and skin color patterns she saw to memory, of everyone she would kill if they harmed her Clan male.

Phalalin heard his Mistress of the Ship's occasional grumbles and grunts, smelled her, knew how she felt, what she planned if things went wrong.

Like her, he belonged to the O'un Tu Clan.

***

Almost done, Marsch sighed. He was closing in on the end of the odd branching pattern. He knew that hours had passed. He had no idea how many, but a subtle presence had been filling his awareness the whole time, keeping him going, alert, and awake. It caressed its cobwebby tendrils against his forehead, pouring strength into him, dispelling fatigue and numbing pain. It persisted with him, and if he concentrated hard enough, he could feel individual impressions.

And they felt feminine.

Marsch tied the last adulthood knife to the neckwear of a short, muscular young Warrior who must have ranked Kidahin by only the slimmest of margins. The rearming ceremony complete, he looked around for the first time since leaving the LAC.

The deck was awash in bright yellow sand. It felt like sand, too. The material resembled sand in every way, but one: no individual grains of sand. The illusion was a holographic one, but the deck felt soft, like a pliable sandbag.

The stuff felt luxurious. So much so that Marsch had to fight the impulse to lay down on it. He looked across the bay, taking in the holographic seashore that surrounded him. The LAC rested on a beach. The still open bay's wide rectangular portal floated on a placid seascape. Sighing in disappointment, he dragged himself back to Melkorka.

Princess slept. For the first time in what seemed like hours, he thought about sleep. He gave the sleeping infant back to Hervorallin and waited.

Melkorka reached out and put her hand on the troop transport's flat leading edge and fondled Del's curved sword. *It all comes down to this*, she murmured to the spirits. Marsch looked tired. He had several wounds: claw slashes, a shoulder injury, a collarbone injury, and she thought he walked as if he had a hip or tailbone injury.

He would receive the rest he needed when he regenerated.

Marsch stood next to her. "Melkorka, I return Kidahin and the twenty-one crewmembers taken from you. I surrender the Lizard ship to the Compact for study. I think…"

"Del," Melkorka interrupted. "You entrusted this sword to me. I return it to you so that you may declare your intent."

Marsch accepted the weapon.

Intent? What was she talking about?

The old sword was a family heirloom. His daughters were dead, and he had no family to pass it down to. It had stood as the physical reminder of his pledge to Melkorka. She and the bulk of the warship's crew echoed in his mind as if they, too, were his daughters well grown. They really were his daughters. Melkorka felt like his eldest, although she was much younger than Phelindra. He unsheathed the old sword and, grasping it by its blade, held it out to her.

"Melkorka, I can't think of a better place for this sword than with you forever and always."

Melkorka jumped for the unsheathed sword, snatching it with an iron grip, and wrapped her tail around the sharp exposed edge, speaking as she did so.

"On behalf of and with the unanimous consent of our society, I declare Delwyn *ar ahoun Unahaillaea Tyreniioroneo*, the Warleader of the Compact warship *Hunter's Moon*."

Melkorka, Phelindra, and Kidahin wrapped their tails around him, Kidahin wrapping his waist, Phelindra wrapping his chest, and Melkorka wrapping his thighs. Held by the three, Marsch stood immobile. They caressed him with their pons, marking him with their pheromones.

The Eyloni rushed Marsch. At the last minute they swerved aside and surrounded him with the dense mass of their bodies as they danced around him. He heard the soft cant of their songs, the swishing of their tails against their bodies, the whispering of air as they scissored across the yellow sand. Large playful eyes looked into his, their ears flipping forward, giving him their undivided attention.

Marsch exalted in their presence, their sound, their smell, their being. By their song and by their dance he became one of them. He felt the toughness of their muscles, felt their empathy born upon their scent, felt included, his loneliness shattering, and he knew for certain their true feelings, for they shared themselves with him.

He swooned as waves of exhaustion and shock flashed through him.

"Mistress of Healers, take the Warleader to Health Center for regeneration at once!" Melkorka demanded.

"Affirm, acting!" Allohindra replied. Wrapping her tail around Delwyn, the warship's chief physician guided the semiconscious, protesting male into the forested depths of the ship.

Marsch dreamed he floated in a jungle of oranges, reds, and golds.

Melkorka twitched her ears in indulgent amusement, marveling at the universal constant females contended with daily: *males were strange.*

In her private mind she sighed, deeply relieved, and gave thanks to the spirits. Delwyn was Warleader. She watched Phelindra, his Protectress, following him.

Melkorka thanked the spirits again. Not only had Delwyn issued a public declaration of his intent to remain with them, but given the choice of any female, he chose her to remain as Mistress of the Ship. Her title proclaimed before her society, she again held command by the Warleader's choice and not through inertia and Kalinn's honored memory.

She watched excited females exit the staging area and head for their stations. She had many things to do herself. First, she must arrange with the Mistress of Saga to transmit updated warship's chronicles to Elleio. No doubt Delwyn would want them to retrieve all Compact assets from the moon's surface. Then there was the mission they had been given before their ill-fated jump into this star system. Their return with a Ni'zakhonii light attack craft would accomplish their mission beyond the Counsel's wildest dreams.

She thought about her homeworld. No human walked the lands of Elleio without escort. Not out of disrespect, but because no human came under the reach of tribal law. The Compact Counsel had assumed responsibility for Captain Lahiri's and Captain Winters's people when they visited the clans. That changed for Delwyn the moment Princess bonded with him. He fell under the laws and customs of the La'huaset Tribe and the O'un Tu Clan. He had absolute freedom of movement now, like any male, subject only to matters of privacy and social courtesy.

Soon the Counsel would inform the people of Elleio, every warship, and every Compact world that Delwyn, an Eyloni who only looked human, was one of The People, and was *Hunter's Moon*'s Warleader. Her people did not take social identity and status lightly. By the time they arrived in Homespace, everyone would know of Delwyn.

"Mistress," the Mistress of Healers called from Health Center, "Delwyn is in regeneration and is resting. I want his complete medical files transmitted to my medical records," she demanded in a harried tone.

"Is there a problem?" Melkorka asked, alarmed. To lose him now was unthinkable.

"No, Mistress," she replied in the same aggrieved tone. "There are just too many people in Health Center now!"

Melkorka smiled. Too many females were 'just happening' to wander into Health Center to look in on their Warleader.

"I see," she said, flicking her ears at the sound of another call, and hit the reply button.

"Repeat, Mistress of Saga."

"Mistress, I need Delwyn's warrior record from the Coalition warship's archives for updating our records and transmittal to the Compact Counsel."

Smiling at a private joke, Melkorka calmed Mirrahindrallin. As the ship's historian and chronicler, she wanted to review the accomplishments and combat honors their Warleader had received while under Coalition obligation. Her job was to record his exploits and make known the valor of his clan. Melkorka smiled again at Mirrahindrallin's obsessive nature when it came to her chronicles.

"Mistress," Hlindredreda interrupted, "Warleader Phalalin signals greetings to you and pays his respects to Warleader Delwyn. He requests permission to jump his warship to the escort honor point off our bow."

Melkorka nodded. "Tell him that I would be honored."

"Mistress, Warleader Phalalin advises that upon jump completion he has critical information to convey to you," Hlindredreda growled in sudden fury. "He says he has information concerning a plot to impede the free movement of Delwyn by Coalition Ambassador Harrison."

"What?"

Ambassador Harrison awoke from a short nap and checked the time. He smiled. His tap on the CMDCC hyperlink relay had picked up Phalalin's comm chatter. His engines had recharged over two days ago, but he remained in Ibeetu orbit. He was probably waiting for Marsch to finish this ritual business. Phalalin could then bring the Eyloni males here and let them argue over who would take command of the warship.

Perfect. Even if Melkorka refused Phalalin's order, her new warleader still wouldn't allow a human male sanctuary aboard his ship. Last he checked, Marsch was down to fifty Eyloni. He should be done by now!

"Harrison to bridge."

"Yes, Mr. Ambassador?" Commander Rodgers replied.

"Is Marsch still at it, Commander?"

"No, Mr. Ambassador. They carried him off the bay just a few minutes ago."

Good. *Good!* Harrison smiled, savoring his triumph.

"When are they returning him to the ship? I want him in the brig, Commander. He's charged with interstellar piracy, remember."

"I don't think you have to worry about that, Mr. Ambassador. They've just made Marsch their warleader."

No! That can't be possible!

"What…what are you saying, Commander? How is that possible?"

"I don't know, Mr. Ambassador. Maybe you should listen to the co-ambassadors. They're talking to the Captain about it now."

Rodgers left the intercom open.

"Anlann, surely this is an honorary title. They can't expect Marsch to assume command of that ship!" Winters was saying.

"Yes, Captain, it is an honorary title. The highest rank a society can bestow upon a male. And yes, they expect him to assume operational command of their warship."

"Do they have the authority to place a human in command of a military asset worth several hundred-trillion United Earth euros filled with I don't know how many classified Compact secrets?"

"Females always choose, Captain," Seralin said. "Delwyn became Eyloni, one of The People, the moment Princess bonded with him. From that point, he was a lawful choice. He fought for them and he fought with them. They know him far better than any male Phalalin has brought with him. I assure you that Melkorka has already informed Phalalin that they have no need for the males he conveyed here."

"And he'll accept that?" Winters asked.

"Of course, Captain, Compact warships are autonomous. That autonomy is absolute unless a Warpact exists, but even during a Warpact, the supplanted warleader never loses autonomy of action over the internal affairs of his ship."

Harrison cringed as he listened to the back and forth between the co-ambassadors and Winters. His heart lurched. Phalalin would back Melkorka's choice. He was sure to tell her about his attempt to have Marsch arrested. He needed a damage control scenario in place before that information became public.

"Commander Rodgers, please tell the captain that I'll be in my quarters in conference with Mr. Parakh on this matter."

"Very well, Mr. Ambassador."

✦✦✦

"Captain! *Fearless* has arrived. The Compact destroyer is maintaining position thirteen hundred meters off Marsch's bow, Sir," Lieutenant Carstairs reported.

"Captain," Lieutenant Romaine interrupted. "Message from Mistress Melkorka, Sir. She's asking for Marsch's medical and personnel files. She also wants his personal effects sent to her ship, Sir."

"Ship-to-ship, Lieutenant."

"Aye, Sir. Channel open. Go ahead, Captain."

Melkorka's figure flashed on the main viewscreen. She sat in her command chair, back straight, Marsch's unsheathed old sword was balanced across her knees, her tail wrapped around the length of the exposed blade.

"Mistress Melkorka."

"Captain Winters," she acknowledged.

"Mistress, I understand that you want Senior Chief Warrant Officer Marsch's personnel and medical files."

"Yes, Captain. Just as your ship has up-to-date records for everyone who serves aboard him, we too need complete personnel and medical files on Delwyn. He belongs to us now. As with any transfer, Delwyn's property must be given to us so we can have it ready for him," Melkorka said, her tone unusually flat for the musical Eyloni.

"Mistress, may I speak with him?"

"No, you may not. About my request, Captain?" she demanded.

Winters turned to the co-ambassadors. The looks they gave him made it clear he had no choice. Marsch was no longer under his command. Besides, by leaving him in Eyloni hands Harrison couldn't very well have him arrested, now could he? And to be fair, Melkorka spoke the truth. Marsch had transferred to another ship.

"Fine, Mistress," Winters conceded, "I'll have my medical and personnel department heads transmit the files to you. His personal effects will be packed and ready for teleport."

"No, Captain," Melkorka interrupted, "I will send a detail over to your ship. They will pack Delwyn's things. You may watch them if you wish, but they must perform the task themselves. We are returning to the moon. You are welcome to orbit there and wait until Delwyn can leave Health Center."

"Thank you, Mistress."

"Captain, please inform the co-ambassadors I wish to speak with them."

"Of course, Mistress. Anlann? Seralin?" Winters gestured them forward.

Seralin frowned and flipped her ears back. Something was wrong. Melkorka's posture, tail, and ears revealed a deep burning fury inconsistent with her words but not with her flat voice.

Anlann held back. Something had happened. Better to let the females argue it out. Besides, with Delwyn aboard the warship, the more appropriate channel was warleader to warleader, not Mistress of the Ship to Warleader.

He listened as Melkorka sang a complex song rather than signing in Battle Language.

So he could hear their conversation, also. Odd for females, they did enjoy their secrets.

Sudden rage overcame him, so violent it was that his scent reeked with it.

Seralin stepped back, wound her tail around him and squeezed his pons with a crushing grip until he got himself under control.

"Anlann, are you all right?" Winters asked, wondering if the co-Ambassador had suffered a seizure. Concerned, he punched a button. "Sickbay, Winters here. Dr. Kerchival? Report to the bridge."

Anlann shook his head. "No, Captain. It is nothing. It will pass."

Seralin turned back to Melkorka and sang a curt reply.

Hours later, eight Eyloni quantum translated aboard *Henri Edda*. Six young Warriors and two intense older Hunters followed Anlann and Seralin to Marsch's quarters. Anlann opened the door and helped them by pointing out fragile items of interest. Seralin held back.

She knew what the Hunters' needle-thin single bright green rank webs meant. Warleader special security. They prowled under the direct command of the Protectress herself and never with the warleader's knowledge.

Their presence aboard another warship violated his autonomy, but Elleio's overwhelmingly female social structure had decreed long before there was a Compact Counsel a single law that forever superseded any other law and custom: that the premeditated intent, without honorable justification, to cause harm to a male must be avenged immediately and by any means necessary. Females were the guardians of males, after all.

"Mistress Seralin," one of the Hunters asked, "with respect, where is Ambassador Harrison?"

"He is on the VIP deck, the guest quarters deck."

"We have warship's business to attend to," the other said. Seralin nodded, and the two Hunters stalked off down the deck.

Anlann ground his teeth, impatient. The Warriors packing Delwyn's things took their time. They gathered together and debated how they should pack their warleader's musical instruments, then his books, then his clothing. On and on it went, as if they intended to tail-chase the time away.

Seralin entered the room, saw them talking excitedly among themselves.

"Anlann? *Anlann!*"

"Yes? I am sorry, Sera, but I do not understand why... *What?*"

"Warleader special security Hunters prowl here, Anlann. They seek Ambassador Harrison!"

"Yes, yes. I am not blind, you know. I am not deaf, either. You know what? These Warriors are so excited that they want to take each separate item out and pass it around and discuss how they should pack it!"

Seralin watched the Warriors. At first she thought they stalled for the Hunters, but the longer she watched them, the more their simple awe changed her mind.

Coalition Ambassador Harrison knew his time was running out.

"How do we spin this, Percy?"

"Well, Mr. Ambassador, I say we lay the blame for our misguided attempt to have Marsch arrested on his mental defect."

"Come again?"

"Sir, Marsch has posttraumatic stress disorder. He's unstable. I had Deering pull the SOG backup copies of his medical records. Winters has been covering for him. Chief Medical Officer Kerchival has been medicating Marsch on a weekly basis for months. But only a few days after arriving on Ibeetu, Dr. Kerchival reports that Marsch stopped taking his medication and going to therapy. We should claim that Marsch fell off a cliff when he charged into that Lizard ship. I mean, what sane person would do that? What sane human would do that for *aliens*?

"You know, that might work. Write a draft for me to review, and I'll have Deering send it to the Coalition Government on our hijacked hyperlink."

The door chime interrupted his musings.

"Answer that, would you Percy? It's probably the co-ambassadors come to gloat."

"Yes, Sir."

Harrison spoke to his omni, dictating notes outlining the cover story and how he would tie any blame to Marsch's mental state.

"Ambassador Harrison?" a furious accented Eyloni female voice demanded.

"Yes, Ambassador Seralin…?"

Several Coalition standard days later, a grumbling Marsch emerged from the Health Center's regeneration chrysalis healed and itching like mad. Similar chrysalises held the two wounded Warriors. He stared, shocked, at their nearly regrown legs, arm, and tail. A crowd waited to escort him. They took turns walking him throughout their warship, showing off jungle scenery like a realtor selling choice land. After the third hour, he decided that 'escort' didn't begin to explain the company he kept. They packed the pathways and trails so tightly that he didn't have to stand on his own. If his legs, still wobbly from the regeneration effect, failed him, then they could carry him along by the press of their bodies. He wouldn't sink so much as a centimeter. Just thinking about it made him stumble, and the Hunters around him pressed against him, a wall of lean flesh.

The warship's layout made it seem much bigger on the inside. The beautiful optical effects fooled his perceptions. All interior spaces were filled with green-less jungle foliage. Holographic projections hugged force field shaped plant life and the physical irregularities built into the walls, ceiling, and decks.

The crew stalked and prowled rain forest paths plucked from an artist's dream, one who favored the warm color spectrum. Marsch could imagine Native Americans on Earth walking forest trails like these, if the forest had yellow, orange, and red leaves and golden yellow and light orange grasses. Subtle hints of potpourri and lilac filled the air, joined by the beagle, bakery, and spice body odors of his crew. Other atmospheric smells, soil, leaf litter, and ozone tickled his nose.

The ship maintained Elleio's high rain forest humidity, lighter than Earth-normal gravity, and temperatures in the thirty-degree Celsius range. Cool mountain breezes gusted from time to time, circulating air containing less oxygen and more carbon dioxide than he was used to. Several hours had certainly passed, but the sun had climbed only slightly in the mid-morning sky, and Marsch remembered why: Elleio was tidally-locked into a day that was over 12.5 Earth days long. EST and TST time standards were based on Eyloni physiology. A gas giant, light blue and as big as ten full Earth Moons across, hung overhead. It, too, had barely moved.

Last of all, they brought him to the command center. Melkorka sat in her command chair with his unsheathed saber resting across her knees, tail wrapped around its blade. She smiled. Her ears followed his progress, her pons twitching with excitement.

Forward of her command chair waited his station, the Warleader's Watch. His piano and a drum rested next to a comfortable chair offset from a supporting console. The Watch's layout suggested that a warleader spent most of his time standing or walking.

Marsch gazed into the holographic main display that projected into the command center. Massive, the thing reminded him of a panoramic cinema screen. The 3-d image filled the width of the display and out into the room, engulfing the Warleader's Watch to just short of Melkorka's station.

He walked into the display and viewed the image from several angles. Ibeetu and the orbiting *Henri Edda* hung there. He walked up to, and around, the image of the carrier. He touched it, and the carrier grew, filling the display with fine detail.

As he studied the toy image, his doubts returned. Was he ready for this? The Eyloni had no doubts. He tried to convince them of his inadequacies from the moment he regained consciousness, but they would hear nothing of it. They thought he exaggerated.

And Phelindra! His Protectress never strayed far from him. But for bathroom breaks, and even then just barely, she followed him everywhere. So enmeshed with his thoughts was she that she turned before he turned: as if she read his mind. She even told him she was going to sleep in his quarters next to him!

They had not put him in Kalinn's old quarters. Those rooms had been sealed. Marsch's quarters looked like the polished inside of a hollow tree, irregular, about fifteen meters across at its widest. It was a split-level tree house. A simulated view looked out and down three hundred meters onto red, yellow, and orange foliaged trees and a wide river that ran over a high waterfall. The days-long morning and evening sun hit the falls exactly right to give the impression of liquid fire roaring over the edge. The view itself overlooked the lands of the O'un Tu Clan, the Fire River Clan.

His Clan.

The one thing that bothered him the most, the combat address system, would take some time getting used to. It constantly broadcasted his voice throughout the ship day and night and could not be shut off! His snoring had already brought warleader special security barging into his quarters twice now.

"Status?" Marsch asked Melkorka.

Phelindra moved to hover behind and to the left of him.

"All personnel and materiel have been recalled from the surface. The Ni'zakhonii vessel is secure. Warship is at Action Ready Status and all stations report nominal. A course has been plotted for multiple direct jumps to Elleio. The jump drive is standing by, Delwyn," Melkorka said.

Marsch winced at the sound of their preferred use of his given name over the nickname.

"That's welcome news, Melkorka. Trebithia, prepare to jump the ship."

"By your command," the Mistress of Pathwalking replied.

"Mistress?" Hlindredreda interrupted. "Message from Captain Winters for the Warleader."

Melkorka perked her ears in inquiry and waited for his nod.

"Accept," she said.

Winters measured the figure standing in his viewscreen. Marsch wore nothing but tan shorts and a small gold earring in his left ear. It was embossed with a triangle, the only rank symbol a warleader wore.

"Delwyn," Winters said, keeping in mind Anlann's warning that Eyloni had a single name, and therefore that Marsch's was Delwyn, not Del. "I wanted to pay my respects and say good-bye. It has been an honor and a privilege having you as a member of my crew."

"Thank you, Captain. It's been a pleasure serving aboard *Henri Edda* and under you. I hope you will do right by the Coalition and accept my recommendation that you serve as acting Coalition Ambassador Plenipotentiary. I don't know how you're going to handle Mr. Harrison's objections with the Coalition Government, but I think the co-ambassadors' and the Compact Counsel's endorsements will help. Captain, how are you going to square it with the Justice Directorate? Mr. Harrison's piracy charge and all?"

"The Coalition Government accepted the Compact Counsel's viewpoint and withdrew the charge on Harrison's behalf. The Compact Counsel explained in confidence that the action taken against the Lizard ship was a Compact military operation. The Counsel also made it clear they had taken a very dim view of the prospect that insult to one of its warleaders might have occurred."

"What about Harrison? No doubt he's been screaming since he got the official word."

Winters paused a moment for effect.

"Delwyn, Mr. Harrison and Cultural Attaché Parakh have been missing for the past few days. You wouldn't know anything about that, would you?"

"Missing?" Delwyn echoed. "How can anyone go missing on a carrier?" He cast a glare at Melkorka, who shrugged with genuine confusion.

"Well, it's possible," Winters supposed. "There are a lot of spaces one could hide on a fourteen-hundred-meter-long carrier. The 'tween hulls areas themselves offer a lot of hiding space. I've seen little nooks and crannies decked out better than quarters by maintenance techs. The co-ambassadors haven't seen him, either."

"Well, I'm sure security will find them eventually. Captain, Warleader Phalalin tells me that Harrison contacted him via hyperlink prior to his last jump into this system. He couldn't have done that from the bridge, and while there are several short-range hyperlink comms on the fighters, betas, and alphas, the only other long range hyperlink is in SOG. I'd recommend you have the TOC communications center's CMDCC interface checked over. See SOG TOC comms command duty NCO Senior Chief River Six. Only the TOC comm staff, Cummings, or Deering could have hotwired the comm for him. One of them might even know where Harrison is hiding for that matter."

Winters nodded thoughtful. "I had a watch put on the delegation, but I canceled it right after Melkorka named you warleader. There didn't seem to be a need to keep it going after it was clear you weren't returning to the ship."

A derisive, insolent trill exploded from Phelindra.

Delwyn turned casually on her and cocked an eyebrow.

"Anything you want to add, Phelindra?"

The Eldest Huntress gave him her best open face, ears perked forward. "No. Of course not. Why do you ask'?"

He turned slowly back to the comm pickup. "Captain, would you put the co-ambassadors on for me, please?"

"Of course."

The bridge pickup focused on the two Eyloni.

"Anlann, Seralin, I guess the time has come to say good-bye."

"Yes, Delwyn, for now. We will see you again, soon. Either on Elleio or elsewhere. Go with the spirits and farewell," Anlann said.

"Warleader Delwyn," Seralin added, "Be well, and may the spirits be with you always. Remember us often, as we remember you," she added, striving to maintain the dignity of a Protectress.

"Until we meet again, whether on Elleio, elsewhere, or with the spirits, I will always remember you," Delwyn replied with equal solemnity. "I, Delwyn, Warleader of *Hunter's Moon*, take my leave of you. Farewell."

Marsch looked upon Ibeetu one last time before turning to his Mistress of the Ship.

"Clear to navigate, Melkorka?"

"Clear to navigate confirmed, Delwyn."

Marsch reviewed what the Mistress of Sails—Anailiatha—his chief engineer, had reported earlier. Undamaged, the warship could make a direct return to Elleio in about 18.5 Coalition days, about 43 TST days, at the maximum jump rate. She warned that her makeshift repairs would serve him well, but that he should not stress them without cause. Compact jump drive technology placed high demands on hull integrity. All the cutting and patching had degraded the hull. Her verdict: they would not be jumping home at their maximum rate. Rather, they would poke along at half that and take about 37 Earth days to reach Elleio.

Phalalin had insisted he match their jump rate and maintain his honor escort all the way back to Elleio.

Anailiatha had also estimated that *Hunter's Moon* would spend about twenty Elleio Standard Time months in drydock for repairs. That converted to about four Earth months of down time.

Melkorka had said they would spend that time selecting new crew replacements. She also reassured him that he would not be without them, either. The crew usually returned to their clans whenever they returned to Elleio for resupply, but this time they would travel with him as he met clan and tribal elders, the Compact Counsel, and a fair amount of the population.

He had time to learn about them.

Melkorka made it clear that his learning was to start once they had completed their first jump.

All of them would take turns teaching him.

Eighty-six days seemed too short a time. He sighed. *Eight-six?* He meant 321 days.

He had to learn to count again, too.

"Trebithia, plot the first direct jump to Elleio."

"By your command. First 3.043 light-year jump plotted, transferred to helm, and ready to implement," the Mistress of Pathwalking said.

"Kidahin, jump the warship," Delwyn ordered.

"By your command, Delwyn. Commencing jump!" Kidahin sang out with joy. She could not wait for them to arrive in Elleio orbit. As the warship jumped, a foreboding apprehension filled her.

What would the Society of Warleaders think of Delwyn?

About the Author

David Michael Martin graduated from
the Ohio Institute of Technology in 1982
and designed PC-integrated laboratory
analyzers. An avid science fiction and
fantasy reader, Mr. Martin successfully
told engaging and entertaining stories
as a games master for several of the
popular fantasy-roleplaying game
systems appearing today.

Mr. Martin returned to college and
pursued his interests in English and the
humanities at Ohio University and
Adams State University.

Mr. Martin has over twenty years' experience tutoring adult basic
education classes for adult students seeking their G.E.D. diplomas. Mr.
Martin currently lives in western Michigan and is training puppies to
be leader dogs for the blind.

This is his first novel.

www.ingramcontent.com/pod-product-compliance
Lightning Source LLC
Chambersburg PA
CBHW032210180726
48284CB00001B/279